MW00414462

THE UNCOMMITTED

(A NOVEL)

To: Megan,
Enjoy!
With Best Regards,
Margaret M Goss
"Meg"

On the bank of the River Acheron, reside the souls of the Uncommitted—souls who chose to live without conviction or faith, without principle or belief. Having made no commitment to good or evil, they wander eternity searching, yet never reaching, the light.

Interpretation
Canto III, Dante Alighieri, Inferno

Copyright © 2015 by Margaret M. Goss
All rights reserved.

Published by
Three Towers Press
An imprint of HenschelHAUS Publishing, Inc.
www.HenschelHAUSbooks.com

ISBN: 978-1-59598-428-9
E-ISBN: 978-5-59598-429-6
LCCN: 2015948786

Cover art by Clarissa Yeo, www.yocladesigns.com
Author photo by Jody Dingle Photography

Printed in the United States of America

To my husband, Pat,
my children, Sean, Mary and Aidan,
and to my sister, Chris.
Their faith in me and their encouragement
enabled me to complete this novel.

CHAPTER 1

JOSIE

PHOENIX, ARIZONA—APRIL 2002

Josephine Reilly cradles her sleeping infant daughter, Anna. The cabin's recirculated air drifts stale beneath her nose. Space on the plane is tight and tests her endurance; another minute may collapse her resolve. The plane sinks lower, and the Saguaro cacti dotting the mountains come into view as do the cars whizzing by on the freeway below. Michael, just two, grows irritable from being confined—several trips to the lavatory are not enough to break the four hours of monotony. The flight attendants rush up and down the aisle, collecting leftovers and ordering all to return their seatbacks to their original positions. The forward movement of Josie's chair jostles Anna. She emits a loud cry, arches her back and pushes her feet into her mother's lap.

"Shhhh." Josie presses the pacifier firmly between Anna's lips, hoping it will relieve the building pressure in her ears.

Michael peers out his window, mesmerized by the swift current of desert passing beneath his feet. "Mama," he says, "almost there?"

"Yes, Michael, almost there."

Josie thinks about her mother. *She should not have gotten this sick so fast.* Her eyes cloud over from a surge of tears. *How could they have missed it?* Chronic indigestion, abdominal pain, backaches—months of warnings obscured by over-the-counter remedies. Was her physician incompetent, unable to map a constellation of symptoms that would have pointed him toward an accurate diagnosis? Or was it her cancer? The sneaky culprit hid behind her stomach, wrapping itself around her pancreas and vital organs in an insidious maze. "Too late," her oncologist said. Stage IV. A week ago he gave her six months. Then after more testing, he revised the terms and six months morphed into two months or less.

The plane touches down and slows. It jars Michael forward and then back. "Whoa ... fun!" he says. His red-brown hair is soft and overdue for a trim. Josie remembers her father's offer, he promised to take Michael to the barber while they are here. At least it will give her father something to do besides hold vigil by her mother's bed.

While the plane taxis, Josie pulls a note from her pocket. *God in his heaven, through death, recovers His own.* Josie reads her mother's words over and over, but they give her little comfort. *He will eventually call all of us home,* her mother wrote—but where was His warning? Josie had expected a sign that would have alerted her to His plans.

Above her, the fasten seatbelt light dings and turns off, indicating the end of her flight, but the beginning of her real journey. She watches the people around her stand-up and shuffle into the aisles. Their faces, eager and pale, are seeking a sun that has been hiding for months under cloudy Midwestern skies. However, she will not find a refuge here from reality. She is here to do what they asked, "they" being her parents. She'll be responsible for administering her mother's morphine, lifting her out of bed, taking her to the bathroom, bathing her and more. It will be arduous, round-the-clock attention. Her nursing experience, limited to emergency care, did not prepare her for this sort of work. Nevertheless, Josie's specialty doesn't matter. She would care for her mother to the best of her ability—no matter how overwhelming it was sure to become.

The difference, though, was the inevitability of death. In the ER, lives were to be saved, not lost; there would be no life-saving interventions here. Above all, deaths in the ER belonged to other people's families. This one belonged to hers.

JOSIE NAVIGATES THE DOUBLE-STROLLER around the airport's milling crowds to find a passable track through the long stretch of terminal. They arrive at the elevators and enter.

"Water, Mama ... want water." Michael reaches out his arms in search of a drink.

"I know, sweetheart, I'm thirsty too." She rummages through the diaper bag and finds all she has left to offer him is a bag of cracker crumbs. "We'll find you some water as soon as we meet your Aunt Nora."

Michael has no understanding as to why they are here, nor does his sister. Despite Josie's best efforts, they will not remember their time here with their grandmother. Josie hasn't any recollection of her own grandmother and thinks it strange how history repeats itself. Her grandmother died when she was two—the same will now be true for Michael.

They exit the elevator and begin their search for Nora. Josie finds her waiting by the last baggage claim carousel. Nora's long black hair is cut in a short pixie, cropped to the base of her neck. She wonders why Nora didn't mention it. Despite the physical distance between them, the two sisters were close, bonded together like an old pair of glasses—each having their own independent lens but connected by the same frame.

"Josie!" Nora waves and walks toward her. "What's the matter?" She stops and examines Josie's face.

"The hair," she says, transfixed by the change in Nora's appearance. She's older than Josie by twelve years but the new hairstyle makes her look much younger. Although, it could be the result of Nora's faithful use of sunscreen. She wore it religiously since she moved to the Valley of the Sun fifteen years before.

"Oh, do you like it? I did it yesterday," Nora says, fussing through its layers with her fingers.

"I do ... but why?"

"I didn't have time for it anymore, taking care of Mom and all. It'll grow back later."

After Mom is gone, Josie thinks.

Anna and Michael are restless in the stroller. Nora bends down to unsnap the buckles securing them.

"What are you doing?" Josie asks.

"Can't you see they want out?" Nora asks.

"Well, no kidding, but you're letting caged animals free."

"Will you relax? I've got 'em." Nora releases Anna first and then Michael. Holding Anna in her right arm, she plunks a new teddy bear into Michael's hands with her left. He clasps his arms around the soft white bear and Nora gives him a tender hug.

"What about me?" Josie asks.

"What, did I buy you a bear?" Nora smiles and reaches out her free arm to hug her sister.

In the middle of their embrace, Josie begins to break down. The imaginary box she uses to contain her emotions is giving way to her grief.

"Maybe I should've gotten you one." Nora pulls back to see her face.

Josie covers her eyes and looks down at the ground, hoping no one notices her crying. The bags descend in rapid succession with methodical plops and thuds off the belt and onto the cycling carousel. Fortunately for her, those nearby appear more interested in watching for their luggage than watching her cry.

"Seriously, you've got to pull yourself together before you see her." Nora hugs her again with one arm, this time tighter while still holding Anna with the other. Michael is toddling around them, squeezing his new bear and patting its back like a baby.

Nora reaches into her back pocket. "Here, take these." She hands Josie a couple of tissues. "I had them ready for you."

Josie takes the folded tissue and dabs smudges of mascara from under her eyes. "I guess I should've worn waterproof."

Nora nods and gives a twist of a smile. "We'll be okay."

"I know, but my kids were supposed to experience having a grandmother. I never knew Grandma. I wanted things to be different for them than it was for me."

"That's life ... what can I say?"

"I'm sorry, I'm ..."

"It's okay, Jos. It's not your fault I haven't been able to have kids of my own. We have to make the best of the hand we've been dealt. And at least they have Mom now."

"Water, Mama," Michael reminds Josie.

"Nora, could you take Michael for a drink of water while I wait for the bags?"

"Sure."

Nora continues to hold Anna and walks Michael to a nearby water fountain. Josie's eyes meander from the baggage carousel to the faces of the surrounding throng of passengers. Her gaze comes back around to her children and Nora. In one-part reality and another part dream, she feels a pull into the distant past. She sees her mother as a young woman in the embodiment of Nora—the curve of her lips when she smiles, the inflection of her voice, and the loving way she embraces her children. The genetic blueprint of her mother's face and shape appear stamped onto Nora's body and manner. It lasts mere seconds but those reflections of her mother present in Nora make Josie feel lost, a stranger to herself. Their mother hasn't died yet but Josie already feels like an orphaned child.

Nora returns with the children and sets them into their stroller, buckling them back in. "Are you ready to do this?" she asks.

"I think so," Josie says, but closing her eyes, she hopes for a different answer, a different time, a different place. She breathes deep, opens her eyes and nods once more.

"Remember my promise," Nora says, "I'll take care of the kids. You focus on taking care of Mom. That's why you're here."

The two sisters flash a wordless glance at one another. They read each other's thoughts as they have many times before. From this day forward, they will not have their parents to count on anymore. The role of parent and child has reached the point of reversal ... whether they are ready for it or not.

THEY ARRIVE AT HER PARENTS' DESERT CONDO shortly before 7 p.m. It is perfect, just one-story for their retirement years and a small, manicured yard. Giovanna chose it because of its likeness to pictures in magazines of small Italian villas even down to the olive tree at the front gate and a flagstone path to the door.

Nora walks in ahead with Michael. Josie holds Anna and stops to read the handwritten sign on the door, *Hidden Camera*. She laughs to herself. Apparently, her mother feels it will repel would-be robbers. There is no camera or security system, only her mother's superstitious Sicilian nature keeping them safe from her imagined predators.

Before she opens the door, Josie straightens Anna's cotton dress down over her chubby thighs and combs Anna's curls with her fingers. "There, you look beautiful," she whispers. Then tells herself, *Suck it up.*

Upon entering the house, the melancholy sweetness of memories and laughter from earlier visits brush the perimeters of her mind. The cherished family painting still hangs in the entry hall—the one her mother will never sell at any price. Giovanna painted it during the height of her art career—a career producing hundreds of watercolor and acrylic landscapes, farms and seascapes. This particular painting was of the Upstate New York farm once owned by Giovanna's father, Giuseppe Rizzo. He lost the farm during the Great Depression but she kept the painting in remembrance—a tribute more bitter than sweet.

Each brushstroke conveyed a story—the story of Giovanna Rizzo before she became a mother and wife, of the little girl who at age seven picked onions in the fields and fed the pigs in the barn. It also depicted a time she grieved deeply. Her father died soon after losing the family farm when the bank foreclosed on him during the lowest point of the Depression Era. While his doctors said he died from a stroke, she always told Josie that he died from the stress of losing his livelihood, despondent at being unable to provide for his family.

The familiar aroma of fresh basil and garlic wafts through the air. Josie's father's signature marinara sauce and meatballs are simmering on the kitchen stove. Its scent reminds her of Sunday dinners during her youth. Her parents, siblings and extended family would gather around the large dining room table, passing baskets of garlic bread and carafes of homemade wine.

Carmelo La Fortuna is waiting for his daughters in the living room, watching the evening news from his leather recliner. When the girls first enter, he is unaware of their presence. Josie notices the dark sunken wells beneath her father's eyes and thinks he looks about half the size of his former self. The room is dim except for a few slivers of light creeping through the drawn blinds.

"Pa," Josie says.

He looks up at her. In what feels like slow motion, his aging body rises stiffly from the chair and reaches for her. "Josie ... we've been waiting for you."

Nora takes Anna from Josie's arms and, like a mother embracing a small child, Josie holds her father. "I came as soon as I could."

The sound of grief rises in his throat. He begins to weep.

"It's all right, Pa. I'm here. I'll help you." She encloses him tighter within her arms.

After a minute, Carmelo steps back from her embrace. He wipes his eyes with the handkerchief he takes from his pocket. He looks to the children. "So beautiful." He smiles and touches Anna's brown curls, giving her a kiss on the cheek.

"Nannu," Michael says. His voice echoes off the room's cathedral ceiling.

"I'm so glad he remembers me." Carmelo bends down to greet him.

"Of course," Josie says. "Michael, please give Nannu a kiss hello."

Michael leans in and gives his grandfather a wet peck on the check. "Ouch!" Michael pulls back. "Nannu's face scratchy."

Carmelo rubs his hand over his beard. It is evident he's lost track of caring for himself. "How's Declan? Your mother and I wish he could've come."

"Perhaps later, we'll see." Her parents loved Declan and fell for him almost as fast as she did. Tough, smart, handsome—every parent's ideal husband for their daughter to marry. Sadly, she knew Declan could not come now. As an attorney for a prominent Minnesota law firm, he wasn't able to leave during critical periods—he had several important meetings in the coming days. His clients paid his firm big money for representation; if he wasn't up to the task they would seek it elsewhere. She hoped her parents could understand.

Anna grows fidgety in Nora's arms and reaches for Josie.

"Josie, go see your mother—the children will lift her spirits." Her father nods toward the bedroom where her mother is resting.

Josie takes Anna from Nora and walks with her down the short hallway. She lingers outside the bedroom door, afraid to go in. She can't shake the feeling that the vibrancy her mother brought into their world is vanishing. Whispers, instead of laughter, now permeate the house so as not to disturb the dying.

Her brother Tony sits in the rocking chair beside her mother's bed. "Josie," he says and gets up from the rocker. He comes toward the doorway where she is standing and embraces her. "It's so good to see you. Ma's been waiting for you."

Tony is Giovanna's only son and, to her mother's dismay, he is "divorced"—a word she utters with shame. He did not seek an annulment. Giovanna still held her children to the same stringent Catholic beliefs she grew up with. In truth, Tony should not have married. He was a successful local guitarist with an ample female following—temptation for him was everywhere.

Tony and Josie approach the bed where their mother is sleeping. It scares her to see her mother so pale and lifeless. Briefly, her mind drifts to the past. She can see her mother painting landscapes from the backyard of her childhood home—the sweet smell of her acrylics, the scratching sound of her pallet knife against the canvas, and the number two pencil tucked behind her ear. Anna begins to babble softly. Giovanna wakes up.

"Josie?" she asks.

"Yes, it's me." She bends down to kiss her mother's cheek.

Michael ambles up to the bed. "Nonna?" His body shifts and leans against Josie's. He hasn't seen his grandmother since Anna was born and the pictures from that visit show a colorful portrait of a woman full of life. Giovanna no longer looks like the same woman.

"Michael, it's all right. Give Nonna a kiss," Josie says.

"He's scared, Josie. Don't push him ... give him time." Giovanna smiles at Michael and then turns her eyes to Anna. "Look at how beautiful they are. They're growing so fast." She gazes at them for a few seconds and then tries to sit up.

"Mom, hold on," Tony says, "let me help."

While Tony positions Giovanna at the side of her bed, Josie glances about the bedroom. It is quiet, no television or radio playing and it smells clean like fresh-laundered sheets. Nothing has changed since her last visit. Her mother's prayer cards lie in a small pile on the bedside stand and her rosary still dangles from a hook next to her side of the bed.

Nora enters. "Dinner's about ready, Mom. Do you want something to eat, some pasta or soup?"

"No, nothing, just bring me a fresh glass of ice water, please."

"Okay, later then?" Nora raises her brows. "You've got to keep up your strength."

Giovanna gives her a mirthless shrug, "For what?"

Nora shakes her head and turns to Josie, "Let me take the kids and get them started with something to eat. I picked up the baby food you wanted for Anna before you got here today. I bought some snacks for Michael too—the ones you said he could eat—Goldfish crackers and cheese sticks. I double-checked the labels, no peanuts or tree nuts in them."

"Thanks for checking, we don't need him to have an allergic reaction today." Josie hands Anna over to Nora and directs Michael to go with them.

"All right, but bring them back when they're done so I can enjoy their company," Giovanna says, appearing frustrated with Nora as she takes the children out the door.

Once they are gone, Giovanna turns again to Tony, "I think I'd like to stand up."

"Are you sure about this? Perhaps you should allow yourself a few more minutes to adjust," he says.

"Please, I'm ready. I want to be in my chair when the children return. I think it frightens Michael to see me in bed ... like I'm already dead."

"Mom—" Josie says, reacting to her mother's black tone.

"Never you mind," she snaps, "Tony, c'mon now—"

Tony concedes. Although she is sick, her will is strong. He lifts her carefully into a standing position. For the first time in her life, Josie sees her mother as breakable. Her thin hand reaches for Josie's. She can feel the bony contours of her mother's fingers, her palms and her wrists and each hollow space in between. Their mother had always been so strong but now her hair is completely white, her skin colorless and drained of life. Josie places her arms gently around her and provides the strength for both of them.

"I'm glad you're here," Giovanna says.

"Me too, Mom."

"I was so worried about you and the children. It's too bad you had to fly all this way alone without Declan."

No matter how old Josie gets, her mother still feels she needs a security guard. But then Giovanna drops it. She doesn't harp on Josie traveling "alone" with her children or the three of them venturing across country without a male escort for protection. She just lets it go.

And that night, Giovanna isn't the one bustling around locking and relocking the doors, checking and rechecking to see if all the windows and blinds are shut. It is Nora and Josie sweeping the floors and making sure everything is in its place the way Giovanna liked it before going to bed. Those little obsessions of their mother's they once considered annoying, they now miss because she can't do any of them—nor will she be able to ever again.

THE CLOCK AT HER BEDSIDE SHOWS IT IS TWO in the morning. Josie is wide-awake, staring at the ceiling and walls from her bed. A slurry of thoughts churn through her mind—her parents, the future and Declan. It's the beginning of a new phase in her life—a phase where her mother will not be there to warn her or protect her from all those things that can bring her harm. The more Josie thinks about how her life is going to change, the more her mind refuses to give in to sleep. She doesn't know whether to feel relief or fear that her mother's long-held and suspicious convictions about strangers, traveling and more will no longer haunt her days. She questions her abilities—will she be equipped to handle an adult life without her mother's apprehensions about her safety?

Her stomach is in knots and her heart aches—fear has become a way of living. How will she go on? She knows she'll have to reprogram her ways of thinking, renounce the abundant and—most of the time—irrational thought processes her mother has impressed on her. But why? Why was her mother always so guarded about the ever-ominous unknown? Did she have good reason? Reasons she chose not to share with her vulnerable daughter?

Josie gets up from bed, snaps on the bedside lamp and puts on her robe. She goes into the kitchen for a cup of water and a few saltine crackers and sits down at the table. She takes a look around the kitchen. Apart from the hum of the dishwasher, she is alone. In the corner gathering dust, she sees a yellowed newspaper and thinks it must've missed the nearby recycle bin. She picks it up and one of her mother's prayer cards falls to the floor. She wonders how it got inserted between the sheets of newspaper and how long it was there. Why was it not with her mother's collection of prayer cards by her bed?

Josie reaches down to pick up the card and observes its faded picture under the light. It is a painting of a friar, holding the infant Jesus. Its inscription: *Saint Anthony, Patron of the Lost.*

CHAPTER 2

Josie's thoughts drift to the St. Anthony card most of the morning. She knows her mother must've left it in the kitchen a long time ago, long enough for the card to become faded and the papers around it to have yellowed. Usually, Giovanna prayed to St. Anthony when something material went missing—like a key or a wallet. But this card was different than the one she remembered. It implied something else. It implied the intangible. She began to worry. Did her mother feel lost as she approached death's door? Or, maybe the card was no longer of any significance? Doubtful. Giovanna prayed so often about important things, things and people who mattered to her, choosing not to waste time on the "inconsequential."

Josie enters her mother's bedroom. Giovanna is sleeping following a visit with Father Jim, her parish priest. He brought her communion, something Giovanna couldn't bear to miss today—Sunday. Three days prior, Father Jim provided her mother with the *Anointing of the Sick*. This gave Josie a sickening feeling rather than a feeling of peace. She still considered it the Sacrament of the Dying, no matter what the church had renamed it.

While her mother rests, Josie folds and puts away the clean laundry. She dusts off the shelves and the portrait of the Blessed Virgin hanging on the wall. In the air is an aura of emptiness. It skirts the edges although it will soon rest fully upon the house once her mother is gone. Josie picks up the calendar on her father's desk. Mother's Day is two weeks away. It will be her mother's last. It seems pointless to buy her anything besides flowers. She hasn't a need for lasting possessions anymore—no tangible artifact or souvenir can accompany her on her journey into the hereafter.

Josie retrieves the morphine drops and a cup of cold water from the bathroom, then returns to her mother's bedside. "Mom." She taps her on the shoulder. "It's time for your pain medicine."

Giovanna's eyes flutter then open.

"It's time." She holds the vial where Giovanna can see it. "If you want, I could come back later if you're not ready?"

"No," Giovanna winces and presses her abdomen. "I can feel it starting up again."

"It's best to stay ahead of it, keep it under control."

Giovanna reaches first for the water and takes a drink, "Oh ... that tastes good." She hands the cup back to Josie and opens her mouth. Josie takes the dropper and places a few drops of morphine into the well beneath her mother's tongue. Giovanna closes her eyes and her mouth for a moment to let the medicine absorb.

Josie places the cup of water on the bedside stand then takes a new pillow and fluffs it.

"Where are the children?" Giovanna asks.

"Nora has taken them to the park and then they were going to the store, just to get them out of the house for a little while," Josie says. "Are you warm enough?" She begins to pull the quilt over mother's shoulders.

"Yes, yes, I'm warm." Giovanna's eyes glance up at Josie. Her mouth opens but no further words come out.

"Is there something else?" It's obvious her mother has something more to say.

Giovanna reaches out her hand from beneath the quilt and touches Josie's arm. "I have three weeks."

"Mom, c'mon. How do you know that?" *Just three weeks?*

"My sisters told me, last night in a dream."

"Just like that, they told you?"

"Just like that."

They were sensitive souls and Giovanna was the last survivor of the five-sister clan. The Rizzo sisters always believed dreams were a vehicle for communication with the dead. Although to Josie, this communication seemed to occur in one direction, to tell the living what the dead already knew.

"Mom, did they say anything else?"

"No." She shakes her head.

Giovanna reaches again for her water. Josie helps her hold the straw but her mind fixes on her mother's revelation. She knows Sicilians, in particular, expected warnings from their dead to allow them time to prepare. She wishes her mother's sisters brought the warning sooner—long before the cancer had a chance to spread to her mother's liver and bones.

"Josie, I need you to promise me something."

"Sure, Mom. What?"

"Do not tell your brother or sister or your father about the amount of time I have left. It will be upon us soon enough; I don't want our last moments to be anxious ones."

"But you—"

"No buts ... this is how I need it to be."

"What about Declan? Can I tell him?"

"No. It wouldn't be fair that he knew and they didn't. If you told him and they found out, they wouldn't forgive you for keeping it from them. I'm not asking you to lie, there's simply no benefit in telling anyone else. It will only make the time we have left more stressful; it will become a countdown and I don't want that."

"All right, Mom" Josie agrees, reluctantly. "So why are you telling me and not them?"

"I'm sharing this with you because you will not be here when I die. I've always known this and I don't want you to feel guilty about it. You do what you need to do. I'm at peace with my life, you need to go and live yours."

"Mom, I can stay, I don't need to go. I will be here when the time comes," she insists. *How does she know all of these things? Why wouldn't I be here with her?*

Giovanna smiles softly. "Please, we've talked enough. Keep me company now while I rest."

Josie sits down in the rocker while Giovanna relaxes into her bed. Her mother closes her eyes, appearing to be comfortable, then drifts back to sleep. Josie thinks about what her mother has shared and it gives her a heavy heart. She rocks quietly and gazes out the bedroom window. She views the distant desert mountains sparsely covered in saguaro and the dry brown expanse that meets at their base. For the last month, rainfall was low even by Arizona standards. The blistering Arizona sun made the desert appear more austere than usual to her, even brutal.

She turns her eyes to the crucifix on the wall and says a prayer, thanking God for her mother's faith. Although, she has never figured out what Giovanna believed in more—the promise of eternal life or eternal damnation. Her mother was convinced that evil lurked behind every corner and insisted her children wear or carry something red to ward off the *m'al occhio*—the evil eye. She claimed that wearing a cross showed the Devil you belonged to Christ.

An hour has passed when suddenly Giovanna's limbs begin to twitch as if she is having an intense dream. Josie touches her mother softly on the shoulder. "Mom, are you okay?" She looks at her mother's mouth and chest. She is breathing normally. The twitching stops. Giovanna grimaces and opens her eyes.

"Josie," she says.

"Yes, Mom?"

"I need to give you something," she whispers.

"What is it?"

Giovanna reaches for a small blue velvet box sitting on her bedside stand. "Keep it with you always." Her hands tremble as she gives the vintage box to Josie.

"Mom, don't strain, this is too much for you right now."

"Please, open it," she insists.

Josie stares at the familiar box.

Giovanna motions with her hand for Josie to open it. "C'mon, now."

She cracks it open and finds an ornate silver cross strung over a delicate chain. It is the pendant that once belonged to her grandmother. Did it truly have the power to protect you from evil as her mother always said? Or was it another one of her crazy superstitions?

"My mother gave it to me before she died ... and now I'm giving it to you."

"Mom, I don't feel right taking this." She doesn't feel worthy enough to hold the heirloom, let alone be its keeper.

"You must wear it. It will protect you. I'm certain of it."

"What about Tony and Nora?"

"You'll need it more than them."

To appease her, Josie concedes. She takes the necklace from the box and places it around her neck, careful not to catch the buttons on her shirt lest it yank and break its fragile chain. "Mom?" she asks.

"Yes? What is it?"

"Oh, never mind."

"What is it? I know you have a question, so ask it."

"It might be too personal."

"I have nothing left to hide, there's no point in that."

Josie hesitates for a long moment. "I found this in the kitchen last night." She shows her mother the prayer card. "It looks different than the other St. Anthony cards I used to see you praying with."

"Yes, this one is different." Giovanna takes the card from Josie's hand, "Ah, I didn't even realize it was gone." She quietly laughs, "The irony of losing a St. Anthony prayer card."

"I know you said you are at peace but be truthful, are you at all anxious about dying? If you're scared, Mom, I'm here to talk to you; you know I will listen and try to help."

"No, I'm not scared of dying."

"Then what were you praying for?"

"I was praying for you."

"Me?"

"Yes."

"But I thought you prayed to St. Anthony for lost things, not people."

"That's where you're wrong. St. Anthony is also the finder of lost souls."

"But I'm not lost."

"We are all lost, Josie, trying to make our way home to Jesus. I was praying that you, your father and brother and sister will find your way home after I'm gone."

Josie smiles. "Mom, you don't have to worry, my soul is safe."

Giovanna raises her brows as if to doubt her. She points to the cross around Josie's neck.

"Wear it. There will come a time when you'll understand the importance of its protection. It may not be now. It may not be tomorrow or a year from now. But the time will come. You can be sure of it."

"I promise, Mom, I'll wear it." Josie swallows hard, unsure if her mother's warning is reality-based or true paranoia.

"There is one more thing."

"Yes?"

"Our parish back home, do you remember it?"

"Of course." Josie recalls her family's church in Upstate New York with its stone columns, marble altar, inlaid gold murals of the Madonna and Child and its twenty-foot stained glass windows.

"You used to say to me during Mass that you saw a glow around people."

"Yes ... that was such a long time ago. I was little." Josie preferred to keep certain memories locked away.

"And poor Rosalie Delmonico."

She knows what her mother is referring to. *I wish she would let this go.*

"One Sunday, you saw a brilliant blue color around Rosalie but said her husband was a dull gray. That's when I knew you were like me."

Josie sighs and nods, feeling sick to her stomach. When she was a child, she was sure she caused Mr. Delmonico to die because she could see his color. There was no way for her to understand it wasn't her fault. And everyone in town knew Mr. Delmonico. He wasn't a nice man. The townspeople used to whisper about his dealings in New York City with his mob friends. Josie understood that much about him, even at her young age. And she could sense the dark spirits around him, laying claim on his soul. A shiver ripples across Josie's arms.

"Please hand that to me," Giovanna reaches for her rosary. Josie hands it to her; her mother holds it to her heart. "That doesn't happen to you anymore, does it?"

"No, I've not seen colors around people since ... I was twelve or thirteen. Well, except for once, when I first met Declan."

"It was such a gift."

Gift? Josie was relieved she didn't see auras anymore and who would want to know these things? Furthermore, Declan preferred to stay in the dark about Josie's talents. When she told him about her ability, they were dating. She emphasized how the talent occurred in childhood, and that she saw an aura only one other time afterward and that was the moment they had met. He became visibly uncomfortable with the information. In his words, "The supernatural is not something I choose to entertain." From that day forward, she decided, for the health of their relationship it was best she turn off her "weird abilities" ... for good.

"I still see auras. That's how I knew I was sick months and months ago." Giovanna's voice heightens and strains. "But the doctors never found it. I could see the sickness in my own aura."

"Did you know you were sick when you came to visit us after Anna was born?" Josie's stomach twists and her body aches. *How could I have missed it?* While she hadn't tried using her "gift" in years, she was still a nurse and what kind of a nurse was she if she couldn't see that her own mother was sick?

"Yes, I knew even then, at your house. I knew it was there. I kept going back to the doctor and they would run test after test. They never found it. But I knew and they said it was just diverticulitis," she sneers in disgust. "Josie, you must always listen to your inner voice. It knows. Remember, you are also a Rizzo. You feel things, things that other people might not notice."

Admittedly, once Giovanna's diagnosis was out in the open, Josie's own psychic dam started to crack. It emerged with a full-fledged vision of her mother's body going up in flames like a maple tree being lit by a torch and swiftly consumed by fire. In her abdomen grew an inexorable and incapacitating pain which radiated straight through to her back. If she could suspend her logical mind, it seemed to her that it was *her mother's* pain manifesting in her body. Josie pushed the vision back behind the dam. *No. Not again. Not now.*

"You know, I've always wondered about that boy ..." Giovanna's voice trails off.

"What boy?"

"Your friend who drowned."

"Andy?"

Giovanna nods.

"What's there to wonder about?" Josie is only half listening, still shocked by the intensity of the vision she'd just had.

"Lots of things. What happened to his mother and father?"

"I don't know."

"I think he was only eleven. I've lived so long, I wish I could've have shared some of my years with him. Why doesn't God allow us that?"

"I don't have the answer for you. I wish I knew."

"Do you ever dream of him? You used to, you know."

"No," Josie shakes her head. She realizes she hadn't dreamt of him or even spoken his name in at least twenty years. Her dreams of skating with him on the neighborhood pond were once so vivid she was convinced they were real.

"If only we went with him. He wouldn't have been upset and gone off alone. I was too busy, too busy to pay attention to that poor child." Giovanna begins to weep.

"Mom, it wasn't your fault."

"And there he went to the pond alone only to drown in the icy water." Giovanna's cry grows louder. "Something didn't feel right to me when he walked away. I should've called his house to make sure he got there safe." Her tears trickle down her cheeks.

"Mom, stop. There was nothing we could've done."

"Yes, there was. I knew something wasn't right. I should've helped him."

Nothing Josie says will change how her mother feels. And Josie missed it too. She never saw Andy that cold dreadful day. She was upstairs picking up her room when he came by. Maybe she would have known if only she had seen his color.

"I could've done something, I should've listened to my gut," she whispers. Giovanna's eyelids grow heavy and begin to close. The conversation is taking too much of her energy. "Josie, do me one more favor." She reaches again for Josie's hand.

"Yes, Mom."

"Watch and listen for me. I'll send you a sign to let you know that I made it."

Josie swallows and nods.

"And, if I'm allowed a choice, I'll come as a cardinal. It'll be my sign to you."

"Okay, Mom, I'll be watching for you."

Giovanna closes her eyes and returns peacefully to sleep.

ONCE HER MOTHER IS ASLEEP, JOSIE CREEPS OUT of her room. Michael and Anna have just returned home. Carmelo is sitting on his recliner, playing a game of patty cake with Anna on his lap. Michael is nearby playing with a new toy Nora bought him at the store. Josie goes into the kitchen and prepares a snack of cut-up banana and toast for them. She mulls over her mother's words. She understands she shouldn't be surprised—this talent for communicating with the dead is inherited, but is it gift or curse? She has always been aware of her ability but decided early in life to ignore it. With her disregard, her ability eventually disappeared from her consciousness. Besides, it never felt like it was much help to anyone—it certainly didn't help her mother save Andy. And now, it couldn't help her save her mother from cancer.

"Dad, could you bring Anna to the kitchen? Michael, time for snack," Josie says.

Carmelo places Anna in her high chair. She begins to kick her legs as soon he buckles her in. Josie places her snack on the tray. Anna picks up a piece of the banana with her plump little fingers and plunks it into her mouth.

Will Anna and Michael be like me? Will they see auras, too? Josie's mind flickers through her childhood memories. She sees Andy talking to her as if he were still among the living.

At the kitchen table, Michael sits in his booster chair gulping cool milk from a sippy cup. Josie smiles and tosses a finger through his soft hair. Joyful and innocent, she prays he and his sister won't inherit this special gift. The ability passed from generation to generation on her mother's side of the family, though not everyone was touched by it. Whether by predetermined fate or fluke of chance, Tony didn't inherit the gift and her sister didn't manifest it to the same degree Josie did as a child.

Maybe, she thinks, *my kids will be like Nora. Maybe it gets diluted as it passes from generation to generation.* Yet, sitting there, resting her chin in her hand and watching her children eagerly chew each piece of their snack, she realizes the inevitable. There will come a day when her past will burst to light, when her skills will refuse to be trapped anymore.

CHAPTER 3

ANDREW

The seaside flags flap in the morning breeze. A fine ocean mist trills over the surface of Atlantic shore, the waves brush up against the boat's hull. The boat creaks and sways, tethered to the steel dock. Captain Andrew Chase walks from one end of the damp wooden deck to the other, preparing for the day ahead. He anticipates seven fishermen in all, chartering an expedition off the coast of Cape May. Hundreds of shorebirds—whimbrels, black-bellied plovers, and sanderlings—who have wintered in the surrounding forests and marshes, fly over, and land on the beach. The song of the native warbler pierces the quiet.

The month of May is especially demanding for the captain. Chase Fishing—one of the oldest charter boat companies in South Jersey—plays host to novice and skilled fisherman from all over the eastern seaboard. With the water temperatures growing warmer, the ocean holds abundant striped bass, weakfish, flounder and even bluefish. Andrew has become the permanent fill-in for his father, Joseph, the owner of Chase Fishing. Joseph, now seventy, had grown tired of captaining the expeditions. It was hard on him physically to keep up with the job's demands. This was an unfortunate reality of old age and the passage of time and generations. Andrew's great-grandfather, Thomas Chase, had founded the company in 1903.

But today, before Andrew begins to accept guests onto his boat, his father steps on board.

"Are you joining us today, Dad?" Andrew asks. Puzzled, he notices his father isn't dressed to fish. He is wearing navy trousers and a gray cardigan sweater.

"No, I've got work to do back at the office." He places his hands in his pockets and watches Andrew prepare the lures and bait.

"Too bad, the waters are calm and I've seen bluefish popping up everywhere—should make for a rewarding trip for our passengers."

"I did want to talk to you though ... before you set out," Joseph says, somewhat awkwardly.

"Is everything all right?" Andrew stops working and looks at his father. He is well-aware of the rarity of Joseph's visit. Whenever he came onto the boat, he came to fish. He wasn't one to come to chat.

"Yes, yes, everything's fine but I do want to talk to you about your future."

"Do you mean your plans for when I take ownership of the company?" Andrew crinkles his forehead as he had assumed, perhaps wrongly, that his future was to become the next president of Chase Fishing—he was his father's sole heir. They were meeting with their lawyer next week to determine the details of the transaction.

"Andrew, I want you to be happy. I want you to live your dream."

"My dream?"

"I know you've wanted to use your medical degree for a long time and I appreciate your coming home with the intention of allowing me to retire. But I know—in your heart—this isn't what you want. In all honesty, your mother and I've known this since you were twelve, when you started ... healing people."

By the act of laying his hands on a person's injury accompanied by a silent prayer, Andrew could heal wounds. The gift arrived in the early morning hours of Good Friday when he was twelve years old. He woke-up screaming with extreme pain in his hands. Witnessed by his parents, puncture wounds formed on the inside of his palms. It was if they were being driven open by invisible wide-bore nails. The wounds bled for eight terrifying minutes. Certain his son was dying, Andrew's father tried calling for help but the phone was dead. By the time they got Andrew into the car to find emergency care, the wounds spontaneously healed as if the perforations never existed. And that was just the beginning.

The wounds returned every year at the start of Holy Week, precisely at 1:53 a.m. and disappeared eight minutes later. They left no residual scar. However, beyond these peculiar painful wounds, Andrew's gift of healing developed with each passing year. He found himself able to heal open gaping wounds, broken bones and scars. He didn't use it often, only on his mother, father, animals and a few unsuspecting friends. It was their secret because they knew if it got out that he was a healer, Andrew's life would cease to be normal. He'd be deluged with strangers looking for a miracle worker.

"But Dad, this is my duty. Running the company is what you raised me to do."

"Yes, this is what we raised you to do, but not what God intended you to be. You were born a healer. You're a gifted fisherman but your calling—your vocation—is to be a doctor."

Andrew walks over to his father and embraces him. They hold each other tight but Andrew is reluctant. He doesn't want his father giving up on him. "Dad, you don't have to do this for me. I'm young ... there's time. I'll be a doctor one day and my son will take over the business for me."

"I appreciate your optimism. However, you don't have any children ... and before you have children, you need to find a wife. I don't think you're going to find her here working in this industry." His father laughs, only partly in jest.

Andrew nods and returns a smile to his father. He knows he won't find his wife here on the Jersey Shore. He had visions of her over the years and none of the visions showed them in a place he recognized. The visions showed a faraway desert-like place, perhaps in the Middle East, and she may have even belonged to a different time.

"Look, business is good, your mother and I will able to sell it. Our fleet is sizeable, our name and reputation is solid. We have twenty-one boats stationed from Cape May to Ocean City–"

"Yes, I know but it's not the time to sell."

"Andrew, it's time, we've done what we can. Three generations is enough."

Andrew stares at the ocean in front of him. The waves roll in and roll out, tumbling and free, but they are always obligated to return. This was how life was for him. He always returned home after brief periods of freedom because he had always been bound to this life. And this meant the end to the family company,—a legacy lasting almost a hundred years. But he knew if anyone was to break the line, it was up to his father. Joseph would never place that burden on Andrew, and he knew Andrew wouldn't sell the business once it was in his hands. Andrew was adopted—he would never think to let his adoptive family down by dissolving the company. In the absence of other blood heirs, his father was right. The time had come.

CHAPTER 4

JOSIE

PHOENIX, ARIZONA—MAY 2002

"I have some news but just know that I'm okay," Declan says over the phone.

"What is it?" Josie asks. "News?" Her heart beats faster.

"I was in a car accident this morning," he says.

"Are you all right?" Her mind tumbles through a mess of terrible and anxious thoughts.

"Sort of."

"Sort of?" She imagines his wreck and pictures him on a hospital gurney sprawled out with broken bones, all by himself.

"Settle down. I'm fine, you can hear my voice, right?" Declan asks.

"Yes, but what do you mean by sort of?"

"They think I have a concussion."

"A concussion? They? Are you at the hospital?" A note of concern makes her voice rise.

"I'm in the emergency room at St. Catherine's."

"Oh, geez! How did this happen?" she asked.

"I was on my way to work when this guy cut me off."

"Please tell me it wasn't at the merge from Hiawatha to 94—"

"It was."

"I hate it when you go that route, it's so dangerous!" she says with a touch of vehemence.

"Except for this concussion and the soreness in my neck—"

"Your neck? Did they X-ray it?"

"My neck's been cleared. Just sore, no fractures anywhere. Some cuts and bruises, that's all."

"That's all? What about the concussion? Do you remember any of what happened?" she asks.

"That's why they think I have a concussion. The last thing I remember was getting in my car to drive to work. I don't remember much after that until one of the guys who saw the accident opened my door to ask me if I was okay. He told the cops he saw me try to avoid the other driver but we ended up colliding," he explains.

"Did you crack the windshield? Is that how you hit your head?"

"That's what they suspect."

"Were you wearing your seatbelt?"

"What do you think? Of course."

"I told you shouldn't be driving that old car anymore! There aren't any airbags in that thing."

"Doesn't matter now, Josie. My Prelude's totaled. I couldn't drive it if I wanted to."

Declan goes over the few details of the accident he was given by the officer at the scene. Josie's cycles through what she should do next. Go home and leave her mother?

"I didn't want to have to tell you about this and stress you out more but I knew you'd be pissed if I didn't," he says. "Since you're not home, the ER doctor thinks he can get me admitted for 24-hour observation, but I've got so much to do at office—"

"Dec, you've got to take care of yourself. Work will wait. We'll come home."

"No, don't. I'll be fine. Your mom needs you," he insists.

"You have a concussion. Plus, you can't drive while you have a concussion, much less leave the house for a time. What if something happens? What if your condition worsens and no one is around to help?"

"Yeah, but I'll be staying in observation for at least a day."

"But what then? You could have symptoms later and no one's home to keep an eye on you." Declan's immediate family was not an option. His parents were deceased and his sister lived in California.

"Well, if you come home, I'd want you leave the kids with me and head back to take care of your mom."

"I can't leave the kids with you. You'll be in no condition to take care of them."

"We can cross that bridge when we come to it," he asserts.

As they talk, Josie mentally accounts for the time her mother predicts she has left. She's been with her parents almost two weeks—if her mother's right, she has about ten days left to live. Maybe her mother will be wrong?

Josie peeks into her mother's bedroom from the hall outside the door. She appears to be asleep. Josie starts to walk away when Giovanna asks, "Is everything okay?"

Josie comes in the doorway and makes the so-so sign with her hand.

"What's going on?" she asks.

Josie holds up her index finger as if to say in one minute. She nods while Declan talks on the other end of the receiver. She steps back into the hallway for privacy. Her mind wanders to the night she met him. She was waiting for a cab outside a Minneapolis Hotel. Declan drove up and got out of his car and offered her a ride saying, "I don't think it's safe for a beautiful woman to wait alone at night for a cab." While she didn't get in his car, she was captivated by his aura. She hadn't perceived auras since she was a child. His was an incredible turquoise color and it put her at immediate ease. She knew he was more than someone special and for the first time in her life, she felt confirmation from above. This was the man she was meant to be with.

"Josie?" he asks on the other end of the receiver.

"Yes, I'm here."

"I thought I lost your call for a minute."

"My sister and Tony can help for a short time and then I'll return to take care of my mom," she says but the minute she speaks these works, she is regretful.

"Jos, you're the one with the nursing skills. She needs you."

She'd want me to take care of my husband. It's a few days, there'll be time. I can still be here for her. "I'll come back to take care of her, I won't be gone long."

JOSIE FINISHES PACKING HER BAGS. IT IS SUNDAY MORNING, Mother's Day, May 12, 2002. Outside, the weather is warm and the sky, clear blue, a typical Arizona day. Her father paces and mutters, wandering from room to room, fixing things and fidgeting with gadgets around the house. Josie knows her leaving is breaking him inside. For the last fifty years, his life has orbited around her mother's. Giovanna has directed their routine and all of their activities. Josie's presence has allowed her father to avoid his impending solitude, and her absence will only make this reality more apparent.

Tony brings their mother out of her bedroom and assists her to the living room couch. Josie thinks it's good to see her up and out of bed. Giovanna has some rosy color in her cheeks. She remains a beautiful slender woman, even in her old age. She places a graceful smile on her face for her grandchildren. Her skin is creamy and smooth and she appears almost radiant except for the dreaded disease that overshadows her every movement.

Carmelo continues to wander, not knowing what mind-occupying activity to perform next. At least, Josie thinks, he is clean-shaven and well-fed. This gives her some peace of mind, and knowing that Nora and Tony will keep a close eye on him as well as her mother.

Nora sits with Giovanna on the couch. They watch Anna and Michael playing on the floor with a few toys.

"Josie, it's time to get going. I'll start putting your suitcases in the car," Tony says. He picks up her bags parked by the front door.

Josie nods. *This is it … be strong.* She directs her eyes toward the floor, not wanting her mother to see her cry. She busies herself with gathering her carry-on bag stuffed with diapers, snacks, and toys for Anna and Michael to have on the plane. She wipes her eyes and walks over to her mother sitting on the couch. "Mom, I'll be back, okay? Once I know everything is clear with Declan, I'll come right back."

"You will?" Doubt is heavy in Giovanna's voice.

Josie's heart sinks, knowing well what her mother is thinking. She will never see her alive in this life again.

PART II

He who seeks, finds, and sometimes what he would rather not.
—Italian Proverb

PREMONITIONS

"Am I dreaming?" It feels too real to be a dream. The air is cold and still, the ground damp and hard. The crescent moon is high above and sheds almost no light on her surroundings. Her body becomes heavy and her neck aches as if two hands have left their mark. She hears a shovel scraping against rocks and dirt. Her body is broken, her breath is gone. She feels the earth burying her. Beneath the rubble, her heart beats its last beat and while she knows she is no longer alive, she is still aware. Then, in an indecipherable instant, she finds she is no longer in the grave but watching a stranger dump shovelfuls of earth on top of a woman's dead body, not hers but another's, in a shallow pit. She hears a pleading voice.

"Tell my mother I was drunk. I didn't know what I was doing. I didn't mean for this to happen!"

A thin young woman with hazel eyes appears next to Josie. "I'm sorry, Mom! I was so stupid for going with him!" the woman cries.

The man does not see the dead woman's spirit, nor does he see Josie. She doesn't recognize the woman—or the man—but knows the woman is about twenty-two. Before the woman vanishes, she grabs Josie's arm, locking on her eyes, "Please, show my mother where he buried me."

The man coughs and clears his throat, packing soil over the woman's shattered body and covering it with the brush of the surrounding woods.

CHAPTER 5

JOSIE

ST. PAUL, MINNESOTA—MARCH 2006

osie pulls her robe snug around her body, bracing for the chill. She opens the front door and picks up the newspaper on the porch. She heads back into the kitchen, sits down at the table and begins to thumb through its pages. She sips her morning coffee and feels a subtle ripple of pleasure flow through her body. The night is over, her restless dreams are done. This is the time of day she cherishes because it is her time, belonging to her and no one else. She holds onto it like a prized possession, sharing it only with Jamison. The trusted terrier lies at her feet like a warm pair of slippers, occasionally jingling his collar when his hind leg reaches to scratch behind his ears.

As she reads the paper, she avoids looking at the date. She already knows well what day it is—March 2nd, what would've been her mother's seventy-fifth birthday. The weight of her absence sinks in. Josie's third baby, Jacob, is fourteen months-old. He will only know his grandmother through photos, paintings and the stories Josie will eventually tell him once he is old enough to understand. She closes her eyes and mumbles an *Our Father* to herself and then, making the Sign of the Cross, opens her eyes again to look out the window, looking for her mother's messenger—the cardinal who perches in the tree by the kitchen window. Where is she now? Where does her spirit go when she isn't whispering to her in her mind and living in her dreams? Josie wonders, *What if? What if*

Mom had lived? Would her father's dementia have gone unnoticed? Would her mother still be making excuses for his forgetfulness? *Thank God for Nora*, who now guards Carmelo's affairs. And what about Josie's premonitions? Would they be happening if Giovanna was still alive?

Josie takes a tissue from her pocket and blows her nose hard. It's time to get on with the day. She paces through the newspaper's headlines, reading a blurb here and there, from the city's politics to the unsolved crimes in the area. She takes special note of national and world events, terrorism and even unusual weather. She jots down her thoughts on a piece of scrap paper for no real purpose except for the sake of keeping a record. Every morning she takes her handwritten notes and tucks them into her robe pocket. She saves them for later to review against the notes she keeps in a journal; a journal that is busting at the seams and hidden in a drawer beneath her lingerie.

Time and again, morning after morning, year after year, Josie reads the news, and with each passing day, as her mother warned, the news fails to shock her. Her warning came via letter, about a month after her death. Nora found it when cleaning out Giovanna's bedside drawer. The letter hadn't been finished. There was no closing, no good bye. It just trailed off. Giovanna's once beautiful handwriting appeared much weaker. The sentences were uneven and scrawled across the page, her penmanship shaky. She wrote in short disconnected sentences. *"I know your gift arrives soon. The leaves will be orange and red. My sisters come to me in dream after you left. Nora, Tony do not have the gift as you do. You were destined to be parent, mother. You experienced it young to prepare for your life after my death. The gift finds those who can pass it on. After I die, my gift passes to you ..."*

And Josie's premonitions began to increase exactly as her mother warned. Within a few months of her mother's death, major and even back page news began to reveal itself in pieces and portions through her dreams, days and sometimes months, before they happened. It felt as if she were standing in the middle of events as they occurred—the sense of dread, anguish and even, sometimes, physical pain. It was much like watching a movie trailer for a coming attraction or listening in on a clandestine conversation.

Occasionally, Josie became the victim and looked through their eyes, feeling their torment as her own. She became the captured child trapped in a predator's closet; the inebriated teenage girl on a nighttime beach raped, beaten and left for dead; and the blindfolded hostage with her hands tied behind her back and a gun pointed at her head. These events were already set in motion, their energy preceded them. The other realm contained the whole story while her unrestrained spirit dipped into the chapters of time, placing its impressions on her consciousness.

But over the years, she did nothing with this information. Correction, twice ... but did so in secrecy. She gave two anonymous tips to the FBI on the whereabouts of remains of two missing children. She was terrified to tell them who she was, afraid her husband would discover her tips and afraid she'd find herself on the FBI's list of lunatics. She revealed the longitude and latitude lines of the body of missing Florida teen, Amanda Kinsley, who disappears on her senior trip to Cancun in May 2005 and, Joshua Tegstad, who vanishes after his mother drops him at his elementary school in June 2004. There are more ... more than she wants to remember.

Over the baby monitor, she hears Jacob stirring, marking the end of her solitude. She sets aside the paper and gets up to retrieve him from his crib upstairs, and then tiptoes back down the steps in attempt to let Anna, Michael and Declan sleep a little longer. Jacob is the easiest member of the family to please at this early hour; he can be made happy with a bottle of warm milk and a cozy position in his mother's lap.

Jacob snuggles with her in the kitchen chair, drinking his bottle. She continues to read when something catches her eye and this time it isn't a headline. It is a photograph. She examines it closely—a man with graying hair, a white lab coat and wire-rimmed glasses. Below his picture, she notes his name, *Dr. Daniel Sheppard, MD, PhD, Afterlife Scientist, University of Colorado at Denver*. Her eyes drift to a small bold print headline, "Scientist Claims Proof of Life after Death by Capturing the Thoughts of the Dead." She stops. Her mind goes wild. Her fingers begin to tremble and then, without noticing, she releases Jacob's bottle. It falls to the floor.

"Mama," Jacob cries.

She tries to shake off her surprise but she cannot contain her astonishment.

"Mama!"

She reaches down in a daze and picks up Jacob's bottle. Without washing the tip, she sticks it back in his mouth. She can't think of anything else but this man, this photo, this unbelievable revelation. *Proof? Is he serious?*

She bounces Jacob softly on her lap and begins to read:

In the modern age, particularly among Western cultures, encounters with the spirit world are often trivialized. Yet, it's widely known that police departments utilize mediums periodically to assist them in criminal investigations and the United States military utilizes them for defense prediction strategy. Their titles are usually cloaked into more 'acceptable' terms, such as spy, profiler and most recently, mentalist. Now, to clarify, not all spies, profilers or mentalists are psychic. Some are skilled in the art of statistical prediction and analysis and utilize computer-generated models to help them do their work. However, many are indeed psychics or mediums by trade. And yet, as a society we refuse to accept that such abilities are present and possible among human beings. Above all, we refuse to listen to the voices calling from beyond the veil of the physical world.
—Daniel Sheppard, MD, Afterlife Scientist

Could it be true? Is there really a legitimate resource in the United States? And, at a university no less, studying the power of communication between the living and the dead? From his statements, she understands—psychics are everywhere, working in reputable capacities using masked identities like profiler, mentalist and spy. *Why is that?* She tries to convince herself that the Western view, the one that says, "If something can't be seen, it doesn't exist," is the one to trust. That by believing in unseen realities, means you must be clinically insane. Yet, Josie knows love is real, radio and sound waves are real, and air is real ... and they're all invisible to the naked eye. Couldn't the same be true of thought?

She reads further.

> *The University of Colorado is permitting Dr. Sheppard to expand his study as there continues to be heavy skepticism among his fellow researchers. With grant funding from an anonymous donor, the larger study will involve a greater number of mediums—increasing it from the current level of fifteen to a population of seventy-five mediums. The larger population will allow for more rigorous statistical testing and provide findings at a higher level of statistical significance.*

Josie ponders but it isn't long before her thoughts turn to grappling. What should she do? Should she contact this man? What will Declan think? There is a website listed at the end of the article. She knows she must look it up or go crazy with wonder but it's essential she be patient. She closes the newspaper and creases it back into its original folds. It is ready and waiting for Declan to read before work, leaving no trace of her discovery.

LATER IN THE MORNING, AFTER DECLAN LEFT FOR THE OFFICE, Josie sits down at her computer. Before she goes any further, she thinks about her husband and their life then clutches the silver cross she wears around her neck. She remembers what it was like when they were first married. He would bring her spontaneous and thoughtful gifts—sugar cookies from her favorite bakery, cute pairs of fuzzy socks for her cold feet on winter nights, a coffee warming plate because hers always grew cold before she finished it. And there were the flowers—roses, orchids, carnations, lilies— depending on the season and sales. He was romantic yet practical. Now they were so busy with the kids and his job, the little things got overlooked.

Maybe it was beyond them being busy, maybe it was beyond her being taken for granted, though she tried not think about their life together in those terms. It was too discomforting. However, it did seem to her that something changed in him and he was often missing from their family life. He'd travel for work for days at a time, to and from Chicago, Seattle, Madison and, on occasion, Manhattan. The more travel, the more pressure, the more pressure, the more he drank, the more he drank, the more distracted from them he became. It became no use for her to hide his drink of choice—bourbon, straight. He would leave to buy more, thinking he had run out.

She could feel her insides tearing apart—a spiritual tug-of-war—she loved him and yet, she couldn't approach him about this study. He knew little about her abilities, nor did he want to, and she knew he would never support her venture into the unknown. Why? He was a corporate attorney and, as such, their family conformed to accepted societal norms. It was an imperative part of his image that they lived a life free of controversy, one grounded in traditional values. Her unusual talents didn't fit within the confines of anything conservative and least of all, normal. And after all, when they married she had assured him that was all over for her.

A few minutes pass before Josie finally shakes off her uncertainty. She types in the website, deciding she can erase the browsing history later. The website comes up on her screen. She sees the doctor, the same one from the newspaper photo. He is slim and short in stature, and from his picture, she surmises he looks benign enough. To the right of his picture, it reads:

As a child, I was always curious about this thing my parents called the soul. They claimed it belonged to Heaven while the body belonged to the earth. It was an abstraction and I, a budding scientist, found this answer to be insufficient. It seemed logical to me to find evidential proof of the survival of consciousness following the body's physical death. — Dr. Daniel Sheppard, MD, PhD"

Incredible, she thinks, *here's a man with doctorates in psychology and medicine from Cornell and Harvard. Impressive qualifications.* If she had any shred of hope of enrolling in this study, it had to be a legit scientific experiment. Otherwise, she didn't have a leg to stand on with Declan.

She swallows hard. She wants to send him an email and inquire more about his study. Her conscience starts screaming at her in two directions, *"Go for it!"* and *"Stay put, you gutless waif!"* A compromise is out of her reach ... momentarily. She is willing but afraid. Should she wait for a better day? In her heart, she knows there will not be a day better than this one. She decides she can blame herself later if this all blows up in her face.

Her life has come full circle, the skills were there as a child, dormant for years, and then returned again, but now in a downpour. And emailing him isn't necessarily an act of disloyalty to Declan. She isn't offering her services to the good doctor. At this point, she seeks guidance—she needs to know more about it and needs to get it out of her head, to unload it on someone who understands what's going on with this sixth sense of hers. Perhaps Declan will surprise her and overlook her indiscretion. She isn't being dishonest, just omitting some information until she feels able to confess it to him later.

And then, her fingers do the walking as if some independent third person is acting on her behalf. She begins to type her message:

Dear Dr. Sheppard,

I'm interested in learning more about your research. I read about it today in our local paper here in St. Paul, Minnesota. I'm hoping you can offer some guidance on this matter of spirit communication. Since childhood, I've had what I now believe to be encounters with those in spirit, mainly deceased relatives, and mostly during dream state. Recently, my encounters include a message or vision of some future event—predictions of death, accidents, severe weather, or even, simple human interactions that are going to take place. Oddly enough, I saw auras as a child but I don't anymore. Rather, they've been replaced by vivid premonitions.

Since my mother's death from cancer about four years ago and especially since giving birth to my third child last year, I've noticed my abilities have increased significantly. It's spilling into my waking life and I feel telepathically inundated. At this time, I'm having trouble sorting it out and I'm not sure where to go with it.

Currently, I do not work as a profes-sional medium or psychic, and your website indicates you're looking for participants who channel the dead for a living. Rather, I'm a part-time nurse and mother of three children who happens to encounter the deceased.

```
Any recommendations you may have in regard to
these matters would be much appreciated.
Thank you for your time.

Sincerely,

Josephine Reilly
```

As she reads it over, her letter is part-formal request and part-crazy. How does one say "I think I may be psychic" without sounding off their rocker? She tries to make her words sound coherent, but it's impossible. Why would she, some housewife in St. Paul-freaking-Minnesota, have some supernatural gift? That was for other people, more special than she. Josie knows she is ordinary. She is mundane and utterly, unremarkable.

The send icon on her screen appears to vibrate, waiting for her to click on it. She thinks about her family, pulls her hair back tight with her hands then lets it fall back about her face and shoulders. The photos of her children look at her from their picture frames on the wall in front of her. She takes the mouse, moves the letter over to her drafts folder and closes out her email.

CHAPTER 6
ANDREW

D r. Andrew Chase sits waiting on a folding chair inside the human resources office of Doctors for World Relief (DWR)—an organization dedicated to caring for the world's poorest. It's clear to Dr. Chase that their mission starts right here in their sparse, no frills office space in the middle of south-side Chicago. DWR commits their dollars to where they are needed most —to their clinics, supplies and staff located in remote areas all over the world.

"Dr. Chase." The office assistant approaches him.

"Dr. Reinhardt is ready to see you now," she says in a thick Colombian accent.

"Thank you." Andrew stands up and follows the tall, curvy South American woman to an office at the end of a long hallway. She knocks with a firm tap the door.

"Come in," Dr. Reinhardt says.

She enters the doctor's small office, Andrew follows her in.

"Dr. Reinhardt, this is Dr. Chase." She turns to Andrew, nods, smiles slightly and closes the door behind her as she leaves.

"Hello, Dr. Chase, I'm Sam Reinhardt.." He stands up from behind his desk and offers Andrew a handshake.

"Hello, sir ... and please, call me Andrew."

Dr. Reinhardt nods. "Okay, and please feel free to call me Sam. Have a seat." He motions with his hand for Andrew to sit down in the chair across from his desk.

Andrew begins to feel awkward in his suit and tie upon seeing Dr. Reinhardt's attire—a cable knit sweater and khaki cargo pants— far more casual than he expected. Andrew assumed interview protocol was to wear a suit and tie. It's a stretch for him to even be in a suit. He has only worn it twice. The first was for his graduation from his residency program and the second for his job interview at Cook County Hospital. That made the suit at least a decade in age but he figured men's clothes rarely went out of style.

As he sits, Andrew gives a cursory once-over to the medical certificates hanging on the wall. Dr. Reinhardt is board-certified in family medicine and graduated in 1970 from Cornell Medical School. Andrew deduces the senior doctor is in his sixties. Nevertheless, the man has an energy about him that doesn't look interested in slowing down. Similar to the waiting room, Dr. Reinhardt's office is devoid of unnecessary décor. It is equipped with his desk and two chairs, one for the doctor and his guest, a green potted floor plant and a small lamp that sits on the corner of his desk. On top of his desk are numerous small picture frames filled with photos of Dr. Reinhardt and presumably, his wife, in various South American locations along with their patients. The patients appear vulnerable, mostly children and the elderly, but they are smiling almost as if they are emanating love and gratitude.

"Those are some amazing photos." Andrew points toward the pictures.

"Thank you. To tell you the truth, the photos aren't amazing but the people in them are. You have no idea how hard life is in those villages. My wife ... right here," he says, pointing to her picture, "The villagers always flock to her."

"Is your wife a doctor too?" Andrew asks.

"No," he laughs, "Claire's too good to be a doctor, she's a nurse." His eyes light up when he speaks her name. "She's a nurse-midwife. She's probably delivered more babies than there are threads in that fancy suit of yours," he says it with a chuckle but seems to be only half-kidding. "She's delivered a lot of babies in those villages, and many in the middle of the night ... with barely enough light to see the baby's head crown."

Andrew nods, feeling about as tall as a small dog, as he has hardly done anything of service or merit since leaving his medical school program. He hasn't even been practicing medicine for six of the ten years he's been done with his residency.

After a few more words of small talk, Dr. Reinhardt clears his throat, as if to signal the formal beginning of Andrew's interview. "So, Dr. Chase," he clears his throat again, "I mean, Andrew ... I understand you've captured the eye of one of our top physicians— Dr. Peter Ramzi. He holds you in very high regard and he's not an easy guy to impress. He's even called you a *'healer'* in his letter of recommendation."

Andrew swallows and shifts in his chair. He doesn't like it when the word *healer* gets thrown out there. He wonders if Dr. Reinhardt is on to him and his supernatural talents or if he is simply referring to his skills. As far as he knows, Dr. Ramzi isn't aware of his healing hands. "I work hard for my patients and if that makes me a healer, then I'm honored to be one. Although—I wouldn't consider myself in a league with Dr. Ramzi." Andrew reflects on Dr. Ramzi—a renowned trauma surgeon. He took Andrew under his wing when Andrew was in training at Cook County Hospital and where he now worked as an ER physician.

"You know, Peter and I go way back; we've collaborated on many cases together. He would travel from village to village, helping us local doctors in the stabilization and repair of complex wounds and fractures. Without Peter, I'm certain many of my patients wouldn't have made it."

Andrew had a similar feeling about Dr. Ramzi. It was over the most complicated trauma cases when Dr. Ramzi and Andrew grew into colleagues and friends. He shared with Andrew his experiences of spending twenty-plus years, on and off, working for DWR. Through DWR, he operated on victims of both natural disasters and war in the remote regions of the Andes, and the jungles and rainforests of El Salvador and Guatemala.

After listening to Dr. Ramzi's unusual, and often, perilous stories, Andrew began to feel like DWR might be the answer to the calling he spent his life searching for. He dreamt about travel to exotic places with expansive natural landscapes, picturesque mountains, clear rivers and plenty of wildlife. And, upon midnight conversations over victims of inner-city violence, Dr. Ramzi urged Andrew to apply for the job with DWR.

"Tell me Andrew, what makes you want to dedicate a year of your life to DWR? You do know it's a minimum of a one-year commitment?" Dr. Reinhardt asks.

"Yes, sir, I do," he says.

"And?"

"I feel it's time for me to make a contribution not only to my profession but to humanity. Chicago's been a great place for me to learn and to train, but I'm ready for more. You know, I was raised Catholic so that might have something to do it ... I've always wanted to serve the poor."

Sam nods. "I do believe, however, that the inner city of Chicago has its fair share of the poor."

"Of course, I mean, in particular, the poor who do not have any structured access to health care as in certain regions of South America, Africa, and the like. I know we don't have an optimal system here in the U.S. but–"

"I understand ... more than you know."

Andrew tries to gage Sam's response by his body language but Sam is difficult for him to read. Did he mean he understands that Andrew doesn't have a clue about destitute poverty? Or that he understands Andrew's desire to serve those who have no alternatives, where the absence of basic health care is felt even more than it is here in our own country?

"Andrew, your wish to serve the poor is right on the mark for someone who wants to work for us. That said ... I have concerns."

Andrew feels his heart sink. "Concerns?" Perspiration builds under his arms and his skin sticks to his dress shirt.

"You've only been working in your current position for three years. Are you sure you would be ready to work independently, without a major support network, in the remote areas we will send you to?"

"Yes, I'm sure."

"Well, that's good. However, it's my job to make certain you're sure ... and I can't be certain until you have a more lengthy work record in medicine."

Andrew's expression falls into disappointment. This interview isn't going as well as he hoped it would.

"Nevertheless, Dr. Ramzi believes you are qualified for this job and I respect his opinion. Plus, you're in decent physical shape. I suspect you'll pass our physical examination with flying colors."

"Are you talking about a routine physical?"

"Yes and more. We'll put you through the paces. DWR has various strength and endurance tests that you'll be required to pass before you could come on board."

"Oh," Andrew says, unsure whether or not to feel good or bad yet. Is Sam saying he appears physically capable but not mentally capable?

"The physical exam will tell us if you have the energy to do the job. Physical capacity will be as important as your ability to care for a wide range of patients with diverse ailments."

"I think I could pass those tests without a problem," Andrew says, thinking it's probably all right that he speak with confidence about his physical fitness, even if it isn't in reference to his medical skills.

"Of course, there remains the issue of you're leaving medicine and coming back. Tell me why you came back."

"It's a long story." Andrew isn't sure how much of his story was necessary. He believed in saying only enough to satisfy another's curiosity.

"Go ahead, we've got time."

Andrew nods. *Oh, boy.* He straightens up in his chair and tugs his pants at his thighs as if to remove the creases. *Talk about the family business.* "My father wanted to leave our family's fishing business to me. It was a rather large charter fishing boat business started by my great grandfather in the early 1900s."

"Hmm." Sam nods.

Andrew continues, "And although they sent me to medical school, it was the plan that I'd take over the business when my father retired. He and my mother viewed med school as a kind of back-up career if our company ever failed. But when I returned after my residency, my father and mother realized how unhappy I was— they could see that I truly loved being a doctor. I do enjoy the outdoors, fishing and being on the water, though."

Sam nods again.

"It came down to a commitment I made to my parents and I intended to see it through. However, they were more concerned about my happiness—and the tabling of my medical degree now that I had it—so, they decided to sell the business. It was then I returned to medicine."

"I see. I'm glad you could set me straight." Sam rubs his hand over his chin. He gets up from his chair and walks toward the window, with his back to Andrew.

Andrew sits quietly, fearing he has ruined his chances and thinking he has provided Sam with too much damning information.

Sam turns around to face him. "The thing is, Andrew, I've got a responsibility to send physicians with experience and I've got to be confident in your abilities to work solo. It's critical you're prepared because you're on your own out there ... we send our doctors into very isolated locations. You'll have some skilled staff assisting you but it's not guaranteed. Many times, you'll be training the villagers to help you with procedures."

"Yes, sir, I understand." Andrew bows his head at Sam's disheartening words.

"And you may not always have a translator around to assist you." Sam sits back in his chair and lets out a long sigh as if in deep thought.

Andrew looks back up at Sam, hanging on his every word and gesture but keeps further comments and explanations to himself.

"Andrew, I like you and I think you've got potential but I believe you need to spend a little more time getting experience here in the States."

"Okay." But another year at Cook County is not what Andrew has in mind; he needs a change of scene. After working with so much gang-related trauma and death, he is ready to trade his urban, inner-city practice to one where the problems are different—be it trauma from environmental disaster and yes, sometimes war. Where he can provide care to children who haven't had access to the basics—like physicals, antibiotics and immunizations. Perhaps, there will also be room for him to think—space he hasn't had room for in a long time.

"I have an idea. Would you like to hear it?"

"Of course," he smiles from hearing the sudden lift in Sam's voice.

"Here's what I propose—I have an ER physician in the Twin Cities who wants to work for us but he can only commit for the year. And while we say it's a one-year commitment, we're always hoping for more than that."

Andrew nods, "Okay ..."

"The problem is if he takes a year leave from his ER position at the hospital, they won't guarantee his job on his return unless ... they can find him a temporary replacement. It's hard to find doctors willing to take such a limited post. However, given your situation, this might make for a good trade. And I did promise this doctor I'd see what I could do for him."

"Hmm," Andrew says but he is still unclear regarding what the trade will entail.

"Would you be willing to work in this doctor's place in St. Paul while he works for us for the year?"

"I think so ... ," although he is unsure of what he is agreeing to. He doesn't know what kind of patient population visits the ER there but figures at least it is a change of venue, even if still in the Midwest.

"This way, you will gain more experience and this other doctor could work for us for the year and return to his permanent position in St. Paul when his term with DWR is up. It's a win-win for all of us. I'd be willing to discuss this with the hospital there and see what I can arrange."

"I suppose that could work, although I've never been to the Twin Cities. I guess it's just a smaller version of Chicago, huh?"

"Not quite, but you'll like it. There are lots of good fishing lakes in Minnesota. You know, Minnesota is the 'Land of a Thousand Lakes' and offers a great variety of outdoor activities."

Andrew smiles. "When do I start?"

CHAPTER 7

Snow falls and dusts white onto the cross-rails of the secluded track. The Northwood's pines sway from the soft eastward wind. In the distance, a whistle blows from an approaching train. Josie watches a young man smoking a cigarette, exhaling rings into the cold night air. He leans against the hood of his car—its headlights illuminate the rail crossing sign. He holds a photograph in his hand, looks at it once then places it under the windshield wipers. He steps away, throws his cigarette onto the dirt and with his shoe, grinds it into ashes. The whistle blows again. The locomotive's white light comes into view, its engine thunders and chugs.

The wheels of the rail cars clack and howl, growing louder ...

Josie pleads, "Don't! Your life will get better. It will. I promise—you're too young to realize this yet!"

The young man faces her. He's a boy, not more than seventeen. His face is grim, "It's already done."

Josie looks down at her feet and finds herself standing on the steel bars, alone. The train has passed but the sound of metal against metal still echoes into the night. The boy who stood beside her has faded into the night.

JOSIE

ST. PAUL, MINNESOTA—LATE MARCH 2006

Two weeks pass. While she's been researching the topic of psychic abilities and studies, she's unable to send her letter to Dr. Sheppard. *No guts, no glory,* she thinks. She proceeds to review her notes from the morning and checks them against her notes in her journal, confirming her latest premonitions. The body of a missing Minnesota woman was found where Josie dreamt it would be, under a bridge near the Mississippi River. A dream she had months ago of three dogs perishing in a fire occurred the day prior at a kennel not far from her home, and finally an earthquake in the Philippines that she dreamt of the week earlier did occur late last night. She watched the story unfold on the morning news.

Why do I bother to keep these notes? Either I take the plunge and talk to Declan about this or give it up. She tears up today's notes in frustration and throws them in the trash. Despite her lack of resolve, she's learned that Dr. Sheppard's research program is not alone. Through her own investigation, she's discovered there are two more centers in the United States performing psychic research: Los Angeles, California and Sedona, Arizona. Further, all over the Internet are conversations about an increase in intuitive abilities occurring across all cultures and regions. *Is there something going on—a kind of world-enlightenment?* The whole prospect of delving into this unknown frontier excites her and in her heart, she believes she could qualify to be part of Dr. Sheppard's research study.

Nevertheless, without Declan's blessing, she can't apply to participate in any study or group. If she does, she might as well throw her marriage into a tailspin and send it off a steep cliff. However, if she gains his approval, she'll be able to go forward without feelings of guilt.

THAT NIGHT AFTER THE KIDS GO TO BED, JOSIE RELAXES ON THE couch with Declan and watches the ten o'clock news. She rests her body against his, cuddled beneath the crook of his arm with her head against his chest. It is comfortable, familiar and warm. She knows he had a stressful day at work crafting the legal arguments for his clients, writing contracts and other dealings of which she knows close to nothing about. Not because she didn't understand his work, but rather, Declan's time at home was his time to escape the rigors of his job.

She turns her face to his and begins to stroke his wavy hair, noticing the gray strands growing at the edge of his temples. His eyes, subtly dabbed by the fine lines of stress and age, linger over her face and lips. He pulls her closer to his chest and kisses her, his hands caress a path over the curve of her spine. His arms tighten, pulling her onto his lap and encapsulates her in the warmth of his embrace. His lips slide smooth over the surface of her ear, she arcs her neck as his warm breath passes over her skin, then presses his lips again to hers.

It has been ages since he's kissed her in this way—with such hunger. Yet, she struggles to engage her passion. How does she let herself lose control and forget all that she needs to tell him? Can it wait? Her thoughts hold her body in a vise. Should she wait until his passion is fully satisfied? Logic tells her she must stop before things go farther. It isn't fair to seduce him, although this is not her intent. Nevertheless, he will see it this way—arousing his physical thirst in order to allow her to have her way. She must share her discovery about the Institute with him. There is no use in stalling. It's a gamble she must take. She pulls back from him, not harshly, but enough so that his tenderness rocks to a halt.

"Declan, I have something to tell you."

His expression alters from one of liquid passion to confusion and concern. His skeptical blue eyes examine her face. She slinks off his lap and into the couch cushions, losing her nerve. She should have kept her mouth shut awhile longer only it's too late to retreat.

"Okay, Jos, what did you do now? Back into something with the van again?" He speaks like a father addressing his mistake-prone teenage daughter. She can't hold this against him after all the times she backed the minivan into things such as parked cars, the garage door, and snow-covered rocks. It is a good guess on his part but for once, it is not the van.

"No, nothing ... like that." Telling him about this is worse. She might as well tell him she's having an affair with the postman.

"Okay ..." His back straightens, all joking is put aside.

"I read in the paper about a research program in Denver at the University of Colorado. It's studying people with psychic abilities." There. She blurts it out in full force, *psychic*—the dreaded word she never speaks around Declan. He is far too practical and rational for it; her association with anything "New Age" is the equivalent of calling herself a tree-hugging liberal.

"And what about it?"

She notes his tone and treads carefully. "Well, you know how I sometimes tell you what's in the newspaper before you pick it up to read it?" While she doesn't do this often, she figures it might help her to make her point.

"Yeah?"

"They're recruiting research subjects."

Declan takes his thumbs and rubs them over his brow line until they press hard on his temples. "Please tell me you didn't contact them and volunteer."

"Of course not. I wanted to talk to you about it first. I want to know what you think about it."

"Hon, you can't, it won't fly. I'm sorry. If it got out, it will affect my position in the firm."

She lowers her eyes. *Guilt by association.* Having a wife with psychic pursuits, no matter how legitimate, will jeopardize his reputation as one of the most solid, reliable corporate attorneys in the Twin City area. And no conservative corporate lawyer with half-a-brain would consider flirting with the occult. Such activities could create undesirable perceptions among one's colleagues and clients. Declan was all about respect and professionalism. The mere question of inappropriate behavior off the job—by him *or* his wife—would not bode well within his firm.

"I only wanted to look into being a research subject."

"No."

"Why?" she challenges. "It sounds like something I could do!" She hears herself and thinks she sounds like an adolescent begging for a chance to go to her first rock concert.

"Jos, talking to the dead is not a hobby or a profession. Remember who you are—you're a mother and a nurse. Our family needs to be your first and foremost priority."

"Declan, of course, this doesn't change my priorities. But, you ..."

"End of conversation."

She falls silent and looks away from him. The weight of those words—"*end of conservation*"—meant one thing. There would be no compromise. He gave his order and any further pursuit on her part would be an outright act of betrayal. She knew it would go nowhere but a deeper grave. The hole was dug. It was time to bury it. She gets up and goes upstairs to bed.

CHAPTER 8

The liar needs a good memory.
—Italian Proverb

I
t is early morning and Josie is the only one awake. She returns to the Institute's webpage and locates the link to the application form. She stares at her screen, knowing full well if she opens the link to the application document, she will cross the forbidden line, the line Declan drew. She grapples, *should I or shouldn't I?* Is she the dutiful wife or a disobedient psychic mom? Perhaps a little of both. The choices swirl in her head. Then with one click of the mouse by the independent motion of her index finger, the document opens. She begins to read:

```
Dear Applicant:

Before proceeding further, please be aware of
our application requirements:

You must be a United States Resident and be
at least 18 years old to participate in our
study.

All prospective mediums are required to
complete three readings for three randomly
assigned candidates. Details of each reading
must be documented according to the specifics
outlined in Application Attachment 2.

If you aren't capable of performing these
readings, then please do not apply.
```

She stops and reads the sentence again. *If you aren't capable.* Self-doubt creeps in.

Someone taps her shoulder.

"Hi, Mommy," Michael says.

She turns, foggy from being lost in her thoughts. "Michael." She smiles and gives him a peck on his soft, rosy cheek. "It's early. Did you sleep well?"

"Yes." He gives a stretch of his little boy arms. "I'm hungry. Can you get me some breakfast?"

"Sure. What would you like?"

"Cinnamon squares ... the ones you bought at Wilson's."

"And what's the magic word?"

"Pleeeease ..."

She closes out the page, deletes her recent browsing history and heads into the kitchen with Michael. She pulls the box of cinnamon squares from the cupboard and scrutinizes each individual ingredient listed at the side of the box again just like she did at the market.

He ambles into the kitchen and plops down on a stool by the counter. "Mom, I wish I didn't have peanut allergies." He watches her pour the cereal into a bowl for him.

"I know, Baby ... and I wish I could make them go away for you." She frowns—*Someday there'll be a cure.*

Michael shrugs and switches on the kitchen TV, turning the station to the Cartoon Network. Josie enjoys seeing him there with his freckled nose and dimpled cheeks, almost a carbon copy of his father as a boy.

A few minutes pass when Michael pipes up again. "Mommy, who's Jerry?"

"I don't know. Is that someone in the cartoon?"

"No, a name I heard."

"At school?"

"No, just now. I heard it in my head."

That's weird. "You heard it in your head? What do you mean?"

"I don't know, like a voice," he says, blankly.

Josie's stomach turns. It is a random question as if a speck of dust flitted across his mind.

"Hey, Mommy, could I have some orange juice?"

"Sure, honey."

Josie isn't sure if she should pursue him with more questions about the voice. She decides it's likely nothing more than the random thoughts of a child. She pulls out the bottle of orange juice from the refrigerator and pours the juice into a cup for him. He is still watching his cartoons and munching away.

She gazes at him and ponders. *Is it worth it? Do I go ahead and attempt the prerequisite readings? Where is my self-confidence? Oh, yeah, I have none. Why isn't being a mommy enough for me? Lots of moms work. Although, those moms are doing regular jobs and this job is not exactly regular. No, being psychic is definitely out of the range of normal.*

Josie hears more shuffling steps and turns to see Anna entering the kitchen holding her "blankie" and "lammie," her stuffed baby lamb.

"Hello, my dear," Josie says.

Anna crawls into her lap and clasps her arms around her, giving her a light kiss on the cheek.

"How did you sleep?" Josie asks.

"Good, Mommy," Anna says. Her long, wavy hair relaxes in tresses about her face and across her back.

"Hey, you slept in your bed all night, I'm so proud of you."

"Yes, Mommy, I did." Anna grins wide, pleased by her achievement.

"That's my girl." Josie knows it's important to praise her daughter's independence. Plus, she didn't much like having Anna sleep in the same bed with her. Not because she didn't want to snuggle with her daughter but because it triggered even more graphic dreams for Josie than usual.

She hears Jacob calling, "Maaa-maaa, Maaa-maaa" from his crib upstairs.

"Anna, I have to go and get Jacob," Josie says.

"Why? I want to sit on your lap some more." She tries to keep Josie in place so she can't stand up.

"I know. I'd like to sit with you longer, honey, but Jacob's awake." She stands up and places Anna's stubborn body onto on the floor. Anna purses her lips and clutches her blanket and lamb tight in her small hands.

Josie walks up the winding staircase. She slides her fingers over the hard oak banister. She thinks about how blessed she is to have three healthy children and a beautiful home. When she reaches the top, she hears the water running. Declan is showering and singing along to the music over the shower radio in the master bath.

"Mama," Jacob calls as he sees her coming through his bedroom door. His arms open wide and reach for her.

"Hi there, mister." She lifts him out of his crib. "Oh, you're wet. We've got to change your diaper." She sets him down on a changing pad and pulls off his wet diaper. He babbles and chatters while she cleans him, appearing to enjoy the sound of his own voice. Of her three, Jacob looks the most like her—fine brown hair, large blue eyes and a full round face. Above all, he is solid. It pleases her to know that some features from her side of the family will continue on.

As she dresses Jacob, Declan enters Jacob's room. He has a towel tucked around his waist and dries under his arms and his back with another.

"Hi, buddy," Declan says, peering over her shoulder at Jacob on the changing pad.

"Dada!" Jacob beams.

Declan bends down and gives him a gentle peck on the forehead.

"Dada!" Jacob kicks his sturdy legs up and down.

"Now that's my beautiful boy." Declan reaches over Josie and picks Jacob up off the changing pad.

Josie finds it hard not to notice Declan's arms flex as he picks up their son. These days, not only is Declan stubborn like a rock, he is built like one. While he ran a marathon every year, this year, he alternated running with rigorous strength training using the weight machines at his firm's fitness center. Although fast approaching forty, Declan had never been in better physical condition. Josie, on the other hand, feels frumpy and old. She wonders to herself if his training is the reason for her own restlessness. He has interests apart from them as well as a rewarding job. What does she have? She reminds herself—she's the mother of three beautiful angels and the wife of a successful, handsome man who loves her. Why isn't this enough for her?

Declan breaks the apparent spell she is in, "What are you guys up to today?" he asks, appearing to forget the divide they encountered the night before.

Josie says nothing. Her mind wanders.

"Josie, hello, are you there?" he says.

"Oh, sorry, I was daydreaming." She folds and puts away the changing pad.

"Not about that program again? You've let that go, right?"

"Of course. I'm still trying to wake up ... that's all. I didn't sleep very well." She tosses Jacob's dirty diaper into the trash.

"What's your plan for the day after you drop Michael off at school? It's supposed to be a nice day."

"I've got to run Anna to preschool this morning and after, I'm going to Wilson's. We're out of a lot of basics ... bananas, coffee, bread ..."

Hey, could you pick up some steaks? I feel like grilling out since it's supposed to get up to fifty today."

"Sure. What time will you be home?"

"The usual, six o'clock."

"Okay, sounds good, hon," she says, smiling slightly in attempt to conceal her hurt feelings.

He gives her a soft peck on the forehead. "I gotta hurry up and get to work." He hands Jacob back to her and leaves the room.

Josie finishes dressing Jacob and carries him down the stairs. When she arrives at the kitchen, she finds Anna pouring herself some Cheerios and most of it is landing on the floor, not in her bowl. The dog is doing his part, gobbling up the cereal mess on the floor.

Josie puts Jacob into his high chair then kneels down to pick up the cereal. "Anna, you need to wait for Mommy to help you."

"I was hungry, Mommy. You took too long," Anna whines.

Jamison is still acting like a vacuum, scarfing up the pieces. "Jamison, go lie down!" Josie orders. The dog takes off and huddles into his kennel.

Nevertheless, Josie's mind continues to be elsewhere. She thinks about the challenge the Institute has set forth and all the "what ifs." *Declan doesn't have to know, does he?* Although keeping secrets from each other wasn't part of their marriage thus far and to start now doesn't seem like a wise plan. She sighs. *Why me? Why can't I be normal like other wives?*

The morning is off and running. Josie's daily schedule of plans and obligations will go on as they do every day. But today, the voices in her head are urging her—*Spread your wings in a new direction.*

CHAPTER 9

Josie arrives home from her errands and puts away the groceries. Her daydream spins like a spider's web, thinking about all the convoluted ways she might be able to justify her application to Declan. *What if I apply to the institute, do the readings they assign to me and I'm actually successful? Would Declan reconsider? Will he come to see the light?* Never. Her chest feels heavy with disappointment and worse, there is a growing bitterness about her. She feels herself starting to resent him. She once thought they made decisions as a team and wonders if this is true anymore. Or, is the image in her mind of their marriage a delusion? An artifact of their past?

Josie grapples, to rebel or not to rebel? It eats away at her until it arrives in a single and obvious truth—she is gutless when it comes to her husband and deep down, she knows—he always has the final say. Above all, she doesn't know how she would survive without him. If she was a ship then he was her shore. And even though he depended on her to run the house and take care of the kids, she depends on him a hundred times more. With her mother dead and a father incapable of caring for himself, Declan and her children are her life, her stability, and her anchor. She lives for them and she hopes they do for her. Without them, she would be adrift. Lately, though, Declan had more of a life apart from her than with her and her children had their own friends and their own futures to plan.

Josie's thoughts spiral, her ambivalence feeds her resentment. Can't Declan see she has aspirations and goals of her own to achieve? Can't he find it in his heart to respect her needs and desires apart from them as a couple? The bitterness takes hold and she refuses to be its prisoner.

She returns to her computer and clicks on the application form. She rereads its introduction. *"If you aren't capable of performing these readings, then please do not apply."* She closes it. *There, it's done. Silly dream over and back to my life of laundry, cooking, cleaning, and carpooling.*

The phone rings. Josie sits in front of the computer and stares at its screen. She counts to ten and then some more. The phone keeps ringing. She quits counting and decides to answer—she knows it's Nora. She is certain that Nora will drill her about why she hasn't called her in the last couple of days. Josie swallows hard and hits talk, "Hi, Nora."

"How did you know it was me?" Nora asks.

"An educated guess and ... Caller ID," she says.

"Oh, yeah, I always forget about that. Couldn't you at least pretend you're surprised to hear my voice?" Nora sounds annoyed but continues without stopping, "Hey, I heard the funniest thing today on the news."

"What's that?"

"There's this study being done in Sedona with people who have psychic abilities."

"I read about it too, there was an article I found on the Internet a couple days ago."

"I thought about you, of course, but you know the weirdest thing about it? Their logo is a cardinal."

"A cardinal? That's funny. I completely missed it when I was reading the article. I wonder why it's not something more southwestern like a cactus or a coyote."

"I know, strange they would use a cardinal for a project in Sedona. However, I thought of you right away. I think it's a sign from Mom. You should look into it."

"I can't, I talked to Declan about a similar study in Denver. He doesn't want me to apply to it or any study. He thinks it would cause problems."

"Problems? For who?"

"For us at home and especially for him at work."

"Oh, come on. That's crazy. Does he think it would jeopardize his job or something?"

"Pretty much. He feels it could be damaging to his position in the firm if it got out that I was a budding clairvoyant."

"For real?"

"Reputation is everything when you're an attorney. I get that."

"I don't see what the big deal is. Again, I don't think you can ignore it. Mom is sending you a sign, or why would a Sedona psychic research center pick a cardinal? It's just too much of a coincidence."

"It's out of my hands. Declan's not going to change his mind. The most I can hope for is maybe in time, his opinion will soften, but I'm not counting on it."

In between the words they spoke to each other, Josie knows full well he's never going to change, not a single solitary degree. Nora knows it too. No matter how Josie presents it to Declan, try as she may to twist the words into some semblance of a legitimate and worthwhile endeavor, it didn't matter. It wouldn't change anything.

Nora sighs. "I guess you have to do what you have to do. If he's that against it, it's not worth destroying your marriage over. It's too bad he can't open his mind, even a little, to the possibility–"

"Nora, please ... drop it."

"Okay. I get it."

Their voices fall silent for several seconds.

"What else is new?" Nora asks in attempt to move on.

"Nothing ... looking for a new hobby I guess," Josie says.

"I've read a couple of good books lately. I could send them to you if you're interested?"

"I'm not in the mood right now. Save them for me, maybe I'll change my mind in a few months." *Or in a few years.* The books Nora read weren't "junk food for the mind" books. They were about deepening your spirituality, studying your inner purpose, and topics far too deep for Josie right now. She required lighter reading, books without demands on her thoughts or her morality, ones without intimate evaluations of her life and behavior. A trashy romance novel might do the trick, she thinks—certainly not one causing her any expenditure of mental or emotional energy.

Suddenly, Josie hears a scream and a cry. "Nora, I gotta go. I think Jacob's hurt."

She hangs up quick and finds Jacob sitting on the kitchen floor. He has a welt on his forehead and it swells before her eyes.

"What happened, little man?" Josie bends down to comfort him.

"Mama!" he wails. His hand is on his forehead.

"How did you get hit?"

"That!" He points to an open kitchen cabinet door. Josie realizes she left it open. She assumes he collided with it and whacked his head. She goes to the freezer to get him some ice. *Declan is right*, she thinks. *This venture would divert my attention from my kids—it already has.*

As Josie examines Jacob, his eyes are still spilling tears. She tries to comfort him with her hugs and kisses but inside she feels truly selfish. This life is all she ever wanted, to be a wife and a mother but this yearning for something else is growing inside of her. She wonders if she can go back to being plain old Josie and keep her secret safe in her subconscious mind. Will she be able to pretend she's unaware of the invisible world? In truth, she's never been totally unaware. It was whispering to her all along. It was an embedded and intricate part of her.

The lioness has escaped her cage. Somehow Josie will have to tame her ... except she isn't going for it.

CHAPTER 10

Better one day as a lion than a hundred as a sheep.
—Italian Proverb

At midnight, he wanders the grounds of the cemetery, looking for his children. His throat slit from the burn of a rope pulled too tight and left too long, branded in memory of the revulsion he held for himself. The frozen chill of his hollow black eyes watch her standing at the edge of the gate. He approaches. "Do you know where my children are?"

She observes his skin. It is pale and thin, appearing to have the texture of loose sand. "No," she says.

"My wife took them from me!" He clutches his head then releases an anguished cry.

She says nothing. The fringe of her nightgown clings about her legs. Leaves swirl and flirt with the damp earth, floating over the field of gravestones.

In the darkness, he cries, "I didn't mean to hurt them! Tell her I loved them ... with all my heart but I lost control! I'm so sorry ..."

His form dissolves into vapor as if swallowed by the ground beneath her feet.

Days pass and Josie's emotions cycle erratically between feelings of anger, reluctant acceptance, self-doubt and uncertainty. She wants to stand-up for herself but she's forgotten how. So, she fakes normalcy, hiding her visions and dreams, and functioning day-to-day without anyone, especially Declan, noticing her internal struggle. While she continues to document her experiences in her secret journal, she believes it is an utter waste of time. Who is she helping? She hopes, at the very least, that someday her visions could help those left behind to heal. But beneath the surface of her daily routine and ordinary life, she feels cheated out of a dream—a dream her husband cannot accept. Her spirit crushed, she tries to move on to other things. At least Declan appears content with her, as if her psychic venture never came up.

She peers out the kitchen window into her backyard, looking for a sign, anything to give her a new direction, but no answer comes. She reconciles her uncertainty with the one clear-cut decision she can find. Her mother taught it to her at a young age—to turn her struggle over and release it to the Will of God. In time, she knows the answer will reveal itself, not readily or on demand, but with patience and prayer. *Things will get better*, she thinks, and while optimism isn't one of her finer qualities, she figures today she will give it a shot.

It is time for lunch and time for her to snap into mommy-mode. Anna and Jacob wait at the table for Josie to dole out their macaroni and cheese and sliced apples. Josie's mind flits to Michael as she scoops heaps of orange pasta into their bowls. She hopes he has a friend to eat with at lunch today. It makes her uneasy to think of him eating away from home. She doesn't feel completely secure having others keep an eye on him during a meal, even if he is sitting at the school's *peanut-free* table. She pacifies her worries by keeping his lunches simple, avoiding anything that could prove lethal—a cross-contaminated cookie, cracker or mislabeled snack.

With Declan at work and her two youngest now occupied with their lunches and cartoons on the kitchen TV, Josie goes to the family room and perches on a chair in front of the computer. She rubs her eyes and places Sedona psychic research into the search engine. The Center for Intuitive Research comes up, location, Sedona, Arizona. She opens the link and notices the cardinal logo at the top right corner of her screen. How she ever missed it the first time is a wonder to her. *Could I do this? Should I?*

Josie isn't used to entertaining such complicated life questions. The most perplexing questions she faces of late pertain to her children, such as what to feed Michael and how small to cut up hot dogs so her kids won't choke on them. However, she doesn't feel like the same person anymore. Like someone stole her brain and put a new one in its place. Her heart is the same. She still loves her children with her entire being. She still loves Declan even though he's being difficult. But her mind is different. She no longer thinks the same way. Her view of the world has changed. Internally, she can sense it but there are still too many unanswered questions.

And then, it hits her. Maybe the best way for her to feel comfortable with her skills is to practice. *Maybe I should try it out on some of my friends? Maybe I could do my own readings for a few friends and see how well I do? I've got to prove to myself that I can do it. Then, once I have the confidence, I will approach Declan one more time.*

This idea gives her comfort and hope. She was born this way and to fight it is to fight her own nature. It's who she is; she can't shut the door on it now that it's been opened. She can channel with or without applying to any study. She can even do it without Declan knowing. He missed this technicality.

But now what? Josie's internal tug of war returns. Is it egocentric to allow herself this adventure? Couldn't this be a career opportunity? When she became a wife and mother, it meant giving up most everything that may have meant something to her before in return for something greater and more meaningful than careers and adventures. Motherhood is the role of her life, the role she waited and longed for. She cherishes it. So, why isn't it enough for her?

"Ugh!" She lets out a sigh and shakes her head in disgust. She repulses herself. Deceit is not a concept she's accustomed to, it's not in her nature and practically speaking, she's a terrible liar. And intentionally, she forgets that every foolish decision ever made was based on "could" and not on "should." Every question sat somewhere on the spectrum of could versus should, yes versus no. This decision met all the criteria of a foolish decision. She sees her mind moving in the direction of "could" and ignoring the "should."

The doorbell rings and returns her to her present reality.

"I'll get it! It's them!" Anna jumps out from her chair at the kitchen table and leaves behind what is left of her lunch.

As Anna runs to the front door, Josie follows in case it isn't the friends they are expecting. Josie peeks through the peephole of the door. She sees her old friend Maureen and feels a surge of relief. She looks forward to having a break from her ruminations—Maureen will give her a serious dose of normal.

Josie unlocks the deadbolt and before she can open the door, Anna grabs the knob and swings the door open. She barely misses Jacob with it.

"Anna, settle down," Josie says, crossly.

"Hi!" Ronan, Maureen's son, bubbles with excitement.

"Ronan! Will you play Barbies with me?" Anna asks without mincing words.

"Anna," Josie says, "you should ask Ronan what he wants to play first. Maybe he would rather play with the trains or the Power Rangers?"

"No ... Barbies are okay with me," he says, showing a semi-toothless grin and pudgy freckled cheeks.

"Don't tell his father he said that!" Maureen laughs.

Definitely not! Barbies are not for boys!

"What?" Josie's hand goes to her forehead, her eyes scrunch. She mumbles, "What was that?"

"I said don't tell his father he said that," Maureen repeats and raises her brows. "Are you okay?"

"Uh … yeah … I think." Inside of Josie's head entered a voice that wasn't her own. It was deep and masculine.

She remains somewhat dazed though the voice has dispelled. Maureen appears apprehensive. Nevertheless, their collective three are more concerned with getting their play date started. They blow past their mothers and bound down the stairs to the basement playroom.

"Are you sure?" Maureen asks.

"I'm sorry," Josie says, attempting to talk herself back into reality. "Let's go in the kitchen, I think I need some water."

Maureen follows Josie into the kitchen. "You know, we could come over another time. We have tomorrow free."

"I'm fine. I just have mommy brain today."

"I think I have that every day!" Maureen laughs, her smile is infectious and her laugh calms Josie's nerves.

She guzzles a glass of cold water and then offers Maureen a cup of hot herbal tea. She shows her the choices of lemon or raspberry.

"I'll have the lemon," Maureen says.

Josie turns to place the teapot on the stove when a shocking sensation strikes at her temples. The teapot falls out of her hands and lands with a bang on the stove.

"Josie?" Maureen asks, alarmed.

Josie's color changes from rosy to ghost white.

"Are you okay?" Maureen walks over to her and touches her arm.

Her mouth hangs open and her eyes glaze, staring off into a blank space in front of her. A heavy force presses on her chest. Her right hand clutches the fabric of her shirt over her heart.

"Are you having a heart attack? Do you need an ambulance?" Maureen's eyes are wide with concern. "Seriously, let me call you an ambulance—you don't look right."

"No, I'm ... I'm fine." Josie plays down her pain. *Am I having a stroke? A heart attack? Or both?*

"You don't look fine," Maureen insists. "We need to get you to a doctor."

"I'll...I'll be fine, I just got a sharp pain in my chest, that all. It's gone now. I must've stretched a muscle lifting Jacob. He's getting too heavy for me." In truth though, the pain wasn't sharp—it was crushing and dissipated as fast as it came on.

"Well, only if you're sure?" Maureen appears reluctant. "But still, your color isn't so good."

Josie nods. "I'm fine ... really I'm okay." Color is returning to her cheeks.

"Either way, you should sit down, let me take care of getting the tea." Maureen directs Josie to sit down at the kitchen table.

While Maureen takes over the fixing the tea, Josie rests in a chair and places her feet up on the chair across from her. The conversation between them meanders. They chat about easy topics such as Anna's new ballet class at the YMCA and Ronan's budding interest in soccer.

Outside the large kitchen window, the sky is drab and overcast with thick clouds. Suddenly, a cardinal flies in front of the window and lands on a tree branch facing them.

"That's funny," Maureen says while pouring the hot water into their cups.

"What is?" Josie asks.

"The cardinal." Maureen places the cups on the table and points to the bird. "It's looking at us." The bird is singing loudly, so piercing it can be heard through the dual-paned glass. Then abruptly, the bird takes flight.

Josie fixates on the bird's visit and remembers the transitory pressure in her chest. Maybe she's having a heart attack. Maybe her mother's cardinal is sending her a message. *Weird. What healthy 35 year-olds have heart attacks?*

Maureen hands her the cup of tea and sits down at the table with her. "How did Michael's appointment go the other day at the allergist? You never told me what happened."

"I didn't? Not so good, Michael still has his peanut allergy and he's not showing any signs of outgrowing it."

"Oh, geez ... that poor kid." Maureen shakes her head.

Josie frowns and thinks of how they live in a perpetual state of hyper-vigilance. She and Declan must monitor every bite Michael takes. Because of his peanut allergy, he twice had received shots of epinephrine to save his life and ended up in the hospital. There was no room for mistakes.

"But how about you?" Josie switches the topic of conversation. She doesn't want to monopolize their visit with the mystery of Michael's peanut allergies. They would not solve it, at least not today. Plus, the deep voice she heard at the door and the pain in her chest remains ever-present in her mind. *Who the hell was that?* While her *own voice* would tell her things, she didn't normally hear *other* people's voices in her head. And this voice wasn't the least bit familiar to her.

"I do have some good news to share. My mother's engaged ... it happened last weekend. She's getting married next May," Maureen says.

"She did? That's wonderful news." Josie's eyes brighten.

"Yeah, it's almost seven years since my dad died ... it was time ... you know ... for her to move on."

Josie nods. "I understand."

"I'm glad she met someone. It's no fun living alone—especially since none of us kids live near her anymore."

"Are you happy for her?" Josie can't tell. Maureen's expression is flat.

"Of course, I am. It will be different though. This Wednesday is the anniversary of my dad's accident." Maureen's eyes look down toward her tea. She grasps the cup in her hands as if holding it for strength.

"I'm so sorry, Maureen."

"It makes my dad's passing feel so final. That phase, that chapter of my mother's life will be forever closed."

Josie feels the death of Maureen's father's was, in a way, worse than the death of her mother. Maureen had no warning of her father's death. He died in a car accident when he was hit head-on by a drunk driver.

"What was your dad's name? I'm sorry, I don't remember," Josie says.

"Gerald ... but my mom and all his friends called him, Jerry."

"Oh," Josie nods as it feels familiar to her but she can't put her finger on why.

"Maureen, can I ask you a question?" She finally musters the confidence to come out with her request. "Have you ever wondered what it would be like to contact your father now that's he's on ... the other side?"

"Well, sure, I think I've heard from him from time to time, you know those little coincidences that happen at those times in your life when you need it most."

"Have you ever thought about actively trying to contact him?"

"Are you referring to a séance?"

"Not exactly, nothing as spooky as a séance. More like having someone perform a reading for you, like a psychic, someone to validate he's still around, only in spirit form."

"I don't know how you could validate it, isn't that where faith comes in?"

"Of course, I have faith my mother still exists even though I can't see her. But in addition to my faith, there've been times when I've had the unmistakable impression that she's present and I can even feel what she's thinking."

"Are you serious?" Maureen raises her brows.

"Yes. I haven't told anyone about it. Well ... except for Declan and my sister."

"Did this just happen?"

"No ... I first encountered my mom's spirit the night before her wake. You see, I never got to see her the day she died because my flight arrived late. I think she tried to hold on for me but it wasn't meant to be. I guess you could say there was unfinished business between us."

"But I thought you were with her when she was dying?"

"I was for a time but I returned home for a few days and it was then she took a turn for the worse. I wasn't gone long when her condition deteriorated."

"Oh, geez, I guess I didn't realize how it all played out. So, tell me what happened when you met her spirit?"

"She came to me in the guest room of her house where I was sleeping. She woke me up by tapping on the window and told me to make sure the undertaker did a good job with her eyebrows. You know ... for her viewing."

"Oh, now that's funny." Maureen laughs. "Your mom came to tell you that of all things!"

"What can I say, that was my mom. She was meticulous about the care of her brows." Josie chuckles. "She visited me again on the date of her first birthday following her death. I woke-up and saw her standing next to my bed. She looked exactly as I remembered.

Well, she was a bit transparent, but not like a ghost or at least not the Hollywood version of a ghost. It's hard to explain. She seemed almost ... holographic."

"Wow! That's kind of scary." Maureen's expression fluctuates between disbelief and utter astonishment. "Have you seen her since?"

"Not in the physical sense, mostly in dreams. From time to time, she sends me messages in my thoughts."

They sit quietly for a long minute, mulling over the words, seeming too unreal to be true. "You see my kitchen door over there which leads out to the deck?" Josie points to the door.

"Yeah." Maureen is sitting with her back toward the door. She turns to look behind her.

"Do you see the tree that stands to the left of the steps off the deck?"

She nods.

"I feel her coming from the direction of that tree."

Maureen looks at the tree and then to Josie, again with astonishment.

"I know it sounds crazy but every time I open the door and face that particular tree, I feel her presence."

"In the tree?" Maureen asks, surprised.

"Sort of, do you remember the cardinal we saw?"

"Of course I do."

"It shows up whenever my mother's trying to tell me something."

"Like what? What about right now? Do you think she's trying to tell you something?"

"I think so. I feel her around us."

"In this room?"

"Yes."

Maureen shudders. "Josie, did this ability of yours arrive after your mom's death or did it happen before she died?"

"Honestly, it's been going on my whole life to one degree or another and it's not all the time, it comes and goes. But it's been more so lately. It used to happen just with dreams but then it started carrying over into my waking life. Sometimes I even hear from people I hardly knew when they were alive, like the friend of a friend."

"Bizarre." The whites of Maureen's eyes grow bigger with each of Josie's revelations.

"I guess. I'm getting used to it although I've never pursued it. It just happens. When someone has something to say, they come and say it. It feels like I'm some sort of telephone line."

"Do you see them? The person who is dead? Do you hear their voice?"

"No, not usually. I sense their presence with my mind. Their thoughts become my thoughts in my voice but I know they aren't my thoughts. Often, the information comes to me as mental images. It's difficult to explain."

"Sounds like it. Have you heard from my dad?"

"I don't know, I can't say for sure." Although, Josie wonders if it was his voice she heard at the door. "Would you mind if I tried to channel him? I'd like to experiment to see if my ability could work on demand." Josie takes her two forefingers to place quotes around the words *on demand.* "I've never performed an actual reading on someone other than myself."

"You would do that for me?"

"It's a lot to ask, I know, and I understand if you'd rather not."

"Oh, c'mon, of course I'll do it. What do you need me to do?"

To Josie's surprise, Maureen is more open to her request than she thought she would be. In fact, Maureen appears to embrace it.

"Nothing, I don't want to know anything about him. I already know his name was Jerry, and I know he died in a car accident and was killed by a drunk driver."

"Correct."

"Please, don't give me any more information. I can't allow you to help me in any way because that would mess up the experiment. I need to know how accurate I am once the reading is done."

"Sure, when would you like to do this?"

"I could do it right now, if you feel up for it?" In fact, Josie senses Jerry was waiting to talk.

"Okay, why not? I think I need a drink first though," Maureen says.

While it's somewhat early to imbibe, they ditch their tea in favor of a glass of wine. Josie breaks out a bottle of her favorite Merlot. *It's a party,* she thinks, *and we're inviting Maureen's dead father to join us. Why not celebrate?*

Intentionally, she doesn't reveal to Maureen that she already feels her father's presence. She can tell he is a strong and insistent personality; intent on communicating his message to Maureen. She keeps hearing, *I'm here ... I'm here,* inside her head in a male voice. Josie closes her eyes and tries to visualize him. "Please don't answer yes or no. Allow me to tell you what I think he's communicating and then at the end, tell me how you think I did."

"Okay," Maureen agrees and takes a loud gulp of wine. "Do you mind if I grab a pen and paper? I want to write this all down. I don't want to forget anything you say."

"Sure, it'll be a good idea to see what I get right, if anything." She opens her eyes to point Maureen in the direction of the paper and pens by the phone. When Maureen sits back down, they start to giggle, but it is nervous and jittery, as if to mask their fear of the unknown.

Their anxious laughter subsides when Josie closes her eyes again. She lets her mind go blank. There is a silence so thick, you could slice it but moments later, Josie begins to speak. The thoughts come like flashes into her mind. "First, I need to tell you about his personality. He was a formidable presence in life, intimidating and strong in his opinions. In my mind he looks like he was a tall man with a broad mustache." A minute passes when Josie says some more, "Did he have a dog? Don't answer that. I think I see a German shepherd. Hmm ... for some reason, it's not clear, but the dog was very big and his name began with a T. The name sounds like Toby or Tommy."

More thoughts flood Josie's mind. "I think he liked to fish, he's showing me a small boat and a fishing pole." Like watching a movie in slow motion, each frame of the reel is flashing for a second inside of her mind. She continues to keep her eyes closed. It helps her to focus. "There's something about chili dogs and your dad. I'm not sure why this is important but I keep hearing *chili dogs, chili dogs*. Now, he's showing me a house, and it sits beside a body of water. The house has *white* shutters and *blue* siding, there's a trellis in front of the house. I see a blue pick-up *truck* in the driveway." Josie stops. At times, she feels the words emerging from her throat are vibrating. And, some words vibrate more than others like *white* and *blue* and *truck*. It is as if Jerry is helping her to confirm her conclusions about him. The stronger the vibration, the more right she is.

Josie finally opens her eyes to look at Maureen. Maureen has already downed two-thirds of her glass of wine.

"May I speak now?" Maureen asks, swallowing hard.

"Yes, I believe I'm done, I'm not seeing or hearing much else right now."

Maureen glances at her notes and then back at Josie, "You were dead on—no pun intended. That's incredible!"

"Do you think so?"

"Honest to God. I can't wait to tell my mother."

"Where did I get it right?" Josie has no idea. However, if the vibrations are supposed to be an indicator, then maybe she was on the right track.

"Just about all of it!" Maureen smiles and reviews her notes. "My dad loved to fish on his boat. I grew up in a house that was walking distance from a small lake. My house was blue with white shutters and a trellis in front. Our dog, Tory, was a German shepherd mix. Tory was my dad's best friend." She took a breath and continued, "My dad loved chili dogs. My mother had this awesome chili recipe. She cooked it for him at least once a week."

"And what about the truck?"

"He had a blue pick-up truck ... he was driving it when he died. The police told us he died on impact." Maureen frowns, her voice turns somber. She sips more of her wine.

"I'm so sorry." Josie also takes a long sip of her wine. The reading was intended to be fun but the reminder of his accident was an unavoidable part of it.

"No one could've survived the injuries he had. You see, when the other car hit his, it turned the front of his truck into an accordion. The impact crushed his chest. They think the guy who hit him was going at least sixty miles-per-hour, so fast the roof of the truck blew off and the other car's front end struck my dad's head. It fractured his skull."

"Oh, geez." Josie shudders and closes her eyes as if to shut-out the image. "What a horrible death."

"I hope he died as quick as the police said he did. I can't imagine the suffering—it's awful to think about." Maureen casts her eyes downward at her near empty wine glass.

Josie wonders if this is this why her chest and head hurt before.

"Could I ask you something? How do you know all of this? Did you hear my dad's voice?"

"Some of the time … sometimes I heard him in my head speaking and other times he just showed me things, kind of like images from a movie."

"Tell me what he said. What words?"

"Definitely not."

"Huh?"

"About Ronan wanting to play Barbies … your father said *definitely not! Barbies are not for boys!*"

"You're kidding me!" Maureen laughs. "Yep, that's my dad."

Okay, now this is weird. It hits her—a dead person had spoken to her in her head. She didn't know if she was ready for dead people to talk to her in her head. "What do you think, you know … about me doing this?"

"I think you need to do this for more people. You have a God given talent. Don't waste it!"

"Maureen, do me a small favor though."

"Sure, anything you need."

"Please don't mention this reading to Declan. I need to keep this whole thing quiet for the time being. You can tell your mom but no one else."

"Okay?" Maureen asks, puzzled. "Declan doesn't know you can do this?"

"He has some awareness of my ability and what he knows, he doesn't approve of."

"That's unfortunate. Doesn't he see the good it can bring?"

"I suppose, but he doesn't want me to be the one to bring it. It's a double-edged sword— what I love about him is his ability to stand by his values and beliefs. However, at times, it's also what makes him difficult to live with. He can be pretty darned inflexible."

"Well, if it's any comfort to you, I believe your ability is nothing to be ashamed of, it's a gift, truly it is," Maureen says earnestly.

Josie cracks a small smile as for once, her self-doubt did not overwhelm her. It seemed to be too much detail about Maureen's father, and taken together, couldn't be reduced to mere coincidence. She knew she could do it. It was like riding a bike; she just needed to pedal. The information flowed into her mind like a waterfall. Here, she didn't know Maureen until a few years after Jerry passed. All she knew of him was his first name and how he died. Now, she knew all of these other things, albeit trivial but personal enough that he knew it mattered to Maureen and her family. These are the facts that made her father who he was, the way his family remembered him. Perhaps it was his way of saying to Maureen, "It's really me."

The noise from little feet come stomping up stairs and interrupt them. Anna, Ronan and Jacob all arrive in the kitchen in a line, in that order.

"Mommy," Anna speaks for the trio, "Can we have some vanilla wafers?"

"It's okay with me if it's okay with Ronan's mom."

"Sure," Maureen says.

They go to the cupboard and pull out the box of cookies. And there they were, back to reality. Except, Josie's secret was out. She took the baby step, or more like the leap. She pushed the envelope and succeeded. Only she wonders, *What's next?*

CHAPTER 11

The Devil makes the pots but not the lids to cover them up.
—Italian Proverb

Maureen's reading brings Josie newfound confidence. *Maybe I could do more? Only one ... just one. Well ... maybe two?* She thinks it over and makes some notes for herself: Jerry's favorite dish, the name of his beloved dog, the description of his home and most importantly, the specifics of his death.

She's encouraged by her first "real" success and decides to continue by contacting close friends with a deceased relative—in particular, close friends who will likely be open to her research. Monica, her college roommate, comes to her mind first. The last time she saw Monica was at her mother's funeral. Monica flew in from Reno to attend. However, because of children, jobs and distance, it became harder for Josie to stay in touch with her. Nowadays, their primary form of communication was through email.

Monica currently worked as cocktail waitress at Reno's Bellagio Towers. She had a graduate degree in biology but the tips from cocktailing were too lucrative to give up for a teaching career. And Monica was a wild child, a Monday through Friday job didn't suit her. Without question Josie knew she could tell Monica about her little experiment.

Josie picks up the phone and taps in Monica's number. She waits. It rings and rings. She borders on changing her mind when Monica answers.

"Hello," Monica says, sounding groggy.

"Monica, it's Josie, I'm sorry did I wake you?"

"Josie? Hey there ... I was sleeping but I've got to start my shift at five tonight, earlier than usual." She yawns and sounds like Josie's terrier waking up from a nap.

"I'm sorry. I could call back tomorrow if that would be better for you?"

"It's no problem, Jos ... so what's up? I haven't talked to you in forever. Are you pregnant again?"

Josie laughs. "No, no, that's not why I'm calling."

"So, what's going on?"

Josie hadn't planned to launch into her request so fast but Monica was never good with small talk. It was best she cut to the chase. "I was wondering if you might be interested in a project I'm working on. It's kind of an experiment."

"Sounds interesting. Fill me in."

"I never told anyone in college about this but did you know I'm ... um ..."

"You're what?"

"I'm psychic." She blurts it out like a piece of gum that gets spit out by accident when you talk too fast. There it was flying out of her mouth and landing on the table between them. She couldn't pick it off and take it back without Monica noticing. Josie needed to come clean.

"You are? How so? This is so left field!" Monica emits a giddy shriek. "I didn't even see that one coming. Are you serious?"

"Completely," Josie says, flatly.

"Does Declan know?"

Josie pauses. "Not exactly."

"Oh?" Monica asks, sounding surprised. "What do you mean by not exactly?"

Josie sighs, "Let's not go there, okay?"

"Whatever. I don't pretend to be a relationship expert so I'm not going to judge."

"Thank you."

"Anyhoo ... tell me more about this psychic project of yours. You know, there's a lady at Bellagio's who works the night shift with me, she does palm readings by appointment. It seems like a good job, she makes great money too."

"No, I don't read palms, I more or less read thoughts."

"Whoa, hold on there, sister ... can you read my thoughts?"

"No, I can't read yours—don't get all worried."

"It's just that I have indecent, pornographic thoughts so I thought I'd better warn you."

"Like I'd be surprised," Josie laughs. "It's not so much the thoughts of living people I hear. Rather, it's the thoughts of dead people, although I don't think they're really dead, they're in another form ... spirit."

"Now, that's freaky. I didn't know YOU were such a freak, Josie."

"Is that bad?"

"No, of course not, I'm a freak; I mean not the kind of freak you are! It's nice to know I have a friend who's more of a freak than me. Who'da thought that'd be you?"

It was precisely the kind of response Josie knew she'd get from Monica—the stranger the request, the better. Nothing was weird or off base for her. She had the most open mind of anyone Josie knew.

"So, what experiment are you doing?"

"I'm attempting to perform a few readings for friends. My plan is to contact my friend's close relative, one who has, of course, died," as if she needs to clarify, "and see if I can pick up on any facts about the deceased without my friend giving me any information. It's hard to explain but I'm trying to see if I'm any good at it."

"Okay, I'm game ... sounds like fun."

"Would it be okay with you if I try to channel your dad?"

"Yeah, of course. Just don't try to channel my old boyfriend, Sam."

"He died? Oh, my god, what happened?"

"Oh, he's not dead, at least not yet. I still have a hit out on him, you know after he cheated on me with that redhead."

"Oh, geez, you had me there for a minute. Don't tell me you're *still* not over that?" Josie didn't know whether to be surprised or distressed. She couldn't tell with Monica.

"Oh, I'm over it ... it's the getting even I'm still working on."

"Seriously?"

"Josie, you're so gullible, I was just kidding."

"Phew!" Josie realizes she got fished-in again by Monica's dark humor. "Be serious for a minute. I know it's hard."

"Yeah, yeah. I'll behave, go ahead."

"In reference to your father, I need to know a couple of simple things about him before I do the reading."

"Like what?"

"What was his first name? I don't think I ever knew his name."

"It was Howard."

"Did he die of stomach cancer?"

"Yeah, that was it. That was the nasty bastard that got him. And–"

"Stop, don't say anymore, that's all I need to know."

"I was going to say–"

"Please don't tell me anything more about him, it could ruin the experiment," Josie says and cuts her off.

"Oh, sorry, I won't say it then."

"Thanks for understanding."

While it feels selfish to her, Josie knows she needs to determine if she can do the reading all on her own. Otherwise, she'll never be sure about her ability.

Josie goes about Monica's reading differently than Maureen's. Instead of proceeding on the phone, she asks Monica to give her some time. They chat on about other things for a few minutes and before they hang up, Josie promises to contact Monica as soon as she hears from Howard. After they say their good-byes, Josie starts to think about Howard and asks him if he has a message for Monica. Unlike Maureen's dad, nothing comes to her readily. It is strange, so quiet but she believes he'll come when he is ready. She sends him the request, via thought, and now it is time to wait.

FOOTSTEPS. JOSIE WAKES FROM A SOUND SLEEP. Footsteps— heavy, deliberate and coming toward the bedroom door. She looks at the clock. It is 4 a.m. Her heart pounds. Declan is next to her, immersed in deep slumber and snoring away. She thinks of the children, their steps are not this heavy, nor are Jamison's. The steps close in. Her pulse speeds up. She shuts her eyes tight and pretends to sleep. *Could it be Monica's dad?* Something is wrong. Very wrong.

Panic floods her chest. The presence doesn't feel like a loving parent, it feels like an intruder. She tries to open her eyes but can't. She tries to turn her head but to no avail. She tries to scream but her mouth won't open, she can't make a sound. A force restrains her, it isn't of this world. No matter how hard she struggles, her body won't move. Paralyzed. And then, she moves her left foot. It somehow escapes from the weight of the pressure holding her in place. She brushes her foot hard against Declan's leg and tries to wake him. He doesn't budge.

The presence is at her side of the bed. *Look at the happy couple, aren't they cute?* it says in a low whisper. Then with a sinister laugh, a cold breath blows across Josie's face and chills her to her bone. The presence vanishes. She can move her body again. She opens her eyes and rolls over to look around her. There is nothing and no one there except for Declan sleeping next to her.

CHAPTER 12

When she wakes the next morning, Josie remembers the dark presence from the night before—the unyielding pressure, the paralysis, and still an awareness of all that was happening around her. She tries to shake it off, to convince herself it was just another disturbing dream but her memory reminds it was real. She steps into the shower and lets the warm water pour over her. Her hand reaches for the shampoo. *Bald.* She hears it clear and strong. *Bald, bald, bald.* It replays in her mind. The words come in her *own* voice. She finishes her shower and towels off. Declan's eyeglasses sit between the master bath's dual sinks and send her pulsing vibrations. She picks them up, examines them and sets them back down. "Glasses?"

Taking a sheet of scrap paper and an eye pencil from her vanity drawer, she scribbles the words "bald" and "eyeglasses." *Maybe it's Howard? Maybe he's ready to talk.* On the other hand, she's essentially naked, wrapped in a towel and her hair is soaking wet. She throws a thought Howard's way. *Do you mind? I need to get dressed first.*

She proceeds to her dresser, opens a drawer and pulls out a bra and panty. She visualizes a *white undershirt.* "Ugh," she says, annoyed. She stops and jots "white undershirt" on her list. Next she pulls out a shirt from the drawer and selects a new one she picked up at the mall the day before. The label sends her a vibration. *Italia.* Again, she makes a note of it.

From there she returns to the bathroom. Two rubber ducks are on the carpet. She bends down to pick them up.

"Ow!" she says.

The ducks send what feels like electric charge through her palm. She drops the ducks and rubs her hand. "What the ..." The words *duck, duck, duck* repeat in her mind. She writes it down.

After dressing, she heads downstairs. Anna and Jacob are awake and watching Sports Center on the TV.

"What are you two doing up? It's only 6:30? How did Jacob get out of his crib?" Josie half-asks and half-wonders.

"Daddy got him out. Jacob was calling for you when you were in the shower," Anna says.

"Did Daddy go running?" Josie asks, concerned. *I wonder why he didn't wait until I got downstairs.*

"Yeah, he said you would be here in a minute. I told Daddy I was a big girl and could watch Jacob until you got here," Anna says.

"Hmm," Josie says to herself and decides to let it go. She returns upstairs to check on Michael. He is sprawled out in his twin bed, blankets everywhere but on him. She decides to leave him be as he has at least a half-hour more before needing to get up for school.

Once downstairs again, Anna asks, "Mommy, can you find Dora on the TV? I don't want to watch Sports Center anymore."

"Sure." Josie takes the remote and as she goes to change the station, an ad comes on with a man on a motorcycle. Her eyes fix— the motorcycle sends her a vibration.

"Mommy, look! There's a man on TV on a motorcycle!" Anna exclaims.

"Uh, I see that." *That's strange. Does Anna notice the vibrations too?*

Abruptly, Anna gets up from the couch and walks into the kitchen. She retrieves a box of Cheerios from the cupboard and hands it to Josie. "I'm hungry, Mommy. Can I have some Cheerios?"

Josie freezes. Vibrations come at her from the box of Cheerios. She adds "motorcycle" and "Cheerios" to her growing list.

"Mommy? Who's Monica?" Anna asks.

She didn't overhear me contacting Monica, did she? Anna isn't familiar with the Reno Monica nor does she know anyone named Monica. Furthermore, under no circumstances did Josie want her children to be part of this experiment.

"Mommy, the man's saying 't-shirt and shorts'." Anna interrupts Josie's ruminating thoughts.

"What man are you talking about?!" Her eyes widen, a pit develops and burns in her stomach.

"You know, the man's who's talking in my head. He's yelling at you to write it down!"

"What!" she says and mouths, "Anna?"

"Yeah, Mom?"

Josie doesn't answer her. Trembling, she telepathically shouts. *DO NOT TO TALK TO MY KIDS! The reading is between us. The kids aren't part of the deal!*

With an abrupt halt, the flood of communication and vibrations cease. Howard's presence is gone.

JOSIE WAKES MICHAEL FOR SCHOOL AND RESUMES, THOUGH guardedly, her morning routine with the children. Declan dresses and leaves for work. Michaels gets on the school bus. Josie, Anna and Michael go into the garage and get in the minivan. She will bring Anna to her morning preschool class and run her errands with Jacob in tow. She knows he will want everything he put his hands on and more, so she begins to gear herself mentally for his demands and their "negotiations."

She buckles Anna into her booster seat. "Mommy, the man is talking," Anna says.

Josie's pulse races. *Why is he still here?*

"He wants me to tell you he likes cheap beer."

Josie clenches her teeth and a snarl rips from deep within her throat. It is guttural.

Anna's eyes grow big, "You're scaring me, Mommy."

Josie doesn't answer. She listens with the instinct of a wild animal protecting her young, scanning their surroundings. Maybe she will see this menace, out there in their garage. She keeps her radar eyes off Anna. She doesn't want to frighten her further, only Monica's dad. It is doubtful he'll take form and shape, she thinks. His voice is all he allows them to perceive. Only now it is clearer than before. When Josie stopped talking to him, he continued talking to Anna. Anna could hear him when Josie could not. With fear exploding in her heart, Josie understands what must happen. Anna needs to tell him to leave.

"Anna, tell the man to go away," she says, trembling. "Tell him to leave now!"

"Okay ... but do I have to?" Anna asks. Her eyes are tentative, her face is uncertain.

"Yes, you do, honey. Just do it."

"Okay," she says, warily. She turns from Josie toward an empty space in front of her. "My mommy said you have to go away now. I can't talk to you anymore."

A startling crash emits from the other side of the garage, sending shivers rippling down Josie's spine. She sucks in a breath and walks over to the site of the crash. "Ah," she sighs. *It's just a shovel, it must have tipped over by accident ... I wish.*

"Mommy, I don't hear him anymore," Anna says.

"Thank God," Josie mutters to herself and realizes she forgot to wear her cross today, the one her mother gave her. She grabs the keys from her purse and prays they'll never hear from Howard again.

CHAPTER 13

Early in the afternoon, Josie sits down to write an email to Monica. She decides calling her is out of the question given the circumstances. It is too uncomfortable and she doesn't want to discuss the ensuing details of the nightmare contact with the spirit she identified as Howard. However, Josie still isn't sure if it was Howard communicating with her or not. Besides, if it wasn't Howard, then who was it? Whoever this spirit was, he took advantage of her, her kids and the opportunity. In Josie's mind, he overstepped the bounds of respectful living-dead communications. Then again, she wonders if there were any rules for communicating with the dead.

Josie fingers tap her keyboard at a frenetic pace, fearing the sight of Howard's printed name might bring his unwelcome presence back to her house. *Why would Monica's father try to scare us? Was it intentional?* She couldn't imagine he was the type of person to yell at a child. Then again, she didn't know him when he was alive. *Maybe he wasn't a nice person?* Nevertheless, this "reading" needed a definitive end, once and for all.

```
Monica,

Here's what I got about your dad. Let me know
if I'm right. He was bald, wore glasses, had
a motorcycle, wore white t-shirts and shorts,
told me something about a duck and he men-
tioned Italy. He also brought up something
about Cheerios and that he liked cheap beer.
Sorry it's not more. It's hard to concentrate
```

```
with the kids always interrupting my train of
thought. Thanks for letting me channel your
dad. Let me know what you think.

Josie
```

She decides to leave her message brief. She knows using her children as an excuse is a cop-out but how can she tell Monica the truth? It wouldn't be right to place Monica in a position of responsibility. It wasn't her fault that her father's spirit was so intrusive and far better for Monica to keep the memories of her father pleasant. Plus, Josie would never know with one-hundred percent certainty if it was truly Howard talking to her ... how do you validate a person you cannot see.

Josie becomes more and more wary about her endeavor. She continues to ruminate about Anna—how Anna recited what Howard was telling her and how, in an instant, Josie became terrified at a level she didn't know was possible. She realizes she can't control who these spirits talk to once she opens the door to her home. With her confidence faltering and the potential for her children to be accessed by these troubled spirits without her consent, she questions her intentions. Why is she bothering at all?

THE FOLLOWING DAY, JOSIE OPENS HER EMAIL AND FINDS a reply from Monica:

```
Josie!!!

Holy crap—you are amazing! My dad drank very
cheap but, in his words, extremely tasteful
"Old Milwaukee." He drove a Harley-Davidson
motorcycle. He was nearly bald, more like
receding and yes, he wore eyeglasses. I guess
you might say he looked like an older version
of Al Bundy from "Married with Children."
```

Much to my mom's chagrin, he wore white
undershirts and boxers around the house in
broad daylight. The last trip he took was to
Italy with my mom. And the Cheerios were
probably about what he fed his dog every day.
Oh, and he was an avid duck hunter in his
younger days before my mom wouldn't let him
keep shotguns in the house, even though they
were locked and unloaded! I hope he wasn't
hard on you, he was a bit gruff in life but
he was really a big teddy bear.

Let me know if you want to contact any more
of my deceased friends or family members.
This is so cool. Great work, woman!

Kisses,

Monica

A teddy bear? Try a grizzly, Josie thinks, reflecting on how the reading actually went down. Despite this, she's encouraged by Monica's certainty and yet, she can't dismiss the whole encounter as pure coincidence. Howard was obviously an odd guy in life, at least according to Monica's report. Maybe it was him communicating with me after all? Although she supposes she can find a way to fit those words into about anyone's life and yet, Monica clearly feels otherwise. And she wonders—if it rings true to the family member and it leaves them with positive feelings, is it then a valid reading? Is this evidence of post-death survival?

All of these questions haunt her. As a result, Josie refrains from pursuing further readings for any of her other friends in the days that follow. Further, she decides a few ground rules are in order— she'd have to be crystal clear with the discarnate. She'd help them if, and only if, they left her family, especially her children alone. They were too young and even if they have the gift, she wasn't ready for

them to have it. And, she did have this one advantage over spirits—
she could—and would—hold their message hostage if they crossed
the line and badgered her children. No amount of persistence would
get her to tell their loved ones they made it to the other side. If they
bothered her children, the session was over.

CHAPTER 14

One week passes before Josie is ready to try again. She regains her confidence, sets some boundaries and has new found mental control over her ability. She thinks. She convinces herself by using positive affirmations in order to remain on level ground.

Her next contact is her childhood friend, Katherine. Katherine lost her father to colon cancer when she was in the eighth grade. She married her high school sweetheart, Jeff. She and Katherine were the kind of friends who could lose touch for months, even years, and still come together, picking up where they left off.

Josie knew more about Katherine's father than she did about Maureen's or Monica's. Therefore, technically, he didn't meet the criteria for her self-constructed experiment. But, she felt she should offer Katherine the opportunity to channel him if Katherine wanted to. Of course, if Katherine didn't, that was fine with Josie too. It was more out of a sense of loyalty to their life-long friendship that Josie felt compelled to tell Katherine about the goings-on in her life. She wouldn't feel right telling Katherine about it later. Plus, she knew Katherine's dad well enough to know he wouldn't bother her children. And for that reason alone, Josie believed he was a safe bet.

Josie decides to contact Katherine after Michael leaves for school and Anna leaves for preschool. She wants them to be out of the house when she attempts channeling. While Jacob will still be home, she figures he won't be of much help to a spirit trying to send a message because he has so few words in his repertoire. However, to be safe, she decides to wait until his naptime so he will not overhear or be present for her conversation, just in case.

It is early afternoon when Josie calls her. She assumes Katherine's children will be at school and her husband at work, thus it should be a good time for her to talk. Josie lets the phone ring and ring and ring and ring.

"Hello," Katherine says.

"Katherine? It's me Josie."

"Hey, Josie!" She sounds breathless. "I just got in the door from grocery shopping."

"I'm glad I got you then. Is now a good time to talk?"

"Sure it is," Katherine says, although Josie knows Katherine is not one to indicate if she is being inconvenienced.

"Are you sure? Do you want to unload your groceries and call me back?"

"No, it's fine, I can talk and unload groceries, you know, multitask. So, how's it going?" Katherine is still huffing a bit.

"Pretty good. And you? How are Jeff and the kids?"

"Fine. Jeff's in Daufuskie working on the house. He's putting in a new patio and overseeing the construction of our pool."

"Sounds nice, I hope we can check it out one day. How come you didn't go with him?"

"Ohhh ... the kids are in the thick of their semester and we plan to go once school is out."

"I always forget how much older your kids are than mine."

"Yeah, and it gets harder and harder to take the kids out of school the older they get. Besides, the yard there is all torn up from the construction."

Katherine's husband, Jeff, was a small town boy turned successful real estate developer. It seemed whenever Josie called, they were always engaged in some new fun (and expensive) family project.

They converse for a long while, catching up on the details of their lives without Josie bringing up the reason for her call. Nowadays, they almost never saw each other. Their busy families, and the distance, didn't permit them to get together more than once every few years.

"So, Josie, you've covered Declan and the kids but why are you calling me? It can't be because I haven't talked to you in three months. It usually takes one of us at least a year to pick up the phone and call."

"You're right. I'm calling for a particular reason."

"Well, what is it?"

Josie pauses to think about her request one more time. *Should I ask her or not?* She can hear Katherine breathing on the other end of the phone. "Okay," she says, finally. "Think back to the day when you came with me to Mass at St. Joe's when we were kids."

"Well ... I remember feeling relieved because we didn't have to stand as much like we did at my church." Katherine grew up Russian Orthodox—Mass for her meant standing for two hours and hearing it in a language she didn't understand.

"Well, I've had a few experiences similar to that day, but ..."

"What?" Katherine asks. "Did you see my sister at church again?"

"No, I didn't see Sarah. Something different."

Josie reflects—Katherine's older sister died unexpectedly of a terrible illness sometime before Katherine's second birthday. Yet, before that day at St. Joe's, Josie didn't know Sarah existed. And it was a day Josie would never forget. She saw a golden-haired girl flying in front of the church balcony. The girl had large, iridescent, feathered wings and her dress sparkled like sunlight on fresh snow. The long fabric of her dress covered her feet. Katherine, however, didn't see her and, to Josie, the image was fleeting. When Josie described the "angel" and her golden braids to Katherine, Katherine told her about Sarah, her deceased sister.

"Then, tell me, are you reading auras for a living now?" Katherine jokes.

"No, not that either."

"I swear ever since that boy died, you've never been normal."

"What?" Josie coughs, taken aback. "How so?"

"When Andy drowned you went into a cocoon and I don't believe you emerged until you met Declan."

"What does that have to do with me right now?"

"I know what you're going to tell me. You're going to say you've been talking to dead people."

She should've known Katherine would guess right. She already knew about Josie seeing auras as a child and her dream skating with Andy on the frozen pond. When they were kids, Josie told her that Andy wasn't truly dead—she could see him, albeit in her dreams, but there he was very much alive. Strangely, Josie's aberrant ways were okay with Katherine. She, more than any other of Josie's friends, understood that what was happening to her now didn't arrive out of the blue. Rather, it was a series of experiences, strung and woven together, rooted in an ordinary childhood. Josie's awareness of the supernatural world always lingered in the background and Katherine embraced it.

"Okay, here it is, Kat, I'm attempting my own experiment. I know there are people who claim to be able communicate with the dead. Some are for real and others not. I think I am one of those people who can do this for real but I need to be sure. I thought if I could do a reading for you, I might be able to validate what I've always suspected about myself."

"Does Declan know you're doing this experiment?"

"No, not yet. He's not been very supportive of it, either."

"Then why are you doing it?"

"Good question, for a couple of reasons."

"And what are they?" Katherine asks with a distinctly parental tone.

"You know, Declan has gotten pretty stubborn over the years. He makes decisions without hearing me out. But I don't think I should ignore my ability if I have it, not if it could be of use to others in need."

"I see what you're saying but I don't understand why you would pursue it if he's not supportive though. From what I know of Declan, I'm sure he has some valid reasons as to why he doesn't want you to do these readings."

"All I'm doing is trying to develop my skills, improve them, and when I get good enough at it, I'll show him."

"Okay, I guess, but I don't agree. Are you sure it's worth it? Do you want to risk going behind his back?"

"Well, now, you're making me second guess myself."

"That's my job, Josie. I wouldn't be your friend if I didn't."

Josie pauses for a moment. "All I would like to do is to channel your father. That is, if it is all right with you?"

"Josie, look, I love you but no. I'm not willing to be your accomplice. If anything happens, I don't want Declan coming back to me and asking me why I encouraged you to do this. It's not that I don't believe you can do it. I know you can. I've seen you do it at least with the aura thing. But, if he's opposed to your experiment, then you should find another avenue to channel your psychic creativity. You know, your mom was a great artist, perhaps you could try painting?"

Katherine's right about that, my mom was a phenomenal artist. Perhaps, she wonders, the creativity that surrounds her early life is what leads her to the place she is now—much too in tune with the world. However, Josie realizes she isn't much of an artist. "It's okay, I didn't intend to force you into it." Despite her words, Josie's heart fills with disappointment.

"I worry about you. I don't think it's a good idea anyway, with or without Declan's approval. It doesn't feel right to me."

"You're a good friend Katherine and I appreciate your concern. I promise to think it over some more." *Maybe this isn't the right path for me?* There it is again—"could versus should" rearing its ugly head. Josie knows she could do it but was beginning to question more and more if she should. Katherine, like Declan, seemed to think not.

CHAPTER 15

ANDREW—APRIL, 2006

Andrew arrives at St. Catherine's at 6 p.m. ready to work his third night shift at the established community hospital. Before taking the job, Andrew did some of research on his new place of employment. Unlike Cook County Hospital, he found that St. Catherine's operated in an upscale area of town located on the immediate border of St. Paul's Metro State's campus. Most of their patients carried private health insurance.

Staff to patient ratios in the ER were generous, one nurse for every three patient beds. Andrew figured he could "treat 'em and street 'em" in about half the time he did in Chicago. Plus, mending a drunken co-ed's laceration as opposed to stopping the hemorrhage from a gang-related gunshot wound was going to be a decent trade in his book. To be fair, he found that St. Catherine's had its share of trauma cases but most resulted from a motor vehicle crash or the weekend college-town bar brawl.

On his way out from work on Sunday morning, he stops by the hospital chapel for the 8 a.m. Mass. He hasn't been to Mass since he moved to town ten days earlier. A practicing Catholic, he believes receiving the Eucharist is an essential act of faith. And his ability to heal is directly tied to his receiving Holy Communion on a routine basis.

When he enters the chapel, he notices the attendance is thin. The chapel is small but there is enough seating to accommodate at least twenty to twenty-five. This morning's Mass includes him, three patients and their caregivers, one of which trails an IV pole, and about five other hospital staff members. Andrew doesn't know anyone in town besides his co-workers, and at this point, they are mere acquaintances. Seeing so few people makes him miss the comfort of home even more than usual.

He chooses a pew in the back row, kneels down, and says a prayer. He glances at the faces about the room without realizing he is looking for *her* face. When he arrived in St. Paul, he began to have recurring dreams of the same woman. While he dreamt of this woman many times over his life, it hadn't occurred with such frequency. She features nightly in his dreams and sometimes in visions while he is awake. She is about thirty or so, he thinks, with dark hair and cobalt eyes. *Who is she?* he wonders. Is his imagination fixating on a crazy recurring dream? Or is his need for someone to love becoming so strong he can't beat it back, even in his sleep?

However, in his dream, this woman belongs to another man. This other man calls Andrew, "Brother," and yet, Andrew was adopted. He has no brothers, at least none he is aware of. He decides it must be stress causing him to have these bizarre encounters. He coins them "encounters" because there are instances when he is certain he experiences her presence—he smells her perfume wafting through the air, hears her laughing and even feels her heart beating against his chest. As he continues to kneel in prayer, he beseeches Mary, the Mother of God, to take away these visions or bring this woman forth if she indeed exists. He knows it is a dangerous way to pray, to demand anything from the supernatural, but he can't wait any longer.

After he is done saying his private prayers, a young mother enters the chapel carrying a toddler—a girl not more than two years old. A man, likely the girl's father, is walking beside them and pushing the child's IV pole. The family sits down in the pew directly in front of him. The blonde-haired girl appears to have undergone a recent surgery. Her hand is wrapped in a soft white bandage. While her hand is covered, the exposed portion of her forearm appears to have suffered a severe burn and is in the process of healing.

Andrew overhears the couple whispering. He tries not to eavesdrop but it is impossible not to hear. The mother is tearful and the father is consoling her. Together they hold the child who is somewhat oblivious to their emotional pain.

"Remember, all things are possible with God, honey. We're here for a reason, we have the best doctors. God is providing for us, we just have to trust in Him," the young father whispers to the mother. The mother nods and wipes her eyes.

The priest enters at the front of the chapel and takes his place at the altar. He begins to say Mass. The couple continues to console each other, the father keeps telling the mother to "be strong."

At the close of Mass, one of the caregivers comes over to the young parents on his way out. "How is Amanda's hand doing? Do they think she will regain the use of it?" he asks.

"She's doing better but we don't know if the grafting is going to take and even if it does, she still may not have the use of her hand. We'll have to wait and see ... and pray," the father says.

"Let me know if there's anything I can do," the caregiver says, and then escorts his patient out the door.

The young couple sits in the pew for another minute. Andrew bows his head to pray silently to himself. It is then he hears them ... cathedral bells. Not the chapel bell at the hospital but rather the bells he hears when God wants him to intervene. They ring loudly in his ears but he is aware no one else can hear them but him.

The couple gets up and carries their daughter out the door of the chapel. As they do, they pass by Andrew kneeling in his pew.

Andrew gets ups and follows. He catches up to them as they proceed through the long hospital corridor outside the chapel.

"Excuse me," he says.

The couple stops and turns around to face him. They have a look of surprise.

"Is there something wrong?" the mother asks, noticing Andrew is in his white emergency physician coat.

"Oh, no, nothing's wrong. I'm sorry to startle you. I just overheard you talking about your daughter back in the chapel. I just wanted to say—"

Out of the blue, the girl's eyes brighten and she reaches for him. With no words, it is clear to the adults that the child wants Andrew to hold her.

The father appears unsure, "I think Amanda would like for you to hold her. She loves people, would you mind?"

"Of course, I would love to hold her," Andrew says.

The father reluctantly hands the child over to Andrew who has already said his silent prayer and made the Sign of the Cross at the chapel in preparation for the potential healing. He suspects he is to lay hands on her injury but doesn't know this until he hears the cathedral bells—this is indeed what God wanted him to do.

As he holds the little girl, he gently touches her arm and tries to not be too obvious. "When will they know if her grafts will take?" he asks her parents.

"We won't know for a few weeks. They have to debride portions of the wound every day and the grafts are new. It's so hard to watch her go through this," her father says.

"I had no idea she could reach the stove. She pulled the pot of hot water right over on herself," the girl's mother says, her voice is full of pain. "The screams were awful, I can never forgive myself."

"We're thankful the water did not burn her beautiful face," the girl's father says.

"I will be sure to keep her in my prayers," Andrew hands the child back to her father.

"Thank you," her parents say.

The couple walks away with their daughter now in her father's arms. Neither one sees the child's hand and forearm, though almost fully concealed by bandages, has entirely healed.

CHAPTER 16

*Wherein the Devil habitually meddles so freely in revelations or
extraordinary phenomena that I believe it is impossible for a man
not to be deceived by them, unless he strives to reject them, such
an appearance of truth and security does the Devil give them."*
—St. John of the Cross

Josie mops the kitchen floor on her hands and knees with a rag. Cleaning the floor, though monotonous, is therapy to her. It allows her time to think in peace while Jacob takes his nap. Her older two are at their respective schools and Declan is at work. A week has passed since her conversation with Katherine. The hollow ache in Josie's heart began right after she hung up the phone. Katherine reminded her of what this act of defiance would cost in real terms.

If Josie broke the precious bond of trust she shared with Declan, it wouldn't be something she'd easily win back, if ever. As a result, her uncertainty grew like a cancer and spread—why was she doing this? For what purpose and to what end? Was it because she needed to prove something to herself? Did she feel by doing so, her worth, her value would increase? Didn't motherhood count for something in and of itself?

She stops mopping and takes a break with a glass of iced tea and sits down to catch up on her email. A lump catches in her throat. She has a new email from Monica. *Oh, no. I hope she doesn't want me to do another reading for her.*

```
Hey Jos,

I just want to thank you again for doing the
reading for me with my dad. I think it's
totally awesome that you can do this for me
and maybe for others too. You have no idea
what peace of mind you have given me. I
shared it with my mom and she wants to know
if you would do a separate reading for her
with my dad. What do you think?

By the way, I'm also wondering how the heck
you do this! Can you explain to me how this
information comes to you? It's fascinating to
me. I wonder if it's something I could learn
to do, then we wouldn't have to bug you for
answers!

Anyway, let me know about my mom. She's just
chomping at the bit!

XXOO,

Monica
```

I can't do this. It wasn't confined to her uneasiness about inviting Howard's presence back into her home. The problem has become bigger than Howard—her receptivity has elevated and expanded since her initial readings. The leaking dam burst open in an explosion of force well beyond her novice control. Not only are spirits talking to her at all times of day, they've begun using a new language—symbols and numbers. It is fast becoming their preferred mode of communication with her. She finds it everywhere and anywhere, their symbolic messages launched from some external catapult into her brain.

She enters *Spirit Symbols* into the Google Search engine and lists on a sheet of notepaper all the symbols the spirits keep putting forth to her: the wolf, the hawk, the numbers 11 and 22, the circle, the hexagram, and more. There was always a recurring theme, a repeating message. Each symbol created a distinct vibration, some good and some not so good. The negative symbols created great discomfort and uneasiness in her mind and heart.

What returns from her search is curious. Web addresses for spiritual symbol meanings, symbols and the occult, animal symbols, Native American symbols, number meanings and more. She clicks on a site called SymbolismBeyond.com.

First she researches the symbol of the circle. *The feminine life force and birth?* Then she starts looking up all the symbols they've been presenting her with, one after the other. The color pink represents artistry, blue means intuition. The wolf, teacher, the lion, power and the owl, wisdom. The numbers 11 and 22 represent the highest realms of spirit as both are aligned with the Creator's energy.

While all of this interests her, it is the darker feeling symbols Josie knows she needs to study. Evil possesses its own numbers and symbols, and these are beginning to show up with greater and greater frequency. In particular, the numbers 4 and 6 and the symbol of the hexagram. Their negative vibration grows even stronger when the numbers show up in doubles—44 and 66.

Strangely, her search reveals nothing negative about the numbers 4 and 6: 4 meant stability and 6, harmony. However, whenever she sees these numbers, it brings her no feeling of stability or harmony. If anything, they bring feelings of fear and imbalance.

She closes her search and goes to the window. The cardinal that frequents the tree in her backyard hasn't appeared in days. She is losing touch with her mother due to the noise coming in from the others. Josie can no longer feel her presence nor can she detect her in the dizzying array of conversations taking place in her head.

Thoughts spinning, Josie's returns to her computer and taps away:

THE UNCOMMITTED

Monica,

Thank you for thinking of me (and your mom as well) but I'm sorry to have to disappoint you both. Since we last spoke, I've been barraged, unsolicited that is, from more and more deceased relatives and friends. It's hard to explain but it's much like being the payphone that every dead person wants to use only they don't line up and take turns. They insist on talking all at once and it's been a constant interruption in my life. Until I gain some skills at controlling the input, I don't feel I can initiate new readings.

As for you trying to do readings, I advise you to be careful what you ask for. Seriously. I can't even leave my house without a new barrage of vibrations. They come off of most anything having words such as street signs, license plates, billboards and the like. Even product labels in the grocery store attract my attention these days and it's all part of some random and uninvited spirit's message. Some spirits are downright irritating and intrusive. It's as if I'm being followed by my own personal band of spirit paparazzi! I was both naïve and unprepared for this endeavor of mine. I didn't know the rules of this game and from my recent experience, it appears to me that the unseen world doesn't operate under the same rules we do here, if any at all.

I'm so sorry Monica and please let your mom know I'm sorry too. If anything changes, you'll be the first to know.

Love,
Josie

Josie sends her email to Monica and resumes her endless chores. While she vacuums, new thoughts spring to life in her head. Are all these messages truly coming from the deceased relative in question? Or do spirits lie? Could they be spirit imposters? And what would motivate them to do such a thing? Josie realizes, in a technical sense, she is a blind clairvoyant. *Why do I receive all my information by telepathy? I don't actually see the deceased ... unless they appear to me in a dream. I can't verify these people!* She can't authenticate a discarnate being as you would a visible person. And, for all she knows, in the afterlife, souls may be able to access information of any and all who have lived on the earth. Perhaps life histories could be read like an open book. *I can't play this stupid game anymore. They're gaining the upper hand!*

Suddenly, it comes to her. There must be souls who do not reach Heaven or Hell, but wander in the "in between." Earthbound and bored, these vagrant souls are preying on her. She's their entertainment and it's become her living Hell.

CHAPTER 17

Save me, O God
For the waters threaten my life;
I am sunk in the abysmal swamp
Where there is no foothold;
I have reached the watery depths;
The flood overwhelms me. I am wearied with calling,
My throat is parched;
My eyes have failed
with looking for my God.
—Psalm 69 2:4

Josie's anxiety level ratchets up by the minute as the day goes on. Somehow, some way, she must regain control of her mental faculties. She breaks the strangle hold they have on her mind and thinks clear for one instant. *Am I psychotic? Am I delusional?* She's never experienced serious psychiatric problems before. And why can't she stem the tide of spirit contact? Why won't God answer her prayers? Where is He?

Out of desperation, she turns to her sister, Nora, in hopes she will have an explanation and some advice. She gets her voicemail and leaves her a panicked message. "Nora, it's Josie. I started doing some channeling on my own, like we discussed. I'm scared. I'm getting more than I bargained for. I'm hearing from all sorts of spiritual energies, positive and negative. They show up uninvited at all times of the day and night. The negative ones are especially troubling. I can't shut them off. They won't let up even when I tell them to go away. I think I've pierced the veil pretty deep, deeper than I expected. I feel as though it's sucking me in—like water circling a drain and I can't escape. Things are getting out of control. Call me."

She hangs up and immediately starts to ruminate. *Did I do the right thing? I probably shouldn't have left her a message like that.*

"Mom, Mom!" Michael comes running into the family room where she is sitting motionless in front of the family computer. Michael grabs her arm. "Mommy, look at me!"

She wakes from her daze and looks directly at Michael. "What's going on?"

"The radio upstairs went on by itself!" His hands are shaking.

"Which radio?"

"The one in my room!" he cries.

"Oh, I'm sure Anna or Jacob played with the alarm. It probably got accidentally set to go off." She says it as if there's nothing to worry about. She wants him to feel safe.

"Come and turn it off! Come see!" He pulls her by the arm to get her to stand up.

They proceed up the stairs and into his bedroom. The radio is playing loud. She turns it off and checks the alarm setting. It is set to go off at 4:44 a.m. *What the ... ?* There are the fours, in triplicate. Their vibration is loud and ugly. She shudders.

"Mom," Michael grabs her by the neck, pulling her close to whisper in her ear. "I hear a voice in my head and it's not my own!" His body is rigid, his face is pale.

Josie emits a low growl under her breath and orders whoever it is haunting Michael to *Leave now!* Michael clings to her arm. It's as if he feels the cold energy too; it lurks in the air around them. Suddenly, she hears the rippling tap of fingernails, rolling in a rhythmic pattern across the bathroom counter next to Michael's room. *Bar-ump, bar-ump, bar-ump.* She follows the tapping into the hall. The sound ceases. She enters the bathroom. There is no one there but her and Michael.

Crash!

A hallway light explodes into a million sharp pieces in front of Josie's feet.

Michael bursts into fearful tears.

"It's okay Michael, the light shorted out. It's not a big deal." Josie fakes calm. She picks up Michael and gingerly carries him over the shards on the carpet to the stairway where it is free of glass. "Stay here while I go get the vacuum."

"No! I want to come with you!" he insists.

"Okay, c'mon." She carries him over the broken glass again and places him down on the ground once they are in her bedroom. With Michael following her close behind, she proceeds to get the vacuum out of her closet. She inventories in her head where everyone is in the house: Declan is at work, Anna is in the kitchen coloring at the table and Jacob is asleep in his crib in his bedroom down the hall. She peeks outside through her bedroom blinds—Jamison is outside, his ears are back, his tail is down and he appears to be growling at the air.

Be brave Josie, she thinks. With the vacuum in one arm and carrying Michael with the other, she walks back into the hall. Michael's arms cling and lock around her neck. She sets down the vacuum and closes the door to Jacob's room, trying to keep his room quiet as possible for him to nap. She sets Michael down on a middle-level step on the stairway. "Sit here," she says, "and stay away from the broken glass." She goes to plug in the vacuum in the hall outlet and must remove its childproof cover first. She bends over to grab it when suddenly the cover pops out—by itself. Then the second cover comes out, only this time it doesn't pop. It maneuvers slowly out of the outlet as if some invisible hand is pulling it out.

She hears tapping again, this time it is louder, more purposeful and with deliberate and steady beats. It is still coming from the kids' bathroom. She leaves the vacuum and runs to the bathroom. The bathroom is empty. She remembers she hadn't checked Anna's room yet.

She proceeds to look around Anna's room, under her bed, and in her closet. Again, she turns up nothing. She keeps trying to explain things away, the lights are old, the outlets are loose, the tapping sounds are from a mouse. Yet, her reasons fail to convince her.

She returns to the vacuum. Michael waits patiently for her on the steps. She knows Jacob's naptime will be over once she starts the vacuum but there is little choice—she can't have the kids cut themselves on shards of glass. She turns on the vacuum and pushes it back and forth over the sharp pieces and tiny specs of reflecting glass. For a time, the noise of the vacuum drowns out her fear.

"Mommy, are you done yet?" Michael asks, yelling over the loud motor of the vacuum.

"Almost, you can go downstairs, I'll be right there," she says, calling back.

"No, I'll wait for you!" he insists.

She finishes and winds up the cord. She carries the vacuum back into her bedroom but as she passes through the door, she senses an energy pulling her toward it in the corner of the room by her side of the bed. She smells the odor of burning, like that of incinerated flesh. The waft of a cold breeze slips under her nose. She touches the wall behind the bed. It is icy cold but a burning, pungent odor persists.

She whispers to herself, "What?"

"Mommy, Mommy!" Michael comes sprinting into her bedroom. "Don't leave me!"

"What's the matter? I'm here, I didn't leave." She reassures and holds him.

Michael then takes her by the hand and pulls her into the hallway. Before going downstairs, Josie checks Jacob again and thinks it's amazing he's still asleep. She touches his back, he breathes softly. There's no sign of any disturbance in his room. She leaves his room and closes his door but leaves it open a crack. Michael follows her every step.

"Michael, there's nothing to be afraid of sweetheart," she says as they go down the stairs. "But, Mommy, can't *you* hear the voices?" he asks.

"No. Can you?" She stops. All the blood drains from her face and down to her feet. Her skin turns pale. A shiver ripples up her spine and spreads into her arms. Her worst fears materialize before her—the door she has opened cannot be closed. Her decision is irrevocable. When she refused to hear these depraved and invisible creatures any more, they sought another conduit—her children.

Michael sobs, "Mommy, they say awful things, like they hate you and they want *me* to kill *you*!"

"What!" She covers her face because she knows her expression of horror will scare him. *What have I done?* Without realizing, she invited this evil into their home. These deplorable, warped beings will stop at nothing to be heard—there are no limits to their actions, no principles they honor, and no boundaries they will not cross. It becomes clear all at once—in the world of lost souls, children of the earth are fair game and despite those that leave upon their demand, more come in their place.

Josie drops to her knees and makes the Sign of the Cross. "Michael, pray with me." She reaches for his hand and he kneels down next to her. They pray the Hail Mary.

From their place on the stairs, she hears the kitchen door to their backyard fly open and slam with a force so fierce, the walls around them quake. In the distance, she hears something crash and shatter. Anna shrieks and comes running up the stairs toward them. They huddle together on the landing.

"Mommy, the family picture downstairs fell! There's glass all over the floor!" Anna cries.

"Mommy, they're gone," Michael says. "They started yelling bad words at you when you started praying—they stopped as soon as we said Jesus!"

"How? What?" Josie froze, wanting to curl up and die but she had a duty—to protect her children from these pitiless, hateful monsters. "Hold on," she says and orders the two of them to stay put. She runs back into her bedroom and takes the ancient silver cross that was once her mother's and grandmother's and those before them. She wraps it around her neck and latches the clasp. *Why do I keep forgetting to put this on? Are they messing with my memory too?* She takes the holy water out of her dresser drawer and heads back to the hall. Michael and Anna are still standing on the stairs, weeping uncontrollably. She sprinkles holy water on them.

"What are you doing, Mommy?" Michael asks.

"Just make the Sign of the Cross now, like this," Josie says, showing them. They mimic her movements. "Hang on one more minute, Mommy has one more thing to do."

"Why can't we come with you?" Anna pleads.

"I'm right here. You can watch me. I need to get something in each of your rooms."

"What's that?" Michael asks, still crying.

Deliberately and calmly, for their sake, she goes to each of their rooms. She removes their baptismal crosses from the keepsake box she saves for them in each of their closets. She places each cross out in the open on their dressers while she sprinkles holy water all over their rooms. She remembers what her mother told her and prays she was right. Whoever was haunting them would see they belonged to Christ.

SOMEWHAT MIRACULOUSLY, AFTER SHE FINISHES BLESSING the upstairs with the holy water, Michael and Anna stopped crying. Josie emits a colossal sigh of relief and wipes the cold sweat of fear from her brow.

Anna runs from the hall into the bathroom. "Mommy," she calls to her from the bathroom, "Can you help me? I can't unzip my pants."

Josie turns to Michael, "Please go make some noise in your brother's room—it's too late for him to still be napping."

Anna is in the same bathroom where Josie heard the tapping of fingernails minutes before but now there is nothing, just her and Anna who is sitting on the potty. Michael speeds off into Jacob's room and begins to sing, "Power Rangers roar, Power Rangers soar." He sings it loud and strong and with it, Jacob wakes up.

"Mama," Jacob hollers.

Michael is still singing loudly.

Maybe, just maybe, that's what I need to become, a Power Ranger and kick the living crap out of these menacing wanderers ... if only I could see them, she thinks.

Out of nowhere, she hears Jamison barking. She leaves Anna and looks out the upstairs window in her bedroom. Outside, Jamison stands at the base of the deck facing away from the house. His ears are erect and his tail stands on high alert, recoiling his body and growling at the air. Next to him on the ground in a rock bed is Josie's garden angel. Both of its wings are broken off. Her stomach aches. She knows—whatever or whoever it is haunting them may be gone for good but their kind is in endless supply. How will she prepare to fight those who come next?

CHAPTER 18

"**D**addy! Daddy's home!" Anna calls.

Declan walks in the door. Anna jumps into his arms and plant a hug and a kiss on him.

"How's my girl?" he says.

"I'm good, Daddy, I made you a picture. Do you want to see it?" She skips to the table to obtain one of the pictures of puppies she colored from her coloring book. Michael is outside playing on the swing in the backyard and Jacob is on the living room floor playing with his toy trains. All the fear from the afternoon strangely dissipated from the children.

Declan takes the picture from her. He looks it over and with a wide smile, bends over to give his girl another hug, "Thank you, honey, it's beautiful."

"Will you hang it up in your office, Daddy?"

"Of course I will." He gives her a squeeze.

All the while, Josie says a prayer in silence to herself and cooks noodles at the stove. Her eyes are intent on her stirring; she can't face him or look him in the eye. If she does, she'll fall apart.

"Hi, Jos." He leans in and gives her a kiss on the cheek.

"Hi, hon." She glances up at him briefly then begins to sauté broccoli and mushrooms. She avoids further eye contact with him.

"So, what's for dinner?" he says, though it is obvious.

"Stir fry vegetables over noodles." She says these few words with every ounce of confidence she's able to muster.

"Well, I can see that. What else?" he cracks.

"Do we need anything else?" She shoots him a caustic glance but looks away just as quickly. "What about a little gratitude?"

"How about a little chicken or beef?"

"Ha, ha," she says, in a snarky tone. "I figured you were going for a run after dinner; I knew you wouldn't want anything too heavy to eat." *White lie.* She'd forgotten to unfreeze the chicken for dinner due to the day's horror.

"You're too good to me." He smiles crookedly. His hands pull her by the waist against him and he places a firm kiss on her mouth.

Before she falls into his kiss, she pulls back. "The kids?"

"Fine." Reluctantly, he releases her. "Were you able to pick up my dry cleaning today?"

"Oh, crap ... I forgot," she winces, realizing she'd forgotten that too.

"Jos, I've got to have those shirts and my gray suit for my trip to Madison tomorrow." He removes his bottle of bourbon from the liquor cabinet and pours himself a drink.

"Daddy, if there's a mad-i-son is there a happy-son?" Anna asks, tugging on Declan's dress shirt.

"Anna, good one, hard to explain but no ... there's not happy-son." Declan looks down at Anna beside him, amused by her astute language observation.

"I guess picking them up in the morning isn't an option?" She gathers the strength and makes eye contact with him for a healthy few seconds. She notices how handsome he is especially when he is dressed for work. He always dressed sharp for work, in part, because she picked out his clothes.

"Uh, no, my flight leaves at 6 a.m. Remember?"

"Oh." She didn't remember that either. She looks at the clock. It's already 6:25 p.m. and the dry cleaner closes at seven. She wants to make-up for her oversight but, at the same time, she doesn't want to leave the safe harbor of her home. She knows she'll face a barrage of new messages as soon as she pulls her car out of the garage.

"I'll go get them," he says.

"No, Daddy, stay here! I've been waiting and waiting to play catch with you in the backyard," Michael hollers, coming in the door from the yard.

"I guess this means I'm going." Josie sucks in a breath and sighs. "Can you finish this up?" She takes the noodles off the stove to drain them over the sink.

"We'll eat when you get back," he says.

Josie covers the vegetables and noodles, turns off the stove, and then retrieves her keys from the rack by the door. In the driveway she makes the Sign of the Cross, then braces herself for the next psychic attack.

THE ONSLAUGHT HITS ON HER WAY HOME FROM THE DRY cleaners. There's an upward wind of vibration prompting her to look out and up from the driver's side window. An airplane is flying above a small group of feathery clouds. Images of a fiery crash take over and begin to swarm her. She scowls and grips the steering wheel, trying to erase the horrific premonition but the vision persists. Frantic, she thinks of Declan. *Is this a warning about his trip tomorrow?* The answer comes from an unknown voice in her head— *terrorism, jet liner bound for L.A. from Asia.* In her mind she sees a tall man; his face is rough and pock-marked. She hears the words *bomb* and *cell-phone.*

"How? Hasn't security improved since 9/11?" she asks out loud to the air.

That was almost five years ago. A deep voice speaks in her head.

"Stop it!" she screams.

Then, as if it were a movie trailer cut short, she is assailed by another even more graphic image. This time hundreds of dead are strewn about in a body of bloodied water, but it isn't a plane crash that she sees in her vision. It is a cruise ship with its hull spread out in large chunks across an enormous body of water. She sees a woman with fair skin and narrow features. The woman looks pregnant. The vision transforms and the woman's blouse becomes translucent—a bomb is concealed under her shirt.

In fear and frustration, she calls "Enough already!" Yet she is slammed with another ghastly image: U.S. troops falling ill then dying during a meal in the mess tent. She sees a faceless man in a white apron and hair net stir a powdery substance into pots of hot soup. He pours soup from his ladle into bowls and hands it out to the troops, one by one by one. Outside the tent, there is a desert with smoldering ripples of heat rising from the earth. She shudders. *How can I prevent any of these things from happening?* The information sent to her is too broad. There's nothing she can do to stop it— there are too many images. Who will believe her anyhow?

She re-enters her neighborhood when an ominous force presses hard on her right foot. In a flash, her car accelerates. She frees her foot and just as quickly the car slows. The dark presence mocks her, *"You're pathetic!"* Trembling and crying, she prays a Hail Mary and another and another in futile hopes her prayers will save her.

She pulls her car into the garage and shuts the door. She grabs Declan's dry cleaning and rushes into the house, bolting the door behind her. She can see Declan and the kids out the kitchen window in the backyard playing ball. Her hands shake. She hangs the dry cleaning in the hall closet and goes straight for the open bottle of Cabernet on the counter. She pours it into a coffee mug, a stable fixture, knowing her shaking fear will tip over a wine glass. She doesn't want Declan to see how much she is drinking. It will clue him in that she is not well ... that she is not right. She sucks one glass down and pours herself another, all in order to dull her psychic senses. She thinks she's lucky that alcohol is the strongest drug in the house. She'd have swallowed a bottle of Valium if she had it, anything to cope, to function, to shut off the damned.

She steps outside to let them know she is home. "Hi guys!" she says, feigning calm.

"Good, how much was my dry cleaning?" Declan asks, tossing the ball to Michael who stands ready with a plastic bat.

"I don't know, let me check the receipt." She pulls the receipt out of her pocket to look. "Um, it was $44.66." *Smack!* The numbers and the ball hit her in her face.

"Jos! Are you okay?" Declan runs over to where she is standing.

"I'm sorry, Mommy!" Michael says.

Declan places his hand soft on her cheek at the spot where the ball hit her. "Are you all right, hon?" He strokes his hand over her hair in comfort. "That's got to have hurt."

"Yeah, I'm okay," she says, though startled. He pulls her into his arms; she relaxes her head on his chest and is secure for the moment.

"Michael—please get your mom some ice." Declan steps back to see her face. "It's a little red, but otherwise you're still intact."

"I'm fine, really," she says, though shaken. In the palm of her right hand develops a burning sensation, there's a vibration coming from the receipt. She drops it to the ground.

"Whoops, I got it." Declan picks up the receipt and puts it in his pocket, unfazed.

She watches him, stunned by his lack of reaction to holding the receipt. She's the only one who feels it.

"Michael, hurry up with the ice for your mom. Oh, and grab me a garbage bag."

"Sure. Why, Dad?"

"There's a dead bird over by the tree."

"Which tree?" Michael says.

Josie's stomach turns.

"The one that's closest to the deck by the kitchen door," he says.

Her wary expression starts to give her away. It is her tree. The one her mother's cardinal comes and perches on.

"What's the matter?" He asks, puzzled.

"Nothing," she says if only to cover up her anxiety. "I wonder how it died. Did it fly into the tree?"

"I don't know. I forgot to ask it while it was taking its last breath."

His joking sarcasm fails to amuse her. It's clear she's unsettled by the death of the bird.

"C'mon, it was a joke, hon. Relax. I don't know what happened; I just found it when we were playing ball." Declan rubs her shoulders. He leaves her side and takes the shovel. He scoops up the dead bird; its red feathers fan up from the base of the shovel.

CHAPTER 19

Late in the evening and long after Josie places the children to bed, she returns to the computer in the family room. She is grieving the loss of her cardinal almost as if her mother had died again. Yet, if her mother wants, Josie feels confident her mother will find another way to get in touch with her. Surely, there are lots of cardinals. Maybe there will come a new one to her tree? But who killed her bird? Is this a warning that she should not tread this path?

Declan sits on the couch to her left with his back towards her. He is drinking bourbon on the rocks, absorbed in the Stanley Cup Playoffs and unaware of her ongoing agitation. He voices the occasional "yeah!" and grunts in disgusts when the refs call the play against his team, the Minnesota Wild.

Since he's distracted, she begins to search for more answers to her plight. Numerous websites about intuition come up and she reads them all eagerly, much like a mother looking for a cure to her child's disease. One site explains the nature of true psychic ability. *"It's a marriage between the brain and the spiritual mind. The spirit acts as a conduit of information only when the physical mind is open to it."* Nevertheless, she can't find anything that gives her instructions regarding how to control her ability or how to turn it off.

She reads a few articles by some, more famous psychics. Each one has their take in dealing with negative energies. *"Rest assured— you have spirit guides who will protect you from the lower realms of their world. You just need to ask for their help,"* says psychic to the stars, James Vander. Advice from nationally renowned psychic, Maria Coulier, says *"Sometimes your teachers in spirit will allow messages to come to you from the lower realms in order to train you in the ability to recognize the difference between the higher realms of spirit and the lower realms. Don't be afraid of negative messages, it's all part of the lesson."* Tom Porter, the well-known FBI mentalist, advises, *"Our own self-doubt will play mental tricks on us, cause us to think we are channeling negative energies when in fact we're the negative energy we are channeling. We mediums can be our own worst enemy."*

His words give her pause. Is Tom Porter right? Is her own self-doubt causing her to channel symbols and messages about darkness and evil?

She deletes the search history. It will irritate Declan if he sees she's researching the topic. Could she be the source of her own havoc as Tom indicates? If her guides are trying to teach her a lesson, as Maria states, why would they do something to cause her such distress? And who are these guides they speak of? James Vander sounds so confident in these so-called spirit guides.

Josie grows weary. She wonders if all of this is happening to her because she is a "novice." Once she engaged in this supernatural conversation, did she begin to perceive the invisible as it actually exists? A mega-conglomeration of thoughts and energy. Maybe it streams through her because she hasn't developed an intrinsic filter or any internal controls? She hasn't the skills to silence the souls who are miserable, suffering and evil—yet. She wonders if the lower realms of spirit are people who were morally corrupt in life. Are they then lost forever in a transitional state of existence where they wander eternally in the ether, neither good enough for heaven nor bad enough for hell? Although, it seems to her the longer they wander, the more demonic they become. And given she is able to perceive them, they don't appear inclined to leave her alone.

"Jos… Josie!" Declan says.

Josie startles, reflexively.

"Aren't you going to come to the phone?" he asks. "It's your sister."

"Oh ... sure." Josie hadn't even heard it ring.

"Hi, Nora. What's up?"

"I didn't hear from you this morning so I thought I'd check in with you."

"Oh, sorry, I've been busy." *Excuses, excuses.*

"Is now a good time to talk?"

"Not really. Um…"

"You can't talk right now?"

"Um, yeah."

"Okay, call me tomorrow then. I was wondering if you've given more thought to applying to Sedona institute. Before you hang up though, I have to tell you something important about Dad."

"What ... what's going on?" Josie stutters.

"We have to move him out of his apartment to a nursing home."

"But why?"

"This morning, he wandered out of his place and ended up on the other side of his complex in some stranger's apartment. When the assisted living staff found him, he was completely disoriented. He couldn't even tell them where he lived. He knew his first name and that was about it."

"Oh, no—"

"Oh, no is right. They called me right after it happened. I picked him up and took him to the doctor. I was worried he had a stroke or something. He was so confused."

"What did the doctor say?"

"Just what I told you—Dad needs to move where people can keep an eye on him 24/7. He said Dad can't be left alone at all anymore."

"Where is he now?"

"He's staying here with Jason and me until we find him a place. Tony said he can help too. Unfortunately, though, in the process of his wandering, there was a casualty."

"What sort of casualty?" Josie's stomach lurches.

"Dad lost his wedding band. He hasn't taken it off since Mom died but I noticed it was missing when we were at the doctor's office."

"Did you search his apartment?"

"Yes, and I called the staff at the complex. We can't find it and at this point, it could be anywhere."

"Do you need me to come out there?"

"No, we can handle it. You can come later—once we have him settled."

Josie hangs up the phone, overcome by sadness. She wonders what her father would think of her now. Would he be proud of her, or would he consider her to be some lying cheat of a wife, disobeying her loyal and devoted husband? She grows more and more despondent over her father's state of mind and for the poor choices she has made. She hopes her father will never find out or understand. No matter what he believed about her mother's gift, in her heart, she knows he would not approve of her going against her husband's wishes.

CHAPTER 20

Next to her on the nightstand shouts a vibration of light. She opens her eyes to see it's only her digital clock. It reads 5:22 a.m. in large bright red numbers. It isn't time to get up. She wonders why her body is waking up now. She only feels the distinct vibration of numbers, particularly 22.

The bedroom is dark, although not completely. She can make out the shapes of objects from the nightlight in the hall. She rolls over to see if Declan is awake, but he is gone. Confused, her eyes probe the darkness and then her mind clears. She remembers he left to catch a 6 a.m. flight to Madison. It's apparent he hasn't been gone long, because the scent of his cologne, a mix of citrus and pine, still lingers in the air. The air is humid and warm, a left-over from his early shower.

Declan will not return until late Friday night, which means she has nearly two days alone with her children and the telepathic disruptions plaguing her mind. He'll be gone less than forty hours, not a long time, but she already misses him not only because she loves him but because he is her protector, her security. When Declan's around, the invisible intruders appear to relent as if intimidated by his presence. He is her Knight of the Templar, his soul shielded by both his armor of faith and a body of muscular steel. He never feared demons because he never considered them to be real. As long as he doesn't pay them heed, they don't exist. She takes his pillow, smashes it to her chest and hugs it tight, all in futile attempt to avoid the frightening burden of her impending hours of solitude.

Along with her fear of being alone is a nagging undercurrent of anxiety. She thinks of her unsettling premonition from the evening before. Although she knows it isn't his plane in her vision, it still scares her. Should she have told him not to go? Should she have warned him? Her record of prediction was far from perfect, and there was the issue of her premonition's source—a mocking evil spirit.

Worse, she can't remember if Declan kissed her good-bye. She hopes he kissed her even if she was asleep. She wants to remember his last kiss but her mind keeps gravitating toward the memory of a vivid dream she had before waking up. In her dream, her ears are flushed out with a syringe of water, the blue bulb kind of syringe used to clear out mucus from a newborn's nose. A person whose face she can't decipher squeezes the syringe of water vigorously into her ears as if they are clogged and full of wax. She can feel the sensation of water rushing through her ear canals and popping her eardrums open, like the feeling of being on an airplane when it begins its landing descent.

"Josie."

She hears the voice of a woman. *Wait*, she thinks, *that voice sounds too real.* Josie stops and starts listening. This voice isn't part of a dream.

"Josie," the voice speaks again. Out loud.

Who's here? Josie's heart beats faster. The only other female in the house is Anna and she doesn't sound that mature. Anyway, she'd have called her 'Mommy' not Josie.

"Josie," the voice says a third time.

"She knows my name?" she whispers. Josie can't see the source of the words but it sounds as if it is approaching her from the doorway and coming closer to her bed. She presses her eyelids together tight, pretending to be asleep, or dead.

"Josie, listen up!" The voice becomes louder and more insistent.

"Okay, okay, I'm listening." *Enough already! Tell me what you want before I have a heart attack!* Josie trembles, nearly hysterical. The voice is real and it scares the living crap out of her. She pulls the covers over her head and tries to hide.

"Don't talk to strangers!" The disquieting female voice gives her an order. It is right over her head.

I know that voice, she thinks. It is her mother's. It is no longer telepathy. Her words are audible. Josie touches her ears, astounded at this newfound change. Why is she hearing her mother like this, in this way? Why is she telling her not to talk to strangers? If she wasn't so afraid of hearing her mother's voice because she was dead, she would've rolled her eyes at her, like she did as a teenager, to her always over-the-top personal safety directions.

"Be on guard and pray, pray without ceasing!" her mother bellows. Josie quivers under the covers. "And wear your cross! Don't forget to carry something red ... ," She sounds distant now, trailing off.

Josie gathers the nerve to throw back the covers. "Mom, Mom," she calls, "Where are you? I can't see you." She waits but there is no answer and senses her mother has left. *It had to be her.* The presence and voice were unmistakable.

Out of the blue, Josie hears church bells ringing. *I must be hallucinating ... or is it tinnitus? No, those are definitely church bells.* They sound as if they are coming from the upstairs hallway—they ring soft, quiet and crisp. *Donnngggg ...—donnngggg ...—donnngggg ...*—each sound separate and wavelike, reverberating into oblivion as if each ring of the bell were drifting outward into silence before sounding again. The bells ring for one long and endless minute. Then they stop. She looks at the clock. It is now 5:33.

She pulls the covers back over her head. *What if it wasn't her? If it was, why did she come to tell me these things? Be on guard? Wear my cross? Carry something red? Don't talk to strangers? Am I in danger?* Is her mother still paranoid about her safety in the afterlife? Maybe she knows Declan is traveling for work and wants to remind her to be careful. However, she has a feeling her mother's visit has more to do with the riff raff spirits who skulked through Josie's house the day before and whoever tagged along on her trip home from the dry cleaners.

Josie tries to go back to sleep to no avail. She knows her mother doesn't mean to scare her, but inevitably she does. Why isn't she being protected? Where are those spirit guides she read about? Doesn't she have guardian angels looking out for her? Is her mother one of them? Why do these nuisance spirits bother her? And why did the more famous psychics make it sound so easy to deal with the lower realms? Maybe she isn't as a good as they are? They apparently can do their work, find the missing, solve unsolved crimes, and connect loved ones across the veil, all without the spirits of hell ripping through their train of predictions. Why was she so different? It's as if she hit an invisible wall. No way, no how, could she penetrate this wall of lowlifes. In fact, they seemed to enjoy battering her as if she were a ball being tossed about for their amusement. *Why me? What did I ever do to them?*

Her mother's words overwhelm her. Josie was under attack from a full-fledged mental assault by wandering souls. Is it a question of endurance? Will she pass this test before the wicked devour her and lay her to waste? She thinks she may not be worthy enough to channel the higher realms of spirit. Is she just an ordinary psychic groupie trying to get a back stage VIP pass to purgatory? *Maybe I'm not invited.* She envisions growling razor-toothed dogs on leashes held by violent roadies standing guard. *Of course, things like this only happen to me. I must be cursed, cursed to channel only the dregs of the afterlife.*

Then she does what her mother advised. She begins to pray—a whole decade of the rosary—one Hail Mary isn't going to do it this time. She feels better after praying and dozes off.

HER ALARM CLOCK SOUNDS, A LOUD BUZZ. SHE MUSTERS THE courage to push back her covers and shuts it off. She looks at her clock. It is now 7 a.m. Sunlight distills through her windows and drapes and casts rays of radiant light onto the carpet. It is time to get up, shower and start her day. She rises out of bed but not without wariness or hesitation. She waits for a few seconds to see if she hears mother's voice, but no voice comes. She proceeds into the bathroom and uses the toilet. *Nope, no voices in here,* she thinks, *and no sound of church bells either.* She flushes. *Maybe it was all a dream.* Once again, Josie tries to find some explanation and one fitting within the parameters of a tangible and physical reality but can find none.

She turns on the shower and forces herself to keep her focus on the day ahead. She lets the warm water run down over her body and feels it erasing away negative energies, sending them right down the drain. She shampoos her hair and mentally tallies what she needs to get done today. *Drop off Michael at school, take Anna and Jacob to meet Maureen and Ronan for a morning walk at Como Park, return movies to the video store, drop off bills at the post office, pick up milk, strawberries and grapes at Wilson's....* Josie enjoys reviewing the ordinary day she hopes she'll have. She fervently prays no invisible intruders will wreak their havoc on her brand new day.

"Knock, knock!" a child's voice calls to her through the shower door. Abruptly, the shower door swings open.

With a jerk of surprise, Josie sees Anna staring at her. "What are you doing up so early?"

"I couldn't sleep, Mommy. Can I lie down in your bed?"

"Sure," she says as she washes her face. "But I'm going to finish my shower, okay?"

"Oh, that's okay, Mommy. I'll wait for you."

"Anna, I won't be lying back down, I'm up now ... for the day."

"Oooh, I'll go lie down then by myself and wait for you to come out."

Josie finishes her shower, a bit on edge after the jolt from Anna's greeting. Nevertheless, she reasons it's good Anna's up. If she hears anything she can't explain, she can attribute it to Anna. It's worth a try.

Chapter 21

Josie pulls into the parking lot at the Como Park Zoo and Conservatory. She sees Maureen and Ronan over on the sidewalk by the Park's main entrance.

"Hey, they're here already. They must have gotten here early," Josie says from the driver's seat to Jacob and Anna. They are sitting in the backseat watching a DVD.

Josie waves to Maureen and parks. She gets out and walks around to the back of the van to retrieve the stroller. Once more, the vibration starts. She has recited at least ten Hail Marys and five Our Fathers on her drive over to Como. She hoped her prayers would keep the riff raff spirits away, but it isn't working. Josie pops open the stroller, attempting to ignore the vibratory pulses, but it proves difficult.

"Jacob, do you want to ride or walk today?" she asks.

"Walk, Mommy."

"All right." She takes the stroller along anyway, in case he changes his mind.

They cross the parking lot to meet Maureen and Ronan at the gates.

"What a great day for a walk," Maureen says, smiling. "Let's start in the gardens and then catch the merry-go-round. We can go to the zoo afterwards. Sound like a plan?"

"Um, sure." Josie tries to anchor her mind in the present physical reality, praying Maureen and others can't perceive her mental turmoil.

"Hey, don't you guys look adorable all in red. You'd think you were Wisconsin Badger fans or something." Maureen laughs.

"No way, Declan would have a fit! It's a coincidence that I put us all in red today." *And to ward off the evil spirits. You know, per my mother's early morning bedside visit.*

"You're wearing a beautiful cross. I don't think I've ever seen it before. Is it sterling silver?"

Maureen is noticing a lot today. Josie wonders how she can expect to hide her restlessness and anxiety from her.

"I've had it a long time. My mother gave it to me before she died." She reaches to clutch the silver chain and pendant in her hand.

"It must mean a lot to you."

She nods and suddenly finds herself consumed by an image, one of Jesus on the cross. *This man died for me. Why me?* In so many unanswered ways, this "why me" question takes on a whole new meaning with various unexplored and converging angles. Out of the blue, an unexpected wave of calm comes over her. The vibrations stop, the convoluted thoughts and messages vanish. The key word again, or rather, the key vision, seems to be Jesus. It appears the evil spirits didn't like their "messenger" invoking the Son of God.

Josie, Maureen and the children follow the first pathway into the Conservatory. The sun shines bright and warm, the sky is clear. Josie reaches into the stroller pouch for her knock-off Ray-Bans—a cheap indulgence to satisfy her material vanity.

Today, the park is especially magnificent although not much is in bloom. The long Minnesota winter has brought a late spring, yet the gardens are emerging with new life. The buds on the surrounding trees and bushes predict a garden that will soon be bursting in amazing brilliance. The grounds are already greened-up far beyond the lawns of the city dwellers. And of course, each patch of grass, each bush, tree and shrub is faultlessly manicured. Como's stone walkways are pristine, as if having been precisely polished and buffed. Everything smells fresh, fragrant and clean, and the sound of birds and water fountains fill the air.

Josie loves going for walks at Como Conservatory because it is peaceful, her children can run and needn't worry about cars or crossing streets. For the moment, she feels especially blessed. Her mind is surprisingly quiet. She is able to take in the surrounding flawless beauty without the intrusions of invisible strangers.

Ah ha! A new and different thought falls into her mind. *Strangers.* This is what her mother is referring to, those menacing spirits who bother her. *But they talk anyway!* Josie calls to her mother silently. Maureen sees Josie switching gears by the new grimace on her face. They stop to watch a mother duck and her ducklings swim by in the park's stream.

"Josie, is everything okay?" Maureen asks.

"Yeah, why?" Josie tries to appear natural, but she isn't successful.

"You look a little spooked." Maureen's brow rumples.

"I was thinking of something that happened this morning."

"What was it? Do you want to talk about it?"

"It's strange. Are you sure you want to hear?"

"Well, sure, if you feel like sharing."

Josie knows she can talk to Maureen about anything and decides it's probably wise for her to share her distress rather than bottling it up. And Maureen could keep a secret like a sealed tomb buried six feet under.

"Let's go to the meadow, the one near the middle of the Park and let the kids run around. I don't think an audience is a good idea, if you know what I mean." Josie looks down at the kids. Her Anna and Maureen's Ronan are already highly perceptive and increasingly nosey about adult conversations. Josie fears scaring them if they overhear her story.

"Sure, let's go," Maureen says.

They turn the corner on the flagstone path and it leads them back to center of the Park. Much to their surprise, they encounter a group of brilliant violet-blue flowers in full bloom growing at the base of a boxwood tree.

"Check these out," Maureen says, "I wonder what kind they are." She bends down to read the nameplate in the ground. "Hmm ... they're called *Chinodoxa* or *Glory of the Snow.*"

As they marvel at the patch of sparkling Chinodoxa, a gardener approaches them. His worn leather gardening gloves hang loosely from the side pocket of his faded jeans. His visor tips over his eyes and blocks the sun. He holds a clipper in his right hand and some dead brush in his left. He drops the brush in a wheel barrow sitting across from them.

"Those flowers bloom early ... the earliest of all the flowers around here," he says. "They'll actually poke through the snow, especially if the snow sticks around too long."

"Interesting," Maureen says. "Look at this." Maureen points toward another plate in the ground next to the flowers. She begins to read it aloud. *"What though the radiance which was once so bright be now for ever taken from my sight ... though nothing can bring back the hour of splendor in the grass, of glory in the flower ... we will grieve not, rather find strength in what remains behind."*

"That's beautiful, who wrote it?" Josie asks.

"Wordsworth," the gardener interjects. "It's a memorial plaque."

"Oh," she nods.

"Have you ever read Wordsworth?" he asks.

"No, I haven't, but perhaps I ought to." Josie looks down and away, ashamed for missing something of such literary importance.

"I have," Maureen says, "at my father's funeral, the very same poem."

"It's called *Intimations on Immortality*," he says.

As the gardener walks away and returns to his work, Josie hears them—tolling church bells. *There must be a church nearby. Could I be hearing St. Paul's Cathedral bells all this way down Como Avenue?* She looks at the time on her watch. It is 9:22. *There's that 22 again, weird, not a usual time for church bells.* "Do you hear that?" she whispers to Maureen. The gardener is still within earshot.

"Hear what?" Maureen asks.

"Church bells," she says, this time louder as the gardener is now further away, trimming the shrubs down the stone path from them.

"No." Maureen laughs. "I don't hear any bells. Do you?"

"Oh, I must be having ringing in my ears."

"You should go see your doctor about it."

Maureen's probably right. She tries to brush them off, but the bells are still ringing. *Donnnggggggg ...—donnnggggggg ...—donnnggggggg ...*

How can she not hear them? They're so freakin' loud! Once again, each sound is separate and wavelike.

While the bells are still ringing in her ears, they admire the starry-shaped flowers. They grow in small sprays of violet-blue blooms but each individual bloom doesn't crowd the space of another. Each has room to open toward the sky and take in the sunlight as if it were aimed directly at their delicate white centers.

"I come here and walk with the kids every summer and we find many incredible and unusual flowers," Maureen says, continuing to talk.

Josie appears to be listening but in truth, Maureen is becoming a blur. She can barely focus on her words because the church bells continue to ring, *donnnggggggg ... —, donnnggggggg ... —,* but instead of growing closer, they seem to be moving away from her.

"Josie. Josie?" Maureen notices Josie isn't paying attention. She is still lost in the space of her distracting ringing church bells.

"Oh, yes, you're right." Although, Josie isn't sure what she is agreeing to.

Finally, the church bells stop. *Thank God ... maybe now I can focus.* Josie bends down to get a closer look at the Glory of the Snow. Without touching the fragile fabric of their petals, she breathes in their scent. Their fragrance reminds her of the odor of lilacs mixed with the morning dampness of spring grass. *What do the bells mean? Why did they ring after we found this patch of flowers?*

After a short time, they resume their walk on the stone path to the small meadow. When they arrive, Anna, Jacob, and Ronan race off into the meadow. Maureen and Josie sit on the ground and let the warm spring sun beat down on their arms and faces.

"So, what's going on?" Maureen asks, starting the conversation for her.

"I don't know, it will sound bizarre. I can't believe it myself." She tries to garner some self-confidence but it is hard to find.

"What is it?"

"I think I heard my mother's voice this morning ... in my room," Josie says.

"Seriously? Not what I expected you to say. And bizarre, I'll give you that."

"I know—it sounds crazy," she says, her self-doubt creeps in louder. "It all started when the light on my digital clock woke me up, it was vibrating."

"Vibrating?"

"Yes, vibrating, it's hard to explain. And then, I started thinking about Declan. I was worried about his trip today."

"Why?" Maureen's eyes are intent on Josie.

"This is the scary part. I had a vision of a plane crash last night, except I knew it wasn't his plane in my vision. All the same, I still worried it was his."

"Is that why you think your mother came to you? Did she try to calm you?"

"Hardly," she scoffs. "She freaked me out. First of all, I couldn't see her, I could only hear her voice in the dark, and second, she gave me the feeling I was in danger."

"That is scary. Are you sure you're not reading into things too much?"

"Well, you tell me—she told me to pray and to wear my cross. Then she reminded me to carry something red to ward off evil spirits." Josie can see Maureen's face growing more concerned— that Josie's grasp on reality is loosening.

"Well, it does explain the red t-shirts today. Are you positive you weren't dreaming?"

"Yes, I'm sure, I was awake."

"What time did this happen?"

"The time on the clock when I woke up was 5:22. The number 22 seems to attract my attention a lot these days."

"Hmm, now that's weird."

"I never thought I'd ever hear my mother's voice again—at least not in this life."

"I didn't mean that. I meant the time—5:22. Isn't that also the date your mother died, May 22nd?"

"You're right. How did you remember that?" A chill brushes across Josie's arms and the hair on her skin bristles. *And how did I not? It was Mom. Maureen should be the psychic, not me.*

"It's just one of those dates I remember. It's an important one. Did you hear if Declan's plane landed yet?"

A sick feeling comes over her—he hasn't called. In a split second, her morning's peace comes to an abrupt end. The vibrations of her surrounding environment kick into full gear, far flung messages start to pummel her and she can't push them off even as she clutches her silver cross. The wheels of worry and panic reflect on her face.

"Josie, never mind—stupid question—you would've gotten news by now. I shouldn't have brought it up. The point is, he's safe and you and the kids are okay. Just let this worry go."

While Maureen is right, Josie can no longer locate a rational thought.

"Josie, worrying is wasted energy and it will only cause you to spiral. So, don't spiral—all it does is fuel anxiety. And don't let your mother's words haunt you. She was probably trying to let you know she was there and watching out for you."

Maureen's earnest words fail to comfort her and the sides of Josie's mouth turn downward. Everything hits her at once. Her bottom lip quivers and her eyes burn with the salt of her tears. She doesn't know where to turn or where to go. Fraught with obsessive thoughts about death and destruction, she is losing her grip. Her world and the supernatural converge into one collective explosion of insanity. It feels as if her mind has gone missing. She lives in two worlds now, the one pulling her away toward the polluted souls dwelling in this earthbound hell and the one struggling to grasp the tangible here and now.

Suddenly, Josie hears the brash sound of ringing. This time it's her cell phone. It sounds so brazen, so harsh, that it stops her from slipping further into the abyss.

"Oh, shoot, that's my cell," she says. Her hands are shaking as she jumps to retrieve it from the stroller pouch. She's so quick to answer that she doesn't stop to see who is calling.

"Josie? It's Kim at Jefferson."

Her heart sinks. "Kim, what's going on? Is there something wrong with Michael?"

"Is that the school nurse?" Maureen whispers.

Josie nods anxiously.

"First, Michael's okay … but he did have a reaction," Kim says. "I gave him his EpiPen and Benadryl right away. We think he reacted to this morning's snack."

"What? But I checked the snack when I dropped him off. It was cheese crackers. What happened?"

"We called the ambulance. He's on his way to the hospital right now. Janine Thompson is with him."

Josie grips the phone at her ear, her eyes brimming with fear. Maureen waits expectantly to hear the news about Michael. Anna, Jacob and Ronan are still playing and running through the small field, oblivious to the sudden change of events.

"What happened? I don't understand? How on earth?" Josie replays in her mind the morning's drop off at school. Michael's teacher, Mrs. Thompson, handed her the box of crackers. She read their ingredients … twice.

"The reaction came on quickly. Michael complained almost immediately that his tongue hurt and his lips were itchy. He didn't even swallow the muffin, he spit out the piece he bit off," Kim explains.

"Muffin? I didn't say he could have those muffins! In fact, I told Mrs. Thompson not to give him one—that's why we put them to the side of her desk, apart from the snack bin!" The snacks Michael could eat went into the "approved snack bin." Anything else stayed out and either got returned to the parent or was distributed later in the lunchroom away from Michael.

"There was a mix-up and the sub gave him the banana muffins instead of the crackers you approved for him this morning. Apparently, a student in Michael's class brought the muffins in for a birthday treat. We think they may have contained some nuts or peanut residue, which caused him to react."

"Banana muffins with nuts? And Mrs. Thompson was there this morning. I wasn't told she was having a substitute today!" Josie always knew ahead of time when his teacher was going to be absent because of Michael's severe allergies.

"Janine was in the next room performing reading evals. I know, it's no excuse but I wanted to be clear with you about what happened."

"Is he going to St. Catherine's?" she asks. She tries to pull her shattered self together.

"Yes, he's headed to their ER. If it helps, Michael was responding well to the medication when he left. He cried because of the shot but his reaction started to reverse as soon as he got it." Kim's attempt at playing down the situation is futile. To Josie, all the precautions they took at school still failed to protect her son.

"Are you certain he's stable? Is he able to breathe?" Josie voice cracks from panic.

"Yes, Michael was breathing normally when he left, I didn't hear any wheezing when I listened to his lungs," Kim reassures her.

"Did anyone notify his allergist, Dr. Neal?"

"We called him right away after we contacted 911. He said he'd meet Michael at the ER."

Josie is barely relieved as she knows the effect of epinephrine wears off quickly. If his body is resistant, a second attack will follow with even more violent force than the first one.

She says a good-bye to Kim and hangs up the phone. She needs to see Michael for herself.

"You better get going, Josie. Leave Jacob and Anna with me," Maureen says. "We'll follow you to the car to get their car seats."

"Thank you." Josie hugs her. It's imperative she get to the hospital now, and fast.

CHAPTER 22

ANDREW

"What an insane shift!" Dr. Chase says to the oncoming ER physician.

"Thank you so much for covering for me," Dr. Dee Patrick says. "I'm sorry you had to be here three hours too long but you, my friend, are relieved of your duties. I'll take over from here."

"I've got nothin' but time and no one needs me at home like you do. How's your daughter doing?"

"She's much better. It's her first ear infection, and I'm so new to this."

"But you're an ER doc. You see ear infections all the time," he says.

"No, I mean being a mom...it's still so new to me. It's different when it's your own kid that's sick."

"I wouldn't know, don't have any."

"Well, someday you'll get it."

"Oh, you've got faith in my future fatherhood?"

She smirks. "I just consider myself lucky that we made it through her first year of life without any ear infections until now."

"So she's on the mend?"

"Yup, and my husband is home looking after her. He'll call me if anything changes."

"She's lucky to have you."

Dee smiles. "So, tell me what we've got." Her eyes glance to the patient rooms surrounding the perimeter of the ER.

Andrew clears his throat and proceeds. He hands each chart to her as he reviews them. "Room one has a thirty year old man with a corneal abrasion, he works in a mill and a piece of wood grazed his left eye, we're waiting on an ophthalmology consult; room three is a 22 year-old woman with a migraine, she had her last dose of Phenergan at 9 a.m.; room eleven is a 63-year-old gentleman with flank pain, probably a stone," and so on. After each patient's report, Dr. Patrick pens some notes and accepts responsibility for the cases from Andrew.

"Thanks, Dr. Chase," she says and gives him a nod. "Now go home and get some sleep."

"Oh, wait, there's one more coming by ambulance. We got the paramedic call just before you walked in. It's a six-year old boy in anaphylaxis. They say he's stable but the kid's had two doses of epi—one at his elementary school and one en route. They should be arriving here with him any minute."

"Do they know what happened?"

"The school nurse told the paramedics that the boy has a food allergy—I think to peanuts and tree nuts. Apparently, someone gave him a snack at school that contained walnuts or something to that effect. It obviously triggered the reaction."

"Hmm, that's scary. You'd think the staff would be more careful."

"Yeah, I don't know ... hard to say how it all happened. I can stick around until he gets here, if you want, and get his work-up started."

"No, no, you've done enough for me already. Go home. Really, I got it covered."

CHAPTER 23

Strength does not come from physical capacity.
It comes from an indomitable will.
—Gandhi

Josie drives to the ER and prays her spiritual Power Rangers will come to Michael's rescue as well as to her own. No amount of Hail Marys or Our Fathers will ever be enough, but she prays continuously. Eventually her words become a pulsing meditative chant like a guitar strumming through the same chain of chords over and over again. It forms an urgent stream of appeal, asking God to keep her son strong and to conquer the wave of anaphylaxis now threatening to overwhelm him. Simultaneously, she begs for mental quiet as she waits at every interminable red light. She taps her fingers on the steering wheel and touches her foot on the gas ever so slightly and creeps forward into each intersection. When red turns to green, she drives off like a bat out of hell.

She arrives at the hospital and parks illegally right outside the emergency entrance. She pauses momentarily. *There is no point in worrying him—yet.* She resolves to call Declan after she sees Michael with her own eyes. It's important to have the facts, especially her own assessment, before she calls her husband.

As she exits her car, the static of her distracting and racing thoughts escalate and threaten to pull her away. She feels vulnerable and defenseless, a poor excuse for a mother, and hardly the rock Michael needs her to be. Her mind becomes lost in a flickering mess of unrelated and idiotic premonitions, about nothing that matters, at least not to her. She tries to pull herself together, to think straight, but the thoughts are still coming in a mosaic of mismatching pictures, none of them are connected, relevant, or even notable. She garners her strength and angrily pushes them back.

When she enters the lobby of the ER, her empathetic sense goes into overdrive. As if on cue, she becomes entranced in the emotions and odors floating in the air around her. The medicinal scent of the hospital burns the lining of her nose and heart-pounding fear engulfs her being, giving her the impression of impending doom. It is difficult for her to breathe, so she breathes faster. She can hear Michael beckoning "Mama," not with her ears but resounding in her soul. Her stomach turns into one giant knot and sends waves of nausea into her gut.

She sees the ER clerk, her eyes focused on a computer screen on the admission desk. Josie attempts to ignore her and darts toward to the insulated ER. However, the clerk spots her and jumps into her path.

May I help you?" the clerk asks. She carries a pen and a clipboard, using them like a shield to block Josie's ability to move past her.

"Um, yeah," Josie says, feigning surprise. "My son, Michael Reilly, was brought in by ambulance?"

"Yes, he just arrived. I'll walk you back to his room. I thought you must be his mother when I saw you come through the door."

"Thank you," Josie says. *Maybe she's a mother, too.* Perhaps, the clerk recognizes her determined and panic-stricken face—the signature look of a distraught mother looking for her ill child. Or she comprehends the threat—Josie will lunge for her jugular if she attempts to interfere any further.

The double doors to the main ER open with one simple swipe of the clerk's ID badge. It is then Josie realizes she couldn't have avoided the clerk anyhow. The ER was far more secure than it ever was in her day—with its programmed ID badges, double-locked doors and security cameras capturing every point of entry. They pass the central desk of the ER. Josie scans the surroundings to see if she sees any familiar faces. The cardiac monitors hum and beep. The nurses and doctors are all engaged in their work, coming and going in a scatter of directions. The unit clerk is on the phone trying to locate a bed upstairs for an admission. It is just as Josie remembers.

They walk down a short hall to a new pediatric wing of the ER. It has its own quiet feeling, neither intimidating nor brimming with activity like the rest of the ER. It is a peaceful and private refuge with brightly colored walls of yellow, sky blue, periwinkle and white. In the middle of the hallway against a wall sits a cart full of new teddy bears wearing miniature hospital gowns and a shelf replete with children's books and movies. With each steady step closer toward Michael's room, Josie feels a gradual falling away of the stress that enveloped her seconds earlier. She can't discern if it's because he is within her reach or if she is calming down because of the serene environment.

The clerk stops walking and turns to her. "May I bother you for your insurance card? I'll make a copy of it while you're visiting with your son."

"Sure, I have it right here." Josie pulls it from her wallet.

"Thank you, Mrs. Reilly. I'll bring it right back." The clerk takes the card from her and then pulls the curtain back on the doorway beside them.

Josie stands in the doorway, looking into Michael's room. She notices Michael is alert and sitting up on the gurney. He wears an oxygen mask and, much to her relief, she can see his beautiful smile through the mask. The nurse is taking his blood pressure. Initially, he's unaware of Josie's presence looking in from the door. His face appears its normal color. She doesn't see any hives, at least none that she can see outside of the facemask, but he has a trace amount swelling around his eyes sitting above the ridge of the mask. He is connected to a cardiac monitor. However, this doesn't surprise her because he has received epinephrine—a drug known to affect the heart.

"Mommy!" Michael says. His voice muffles through the oxygen mask. His eyes are tearful.

"Now, Michael, you were just smiling. Why are you sad now that I'm here?" Josie reaches over the bedrail and embraces him. She kisses his forehead.

"I'm scared, Mommy. Am I going to die?" he whispers.

"No, of course not—you're going to be fine. The doctors and nurses here are the best and they'll take good care of you," she whispers back and looks him in the eyes.

On one side of his bed stands his nurse and on the other stands his teacher, Mrs. Thompson. She is taller than Josie by a couple of inches, with long dark hair and an infectious smile. Her hands curl around the bedrail, as if holding Josie's place until she arrives. Josie isn't surprised to see that Janine has accompanied her son to the hospital—Michael loves his teacher. No doubt he clung to her when the paramedics arrived at his school.

"Josie," Janine says, her face serious. "I'm so sorry—I don't know what happened, I truly thought it was covered. I told the sub to give him the snack in the approved snack bin where I had left the crackers—"

Josie interrupts her apology. "These things can happen," she says. Nevertheless, she wonders how the mix-up occurred. She knows Janine is human but the mistake could've proved fatal.

"I know this might not be an ideal time but I need to talk to you." Janine tilts her head and motions with her eyes toward the doorway. She pushes a strand of her hair back over ears. "I promise. It'll be quick."

"Sure." Josie turns to Michael. "I need to talk to Mrs. Thompson for a minute. Okay?"

He nods. The face mask with oxygen still lightly whooshes over his face.

"I'll be right over here, just outside the door," she says, reassuring him.

"Okay, but ... you'll be where I can see you, right, Mommy?"

"Of course." She squeezes his hand.

"Did I do something bad?"

"Honey, of course not. You didn't do anything wrong. I want to talk to your teacher—that's all."

Michael's nurse, a veteran as indicated by her ID badge— *25 years of service*—looks at Josie and then to Michael. "Don't worry, I won't bite. I'm only here writing on my papers."

Josie follows Janine toward the door and meets her outside where Michael will not be able to hear them talking.

"Janine, what's going on?" she asks in low whisper. She's unable to imagine there was more to this mistake.

"Josie, I know this is going to sound strange, even impossible ... and honestly, I can't explain it. You see, I removed those muffins from the room when I left to perform the reading evaluations with some of the children. I took the muffins myself down to the kitchen by the cafeteria to be stored—I planned to pass them out to the kids at lunchtime like we do with the other birthday treats that Michael isn't able to eat."

"I'm not sure what you're getting at."

"The crackers—the ones you approved for him in the morning—were still in the snack bin when I left the classroom. I left them for the sub to pass out at snack time."

"So, how did the muffins end up back in the room?"

"I don't know. This is what's strange. The sub doesn't know either. She never saw any crackers. All she saw were the muffins—she assumed *they* were safe."

Josie's eyes grow wide with alarm. "Are you saying they made it back in the room on their own?"

"We thought it could've been one of the children in the class but no one left the room other than the kids I removed for testing. All the children were accounted for and someone would've seen them wandering down toward the cafeteria. In fact, there were only two kitchen staff and they didn't see anyone else in the kitchen prep area besides the two of them."

Josie notices Janine's hands are trembling. Out of the blue, the horrible, sick feeling Josie experienced earlier returns, but now it comes with a growing rage. Her chest rises up and outward, pulling in as much air as she can to stifle the fire of her suffocating anger. She lets it out in one heavy and frustrated sigh. It is all she can manage. Her stomach turns inside out and upside down in a wild flurry of anxiety and horror.

"And that's not all," Janine continues.

"There's more?" Her worst fears are coming to fruition. Who would intentionally bring harm upon her innocent son?

"The crackers are missing, gone, disappeared."

Josie closes her eyes tight and rubs her fingers over them as if she's been struck by a massive migraine from the terror now striking deep within her heart. "Do you think someone maliciously tried to give Michael this snack?"

"I don't know, Josie. I hope not but I can't explain it." Janine's face is tense—she can't offer Josie any clear account of the events.

Josie's arms grow weak, her legs buckle and her body nears collapse.

"Josie, you're pale. Why don't you sit down?" Janine grabs a nearby chair and pulls it over; she helps place Josie's stunned and immobile body into it. "I'll go get you some water."

"No, but how, how can this be? Is there someone tha ... that evil, and conniving, at school? Why ... why ... would someone try to kill my son?" Josie's words stream out in one long stuttering and babbling jumble. She can barely form a sentence. All she can do is shake her head in disbelief.

"We don't know, Josie. It could've been an honest mistake, a mix-up. Although, it does seem unlikely that it was done by a classmate, it's too complicated for a kindergartener to have pulled off, or even a fifth grader."

Pulled off? Pulled off! If it wasn't another student, then who? The wheels crank in Josie's mind. Did some entrusted adult do this knowingly? *What sort of sick, perverse individuals are working at Michael's school?* The teachers, she thought, were legit, and volunteers had criminal background checks. She thought his school was the one place besides home where he was safe. Had she deluded herself into thinking all the precautions necessary to protect him were being followed? Clearly, the plans she made for him were not airtight. They were only as secure, and sane, as the people around him.

"Josie, if it makes you feel any better, Mr. Bauer is on it. We're going to get to the bottom of it. Don't worry, we'll figure this out." Principal Bauer was a man who stood all of five feet two but ruled his school with a stern hand and a firm unwavering discipline. Above all, he had zero tolerance for bullying. No one dared to cross him. "Mr. Bauer is talking to the police about it. He thought we better report it since we don't know if it was a just a kid playing a dirty trick or an adult with some sort of ... harmful intent," Janine chokes out the last two words.

A dark cackle of laughter echoes down the hall toward Josie. She hears a deep mocking voice speaking out loud, "Hey you.

What's the matter, cat got your tongue? Tired of my dirty tricks? Why don't you admit I've won?"

Josie's back straightens as if quills are growing along her spine. Slowly, she rises from her chair to see whose voice is hissing.

"Ha, you'll never win," a female voice returns bitterly, and again the voice is out loud, not in her head.

"Josie, where are you going?" Janine calls to her as Josie goes to the end of the hall and stops.

"Next time, you won't be so lucky," a male voice adds in a decidedly sinister tone.

When Josie looks around the corner, she sees two nurses, a man and a woman. She wonders if it is their voices she hears but these words, though may have been uttered by them, seem to be meant for her.

It is then that she understands. They will never find a material person who did this to Michael. All this time Josie spent fighting evil in the invisible, in the abstract but now, evil was incarnate and fully concrete. It has crossed over from taunting to dangerous. It is prepared to maim and kill without remorse or shame.

She knows what it wants—her mind, her soul, her life. Michael is its hostage; he's a pawn to get her to succumb to its misery. Once more, it hits her solidly on the head, like a brick falling from the top of ten-story building: Demons have no scruples, no boundaries, and children of the earth are fair game. Demons don't discriminate, which would require an ounce of good intent. Josie's growing paranoia and madness are their thrill and amusement in their vacant, empty, frigid existence.

Why me? What for? And why do they want my soul so badly?

CHAPTER 24

"How's my boy?" Declan bounds through the pediatric room doorway. He is still wearing his navy sport coat but his tie is loosened around his neck.

"Daddy!" Michael exclaims and throws up his arms to hug his father, who is now standing beside his bed. The two embrace. Michael's facial swelling has all but disappeared in the seven hours he's been hospitalized. He looks like his young self again.

Declan leans over and kisses Josie's cheek where she's sitting in the recliner next to Michael's observation bed for the night.

"You must've driven pretty fast, Dec," she says as she stands up and straightens out the wrinkled shirt and pants she's been wearing throughout the ordeal.

"That I did. What can I say? There weren't flights that would get me here quicker than driving."

"Or at least, not driving the speed you do," she says, appreciatively.

"Ha, ha," he says.

"Did you get a ticket?" she whispers in his ear.

"What does it matter?" He shrugs. "I was worried about my boy." He smiles and brushes his hand over Michaels head.

"What do you have in your hand, Daddy?" Michael asks.

Declan is holding a white plastic bag smelling distinctly like fried food.

"Did you bring me Culvers?" Michael's eyes brighten.

"Of course."

"With lots of ketchup?"

"That too. I even brought your mom a salad."

"Thanks, Dec," she says, "I haven't eaten all day."

Culver's was the one restaurant in the area with full allergen declarations on their ingredient lists. They knew what items Michael could eat safely from the menu and what items he couldn't. The three of them ate dinner together sharing the hospital tray table.

"What about your meetings? Do you have to go back to Madison tomorrow?" Josie asks, munching on her salad.

"No, I cancelled them and we can reschedule next week." He takes a long slug of his soda.

Josie's surprised that Declan appears to be so relaxed about rescheduling his meetings but is pleased his concerns for the time being are centered on Michael.

After they are done, Declan gives Michael a kiss good night and leaves to pick up Anna and Jacob at Maureen's. They have been with her since Josie left Como Park earlier in the day. Josie stays behind with Michael. The two of them settle in. Michael gets cozy under his blanket and falls asleep watching the Nick Junior channel. Josie rests in the recliner by Michael's hospital bed. Before she shuts her eyes, she notices everything is quiet—not only around her but inside of her head.

It is a peaceful silence. All of her disruptive thoughts are gone, as if her consciousness were emptied. She feels protected and shielded from intrusion. The barrage she's endured on and off for days, and in particular, this morning, vanishes. Gone are the visions and messages, gone are the voices. Above all, Michael is safe. His skin is a pale rosy pink, his face is ethereal. She watches him sleep.

She wonders at the silence, though. There must be some earthbound spirits wandering the hospital floors. Surely, many deaths have occurred within the hospital building. Are the spirits not disturbing her because she is on the pediatric wing? Are guardian angels protecting the children, keeping the riff raff at bay? Maybe her prayers, or rather her desperate pleas, have been heard and answered by God above.

A nagging thought settles in her bones. The unseen world is ever more part and prevalent in this life here on earth ... but it isn't the cream of the crop that lingers here; they're the ones left behind.

CHAPTER 25
ANDREW

Dr. Chase stands at the entry doors of the ER looking outside. The street lights shine on the sidewalk. The circular drive into the ER parking bay still has an ambulance blocking the entrance from the last patient it delivered. He steps out into the darkness and says out loud to himself, "Cities don't sleep... apparently neither do I."

Sleep has never come easy for Andrew and when it does, it isn't restful. He gravitated toward nightshift work, not just because he was the low man on the totem pole but he figured he might as well be doing something productive if he was going to be awake. Besides, nighttime was supposedly when the zombies showed up, at least in the books he read, and he didn't want to miss out on the opportunity to see one.

The night air flows cool over his face. He thinks about his last patient, an old man who lived a long, long, life. "Ninety-two years. All brought to a close here tonight," he says out into the nothingness.

The old man's wife had already died. He was sent in by ambulance from his nursing home and met in the ER by his seventy -year-old daughter—a daughter still clinging to her father and unwilling to sign Do Not Resuscitate orders. He was immortal in her eyes, a man with more to offer this world. So, Andrew and his staff did all they could and worked to save his life. But all the while he wondered. *Would the old man want to live any longer?*

It sinks in, his own private hell, watching others like this old man who have led full lives with families and children who love them. He will never have a normal life because he can't. There are always too many questions that he can't answer. He strives to be of help to others and yet, he's forced to hide the truth about himself. Inevitably, he is left without the intimacy and bonds of true human friendship. While he's been raised by parents who taught him that his healing ability is of the light, he worries. *What if they're wrong?* What if he's been tricked into believing he's a good guy but it's all just a trap? What if his healing power comes from the dark? In this life, there are no answers for him, only questions. He trusts that God is leading him, but he can't say for certain. Faith is all he's got.

A nurse joins him in the parking bay of the ER where he is looking up at the sky. "Are you okay, Dr. Chase?" she asks.

He turns to her but says nothing.

"Dr. Chase?"

"Yeah, I think so. I'm not sure why this one is hitting me so hard."

"I understand, sometimes the deaths we take especially hard are the ones we expect ourselves to dismiss as part of the job."

"Hmm…" he nods.

"It's quiet for the moment, and it won't likely last," she says. "Why don't you take a rest in the sleep room? We'll wake you when we need you."

He looks back up at the night sky and then back to the nurse standing beside him. "I'm not much of a sleeper."

"Take a break. We've got everything covered for the moment."

He nods again. *She's nice and pretty. Why not her?* It dawns on him that he doesn't know her name. He has another eleven months at this place. He could start a relationship; it didn't have to be anything permanent necessarily. He knew he couldn't offer her any kind of commitment; a temporary companionship would be the extent of it. And there was one other minor detail. His heart already belonged to another woman, a woman he hadn't met in the flesh ... the woman of his dreams, literally.

She goes back inside and he follows. He enters the room set aside for the doctors to sleep on their long shifts when time, albeit rarely, permitted.

He lies down on the cot, rolls onto his side and bunches the stiff hospital pillow under his head. "Why am I here?" He doesn't know, except that it appears to be the middle ground on his path to a larger journey. But what happens once he gets there from here? He closes his eyes and chooses not to think about it.

HE TURNS OVER TO SEE A SHADOWY FIGURE AT THE FOOT of his bed. He makes a startled jump. "What? Do we have patients? How much time has passed? I wasn't even asleep yet." As his eyes focus, he sees the shadowy person is a little boy. "Are you lost?" he asks the boy.

The boy reaches for Andrew's hand. "Come with me."

The boy is young and this puzzles Andrew. "How did you get in here? Where is your mother?"

The boy leads Andrew out into the light of the ER. They pass the unit clerk's desk and Andrew looks at the patient board on the wall. *No new patients? That's odd. What time is it?* He sees the ER clock, ticking away. It's 3 a.m. Then he sees the nurse who told him to take the rest. Her name is Kylie, according to her ID badge. She is purging an IV line with normal saline. He and the boy walk out the doors of the ER. He calls back to Kylie, "I'll be right back," though she doesn't seem to hear him.

"Where are you taking me?" He says to the brown-eyed little boy who is wearing a hospital gown. "How did we ... ?" With no transition, he's finds they're on the pediatric wing of the hospital, two stories above the ER. The boy leads him into a patient's room.

"Little boy, where is your mother?" Andrew asks him again.

He sees a woman asleep in a chair next to the bed. There is a boy in the bed. Andrew looks at the boy beside him and thinks the boy in the bed resembles the one who brought him to the room. He looks back to the bed. "Is this sleeping boy your twin?"

But there's no answer. The boy who led him to the room has disappeared.

Donnnggggg ... donnnggggg ... donnnggggg ...

"There they are," he whispers. The tolling of cathedral bells but he's here in a child's room, in the relative darkness during the middle of the night where there is no cathedral. He kneels down and says a prayer, gazes up at the ceiling and then to the wall. There's a crucifix on the wall beside the boy's bed. He doesn't know why the boy in the bed is here. He rests his hands lightly over the boy's heart and asks God to bring the light of His healing power upon the boy. A surge of something like an electric current flows through him. It's more forceful than he's felt when he's attempted other healings.

The mother of the child rests peacefully, not conscious of Andrew's presence. He thinks she looks like someone he knows, someone he has seen before although due to the darkness, he can't see her features in great detail. Tears pool in the corners of his eyes. But these aren't the tears of sadness, rather these are tears of joy, of recognition and reunion, of love lost then found. He hasn't had the privilege of experiencing such joy. To him, joy belonged to other people—young families and people in love. He gives in and allows the emotion to flow through him. Instantly, he's back in the sleep room and lying in his bed.

There's a knock at the door.

Confused, he sits up and rubs his eyes, then straightens out his white lab coat.

"It's Kylie, you have a patient," she says through the door.

"Oh," he clears his throat. "I'll be right there." *That was bizarre.*

He gets a drink of water from the sink and splashes his face with cold water, then dries it with a towel. He exits the room and returns to work, uncertain what it was he just experienced.

CHAPTER 26

JOSIE

The next afternoon, Friday, Michael has made a full recovery and is discharged. They enjoy a normal evening together as a family at home. Since the weather outside is warm and beautiful, Declan takes the children out to play in the front yard while Josie stays in to clean-up after dinner. Lately, she dislikes being alone in the house but she takes the opportunity to catch-up with her housework. With five people in the house, it didn't take long for the laundry to grow into multiple giant heaps.

First, she tackles laundry and dishes and leaves the picking up of the toys for last. She hasn't organized the toys for some time, in part out of avoidance, in part from her being severed from her maternal routines. Her channeling "adventures" caused her to neglect her duties as chief toy manager.

The primary location of the toy mess is in their basement, a place where she sometimes feels uneasy. It is a silly and child-like fear unfounded in any real experience. As she thinks about going down to the basement to clean, she sighs and pushes aside her second thoughts.

When she opens the basement, there comes a trampling of footsteps behind her. Barking and wagging, Jamison comes running down stairs. Once at the bottom, Jamison faces her in an excited crouch and appears ready to play.

How could I have forgotten Jamison? She shakes her head in amusement and relief. *Surely, he'll keep me company.* From where she stands at the top of the stairway, Josie can see the kids' toys strewn all over the floor. "This is going to take me awhile." She places her hands on her hips in irritation but knows expecting more from her children at this stage in their lives isn't realistic. They're too young and she's too fastidious—another quality she inherited from her mother and one that isn't easy to change.

As she takes a step down, she feels a cold draft wafting up the stairs. It passes over her in a colossal wave, causing her to chill. Her body teeters mildly and then she regains her balance. *What's that?* Baffled, she wonders if Declan has left one of the basement windows open.

She takes another step and stops. Her mouth grows dry and her throat becomes sharp with thirst. *Maybe, I should forget this and clean up tomorrow.* Jamison looks up at her, his tail has stopped wagging. *Oh, c'mon Josie, you're being silly,* she bickers with herself. No matter how crazy the last few days were, today had contained a renewed flavor of normality. It gives her confidence. "Stop obsessing, Josie," she tells herself, "you're being irrational."

She proceeds onto the next step and the next, but the temperature drops further with each forward step. The cold seeps in through the walls around her.

"Brrr …" Her lips tremble.

Jamison emits a high-pitched yelp and begins to howl.

Josie's knees lock up, her left foot twists. She tries to right herself but tumbles the rest of the way down and lands at the bottom of the stairway.

You're easy to push. A menacing male voice speaks to her in her head.

"What?" She says, dazed. She stands up but her legs are shaky and weak. Her right forearm is bruising already. Her shoulder and upper arm ache. Suddenly, the bruises on her arm begin to form a pattern—the pattern of an animal's claws. Audible, piercing cackles call out her name—*Josie, Josie, Josie*—the voices mock her with insults and curses. A rumble of fingernails taps the concrete wall next to her. Outside, the sound of crows baying and squawking grow louder through the basement windows. She stands, frozen like a statue from the invisible threat, contemplating a run up the stairs, worried her legs won't hold her.

Hmm, Josie, was it curiosity or fear that killed the cat? Another menacing, mocking voice speaks out in her head.

She shivers, aware she's being watched and yet, there is no one she can see. The basement is dismal and odors of must and rot punctuate the air. Before now, their basement was a warm place. She had it decorated for the kids with throw rugs, children's furniture and bright lighting. The concrete walls were covered with posters of Sponge Bob, Elmo and Barbie as well as the children's colorful art work.

But tonight the basement is dark even though the lights are on. And it is freezing. She might as well be in the dead of a Minnesota winter, but it is April and 65 degrees outside. The basement looms large, gray, and ... predatory. She knows she isn't alone, and she's not counting Jamison. The posters of Elmo and Sponge Bob begin to look freakish. Their eyes follow her every move. She smells something rank and burning, like the foul stench of cauterized skin. She searches for the source of the vile odor, under the toys, behind the closet door, in the back storage room and even inside the furnace. She turns up nothing. Jamison howls wildly at the walls and the ceiling—his ears stand on end and his tail is straight on high alert.

The longer she is there, the worse she feels. Her tongue takes on the texture of leather and the ache of her thirst blazes with the intensity of fire. Hunger scorches her stomach, while her head throbs. She realizes what is happening. She can feel what these vicious and cruel fiends are feeling, their parallel world creates a thirst and hunger far beyond what any human concept of it is. It is brutal and ceaseless, a suffering without end or relief.

And then, without any warning, she is overwhelmed with a driving and heartbreaking flood of tears. It closes in and consumes her. It's as if she's been slaughtered by the emotions of sadness, grief, and despair—all occurring in a marked disharmony.

Josie, THIS is the stark absence of hope, the strange voice hisses out loud.

Her heart races frantically; she takes her head in her hands and holds it tight. Frost begins to form on her lips and lashes. She can see breath billowing out her nose. The steel ice of pure stinging hate is upon her like a swarm of insects and thorns. She trembles with the rush of another frigid breeze against her skin. Something pierces her heart but there is nothing. She screams but no sound comes. She is alone. No one will rescue her. She hears sneering and multiple voices mocking her and flinging obscenities as if she's a woman being stoned.

The sensation of snakes, though invisible, wind around her feet and slither up her thighs. Unseen insects gnaw and bite at her arms and face. She smacks them and grabs them, flailing as she tries to pull them off ... but there is nothing there. Josie feels it in her heart. It is here, in her house, in her very basement—the doorway to Hell.

In horror, she scoops up Jamison and breaks free. She flees up the stairs with her dog snarling in her arms. She scrambles to the top as the snakes fall from her legs. She slams the basement door behind them, hoping it will contain the feral vermin lurking below her.

Leaning against the closed basement door, her mind spins wildly. On the brink of insanity, she berates herself. *Is this what the experts mean by 'don't try this at home?'* What was she thinking? She has put herself and her family in this sadistic situation without understanding the risks in channeling the dead. Be it unintentional, she made them the victims of these barbaric, invisible creatures. All she wanted to do was to test her ability. Instead, she brought this rancid mess into her life and now she can't get *THEM* to leave. Or, were these deranged spirits here all along?

Her heart is filled with guilt. Undoubtedly, she's deceived Declan. Why did she do it? To prove ... what? These people have lived their lives and if they didn't say what they wanted when they were living, then whose fault is that? It isn't hers. It isn't her job to make things right for them. And now, she hasn't any ability to save herself or her family from this netherworld. Will this game ever come to an end? The weight of her personal hell is more than she can bear. She falls to her knees and begins to pray.

Holy water. Crosses. Go get them. A soothing female voice speaks to her. The voice says it again and again. The voice is loving.

Josie in her confusion heads to the window by the front door. Declan is still outside playing with the kids.

"Go get the holy water!" the voice insists out loud, perhaps in attempt to wake her from her mental haze. It's her mother's voice. Josie sprints up the stairs to her bedroom and retrieves the holy water from her dresser drawer. Trembling, she takes a deep breath and makes the Sign of the Cross. She goes back down the stairs, opens the door to the basement and braves the freezing cold once more. She sprinkles holy water all the way down the stairs, on the walls and all around the basement. Jamison follows her, barking, but this time his bark is hostile and his snarl is guttural. While she still can't see the entity, she can taste it. The basement is saturated with the basest of energies which gust past her, fleeing the bottle she holds before her.

The front door blows open and slams shut with a boom. The house vibrates and rocks. A picture on the wall falls and shatters.

She runs back up the stairs with Jamison leading the way. She slams the basement door behind them.

Gingerly, she leaps over the broken glass in the foyer and peers out the window of the door toward the front yard. Declan is in their driveway, picking Michael up from the ground—he is wailing in pain. Josie sees blood. Declan carries Michael toward the house. She stands and watches in silent terror as they approach the open front door. Declan calmly hands him over to her.

"What happened?" she asks. Her eyes are wide with panic. Michael's left cheek has a large abrasion and is bleeding, apparently scraped by the concrete of the driveway. His hands are bloody.

"He fell. He lost his balance and tripped, falling right on his face."

"What, he fell off his bike? Or his scooter?" Josie asks, anxiously.

"No, I said he tripped, Jos, he was just walking." Declan huffs.

"Mommy, something knocked me down!" Michael interrupts.

"What! What do you mean?" She knows exactly what he means.

"Michael, nothing knocked you down. I saw you trip and fall, all by yourself," Declan says.

"No, I felt it. It pushed me! Like a strong wind, Mommy!" Michael cries.

"Well, that was one strong wind then, buddy." Declan looks to Josie and faintly rolls his eyes.

"Dec—just leave him to me. Go back and keep an eye on Anna and Jacob." She knew Declan didn't understand why Michael was so frightened. He couldn't perceive what they could.

Declan surveys the foyer's tile, hesitating before going back out outside. "Geez, Jos, what the hell happened? What's all this glass on the floor?"

"Um, yeah, that. The picture fell. I'll take care of it."

Exasperated, she hurries toward the kitchen with Michael in her arms. She brings him to the sink and carefully washes his wounds.

"Mommy," Michael whispers, as if afraid to speak any louder. "I'm telling you the truth. Something knocked me down. And it said something to me."

"What, Michael? You can tell me."

"It said 'tell that bitch, we'll be back.' And then it pushed me hard. It felt like a really cold wind, Mommy." Michael's bottom lip quivers, his eyes are red and raw from crying.

Bitch? He doesn't even know what "bitch" means. Who is speaking to my child in this way? Certainly not "Casper the Friendly Ghost."

Hopelessness spins in her mind. What will she do? Who will protect them from these spirits of the in-between? Are these spirits here because they've always been here? Were they left behind by the former inhabitants of their home? Do they need to move? Or will *they* follow?

Maybe the only way to save her children is for her to leave. The waters running deep in her soul are streaming away from her idyllic life, taking her to a place that no one should have to go. She caused this disruption. How can she go on pretending as if it were an accident? The world of lost souls is bent on destroying her and her happy life. *What do I have that THEY want? WHO are they and WHY are they here?*

Their rage was thick and whatever it was that they lost, it is clear to her that it cannot be restored by any mortal being. Their souls are well beyond the horizon of salvation.

Josie, pray. Like a flash of light in blackest of darkness, she hears her mother's voice once more. She reminds Josie to hang on to her faith. There is nothing left for her now but to hope that God will not abandon them.

CHAPTER 27

Josie awakes Saturday morning in a sea of self-doubt, blaming herself for her misery. The other psychics she read about had warned of these doubts but she can't shake them no matter how hard she tries. Alone, she stares out the kitchen window toward the rising dawn and sips her coffee feeling lost to her life and terrified in her own home. The morning's searing silence brings warning that something is still amiss in the house. She can't say what it is, she can't put her finger on it, but whatever or whoever it is grimly lingers with the breath of a determined stalker.

She gathers a strand of faith and prays. If only she could read her aura like she did was she was nine. If she knew the colors she was carrying around, perhaps she could consciously change them. Her complete lack of self-confidence seems to be coloring her aura in such a way that it is making her an easy mark. But it's far too late to spend time buried in self-evaluation. Today, she will find a solution and ask God for the strength to overcome. There is a sounder reality somewhere and she is determined, for the sake of her children, to find it. It isn't an option to go on living this way, to allow these spirits of the in-between to continue ruining her life. *There must be a way to shut them out for good.*

Driving her determination is the underlying knowledge she'll have to find her solution alone. She cannot share her twisted thoughts with anyone, not loved ones, not professionals. If she confides in Declan, Nora, her friends or even her doctor about her experiences with the netherworld, it will come at a great cost and sacrifice. That is, her freedom and her ability to be the trusted caretaker of her children. Her ramblings will most certainly result in a well-deserved order of confinement to a mental institution as well an order to protect her children from her.

While she'd never in a million years try to hurt them, how will Declan or the rest know that? They couldn't trust a mentally unstable mother. Her mind cycles and spins in a torrent of hopelessness and strength, crashing like waves against her soul. She's dangerously close to losing everything that matters to her—her family, her home, her friends, her life as she knows it.

"Mommy," Anna exclaims and taps Josie's back.

"Oh, sh-," She stops short of profanity. Her hand jerks, knocking over her coffee mug. It spills hot coffee over the kitchen counter, but misses Anna. "Anna, I didn't hear you come up behind me." Josie's tone is unexpectedly harsh.

"Sorry, Mommy." Anna frowns, hurt by her mother's reaction.

"That's okay, you just surprised me." Josie bends down to give Anna a morning hug and kiss. "What are you doing up so early?"

Josie grabs the roll of paper towels at the kitchen sink and begins to wipe up her spill.

"I don't know. I thought I heard someone tell me to get up. I thought it was Daddy."

"Daddy? I think Daddy's still asleep." Josie's hands are shaky and getting shakier by the minute.

"Then who woke me up, Mommy?"

"I don't know, Anna, maybe it was a dream?" Josie knows that for most other people and households, this would be true.

"Or ... could it have been that invisible man coming to talk to me again? Remember?"

"Yes, I remember." Josie shudders.

A voice laughs inside Josie's head. *I bet you wish you could forget!* It's the same alien voice she heard in the basement the night before.

You think you can get rid of us with your Holy Water! Multiple voices laugh out in her head.

Go away now! Josie shouts telepathically toward these insidious beasts. *Leave my children alone!*

Why should we? They're much more fun than you! Another beast calls out.

Josie's shaking plumes out and spreads over her limbs and torso. It is hard to hide her fear from Anna, but she tries. No matter what she does, says or prays, she can't locate a single lasting method, curse, prayer or incantation to rid their lives permanently of this nightmare. *When will it end? When will I wake up?* It is not a dream. The holy water and prayers prove hopelessly temporary, and like a boomerang, each encounter returns with ever more power and ferocity.

Josie takes Anna into the living room. She turns on the morning cartoons and adjusts the volume so as not to wake the rest of the house then returns to the kitchen to make a new cup of coffee. She fully loads it with two teaspoons of sugar and a splash of milk in an attempt to dowse her irrational fears.

"Mommy, will you sit and watch T.V. with me?" Anna asks, calling to her from the couch.

"Um ... sure." Josie is hesitant because she doesn't know what to do next anymore, be a mother or a warrior. "Let me get the newspaper first so I can read it while you watch."

She steps outside their front door to retrieve the morning paper on the sidewalk. The air is hazy and cool. The dew on the grass glistens and reflects a rainbow-like mist in the morning light.

She picks up the newspaper, it feels warm and then hot on her hand. Its words impress a scalding vibration into her palm. She drops the paper and it falls to the ground. A forceful wind gusts and opens the paper to the sports page. Its headline, "One More for 44!" blares like an annoying horn.

You're afraid of the number 44? What about 666! The demonic alien voices tease and mock her inside of her head. Other repulsive voices circle her in a taunting malicious carousel. Her surroundings spin, she grows dizzy and her balance teeters as if on the edge of a cliff. She leaves the paper at once and runs back into the house. She slams the front door shut and locks it behind her. She murmurs the "Our Father" under her breath in hopes it will help her to hang on.

Before entering the family room, she inhales deeply and makes the Sign of the Cross. She returns to her cup of coffee.

"Okay, Anna, here I am, I can sit with you now." She sits her trembling body down on the couch and places her mug-free arm around Anna. She continues to struggle against her inner voices.

"Where's the paper, Mommy?" Anna asks.

"I decided not to read it." She takes a careful sip of her coffee.

"Brown coffee, Mama, the man says it stains your soul. It makes it weak—like Achilles."

"What? Did someone say that on TV?"

"No." Anna turns and speaks to an invisible space in front of her. "I don't know how to say that. You want me to tell my mommy what?"

"Anna, who are you talking to?" she grips her by the sides of her arms. "Can you see someone there?"

"I don't know, Mommy. I hear their voices in my head. I can't see them."

Josie clutches the cross lying on her neck and prays in her thoughts to St. Jude, the Patron Saint of the Impossible. Tears spill from her eyes. It is taking all she has to not to lose it in front of Anna.

"The man says he wants you to shut-up and listen and to stop trying to make them go away with your *incessant* prayers!"

Oh, my God. These words are beyond Anna's four-year-old vocabulary. "Anna, tell him to go away, that you can't talk to him, not ever!" Josie exclaims, her voice becomes frantic, terror blooms over her nerves and spreads like wildfire.

"Okay, Mommy." Anna turns from her mother and faces the empty space in front of her, "I can't talk to you anymore!"

A vision flashes through Josie's mind—one of a monstrous, blood-red plant. The plant's leaves open wide. A fly hovers near it. The mouth-like leaves of the plant clamp down, trapping the insect inside its jaws—jaws made of sharp, stiff, tendrils. They lace around its victim and provide no escape.

The vision vanishes and suddenly she understands—she is the unsuspecting prey of a paranormal Venus Fly Trap. The demons are consuming her alive. Yet, Anna doesn't appear the least bit fazed by today's invisible stranger. She acts as if he is an imaginary friend but for Josie, she knows he and his evil friends are after mind control—her mind, her children's minds and whoever else they spend in their wake. They menace her children to show Josie they hold *ALL* the cards. They are stripping her of any and all of the little grasp she has left on the physical world. These nebulous monsters clearly obtain immense satisfaction from watching her go completely berserk.

Time is running out. Their growing interference cannot be allowed to go on any longer. If it does, her life and her children's lives will most certainly implode. The options available to her are not to be chosen lightly. She understands the consequences of each, none of them good. She can confess the whole sordid thing to her husband, that she engaged in psychic readings against his wishes only to find she invited the dregs of the afterlife into their home. She can confide in her priest, Father Anthony, and beg him to exorcise her house of the evil spirits. *Right*, she thinks, *neither are realistic options.* Or, last but not least, she can call her sister and ask her what, in God's name, she should do? Every option entails her certain commitment to a mental hospital and very possibly, spells the end of her marriage. She knows it. However, she cannot ever allow herself or her children to be captured by these bizarre and unrelenting monsters. She can't let them win.

'Jesus! Mommy, ask Jesus to help you," Anna says, out of the blue.

"How did you know?" Josie's face looks upon Anna's wondering blue eyes.

"Know what, Mommy?"

"Nothing, um," she stammers, "never ... mind." At this point, Josie is afraid to ask for fear she'll be mocked again.

"Mommy, why don't you hold my lammie—he'll make you feel a lot better." Anna holds her stuffed lamb in her hands and places it on Josie's lap.

The house becomes full of tolling cathedral bells. Anna doesn't react to the sound of the bells, reminding Josie that she is the only one who can hear them ringing. The bells resonate in harmonic waves, bestowing Josie with a new wisdom—God will show her a way out. Her faith must be placed there and she mustn't give up. Anna is right, faith will win this war. Josie makes a desperate plea to Jesus, the Lamb of God, for help out of the crazy mental mess she is in.

CHAPTER 28

These things happened to them as an example and they have been
written down as a warning to us, upon who the end of the ages
has come. Therefore, whoever thinks he is standing secure should
take care not to fall.
—1 Corinthians 10:11-12

It is early afternoon and Declan is outside working in the yard. Josie's mind is fraught in a frazzled web of confused thoughts from the morning's mental torture. While her invisible terrorists have relented with her ongoing prayers, she knows it is just a matter of time before they resume their assault. Though difficult, she moves forward and attends to her children and home. All the while, she avoids eye contact with her husband. If he sees her eyes, they will give her away. He'll know she's been deceiving him and once he does, he will find her venture into the psychic wilderness unforgivable.

Her only option is to leave the confines of their family home. More than anything, she wants to run away, but from what and where to? They go wherever she goes, there is no escape. She settles on the one place where Declan won't suspect there is anything wrong... she tells him she's going grocery shopping.

Before she leaves, she remembers her mother's advice—always wear or carry something red to ward off evil. So she places Anna in a red valentine heart sweater, Michael in his red Phoenix Cardinal's Football jersey and Jacob in a pair of red socks. She decides the socks will be discrete as she doesn't want it to appear odd to Declan by having them all in matching reds. For herself, she puts on ruby earrings—they were once her mother's. She was saving them to someday pass on to Anna but today she needs them. On the bed, she leaves out a new red long-sleeved t-shirt for Declan, placing confidence in the power of suggestion as she doesn't want to exclude him from her demon-protection plan.

As she drives out of their neighborhood, she encounters a stealthy barrage of new sinister and unwelcome premonitions. There is a young woman setting fire to a warehouse. The warehouse is familiar to her, it is somewhere local. The woman wears a black-hooded sweatshirt with gothic lettering across the back of it. Her hands, ghost-white, are holding a gasoline can and lighter. The vision leaves when Josie gets cut-off by a blue SUV. A vibratory surge comes at her from the SUV's license plate. It says, "HEY YOU" and it is soon followed by another car, a black sedan whose plate reads "CHSPKE." *Chesapeake?*

She turns on the radio. Another car flies past. Its bumper sticker emits the same vibratory pattern as the license plates she just read. It says, "Black Sabbath."

Enough! She shouts out in her mind then turns up the radio, attempting to drown out the thoughts, vibrations and loose connections. It's no use. U2's *Sunday Bloody Sunday* starts playing. She changes the station only to hear Simon and Garfunkel's *Bridge Over Troubled Water.* She shuts off the radio off. Chesapeake Bay Bridge, Sunday, black, bloody ... the images and vibrations keep coming at her. A street sign bellows, "DEAD END," house numbers vibrate "44" and "66," and the demons mock and laugh at her inside of her mind.

Why are their messages always about death and destruction? She wonders. *These spirits communicate about the dark and never the light!*

When she arrives at Wilson's Market, she parks her car. She thinks, *Breathe, Josie.* Before she gets out of her car, she prays ten

Our Fathers and begs for God's help to make *them*, whoever they are, go away. Out her driver's side window, a group of dark clouds collect over the grocery store in a peculiar black haze.

"Perfect," she says. "Of course, the clouds of darkness are following me, why wouldn't they?"

Thunder claps and the sky unleashes a wicked downpour of rain and wind. She searches the front and backseats for an umbrella with no luck and decides to make a run for it. She opens her car door and sprints toward the store. The driving rain pelts her face and body. Once inside the entry, she shakes out her wet hair and stomps her feet to release the water from her shoes. Her cell phone starts to ring. She takes it from her purse and answers, "Hello?"

"Josie?"

"Yes?" she says, breathlessly.

"It's Nora. I tried to call you at home but Declan said you left to go shopping."

"Oh," Josie's voice is short.

"How's Michael? I've been worried."

"I'm sorry, I meant to call. I've been ... distracted." She takes a cart and pushes it toward the produce section.

"Declan said Michael was discharged from the hospital yesterday afternoon. I take it he didn't relapse?"

"No ... he recovered ... thankfully, and he got to go home ... in the early afternoon." The pace of Josie's speech is broken into brief, staccato phrases as if she can't speak a complete thought.

"Whew, what a relief, huh? I'm so glad he's okay," Nora says.

Josie continues to shop, though distracted, while Nora talks about their father and his need for near-constant supervision due to his worsening dementia. Josie passes through the aisles but often returns to the same place more than once to retrieve what she forgot the first time through. Her cart fills with the things she needs and things she doesn't. It's hard for her to talk and concentrate on her list while, simultaneously, attempting to ignore the surrounding vibratory impulses. She ends up not saying a word. Worse, she feels alone even with Nora chattering away in her ear. It is as if she's become unplugged, going through the motions of what needs to get done although it is getting harder and harder for her to hang on to the mask.

"Josie, are you there? Are you even listening to me?" Nora asks.

"Yeah, I'm still here." Josie realizes she hadn't "uh hummed" in some time. New vibrations kept bombarding her, off of cereal boxes and cans of soup.

"You were not. I asked you a question."

"Oh, I'm sorry. What did you say?" she asks, overwhelmed and drowning in bizarre thoughts—like *Mediterranean* noodle soup, *flaming* cheese puffs, *nuclear* jalapeno salsa, and cherry *bomb* cake.

Suddenly, Josie awakes to her surrounding reality and her inner faith prods ... she needs her sister's help. No matter what the cost, she can't avoid telling the one person she's always turned to in times of trouble. And, of all her limited options, Nora will have Josie's best interests at heart.

"Nora?"

"Yes. What is it?" Nora asks, detecting a change in Josie's voice. "What's going on?"

"You're not going to believe me," she whispers.

"What, Josie? What is it?" Nora presses.

"I'm afraid to tell you. You're going to think I'm crazy but I'm not, truly I'm not!"

"Calm down. You can tell me."

Nora's voice fails to soothe her, and she breaks into sobs amid the pizzas in the frozen food aisle.

"Josie, where are you in the store? Can people see you?"

"Yes," she cries.

"Go to the ladies room. Don't make a scene!"

"I think my house needs an exorcism!" Josie blurts, steering her cart past multiple pairs of gaping eyes by the frozen waffles and ice cream. She hurries toward the restroom, directing her eyes away from people and toward the floor.

"You what? I don't think I heard you right."

"Oh, you heard me right. There are demons in my house, not ghosts, not those waiting to get into heaven but those who will never make it in. They're here haunting me and harassing me and the kids!"

"Shhh, Josie, quiet down. You're losing your grip! Now hold on!"

"Our basement last night felt so cold ... like it had frozen over," she says, her voice trembles. Other shoppers continue to gawk when she passes by them.

"Josie, Josie, just stop! You're not making any sense! How can you be so sure?"

"I could feel every ounce of their misery. They mocked me and told Michael to call me a *bitch!*"

A woman standing in the checkout line turns and scowls as if offended by Josie's remark.

"What? Where did he get that? What the hell's going on!" Nora's voice can be heard by nearby shoppers on Josie's end of the receiver.

"Hell—exactly that."

"Oh, c'mon, Michael probably heard the word bitch on TV or something."

"Nora, I mean it. I literally felt the doorway to hell in the basement of my house. It's bitterly cold, not hot, like everyone thinks. It's worse than ice frozen for hours on your skin. But there's definitely an inferno burning, but it burns from inside the body out. I could feel it—in my throat, in my head, in my veins–"

Josie loses her grip on her cell phone. It slips through her fingers and tumbles to the ground. The battery pops off and propels across the supermarket's linoleum. She grabs the phone at her feet and chases after its battery but before she can catch it, someone bends down to pick it up for her.

"Is this yours?" a man asks, holding her cell phone battery in his hand.

She freezes in her tracks. His voice blows through her memory but she doesn't know where or how she's heard it before. While he stands only about six feet tall, his overwhelming presence renders her mute.

"Is this yours?" he asks again.

Her legs wobble beneath her. She lifts the battery from his hand. All at once, reality frays and splinters. His eyes, deep and etheric, pierce the fortress of her emotional darkness. His face, angular and firm, sends her a vision of angels in flight. His skin is somewhat rougher about his eyes but his body is solid and fit. It is none of this that strikes her the most. It is his energy—it swarms her. She hasn't felt anything like it since she was a child.

Energy and colors ran together when she saw auras, and while she still couldn't see his aura, she could *feel* his energy. It was buoyant and warm, like the first day of summer. It was fresh and exhilarating, opening her mind to new possibilities and ideas, flowing over her like a river and then drowning her in its intensity— all in a matter of seconds.

"Thank you." She wakes from her fog. She blinks hard and looks at him carefully. She doesn't recognize him. Nonetheless, it would be mortifying if she did—she was a psychological and physical mess.

"Hey, are you okay?" he asks, "Do you need help?"

You know him.

She shakes her head. "No, I don't." Her hand goes to her mouth and covers it before anything else can come out.

"All ... right?" He raises one questioning brow at her.

She stands motionless, observing his rumpled, unbuttoned flannel shirt. Underneath, he is wearing a gray t-shirt with the words, *The Cure.* "Sorry, nothing." Finally something that sounds like language comes from her mouth. She looks down and away, her cheeks flush from embarrassment.

"Are you certain?" His face carries concern and an earnestness to help.

"No ... I mean ... um ... yes ... forget it," she stammers. *Far better to walk away*, she thinks, before she figures out how she knows him or worse, how he knows her. But as she starts to leave, her balance once again becomes unsteady as if tripping over her own feet.

You KNOW him. An emphatic voice repeats in her mind.

He's a total stranger! Telepathically, she shouts back to the voice. She has no idea how she knows him. Even more disconcerting is the emotion that she misses him, this person she doesn't recognize. She misses him terribly. *But how? Why?* She doesn't recall ever meeting him before in her life, yet her heart is flooded with joy by the simple sound of his voice. His appearance is unremarkably human; he is not angel or spirit or demon. Declan is more hand-some, she thinks. This man's hair is too long for her taste and his sideburns cut too close to his chin. She suspects he could be younger than she is, if only because of the way he is dressed. She turns away and attempts walking again. This time, her gait is stable.

"Hey!" he calls to her.

"That voice," she whispers, "How do I know that voice?"

She turns back around to look at him. Somehow, somewhere, she has met this man before ... but where?

"Oh, forget it," he says.

She musters half a smile and keeps going.

WHEN JOSIE ARRIVES AT THE LADIES ROOM, SHE LEAVES her cart outside and goes into a stall, shuts and locks the stall door. She puts the pieces of her cell phone back together and calls Nora. Amid the flushing of toilets around her, she spills to her sister about the night before. The relief she felt from meeting the kind stranger dissolves back into despair.

"Nora, last night, the spirits left when I got out the holy water. They fled out the front door of our house. They knocked Michael over. You should see the bruising and cuts on his face." Josie's voice cracks and tremors.

"I'm worried about you, Jos. I know this is what you think happened, but ... I want you to get some professional help ... you must." Nora words are firm.

"Ma'am? Ma'am?" A woman knocks outside Josie's stall door.

"Yes?" Josie says, sniffing.

"Is everything all right in there?" the woman asks.

"Yes," Josie says and quiets.

"Who are you talking to?" Nora asks.

"No one," she says.

Nora is silent.

Josie can tell by her pause, Nora is considering her story. "Do you think I'm lying? I'm telling you the truth ... Michael bears the marks on his face and I have bruises on my arm from breaking my fall. What do I have to do to prove it to you? Would you like a picture via email?"

"Oh, c'mon, I know you're not lying but what you perceive to be true could be your imagination."

"Please don't patronize me. I'm not a child so don't treat me like one. I get it. This is for real. My house is being ransacked by a group of demons, poltergeists, or whatever you call these monsters."

"Are you still channeling?"

"No, I'm not, but they come anyway, at least the bad ones do, the ones on their way to hell. It's like they're passing through—my house is some kind of pit stop for the scum of the earth."

"I need to come there. Have you talked to Declan about any of this?"

"No, are you kidding me? He'd think I was crazy."

"I'm beginning to wonder."

"Nora, you're the one person I can talk to, I'm telling you the truth. They talk to me. I hear them. Michael hears them. Anna hears them. They tell me they hear them! This morning Anna said the man told her to tell me that coffee stains my soul! And then she started speaking to an invisible space in front of her!"

"Well, lots of kids have imaginary friends."

"These are definitely not friends."

"Okay, well, if you insist that this is real, how many of these so-called demons do you think there are in your house?"

"I don't know, it could all be the same spirit or more than one, I can't tell. I can't see them. I only hear them, telepathically."

"Josie, that's it. You're hearing voices. Something's wrong with you and I'm saying that because I care about you. I'm coming to see you for myself. I'll book a flight today. I'm very, very worried about you."

"Don't tell Declan why you're coming, please! I'm begging you. I can't tell him, not yet. Give me time. Please, Nora."

"All right, but only until I get there and then you have to tell him. Have you thought about going to see your priest? Maybe he could help until I arrive."

"I have, but I'm afraid he'll have me locked up."

"Well, he might."

"I think I need to have the house exorcised, I'm worried the owners before us left some major, negative psychic baggage."

"Okay, that's one thing, but what proof do you have? And *exorcism?* Seriously? Do you believe that's a realistic solution?"

Josie's mouth sets straight. She replies to Nora's doubts with silence. How can she expect to explain this to her sister or to anyone and have them believe she's still sane? How can anyone understand? And Nora can't hear these spirits. She's never had the ability like Josie. She wouldn't ever understand because she'd never walked in Josie's shoes.

"I have an idea." Nora breaks the silence. "How about asking your priest to come bless your house? At least a house blessing wouldn't set off any alarms. I bet it would help. Tell him that you haven't had the house blessed yet and ask if he'd do it. He doesn't need to know anything else. I think it'd be best to steer clear from the term *exorcism.*"

"I guess I could go to Mass tonight. It is Saturday. Declan and I sometimes go separately because of the kids. Maybe I could catch Father Anthony after Mass." Josie wipes her eyes with a wad of industrial quality toilet paper.

"I think that's a great idea. I'll start checking on flights. I don't care what you say. I'm coming to see you. I won't tell Declan anything ... yet, but you have to go talk to the priest tonight. Do you hear me?"

"Yes."

"And when I get there, I'm taking you to the doctor. We're going to get you some help. Bottom line, I don't think you should continue with your experiment. I don't think you can separate yourself from your inner voices long enough to concentrate on the voices of friendly spirits."

"You don't need to worry—I have no inclination to do any more research or experimenting with my abilities anymore. It was a huge mistake."

"Listen, I want you to get your mind on other things. Finish your shopping before Declan starts to wonder what happened to you."

This was easier said than done. Josie's first priority, given the scene she made, was to leave Wilson's undetected by the prying eyes that viewed her earlier hysterics. Furthermore, she needed to avoid running into the guy with the "The Cure" t-shirt. With her luck he was probably someone who knew Declan. Everyone knew Declan. Yet at the same time, she wanted to see this stranger. For some reason, seeing him made her bizarre world come into focus.

"I'll call you later tonight. I love you," Nora says.

"I love you, too." Josie hangs up the phone and brushes the tears off her face. *Silly girl, better not look for the sideburns guy.* Finding comfort in some random stranger was pathetic and she hadn't sunk that low. Instead, she checked out and headed straight home.

CHAPTER 29

Humanity doesn't have the strength to remove
the tombstone of its own making.
—Pope Pius XII

Josie's anxiety continues to escalate the more she thinks about Nora's advice. She dreads having to tell anyone about her supernatural encounters, let alone her priest or her doctor. She wishes her problems would go away, that she could just let them go, but she's careening toward a cliff. A cliff where there's no belay to put the brakes on her fall. The barricade dividing her natural and supernatural worlds is not sustainable, and like a house of cards, it's on the verge of collapse.

Upon her return home, Josie puts away the groceries and makes a concerted effort to keep her distance from Declan. She speaks to him only when necessary and he appears oblivious to her internal agony. She pretends to be preoccupied with feeding the kids, doing dishes, laundry, and changing Jacob's diapers. The wedge the demons have driven between them is producing a chasm so great that she's beginning to feel the life she has with him belongs to another woman, a woman she no longer recognizes.

Inside, her stomach sickens. She can't think about anything else. *Everything is going to come out and when it does, it's going to be ugly.* How will she explain? What will he say when Father Anthony comes to "bless" their house after they'd been living there for months? That suddenly she felt the need for the house to be blessed? And what about Nora's unexpected visit from Phoenix?

Declan wasn't easily fooled, nor did he appreciate being played a fool. All the dirty details of Josie's expedition into the spirit world were going to come out. Yes, her infidelity wasn't another man but in his view her recent act of defiance would be just as bad ... even worse. She obviously crossed the line of a refashioned truth or a little white lie. It would constitute a major break of trust.

Thus, with every tick of the clock, she waits in her uncertainty until it is time to leave for Mass. She finally leaves their house at five minutes to five, a tad late if she intends to get to Mass on time but she doesn't. She must avoid chance conversations with other parishioners—it might prove disastrous given her mental state. To her dismay, Declan sends Michael and Anna with her. She planned to be alone when she approached Father Anthony but Declan insisted he needed to work on a contract for a client. He couldn't do it with the kids at home. Jacob could stay because he was taking a late afternoon nap. Reluctantly, she agrees. It's essential she keep up the façade.

They arrive at St. Monica's Church a few minutes past 5 p.m. and the church bells have already ceased ringing. She steps out of her minivan and onto the parking lot pavement. A surge of relief comes over her. Finally, she can let down her guard without Declan there to see her.

"C'mon guys, we're late," Josie says to Anna and Michael.

"Mommy, can I bring my crayons and coloring book?" Michael asks.

"Mommy, can I bring my Barbie?" Anna chimes simultaneously.

"Sure, why not." She needs something to keep them occupied when she makes her absurd request to Father Anthony after Mass.

She takes a hand from each child and walks toward the main entrance of the church, her heart pounds harder the closer they get.

Nora's recommendation plays over and over in her mind. *I think you might want to want to steer clear of the term 'exorcism.'* She wants to believe Nora but a house blessing isn't going to be enough. The demons are relentless, their persistence second to none. A house blessing will not keep them from prowling and weaving their wretched claws back into her home and life. She needs the ultimate in supernatural help. *Exorcism* will be the only permanent solution.

"Mommy, it looks like it's going to rain," Anna says and points her finger toward the sky.

Above, a collection of dark clouds gather, much like the ones that formed this morning above Wilson's Market. Josie finds the clouds to be an odd shape, appearing like a pool of hazy-winged creatures. The ends of the clouds have gray wispy tips giving her the impression of reptile talons. She turns her focus back to Anna. Anna is trying to pull the hood of her jacket over her head but can't maneuver it with her doll in her hand. "Mommy, can you help me?" she asks. Josie stops to help Anna and Michael cover up for the potential downpour on their way in to Mass.

On the front lawn of the church, they encounter a large crowd. Father Anthony stands tall on a podium at the front of the silent and orderly crowd. Josie observes him holding several palm branches and his vestments are crimson red. He raises the palms high enough so the people standing in the back of the crowd can see them. His graying black hair blows across his eyes in the cool breeze. He repeatedly swipes it out of his way with his free hand.

It's Palm Sunday tomorrow? Somehow, she's lost all track of time through this bizarre period of her life. Here it is Lent and the beginning of Holy Week. *Is this some weird quirk of fate? A cosmic convergence of good and evil?* Here she is, undergoing the most torturous time of her life and it coincides with Holy Week? *What are the odds?* This can mean one of two things—either her life is about to get better or things are going to get even worse. And in her case, she believes, the probability pendulum is swinging toward worse.

"Looks like I ought to hurry this one along folks," Father Anthony says to the crowd and points to the dark looming clouds.

The thought of Good Friday puts Josie's racing heart into overload. Her fears were planted decades earlier by her mother. Giovanna believed Good Friday was the day of the Devil, when he is loosed to reap havoc all over the earth. Giovanna would clean like a banshee and cover every mirror in the house with a sheet by three o'clock sharp. She said this was to "chase the Devil out." Josie couldn't imagine the possibility of more demons in her house. It seemed to her hell was already empty.

Father Anthony walks the perimeter of the crowd. He takes the palms and dips them in holy water and then waves them so droplets of holy water spray the crowd as he passes. When he approaches Josie and her children, an invisible force pushes her toward the ground. She stumbles over her own feet but catches herself on Michael's shoulder.

HA! He missed you! A familiar demon voice mocks her telepathically. It is the same voice she heard when she fell down her basement stairs. A snickering breath brushes the back of her neck and leaves behind a pungent aroma of decay. She quickly turns around to see who or what is behind her. She finds an elderly couple smiling back at her. They appear humored by her near tumble. Josie nervously smiles back, pretending to be embarrassed but in reality she's hiding her inward horror. The demon has followed her to church and instead of screaming, her natural impulse, she holds tight to the tiny shreds of sanity she has left.

Father Anthony expedites his blessing of the palms as the sky turns darker yet. The low hanging clouds evolve into vapory swarms of spider silhouettes, as if creeping closer to the ground. The crowd files in a long procession line behind him into the church. Josie takes Michael and Anna by the hand and falls into the back of the line. When they reach the double doors of the entry, Josie hesitates. She senses two invisible hands pulling her by the waist away from the doors—she is being repelled from the church.

"Mommy, what's the matter?" Michael asks, looking up into her eyes.

Josie breathes deep. Without answering him, she pushes their way through the repelling force. To her astonishment, the energy working against her holds little power. It is a minor struggle to push through it. Beyond the threshold and inside the church foyer, she feels different as if she has crossed into another world. She finds the closest font and dowses her fingers in holy water. "In the name of the Father, the Son and the Holy Spirit," she says and dabs her forehead, chest and shoulders. She takes more holy water and does the same for Anna and Michael.

"Stop, Mommy, you're getting me all wet," Anna complains.

"Shhh!" Michael says. "Be quiet, Anna, we're in church."

The heavy double doors behind them swing back open on their own. It is followed by a loud gust of wind. The wind holds the doors open for several seconds. Then wildly, the doors slam shut with a force so great that the entire group of parishioners ahead of them release a hushed but startled gasp. Suddenly, there's a loud creak and a crack. The oak pedestal holding the foyer's three-foot statue of St. Monica fractures. The statue tips at an angle downward and left and yet, it doesn't fall all the way to the ground. It's as if something or someone caught it but there's nothing there.

Michael's eyes open wide toward Josie's. "Yikes, Mommy, there's that wind again." He clutches her arm.

"Don't worry Michael, whatever it was, it's gone now," she reassures him.

"Mommy, I want to go home!" he insists.

Anna, sensing Michael's fear, starts crying. "I want to go home too, Mommy!"

"Shhh, calm down, we can't go home yet, we haven't gotten to say any prayers." Josie knows they have to stay. She can't allow the demons who followed them intimidate them into leaving. This is what they would want her to do. And she hopes that by receiving Holy Communion, some peace will return to her life.

Josie chooses a pew toward the back of the church because it will be easier to manage her children. St. Monica's altar sits in the foreground. It is large and formal with tile mosaics outlined in gold. She genuflects and sits down. At the end of each pew are sheaths of palm branches. Josie takes five.

Father starts to say Mass and her breathing slows to normal. *Perhaps the demons can't follow us in this far?* She feels better now that she is here, though still numb from days upon days of haunting. *This must be a safe place.* There aren't any more ominous laughs or stalking breaths on the back of her neck. It crosses her mind to never leave.

Mass progresses from the readings to the gospel and eventually to the homily. Josie listens intently though she can't remember what was said, even a minute ago. Her mind is lost in the existential space between the here and now and who will be waiting for her outside once they leave. Toward the end of the homily, Michael and Anna begin to get bored and misbehave. The two bounce around their pew, whisper to each other too loudly and poke at each other with the palm branches. Josie attempts to get them to settle down but it's to no avail. She contemplates going home but she can't leave yet. Not without receiving communion. And then there's the commitment she made to her sister to talk to Father Anthony. Perhaps, he is the key out of her nightmare.

"Mommy, look, I can make the letter X with these," Michael interrupts her cycling thoughts. He is making X's out of the palm sheaths.

"Mommy, who's Simon's brother?" Anna asks, out of the blue.

"Mommy, did you know St. Andrew was hung on a saltire? It's a cross in the shape of an X," Michael says.

"What? Where did you hear that?" she asks in mortified shock. *How would he know that?*

"I just knew it," he says.

Who's talking to my children! Who are you? Josie demands, telepathically. She thought they were safe from her tormenters while inside the church. No answer comes to her.

"Mommy, when do I get to have communion?" Michael asks. His brows furrow as if he's perturbed.

"You make your First Communion when you're in the second grade," she says.

"Why do we have to wait so long?" he asks.

"I don't know, Michael."

"I want communion too," Anna demands in a voice far too loud for church.

"Shh," Josie says. "If you're quiet the rest of Mass, I'll take you to McDonald's." Irritated by their noise and questioning, she resorts to bribery.

"Will we get to play?" Michael asks.

"No, but I'll buy you a Happy Meal, so, be quiet or the deal's off," she adds, crossly.

When it is time for the Sign of Peace, Josie turns around to shake the hands of the people sitting in the row behind them—a young couple holding an infant not more than a few weeks old, swaddled in a soft blue blanket. The mother appears to be young, not more than seventeen or eighteen. She is stunning with eyes that shine like a prism. The father appears a bit older but not by much, maybe twenty-two. He is handsome, bearded but otherwise clean cut, having short black hair and intense blue eyes.

Josie extends her hand to the young mother first. "Peace be with you," she says. As Josie's hand encounters the mother's, she is struck with a vision—the mother stands on a white cloud wearing pearlescent garments and stars of gold around her feet. She holds an infant in her arms.

"May God's peace be with you always," the young woman says.

Bewildered and astounded, Josie lets go of the young mother's hand.

Then, Josie shakes hands with the baby's father. Another strange and unexpected vision appears in her mind. This time it is of the father walking along a desert road holding the hand of a little boy. "May God's peace be with you always," he says.

Josie looks at the baby in the mother's arms. The infant's eyes are similar to his father's; their color is a calming shade of green.

What's going on? Are they for real? Josie trembles. Uneasy, she turns back to face the altar. She wonders why she hasn't noticed the couple until the Sign of Peace. They seem to have materialized out of nowhere. She is tempted to turn and look again but believes it would be rude to stare.

It was time for Holy Communion. Josie stands up from the kneeler and taps Anna's and Michael's backs indicating for them to stand as well. They file out the pew and walk down the center aisle of the church toward the altar. Josie uses this opportunity and turns to look behind her. The pew behind theirs is empty, the couple is gone. Without so much as a noise, they have disappeared.

"Mommy, where did those people go with the little baby?" Anna asks, catching Josie glancing behind them.

"I don't know, Anna," she says. *Who were they? Where did they go?* Josie's physical world collides with the world of spirit—reality for Josie has officially become a blur.

They arrive at the base of the altar. Father Anthony hands Josie, "The Body of Christ," and inserts into her left palm. She places it with her right hand onto her tongue. She prays *Help me,* pleading for a solution to her plight while she consumes the host. Yet, everything feels the same. She assumed receiving the Eucharist would lift her anxiety and fear, absolve her inner terrors, and grant her new found peace and protection. But nothing happens. Nothing feels different. Dazed, she sinks in utter hopelessness. The same pathetic mental turmoil remains.

"Josie?" Father Anthony asks. The priest's voice breaks through the clouds of her brain as if waking her from a hypnotic trance.

"Father ... would you bless my children?" she whispers.

He nods and places his right palm on Michael's forehead and then on Anna's. Once again, nothing happens. Everything is the same. No cathedral bells ring out, either out loud or in her head. No new vision, simply nothing.

CHAPTER 30

Mass ends. The hollow pit in Josie's stomach has grown so large that she is certain her heart is about to plummet into it. It's time to tell her sordid tale to Father Anthony. Her doubts begin to consume her. *What will he say? Will he believe me? Can he help me?*

She nervously takes Michael and Anna each by the hand and exits the back of the church where Father Anthony is saying good-bye to parishioners. She can't confide in him with people still milling around and it's taking longer than usual for the church to empty out. This evening it appears that every elderly person has something important to say to Father Anthony. She waits a little longer for him before she decides to give-up and leave. She rests her hand against the foyer doorway, ready to push open the doors and abandon her plan, when someone touches her shoulder from behind. She flinches.

"Hi, Josie," a woman says.

"Oh, my, hi, Sister," she says upon seeing Sister Lucia. Sister's expression is kind and warm.

"I'm sorry, Josie. I didn't mean to startle you. How are all of you doing this evening?" Sister Lucia asks.

Josie had forgotten all about the kind, petite sister. Sister Lucia was a modern sister—she dressed in secular clothes—tonight she is wearing a turquoise blouse and gray skirt. Her status is indicated by a simple cross she wears around her neck; it alerts others she's a woman of faith. Her greeting sends Josie into a flurry of delusional but hopeful thoughts. *Maybe I can talk to her instead? Maybe this will satisfy Nora's demands?* Perhaps Father isn't the key out of her nightmare at all but rather Sister Lucia.

"How are you? Is everything all right?" Sister Lucia asks again, her smile changes into a small frown of concern.

"No, it's not all right Sister." Josie vacillates about what to say next. *Surely, Sister has heard of things like this before?*

Sister Lucia guides Josie with her hand into a small room that is set off from the foyer of the church. Josie's arms and legs become jittery and weak.

"Kids, wait here for a minute." Sister points Anna and Michael to a spot just outside the door. "Sit down and we'll be right back." Sister closes the door behind them but leaves a crack open for the children to see that they are within sight.

"Sister, I need help. It's like something out of a movie," Josie whispers.

"What's going on, how can I help?" The worry lines on Sister's forehead deepen.

"I don't know what to do. My home, my children, they won't leave us alone."

"Who won't leave you alone?" Sister asks.

"The dead. They come and talk to us, day and night, meddling in our lives and scaring us. I think my house is possessed, we can't get them to go away, we need Father to come and exorcise our home!"

Sister Lucia's eyes shift back and forth as if searching her brain for an answer or a word of guidance. She is speechless and shakes her head. Her lips press together making her silence more prominent.

So much for her not thinking I'm crazy, Josie thinks.

After a long pause, Sister speaks. "Wait here. Let me go get Father." Sister exits out the door and leaves Josie alone.

Of course, she wants back-up. Who wouldn't? Josie, in her anxious-ness, begins to twist her wedding ring about her finger.

Sister Lucia stops briefly to speak to Michael and Anna. She reassures them they are almost done but takes them along with her and out of Josie's plain sight. Josie doesn't feel comfortable about this but she is in no position to argue and trusts that Sister will keep them safe for the time being. While she waits for Father Anthony to come, she looks around the room.

The room lacks décor, save for a wall portrait of Jesus on the wall and a simple brown throw rug. There are folding chairs leaning against a wall and prayer books lining a bookshelf against another wall. She picks up a prayer book and turns its pages. She is unable to comprehend a word as her mind races. If by chance, Father Anthony actually believes what she tells him, will he be able to help her or is performing an exorcism out of his league? From what she remembers about Catholicism, only certain priests can perform exorcisms. She wonders if there was such a thing as earning "exorcist" credentials.

Her litany of ruminations come to a halt when Father Anthony enters the room. His face appears pleasant and his manner is upbeat. Clearly, Sister Lucia hasn't filled him in on the details of her situation.

"Sorry to make you wait, Josie. Sister Lucia said you wanted to talk to me about something?"

"I have something rather unbelievable to tell you and I know this is going to be hard for you to understand but I'm telling you the truth." A new torrent of tears flows down her face. "I ... I need your help." It takes all she has to muster the courage to utter these few words and she hasn't told him the worst yet.

"Sit down, what is it?" He pats her back and opens a folding chair for her to sit down on. He then opens a chair for himself and sits down.

She swallows and blurts out, "Father, I think my house is possessed."

"What?" He laughs. "I'm sorry, Josie. I don't mean to laugh. It's just I didn't expect you to say that!" He shakes his head and places his hand on his forehead briefly as if thinking of a rational response to her irrational statement.

"You see Father, I'm clairvoyant. And I know the church doesn't believe in that sort of thing but it exists. I can hear the dead, but not any kind of dead. I hear the ... evil ones, quite possibly, demons. My kids hear them too. They've told me they hear voices in their heads that aren't their own." Josie speaks in a near whisper so as not to scare the children in case they can still overhear. While she doesn't know where Sister Lucia took them, she knows enough to be careful about what she says and how loud she says it.

Father Anthony's expression has turned from upbeat to alarm. "This is absurd," he scoffs. "This isn't possible. For one, there's no such thing as clairvoyance. This is out of the question," he says, dismissively. "And you can be certain my dear, demons aren't haunting your house. That's silly—these things don't happen except in the movies. Yes, they happened in biblical times. I suppose, they might happen in other places ... but NOT here, not now and certainly not in St. Paul, Minnesota."

"Father, if you don't believe me, then please, please, come bless my house. That's the least you can do!" she begs.

"Josie, go home. I think you need help but not the kind of help I can give you. The kind of help you need is from a doctor! Should I call your husband?"

"Father, why don't you believe me? Why won't you help me?" she asks almost angrily.

He stands up, shakes his head, turns his back to her and walks out the door.

Josie becomes so distraught that her emotions surge with anger instead of fear. She is furious—with Father Anthony and her church. *How could he! He is God's representative on earth—how can he refuse to help me? Isn't this his job? Isn't this why God called him to be priest?*

She leaves the room and gathers her children from Sister Lucia who are now waiting for her outside the door.

Sister places her hand once again on Josie's shoulder. "Josie, during Mass, could you face the altar?"

"Yes, I could," she says.

"What about the children?"

"Yes ... I think so. Why?"

"Good." Sister says nothing more.

Josie takes Anna and Michael by the hand and leaves for home.

CHAPTER 31

They arrive home about 7:15. It is dusk and the sky at the horizon line is a bright orange red. Josie pulls into the driveway and hits the garage door opener. The door rises and she sees Declan standing in the middle of her parking space. His hands are clenched into fists. His face is red, appearing ready to pounce on her like a panther on a lesser member the food chain. She brakes and places the car in park in the driveway. Declan comes toward the driver's side window. His expression is stern, his steps determined. He swings open the kids' door.

"Michael, Anna, go in the house," he says, firmly and without making eye contact with Josie.

"Daddy, Mommy took us to McDonalds and she even let us play!" Michael says.

"Do as I say." He unbuckles the kids from their seatbelts.

Michael and Anna, confused by their father's harsh greeting, grab their Happy Meal toys and slide out of the car and run straight into the house.

Josie doesn't move an inch. She can feel the heat of his wrath about to come her way.

He opens her car door, "Get out." He narrows his eyes at her.

Josie starts to tremble as she unbuckles her belt. She gets out of the car.

"Where were you?" he growls.

"I took the kids to McDonald's after church. I promised I'd take them if they behaved."

"Why didn't you call home? I was ready to send the police looking for you."

"Police? What? I figured you'd want more time to work. I had my cell phone."

"Yeah and you didn't answer." He crosses his arms against his chest, cutting himself off from her.

"I … I just forgot to turn the ringer back on after Mass. Police?" Josie cringes.

"How did I know you weren't going somewhere to harm the kids?"

"What? What do you mean?" Josie stutters, fearing if he uncrosses his arms that he'll strike her even though he has never laid a hand on her before.

"Father Anthony called me. He filled me in on your insane rambling, Josie. Have you lost your fucking mind?"

"No, Declan, you don't understand, it's not like that."

"Not like what? You think you're psychic and we have demons living in our house. What's fucking sane about that?"

"What?" She can't find a single explanation to offer in her defense.

"He told me everything, Josie, so don't even try to make up a new story." His jaw sets, his eyes are dark with anger.

"All I wanted was for him to come bless the house!"

"Well, you got that. He's coming over tomorrow with Sister Lucia. They're coming at one o'clock. I think they're only coming to make sure I don't kill you during the night. I have a good mind to kick you out of the house right now."

She sobs, "Declan, I'm so sorry, I'm–"

"Sorry isn't going to cut it, Josie. You know what you did. You deceived me! You lied!"

"No, I didn't, Declan, I didn't lie to you! I just didn't want to tell you until I knew I could—"

"Could what? Could get away with using an imagined ability? Bottom line, you fucking kept this from me!"

"Could you watch the language? The kids can hear you, not to mention the neighbors," She walks away from him into the garage. She hears a voice in her head, it is not her own. *He never loved you. The voice laughs and mocks. You're delusional! It's only a matter of time before ...*"

"Where are you going?" he demands.

"A matter of time ... ?" She utters confused into the space in front of her.

"Nice, now you're talking to yourself. You've gone completely nuts!"

She turns and looks directly in his eyes. "What's wrong with you?" she cries. He looks different to her, he is filled with fury.

"What's wrong with me? Are you serious? What's wrong with *you*?" He shakes his head. "Unbelievable. Get your things packed. I'm taking you to the hospital tonight. You need help. And if you don't get help and get over this insane drama you've created, then it's over," he says, scornfully.

"Declan, I'm trying to get help but no one will help me! I asked Father for help and he refused!" She places her heads in her hands and huddles in shame.

"Because, Josie, you need mental health help, not an exorcism!"

"Declan, I will get help, I want to get help. Please don't take me tonight," she pleads, lifting her head from her hands. "Let me stay home tonight. I don't want to frighten the kids. Please, think of them. You don't have to sleep in the same bed with me if you don't want. Take me in the morning, I promise I'll go then."

"Do you have any appreciation at all to what will happen to my career if Father talks to any of my colleagues? It will spell financial ruin for all of us!"

She nods, feeling humiliated, disgraced and all of the above. She can't blame him for hating her. She hates herself. She blindsided him. He only wanted their lives back the way they were before. So did she. Ashamed, alone and afraid, she goes into the house and crawls up the stairs to their bedroom. She shuts the door and cries herself to sleep.

CHAPTER 32

In dangers, in doubts, in difficulties, think of Mary, call upon Mary. Let not her name leave thy lips, never suffer it to leave your heart.
—Pope Pius XII

J osie awakes to the sound of a subtle and lyrical whistle coming from outside her bedroom door. She crinkles her eyes to open them a sliver. The room is dark and the house is still except for the whistle softly blowing. She is afraid to open her eyes further, afraid of what she might see. More curious though than frightened, she opens them a bit more. The night light from the hall glows but there is no one there. To her astonishment, Declan is sleeping next to her. She was certain he wouldn't be sharing a bed with her tonight, if ever again, but for some reason he is here beside her. He is sleeping soundly and sprawled over his half of the bed.

The sound of the whistle stops and she wonders if it is only a remnant from her dream. She rolls over and sees the alarm clock, it displays 1 a.m. As she considers getting up and checking on her children, something tells her to stay put. There isn't a word spoken but rather a sense of overwhelming calm. The sound of shuffling footsteps, distant at first, approaches the foot of her bed. She expects to see Anna or Michael standing there but there is no one. A mist spirals up from the floor to the ceiling, the odor of lilacs and roses fill the room.

A figure begins to take shape. The image ripples in the air like a pebble hitting the water's surface but then it becomes even and defined. It is a woman's form. She appears to be in her late teens, early twenties. Her hair, dark with long ribbon curls, rests on her shoulders. The top of her head is adorned by a thin colorless veil. Her dress is white but its details are difficult to discern because she isn't solid. Through the woman's translucent body Josie can see the physical objects around the room—Declan's dresser, an open closet door, and a roll of crumpled clothes next to the hamper. And yet the woman's image is three-dimensional, similar to a hologram.

Her eyes are crystal blue, reflecting an inner light. Josie senses mutuality between them but it is beyond her human grasp. The woman emanates serenity, comfort, and ease. It rolls off of her without effort and comes toward Josie in waves of brilliant color.

If you profess your belief in the risen Christ, I can drive them out in His name. The woman's words are soundless but Josie hears them aloud in her head.

Yes, of course I believe in Him! Can you help me? No one believes me! My husband despises me! My priest thinks I'm crazy and I can't help my children! I feel so alone! Josie calls back to her telepathically.

The woman nods.

Please help me! Tell me who you are? she pleads.

We are ... old friends. The woman speaks again in Josie's thoughts.

We are? She doesn't understand her cryptic clue. *I must be hallucinating. Is this a dream? Is she the Devil in disguise?*

Josephine, I am real and be assured, I am not evil. The woman overhears Josie's internal quandary. *Take the water.* The woman points her holographic finger toward several bottles of water that Declan has by his side of the bed.

How odd? Josie thinks. *Why did Declan bring so many bottles of water to bed?* She does as the woman directs and places the water on her bedside stand. Josie counts five bottles in all and looks again at the clock. It is 1:03 a.m. She turns to look back at the woman and she is gone. Her pulse races. *Where did you go? Please, help me ...*

A gentle and warm pressure begins to trickle over Josie's head and face. It travels downward like a thousand tingling fingers over the expanse of her chest and arms. It proceeds into her abdomen, then to her legs and out to the tips of her toes. Josie's heart thumps in a wild and erratic fashion as if it is no longer able to keep a regular rate or rhythm. *What are you doing to me?*

Still no answer comes. Limb by limb, the woman proceeds to work but remains invisible. The tingling begins to course through Josie's veins. Her arteries pulsate with the perfusion of what feels to be new blood entering into each of her limbs and the warmth in her vessels elevates until she is hot—burning hot. Steam-like waves rise off of her arms and legs. *Strange,* she thinks, because she is without any pain.

Drink the water, Josie.

I wish I could see you. Josie opens the bottle of water and drinks.

Stop. The woman says after Josie drinks half of its volume. The clock reads 1:12 a.m. Josie places the water back onto her bedside stand, lies back down and waits for her next instruction.

Time crawls for two long minutes as Josie watches the clock while lying on her side. The bedroom is still and ominous.

Suddenly, Josie's body turns onto its back and not of her own volition. The temperature in the room drops sharply. She begins to shiver. A wind howls. It accelerates from nothing to fierce, gusting down at her from the ceiling and across her bed. It rips through the house casting an icy and eerie fog. She hears voices coming from the fog—wailing, struggling, shrieking. The wind rattles her bed and the objects about the room—the light, the dressers, the chair. All is shaking, including the walls. The steel brace of cold and fear grip her as she clings to her bedding. She pulls the quilt over her head and around her tight. The wind stops. She peeks at Declan from under a bend in the blankets. He remains still. If he hadn't been breathing, she'd have thought he was dead.

The clock displays 1:17 a.m. Warmth returns to her body but the heat continues to build and intensify. She tosses and turns to find cool relief. When it reaches the most suffocating and unbearable moment, it subsides. The time is 1:22.

Please make it stop! Josie cries. Nothingness comes for two minutes, she rests in the peace. It will not be long enough. Although, time feels to be accelerating and when the clock hits 1:24, the icy surge pierces the darkness.

Two more minutes pass, she cowers under her blanket waiting for the howling winds and screaming voices to stop. At 1:26, the warmth returns, escalates and reaches a scorching peak. Her throat burns from thirst.

Drink more water, Josie, the woman commands.

Thank God. She can't take much more. She guzzles the rest of the water in the bottle. *Who are you? What's going on? Tell me, I'm begging you!*

Go ahead and get up.

I don't understand.

You must rid yourself of the impurity. The woman materializes her right hand and points Josie toward the bathroom.

Josie realizes she is being cleaned from the inside out. Whatever the woman is doing to her, it now needs to be expelled. Josie does as she commands and uses the toilet. The water flows out of her body like hot steam, but again, she doesn't burn.

She returns to bed and the process starts over, continuing to pulsate and perfuse through every single organ of her body. She knows what to expect by the minute on the clock—the cycle of warmth will last for five minutes, beginning at every seventh minute. Then she'll feel nothing for two full minutes, every time, until the minute strikes four when the Arctic-like cold sweeps in. After she experiences each agonizing and timed cycle, the woman commands her to drink water.

Josie feels every molecule of her body undergoing purification—the electrical conductivity of her brain, the peristaltic movement of her intestines, and the passage of fluids flowing out of each organ and into another. She becomes keenly aware of the independent and autonomic processes of her bodily systems to the point that she understands they are under her control. Finally, the last organ to be cleansed is her heart. It quivers as the purifying energy pulses through it.

At 3:58 a.m., Josie's limbs begin to flail, her body convulses and her heart tremors. A force pushes her body upward. She levitates, thrashing about at least a foot above her bed. Declan rolls over. His arms rise up and pull her back down to the surface. Yet, he isn't awake. It is as if someone is subconsciously telling his body what to do. He holds her in his arms while her body continues to convulse. It's 4 a.m. The thrashing ceases with one sudden jolting halt.

The translucent woman reappears at the foot of Josie's bed. Declan releases Josie and rolls over to his side of the bed. The woman's holographic hand touches Josie's and places it across Josie's chest. She is fearful, unsure of what is coming at her next.

It is time for the final expulsion, the woman says.

Josie has drunk all five bottles of water. She goes into the bathroom and shuts the door. The steaming water flows from her body into the toilet but as it does, her body shakes and trembles from head to toe. In one swift but jerking release, she sees something or someone leave her body. The being stands in front of her—a hideous malformed creature, part-man and part-ferocious dog. He seethes soundlessly and bears his large fang-like teeth at her. However, his anger and apparent hate for her dissolves before her eyes. His image fades until he is completely subdued and sitting back on his dog-like haunches. The woman appears out of nowhere. Under her command, she escorts the half-man half-dog out of the bathroom, passing through the closed bathroom door.

Josie hesitates. *Do I go out the door now or do I stay put?* She feels somewhat safe in the bathroom. She knows it is sometime past four in the morning. Now there will be a four in every minute of the hour. Will she freeze for an entire agonizing hour? Suddenly, the door swings open by itself. In a flash of light, she sees a cherub angel, high in the air. The angel waves to her. Her wings are fluttering and although she speaks not a single word, Josie knows who the angel is. *I should've known my mother would be my rescue angel.* The vision disappears.

Josie returns to bed and curls up under the covers, hoping her purging is complete. She wonders again who the woman in the veil is when suddenly her name is upon Josie's lips, "Therese."

With a loud snap, Josie finds herself hovering over her body. Her body in the bed is motionless and sleeping. Yet she is very much awake in the air. There are two of her and they are joined by a long silvery cord, from the top of her mortal head to the heart of spirit body. Josie turns away from her physical body and looks above her. The ceiling is gone and the night sky is full of brilliant stars.

Instantly, she is thrust forward into the atmosphere, high above the earth. She ascends higher and higher but the rocking vibration of the Earth threatens to pull her back. Looking away from the Earth, the threat relents. She sees the planets rotating, asteroids flying and blackness all around her. She passes the moon and visits the stars up close. It's as if she is one of them, a passing comet of light shooting through space. She has a new body, different than the one she left behind in her bed. She feels elated and free. She accompanies the Earth on its trajectory, then submerges into the Earth's atmosphere. From dizzying heights, she flies through the night sky. She views the rivers of the Earth flowing beneath her and waves crashing upon the coastal shores. She sees the vibrant colors of the world and colors she never knew existed.

The effervescent rays of the sun reach out to her as she passes through a daytime sky. From their touch, she feels hope. She no longer needs the earth or its belongings, the weight of its burdens lift from her. She floats and rises and drifts farther away into the universe. She doesn't want to return to the weight of her physical body—she holds onto the exhilarating freedom of flight.

Snap!

With accelerating velocity, she is pulled toward Earth, passing through a layer of all-encompassing love. It surrounds the Earth with a power so strong, so moving, and so overwhelming that it cannot be constrained by the limits of the human mind. It creates a transparent and iridescent mist. She knows this layer of love is intended for those on the Earth but it can't transcend the barrier beneath it.

As she enters the region of the barrier, she hears the voices from Earth beseeching God's mercy. The barrier continues sucking her in like a swirling black hole from which she can't escape. The sky is cloaked in shadows and the Earth's surface is murky, saturated with grit and filth. She hears desperate human moans, pleading for her to release them from their torment. It isn't a vision she could've perceived from the body, only from the eyes of her soul. The Earth languishes in this darkness, beyond the grasp of the incredible love above it.

As she flies closer to the Earth's surface, she views the eternal fires burning and hears the moans change to shrieking. The echoes of suffering rip through an endless night. There comes a pounding noise, a rhythmic hammering—*thud, thud, thud*—from the driving bitterness of nails being pierced into the hands of a man. Through thick black plumes of smoke emerge humanity's collective undoing. There in front of her are snarling beasts and half-human creatures. They crawl with iron chains, holding them bound to the Earth with the odor of foul, rotting flesh. In anguish, they cry out their names ... *wrath, greed, sloth, pride, lust, envy and gluttony.*

They keep us from finding the ecstasy that waits for us in the light of forgiveness. A woman's voice permeates the darkness; she is certain and sad.

Josie's eyes spring open. She is back in her body. The ceiling is closed. She is in her bed tucked neatly under the covers. She looks around her room. Everything is in its place. She looks at the clock. It is 5 a.m.

She hears another sound, a new and different one and yet familiar. It is the vast sucking sound of a motor, like the sound of a vacuum cleaner.

No, you can't be serious! she thinks.

Every ten minutes, she hears the slamming of doors, the moaning of voices and the crashing of windows. Josie's angelic mother is kicking the rest of the demons out, room by room, with her celestial vacuum and from the sounds of it ... there are a lot of them.

A voice speaks to her.

"Do not fear. I have come to tell you that you have not yet fulfilled your mission," the new woman says.

Josie can see her now, not as a ghost, not as a hologram but as a solid human being. Her beauty though is otherworldly. Her long locks of curled brown hair lay soft upon her shoulders, partially covered by a shimmering blue veil. The regal fabric of her long white dress is from a distant time. She wears a blue sash across her waist. Josie realizes the woman is no longer Therese. The woman is Mary.

Mary speaks to her in a clear and gentle manner. "My child, if you wish to enter heaven, you must rid yourself of all the jealousy, vanity and hatred that lived within your heart. It is gone now and you must never permit it to return. It will be hard, the trials will come and you will see your fallen state before you, but I tell you now, you have fifteen years." The woman then takes Josie's hands and presses them over her lower abdomen.

Cancer? Josie thinks. "But why? Why me? I need to see my children grow up. I don't want them to grow up without me here."

Mary doesn't answer her questions. "You've been given this opportunity to live out your natural lifetime. Your time in another life was stolen from you at the hands of sinners." The Virgin shows her a vision of a woman. The woman is dressed in an earthen-brown robe and she is standing by a cave. There is a crowd of Roman soldiers with swords; they come and drag her away from her children. Her children scream. There is an older woman with her, who pulls the children back.

The young mother screams to her children, saying something in a language Josie has never heard before but she still understands every word. "Go with your grandmother, stay with her. I will be with you again, our Lord has promised. I love you."

The men drag her through the streets. Strange people in long earthen robes throw rocks at her. The men with the swords strip her of her clothing. The stones keep hurling at her from every direction until the woman falls unconscious and blue. Then one soldier draws his sword and pierces it through her heart.

The vision ends. Josie mutters confused, "Was that me? Why?"

Mary provides no answer. Suddenly Michael enters her room as if he is sleepwalking. She gasps and looks to Mary. Mary holds up her right hand to keep Josie from speaking. Michael's eyes are closed but he doesn't stumble coming toward her bed. Mary seems to be guiding him to Josie without even a hand on his shoulder. He crawls under the covers next to her.

Mary instructs Josie, "Touch his heart."

Josie reaches over, placing her right hand over his heart.

"Do you feel it?" Mary asks.

"Yes, I feel it beating."

"Your heavenly Father has heard your prayers."

"He has?"

"He has received the Healer's touch. The Healer will be with you in the days ahead," the Virgin says and then she is gone.

"Thank you," Josie whispers into empty darkness.

Michael suddenly speaks out in his sleep. "Mommy, we don't need the man with the cross to come over tomorrow anymore."

Josie knows he is right. They didn't need Father Anthony to bless their house anymore. It was already done.

Michael mumbles some more. "When Daddy wakes up, he's going to wonder where everybody went." And indeed, the demons were gone as well.

The sound of cathedral bells begin to ring out through their house. It is 6 a.m.

CHAPTER 33

The next afternoon, Declan drives Josie to St. Catherine's Hospital. She sits in the passenger seat, enduring his silence. She knows better than to say anything to him as his body language speaks volumes even though his voice does not. She's become a liability to him, as a wife, a mother, and above all, as a partner. His contempt for her is evident and she fears their marriage is beyond repair.

The hospital looms large ahead of them—a literal and intimidating fortress. Perhaps, this is what it will take to trap her thoughts, to wall them up in this prison standing before her. Declan pulls up to the parking garage entrance and pushes the power button to the driver's side window. Together, they watch it descend. It is something for them to do—neutral—requiring no interaction on either of their parts. He reaches out his window for the ticket and the mechanical arms blocking the entry rise up to allow their car through. Josie sighs, swearing to herself she will she will get better, she has to.

Declan finds a space near the elevators and parks. He turns off the engine and pauses for a few seconds. He turns to look at her. The look in his eyes makes her feel hopeless.

"Are you ready?" he asks.

She replies with a nod. She is ready except for the dull ache of her breaking heart. Although he is with her, she has never felt more alone. To him, she is a broken woman who needs to be fixed. His sole interest is in having her put back together, by someone else, someone other than him. Then they can get on with their lives, the way it used to be. Their life before was enough for him. He had a thrilling career, three beautiful children, and a loving, supportive and most of all, dutiful wife. It was perfect. And then she threw a grenade on it.

"Josie, I'm glad you agreed to the hospitalization. The children need you, remember that," he says. He turns from her and stares out the windshield.

I agreed? Did I have a choice?

Then she notices his eyes more closely—they are red and swollen as if he'd been crying, the darkness she saw in them the day before is gone. She turns away; she's afraid to look at him like this. She didn't expect him to show any emotion toward her other than disdain. He had been so hard lately, so cold. Was something starting to change in him, did he feel the same grief she felt? She opens her door to get out of the car when he touches her arm. She hesitates. Their eyes meet for a second and she sees a glimpse of the man she fell in love with so many years before.

"I need you, too," he says. His voice tells her he means it and he isn't asking her to get better ... he is begging her.

God must be hearing my prayers. She sees the man he is, the man she still loves. He is in there, somewhere. And he and the children need her: mom is the hub in the wheel and they are the spokes. Without her, the spokes hang free, the wheel doesn't go round. The temporary fix is to place Nora in the hub, to limp along until she recovers. Nora's flight arrives at six tonight but until then Maureen will fill the maternal void.

Declan lets go of her arm and gets out of the car. She reaches to wipe her eyes with a tissue when she notices her wedding ring finger is sore. Without realizing, Josie twirled her diamond ring around and around her finger to the point of leaving it nearly raw. Behind her, she hears Declan pulling her suitcase out of the trunk.

Finally, she gathers the courage and steps out into the fluorescent light of the barren garage.

He slams the trunk shut. She reaches to carry the suitcase herself when he intervenes. "I got it," he says and takes it from her hand.

He walks ahead of her toward the elevator. She stays a few paces behind as the distance seems to be what he wants. The moment of closeness they had in the car was over.

Once in the hospital, they follow the signs to the "Emergency Department." Although Josie knows how to get there, she lets Declan lead her.

Prior to their coming, Declan had Josie contact her internist. Her doctor, after speaking with Josie over the phone, encouraged her to go to the hospital for a possible admission to the inpatient psychiatric unit. Now there were two against one, she didn't have a chance. But she'd have to be admitted first through the emergency department. While she didn't understand all the logistics, she knew this—she would take the medication, be hospitalized and more, in order to restore her life. Besides, no one believed she could take care of her children anymore, including herself. It was time she confided in somebody ... other than her priest, other than Nora and especially, other than Declan. And now what? For what reason was she granted this second chance? A second life to do what? Who was she? Despite the cleansing she experienced last night, she still feels she is not well.

They enter the lobby of the ER. It is quiet with a few people milling around. A male housekeeper is vacuuming the carpet in the waiting room. He turns off the vacuum and picks up a newspaper someone left on the ground. Josie watches him fold it and place it on a side table by one of the couches. She realizes she has seen this man once before—yesterday, sitting behind her at St. Monica's with the infant and the young woman. *Strange, he disappeared last night at Mass to reappear here? Who is he?*

"There it is," Declan interrupts her thoughts and points to a bold sign, *Emergency Department Registration.*

They proceed to the registration desk. It is separated from the other desks by tall dividers for patient privacy but today, there is only one clerk on duty.

The clerk looks up at them from her computer. "Hello, how may I help you?" When her eyes meet Josie's, the clerk's smile disappears.

Josie reads the clerk's nametag, "Katrina." She remembers her from the days when she worked in the ER, although she didn't know her well. She recalled Katrina was a gossip. Josie decides not to remind Katrina of how they know each other.

"My wife is here to be seen in the ER. Dr. Goldman sent her. I think the ER doctor is expecting us," Declan says.

Katrina flashes Josie a curious glance, pointing to the chair in front of her desk. "Have a seat and we'll get you checked in." She calls into her desk phone, "Triage!" The page is heard over the ER intercom system. Josie looks down at the floor. She fears she'll also know the triage nurse.

"Full name, please?" Katrina speaks almost robotically, staring at her computer screen instead of making eye contact with Josie or Declan.

"Josephine Mary Reilly," she says.

Katrina begins typing. "Your date of birth?"

"June 7, 1971."

"Do you have your insurance card with you? I'll need to make a copy of it."

Josie looks at Declan who is standing next to her chair, as if standing guard—like she'd try to escape. He reaches into his back pocket for his wallet and pulls out their insurance card when a nurse strides up to the admission desk and eye-balls Josie. The nurse's reading glasses are set far down on the bridge of her nose and she appears to be about the age of sixty. Josie is relieved to see she isn't a nurse she has met before.

"You're the gal Dr. Goldman called about?" The nurse gives Josie the once over.

"Yes," she says and makes brief eye contact with her, praying they continue to have this mutual lack of recognition.

"When you're done here, I'll take you back and get your vitals. No hurry, you look like you're doing okay."

Josie nods. The nurse obviously knows why she's here. Josie is certain the rest of the ER staff on today know as well. While she believes the triage nurse will keep her mouth shut, there is no guarantee of the same from the admission clerk. Katrina recognizes her and Josie knows all too well how the hospital rumor mill works, even with all the confidentiality laws in place intended to protect patient privacy. Josie senses Katrina's mind racing like a greyhound chasing a mechanical rabbit at the dog track. Either she's growing more paranoid or she actually hears Katrina's thoughts. *Remember Josie Reilly, that nurse who used to work here? Did you know she got admitted to pysch? I always knew she was a nut-job.*

After registering, the triage nurse escorts Josie back to an ER room. The nurse directs Declan to wait in the lobby until she gets Josie settled in her room. Josie surmises that the nurse will ask her about Declan in privacy—such as does she feel safe at home or does she fear her spouse? These are asked to determine if there's been prior abuse. Declan has never ever hit her. He wasn't the kind, although, Josie knows she may have tempted him with her behavior.

The nurse first takes her vital signs and types it all into a new computer sitting at the side of Josie's gurney.

"Nice computer," Josie says.

"Yeah, they arrived about two weeks ago. I'm still trying to get comfortable with them. I'm old school, a one finger typist. It's been a bit of an adjustment ... so, what brings you here, Josie?"

"Do you really what to know?"

"Well, what do you want me to type in, what works for you?" she asks.

Josie senses she is on to her. "I'm feeling anxious and sad all the time and I'm having a lot of trouble sleeping." It isn't a complete lie, she thinks.

"That's all?" The nurse raises her brows and looks at Josie over the rim of her glasses.

"Um, I'm having trouble eating, too." Josie doesn't want to reveal everything to this nurse, only the bare necessities.

"Are you taking any medication?"

"No." Josie shakes her head.

"Have you used anything to help you sleep?"

"Red wine."

"How much?"

"About three to four glasses a night."

"That's about a bottle a day. Does that sound right to you?" The nurse smirks as if she questions her truthfulness.

"Okay, maybe more ..." Josie figures if she has a chief complaint of anxiety and depression and reports that she is self-medicating with alcohol—it will be more palatable to Declan's colleagues if word gets out about her hospitalization. This is far better than people knowing about the voices she heard and her paranormal exorcism.

The nurse finishes with her questions and goes to get Declan in the waiting room. When he walks into the room, his face appears calmer to Josie than before. Maybe, she thinks, it's because he's done his job by taking the necessary steps to get her back on track. The time she spends here will return her to her "normal" self in a few days. Or so he hopes. She knows it isn't going to be easy. She's not the same person she was before.

Josie hears someone outside the curtain to her room.

"Hello, it's Dr. Anderson. May I come in?" he says through the curtain.

"Sure, come on in," Declan says.

Dr. Anderson enters and greets her with a handshake. "Mrs. Reilly, I'm Dr. Anderson, the ER physician."

She already knows who he is—the one ER doctor who could never remember her name when she worked there. But, the fact he didn't seem to remember her at all was surely a blessing at this moment. And though he was arrogant, he had the redeeming quality of being a skilled ER physician. He had the graying hair and bifocals to prove it.

"Hello, sir, are you her husband?" he asks, turning to Declan.

"Yes." The two men shake hands. "Please call me Declan."

"Well, tell me, Mrs. Reilly, what seems to be the problem?" Dr. Anderson pulls up a chair and sits down to begin typing on the bedside computer.

"Um, it's Josie."

He nods.

I guess saying my first name still didn't ring any bells for him. "I'm having trouble sleeping and eating."

"How long has this been going on?" he asks. Abruptly, he stops typing and looks over to Declan, "Don't I know you? Aren't you on TV? You're that legal consultant on the Sunday morning show. What's it called again?"

"Main Street Minnesota," Declan says.

Of course he remembers Declan. I was just a nurse who spent many nights working with him.

"I had to miss it today," the doctor says.

"Oh, I wasn't on it this morning. They only do the legal segment about once a month," Declan says, standing at the side of Josie's gurney opposite Dr. Anderson.

"I always enjoy your analysis." Dr. Anderson grins.

"Thank you, I appreciate that." Declan appears embarrassed, and oddly humbled.

The doctor continues to chat with Declan about corporate restrictions due to overreaching government regulations and how it binds the private sector's ability to employ more people ...

Blah, blah, blah, she thinks. Dr. Anderson never asks her another question, not even if she wants privacy from her husband. This surprises her because she always thought Dr. Anderson was better than this when it came to his work. While the two men discuss all the laws shackling corporate expansion, they become oblivious to Josie's presence. Dr. Anderson pulls up her patient gown to listen to her heart, lungs and bowel sounds as if she's a practice mannequin.

As he finishes her exam, a nurse peeks in her head from outside the curtain. "Dr. Anderson, we need you in room seven ... NOW."

"Excuse me for a minute." He leaves the room in a shot.

As he leaves, Josie hears the nurse whisper, "He's having runs of V-tach and his pressure's tanking."

In a peculiar way, she is relieved. This other patient has taken priority over her. It's nice to know someone needed help more than she did. She isn't dying, just crazy. She will get better, if not for Declan ... but for Michael, Anna, and Jacob.

CHAPTER 34

J osie's hands tremble all the way from the ER to the fifth floor of the hospital. She shoves her hands in her pockets to cover it up. Her admission has become reality. Images of white lab coats and shock treatments cause her to break into a cold sweat. Her mind feeds her nonsense. She reminds herself, *this is a safe place*. Her admission is "voluntary," albeit coerced. She accepts her mental state needs stabilizing—it's paramount to her survival. As long as she cooperates, her future as a wife and a mother will be guaranteed to continue. Without it, the life she knows will cease to exist and she'll be left with nothing but her name.

Escorted by an ER nurse, they arrive at the doors of the psychiatry ward a few minutes past 6 p.m. The psychiatry unit is walled off from the rest of the hospital with a pair of locked, solid and wide steel doors. *Ah, a barricade for mutual protection*, she thinks, *us from them and them from us*, although, she would now be one of "them" on the inside. A sign on the door indicates to "Ring Bell for Assistance" and points to a doorbell on the wall beside it. The ER nurse presses the bell.

"How may I help you?" a man asks over an intercom speaker.

"Hi, it's Jules from ER. I'm here with an admission."

As Jules speaks, Josie detects a small overhead camera moving. It rotates toward her and Jules. The camera adjusts, emerging its lens outward and appears to focus on Jules' ID badge. A moment later, the double doors automatically open. Jules, Josie and Declan proceed through. They encounter a check-in window to their immediate left. It reminds Josie of a pharmacy drive-up window. It contains a small portal at the bottom to pass documents or medications through. A clerk with a shaved head sits behind the window. His eyes are directed at his computer.

"Hello," he says and looks up from his computer screen. He makes eye contact with Jules and then with Josie. "Your nurse is Susan. I just paged her, she'll be right here." The clerk accepts the paperwork from Jules through the lower window portal.

Declan doesn't speak. He stands in the background, looking around at the blank walls and appearing to bide his time.

An awkward minute later a nurse with long auburn hair approaches them. She is noticeably calm and looks to be in her mid-to-late twenties. Around her neck, she wears a stethoscope and carries a chart under her right arm.

"Are you Josephine?" she asks. "I'm Susan." She smiles and offers her hand in greeting.

"Yes, but please call me Josie." Josie nods and shakes the nurse's hand.

"Josie, it is then," Susan says. "I'll be checking you in to your room and will be your nurse until about eleven tonight."

Josie observes that Susan is wearing street clothes as opposed to "nurse-wear"—a long-sleeved apple green t-shirt and gray chino pants. Jules, on the other hand, is more medicinal, more sterile, wearing faded blue hospital-issued scrubs. On their way up from the ER, Josie had pictured the stereotypical pysch nurse, *Nurse Ratched.* While she knew her imagination wasn't being fair or accurate, she didn't know what to expect. She had never been a patient—or a nurse—on a psych ward before. Susan was nothing like Nurse Ratched and her presence was rather reassuring. Josie's posture relaxes, her hands stop trembling.

"Thanks, Jules, I'll take it from here." Susan accepts the rest of the ER chart from Jules' hands.

"Good luck, Josie, hang in there." Jules touches Josie's arm and then proceeds out the doors of the psych ward.

If only I could follow, Josie thinks. She turns away from the exit and notices Susan staring at Declan. "Oh, I'm sorry, this is my husband Declan," she says. *Yes, this is my husband who'd rather be anywhere else but here.*

"Hello, sir. How do you do?" Susan asks.

He nods and smiles slightly, "Nice to meet you."

Susan turns back to Josie. "Let's get you checked in and settled into your room. Follow me." Susan starts to walk. "First, we need to complete some intake paperwork."

Josie follows behind her. Declan stays a few steps behind them both. They enter a private room off of the nurse's station. It has windows and the other staff can see in. Josie doesn't ask why but supposes the windows are in case a nurse needs help with a combative patient. The small room also contains a scale, a blood pressure cuff and some other medical supplies—tongue depressors, cotton balls, an electronic thermometer, and such. Susan starts in with another litany of mundane questions. She takes Josie's vital signs and has her step on the scale to get her weight.

"Gee, you're only a hundred pounds. Are you having trouble eating?" Susan asks.

Josie raises her brows, she is surprised her weight has dropped so much since the last time she weighed herself. She couldn't remember though the last time she actually ate a full meal.

"That's much too low for your height," Susan says.

"I really haven't been trying to lose weight." Josie shrugs. "I just haven't felt like eating."

Susan nods.

"She hasn't been eating at all, that's part of the problem, Susan," Declan interrupts.

"I'm not anorexic, if that's what you're implying." Josie's snaps at him, her voice is strong, much stronger than it's been the last few days.

Susan interjects as the tension between them is obvious. "It's not unusual for people to lose weight when they're depressed and anxious. We'll make sure Josie eats while she's here with us." Then, turning to Josie, "You won't miss a meal," she affirms and smiles. "Declan, would you mind stepping out for the remainder of Josie's exam?"

Given Susan's matter of fact behavior and Josie's recent tone, Declan leaves the room. Josie knows this is all too disturbing for him to swallow anyway. It probably wasn't fair for her to snap at him but she couldn't help it anymore. Susan shuts the door after he exits and sits back down across from Josie.

"Josie, do you know why you're here? Tell me in your own words," she asks.

"Yes, I think so. My family believes I'm ... hallucinating."

"Tell me more ..." Susan's eyes remain intent on Josie.

She swallows. It is time to tell Susan the rest but Josie's afraid to admit the truth out loud.

"You can share this with me ... only the psychiatry nurses who look after you and your doctor can read this part of your record. You need to tell us so we can help you get better."

Josie's hands begin to tremble again but Susan's soothing manner reassures her. "This is hard for me to talk about."

"I know and that's why you're here, you're safe with us. We're here to help you get better, not to pass judgment on you or your condition."

Josie nods and after a deep breath, blurts it out. "I think I'm hearing the voices of people who have ..."

"Who have what?"

"Died."

There is a long pause as Susan waits for Josie to add more.

Josie's fingers nervously twist her wedding ring around her finger. "Actually, it's not so much anything I hear out loud as much as the thoughts. Well, I've heard voices but mostly I hear the voices in my head."

Susan's face appears more and more concerned, she scribbles down some notes on her chart. "What do the voices say to you?"

"It depends. Sometimes it's something simple, like *tell my son Ron his mother Betty is alive and well on the other side.* But more often than not, the voice says something awful or gives me a warning to communicate to someone."

"Warnings about what? Can you be more specific?"

"Unfortunately, the warnings are mostly about death, like plane crashes, hijackings, bombs, terrorist plots, you name it." Josie shrugs, her eyes tear up.

"Wow, it must be so upsetting for you." Susan hands Josie some tissues.

Josie takes one and blows her nose hard. "Try terrifying,"

"Can you describe to me any other ways you think spirits may be communicating with you?"

"Many times, they'll use symbols and objects rather than their voice."

"How so?" Susan looks puzzled.

"They impose a vibration to a physical item ... it's as though vibrations are coming from the object toward me and that's how I know it's an important piece to the message."

"Can you give me an example?"

"For instance, sometimes the vibrations come toward me off of street signs. If the sign shows a circle, like on a roundabout, this is a message about the cycle of life. Usually, it means a birth. Or, if it's a stop sign—it means that I'm not getting the message straight and need to try harder or take a different direction. *Dead End* usually means something bad is going to happen—not necessarily death although it has meant that at times."

"Does this only happen with street signs?"

"No. It happens with about any object. It's hard to describe, the best comparison I can make is one of magnetic attraction. It's the same sort of subtle pull or tug."

"Are you able to see the spirit talking to you?"

"No, well, I have seen them, but rarely. Again, it's hard to put into words. I just know they're present."

"How did all of this come about?"

"It started when I was little and mostly with dreams. When my mom died, it started happening more, beyond the dreams. Then, a month or so ago, I came across an article about a research study that was studying people who have psychic abilities. I wanted to look into being part of their research but my husband was against it. That's when I decided to attempt some readings on my own."

"Interesting. What's a *reading*?" Susan voice inflects with curiosity.

"Readings are a term for collecting information from someone who is deceased. A living person like me serves as the conduit or the channel for the living relative or friend who wishes to make contact with the deceased. The actual information exchange is called a *reading*."

"So, are you, or rather, were you a medium?"

"I guess so. However, I wasn't much good at it. I channeled all the wrong types of energy," Josie scoffs at herself as she feels like the victim of a cruel spirit's joke.

"What do you mean? Why do you think that?"

"Before coming here, I encountered many spirits but unfortunately, I think they were imposters ... dark spirits who lie for the sport of it, maybe out of afterlife boredom. I don't know what their motive was other than watching me go crazy."

"It must've been awful for you."

Josie notices that Susan acknowledges all of her statements with objectivity, without inflections of doubt.

"Yes, it was," Josie says. "I know it's hard to believe, this whole thing I'm telling you."

"What I think isn't important. What's important is that we find a way to help you get better and help you return to living a peaceful life."

Josie's confidence in Susan grows and she begins to trust her.

"Are there spirits talking to you now?" Susan asks.

"For once ... no. It's worse when I'm alone though." While Josie believes she can trust her, she isn't ready to tell Susan about the demons. She can't come out with all of it—some things had to be kept secret even if it meant hiding the truth from those who were trying to help her get better.

"How is your family handling this?" Susan asks.

"Not well. My kids are too young to understand or comprehend any of this. And we don't want to frighten them. My husband is frustrated and angry with me. He blames me for screwing up our life. He thinks I brought this on myself." Josie's tears reemerge.

"And what do you think, how are you feeling about all of this?"

"I feel ashamed. I've brought shame upon my family. If this ever got out, it would ruin my husband's career and my family wouldn't look at me the same ever again." She can't keep it together anymore and like a faucet on high, her tears pour heavy. "I know in my heart my husband would leave me and take the children."

"Is that what he told you? Are you certain?"

"He said if I didn't come here for help, our marriage was over." The pain settles across Josie's face. The situation is beyond her control. Yet Declan somehow believes it still is within her grasp. And she knows he has the legal power and influence to get everything he wants in a divorce from her: the kids, the house, everything. But would he? Would he do that? The man she saw in the car, the guy she loved was still in there. That Declan wouldn't abandon her, would he?

"Have you thought about hurting yourself? We have to know this, Josie. We need to keep you safe while you're here." Susan leans forward and touches Josie's hand.

"Yes," she mumbles, "there've been times."

Susan's eyes are sad, she lets Josie cry it out and hands her the box of tissues.

"If I went away, my family could get back to living their lives ... without all the upheaval and strife I've caused them."

Susan rubs and pats her hand softly on Josie's back. "You'll be safe here. We can help. And it's not your fault. Mental illness is a disease like any other. Unfortunately, we still live in a society who treats it like a scarlet letter. You have no reason to be ashamed."

"But, I believe ... no ... I know that what's happening to me is real! There's no way I can be convinced that it's not, I've predicted things that have come true. I know things ... there's no other way to explain them. But my husband wants it all to be turned off. And I don't know how!"

"Let me ask you a question. Do you want to eliminate these thoughts? Do you want them to go away?"

"Yes, of course I do!" Josie's wipes her eyes and nose. "I can't focus on being a mother when dead people are talking to me at every turn! Will you really be able to help me?" At this point, it didn't matter if Susan believed her or not or if she thought what Josie experienced was real or fantasy. All that mattered to her was returning to a level of function where she could take care of her children.

"Josie, we're here to help you return to living your life peacefully and I promise you will. You have my word," she says, earnestly. Her pale blue eyes are full of understanding but not pity. "Are you ready to let your husband back in?"

"Yes, I think so," Josie says, but in truth, she wasn't sure.

Susan opens the door and invites Declan to come in. He sits back down in the empty chair next to Josie's.

Susan looks at Declan and then back to Josie. "I have to collect any personal items which could potentially harm you. I'm sorry but I need to go through your suitcase and your purse, Josie. You'll get all these things back. We'll keep them locked up when you're not using them. We do this in order to keep you safe."

"I understand ... I suppose its policy," Josie mutters. Nevertheless, her emotions are raw. Her privacy in all respects will be violated from this point forward. Now, they are taking away her right to her belongings.

Susan gathers all of Josie's things. "I'll bring back what you can keep with you once I've had a chance to go through them."

Josie nods and looks down at the floor. The shame is more than she can bear.

"I know this is hard, Josie. I need you and Declan to realize that you're being placed under our most careful supervision."

"What?" Josie says in disbelief. "Are you putting me under suicide watch?" She understands exactly what *careful supervision* means. She remembers the term from working in the ER.

"I prefer not to call it a 'watch.' It's more like a precaution. It's all about your, as well as our, safety," Susan says.

Declan's face grows agitated, as if blindsided by this revelation. He clearly had no idea things were this bad, he wasn't aware his wife had considered suicide. He closes his eyes and rubs his fingers across his forehead and brow as if doing so will make reality disappear.

Susan turns to Declan. "There's one other thing you need to know."

He opens his eyes and looks to her.

Our unit is locked so when you come to visit your wife, you'll need to ring the bell and ask for permission to enter the unit."

Will he come to visit me? Josie wonders. *I don't believe he will.*

As for you, Josie, Dr. Shapiro hasn't written off-unit privileges for you. Therefore, if you need to leave the unit, for whatever reason, you'll need to be escorted by one of the staff members."

This is the first time Josie hears the name of her admitting psychiatrist. She hasn't had a need for a psychiatrist before today. Inside she wants to scream as it sinks in. Her freedoms are being taken away. She can't come and go as she pleases. She can't so much as brush her teeth without permission. All because they think she will try to kill herself. But in her heart, she is not that far gone. And it isn't because she isn't depressed enough to do it. She can't get any lower, she's hit bottom and circled the drain. No, she realizes suicide would be the most selfish act. She might've ruined her life with Declan but she wasn't about to ruin her children's.

"By the way," Susan says getting up to open the door, "you have a semi-private room. You'll be sharing it with another female patient."

You've got to be kidding. Josie's stomach turns. She didn't want to have to share her room, and the thought of having to manage her state of mind in the company of another is beyond words. This is the nail in the coffin. No freedom, not seeing her children, not having her things under her control, and now having to room with a stranger. *What did I do to deserve this?* She cries out inside. *I don't belong here! God help me.* Her eyes are red and her head hangs low. "I didn't choose this for my life."

Susan reaches over to touch her hand, "Josie, no one does."

Susan walks Josie and Declan to Josie's patient room. When they arrive, it is almost 7:30 p.m. and Josie's roommate is noticeably absent.

"You're roommate's name is Sandra." Susan switches on the light above Josie's bed. "She's probably down in the unit lounge. In the evenings, we offer movies and card games for the patients to come and socialize. The schedule's hanging up on your door," she says and points to it.

Josie observes there is no TV in her room. *Good grief.* She'll be forced to commune in the lounge with the other patients, the last thing she's up to doing. Her patient room is stark and blasé, in a muted earthy gray tone. There's an obvious vacant aura—no objects available to cause injury to one self or one another—nothing sharp within arms-reach, no ceiling hooks from which to dangle a rope, and no place for the sheets to cling to when tied around one's neck. At least the emptiness created personal space as she got the feeling privacy would become her most precious possession.

"I better get going," Declan says. "I want to make sure your sister got in okay. She's going to need my help getting the kids to bed." He leans over and gives Josie a kiss good-bye on her forehead and squeezes her hand. She is puzzled by his act of kindness, wondering if it is all for show or is her old Declan emerging to the surface. Her sister, Nora, is capable of taking care of their kids without him. Is he looking to flee or is he genuinely concerned? No, she gets the sense he is fleeing.

As he walks away, Josie has a vision of their life together—the shared moments of joy when each of their children were born, the family and home they created together. Is it gone now? Will it ever return? Things will never be the same between them. She didn't mean to have kept things from him but he had grown so rigid. This was not the way she intended her marriage to be and not the way she intended it to end. This wasn't the destiny she sought.

Susan calls to Declan as he exits. "I almost forgot to give you this." She hands him a small card. "It's a parking pass for when you come to visit your wife."

I'm guessing he's not going to visit, Josie thinks. She looks away toward her bed, with its white hospital-issued sheets and blankets tucked ever so neatly into the sides of the mattress. She is here alone. And if she doesn't return to who she was before, Declan won't take her back. She'll have to relinquish her story—she doesn't have a choice. She'll have to accept the diagnosis of psychosis, live her life as if all of this had never happened in order to keep her children and marriage. Or, if not, suffer, lose everything ... but live the truth.

CHAPTER 35

Susan returns with Josie's suitcase an hour later, bringing what little Josie is allowed to keep with her in her room—clothing, some make-up, a comb, toothbrush and shampoo. Sharp objects including her nail clippers, tweezers and razor as well as a few of her "finer things" like her perfume are missing. Although she is saddened by the removal of her belongings, it isn't the time to fight for her rights as a sane human being. There is no one but her who can change the future, no one worth convincing otherwise. Efforts to do so will be futile. Rather, it is time to unpack for her self-imposed nightmare.

She puts away her last t-shirt, her favorite purple one with the *CK* logo, the one that makes her feel a little more with it and less like a mom. Sandra, her roommate, shuffles in. Her pale eyes dart to Josie and then look away toward the linoleum floor. Her skin is waxed paper thin and ghost white. Josie can see thread-like capillaries scattered at its almost translucent surface. She smells of cocoa butter, as if having just applied lotion.

"Hello," Josie says politely.

Sandra mumbles a hello and walks to her own bed. She sits down on the edge of her bed and looks out the window opposite Josie. Josie watches her as she isn't sure what Sandra will do next. Sandra begins to wring her hands and then rises up from the bed. She starts to pace.

Maybe she doesn't want a roommate either, Josie thinks. She notices Sandra is tall, about five foot ten, but difficult to say with certainty because she walks with a slouching gait, perhaps from years of avoiding direct human contact. Her attire is haphazard—a baggy navy blue cardigan over a small-print, knee-length dress. Her slippers make a scraping sound when she paces. Sandra appears to be about fifty but then again, she could be younger, Josie reasons, given Sandra's apparent chronic mental illness.

While Sandra paces, Josie's heart ramps up a few beats. She can't help but feel she said something to upset her roommate but her only utterance to her was hello. Sandra, visibly reluctant, even hostile, doesn't offer to share anything with Josie beyond her first bare hello. She doesn't know why her presence distresses Sandra so much. It becomes clear that whatever Sandra has going on mentally, it is far worse than what Josie is in for.

"They tell me you're Josie," Sandra says, without making eye contact.

Josie nods. "Yes, and you're Sandra?"

"Yep." She swivels her posture toward the window and faces away from Josie.

There is a knock at the door. It cuts the awkward tension.

"Come in," Josie says.

Susan enters. "I see you've met Sandra."

"Yes," Josie says.

Sandra resumes ignoring Josie and now, Susan.

"Josie, I ordered your meds from the pharmacy. They should be up before you go to sleep tonight," Susan says.

Josie wonders what Dr. Shapiro has prescribed for her. Given her limited nursing knowledge in the mental health area, she presumes he must have ordered her an antidepressant and maybe even an antipsychotic.

Susan approaches Sandra with a medicine cup. Sandra snatches it from Susan's hand and dumps its contents into her mouth. Susan gives her a cup of water to chase it down with but there is no actual exchange of words.

"I think I'd like to get ready for bed. I'm pretty tired," Josie says.

"Oh, okay, you don't you want to check out the unit living room? They're watching *Field of Dreams* right now." However, after Susan speaks, she looks at Josie's face and realizes this is a bad idea.

"Thanks but I think I'll skip it." Josie needn't watch a movie about a guy who consorts with dead baseball players and hears voices. It is all too familiar for her.

"Sure, I understand. I'll be back with your bedtime meds as soon as I get them from the pharmacy."

As soon as Susan leaves, Sandra scowls. It's obvious she doesn't care for her.

Why doesn't she like Susan? Josie wonders. *Maybe Sandra doesn't much like anyone?*

"Do you mind?" Sandra asks. Her hand is on a radio button.

"No, it's fine," Josie says.

Sandra presses it on. The volume is on soft. A song is playing that Josie hasn't heard in long time. It is *"Diamond Girl"* by Seals and Crofts.

Strange, Josie thinks. She was once someone's diamond girl, someone's "precious stone," as the lyrics crooned, but now she is more like someone's cubic zirconia. She might look the same, but she feels like a fraud. She will conform to the therapy, to the medication … all of it. She knows some of it will help but the rest will satisfy the powers that be, that is Declan, her sister and her priest. If she wants out, she'll have to embrace a façade. And, in being rational, at least on the outside, she will eventually find her way home.

A LOUD POPPING NOISE WAKES HER. SHE BRACES AND LISTENS closer. *Is that gunfire?* The clock shows it's 3 a.m. The room is dark except for a small nightlight along the base of the wall in front of her bed. She wonders if she's being woken again by more unknown spirits. Will they be good ... or evil? In the bed beside her, Sandra is inhaling and exhaling with loud rushes of air.

Josie gets up, hastily puts on her hospital-issued slippers and goes to the window. She pushes aside the drape. Hail the size of baseballs pelts the glass with the ferocity of war. Outside, the howling wind echoes with moans and wailing.

"Make it stop!" she cries and covers her ears. The sound of hammering ice cripples her, sending her into a frozen panic.

Then, like the rift of a ripe electric guitar, the window explodes in a burst of anger. The impact of glass and ice strike her skull and the bitter, metallic taste of blood trickles into her mouth.

Sandra wakes and emits a horrified scream.

The room closes in on her. *Am I dying?* All goes black.

CHAPTER 36

For my part I know nothing with any certainty,
but the sight of the stars makes me dream.
—Vincent Van Gogh

"Josie ... Josie."

She hears her name muffling through a tunnel-like darkness.

"Josie, Josie," the voice says again. This time the voice is loud and clear. Something taps her shoulder, fast and firm.

Her eyes open into narrow slits initially and then open fully. There in blurry view are faces—unfamiliar faces—and their eyes stare back at her. She is on her back and on the floor. Time and place are beyond her immediate grasp.

"Let's get her up," a woman says decisively.

Josie doesn't recognize her. "Where's Susan?" she asks. "Ouch!" Her hand goes to her head in response to a horrible headache.

"Susan's gone home. I'm Gabrielle, your night nurse. Careful, people," she says to two others as they assist Josie up off the ground and into a nearby chair. The night nurse is petite with tan skin and a soft face. A large gold pendant rests on her neck. It is a Miraculous medal—a medal symbolizing one's devotion to the Virgin Mary. It is then Josie believes she's in good hands.

"What happened?" Josie asks in a daze, noticing her fingers are tinged with blood.

"Long story," Gabrielle says. "First things first. Do you know where you are?"

"I think so. I'm at the hospital," Josie mumbles.

There's a broken window across the room from her with a large, gaping hole in the middle of it. Surrounding Josie's feet are sharp fragments of glass. *What's it with me and broken glass?*

"There was a storm and you must've blacked out. It looks like you were hit in the head by a piece of hail that came through this window." Gabrielle, wearing plastic gloves, holds up a large and melting ball of ice stained with what appears to be Josie's blood. She takes a pack of gauze and presses it to Josie's forehead. With pressure, she holds it in place for a minute or two. When she lets it go, the gauze sticks; Josie's blood is the glue.

Splatters of drying blood cover Josie's pajamas. Out of fatigue and frustration, she weeps. Her efforts are futile. No matter where she goes, pain and misery soon follow. The exploding window and the gash on her head support her theory and despite her exorcism, something dark continues to lurk about.

Sandra is sitting up in her bed when Josie notices her. She utters an almost imperceptible whimper, seeming startled and confused by their chaotic surroundings.

"Let's get them both out of here," Gabrielle tells her assistants. One assistant, "Brian, RN," according to his badge, fits Josie's mental image of a Minnesota deer hunter. "Please see what other rooms we have available." Then Gabrielle turns to her other helper, "Rachel, I will need you to help Sandra."

"Of course," Rachel says.

"Gabrielle, we should page the on-call doctor, too," Brian adds.

Two additional staff members enter the room. One of them, a taller woman with short blonde hair, is pushing a wheelchair. On its seat is an icepack.

Josie watches the staff scurry around her, holding the gauze and ice pack to her head with her hand. While she is the object of their attention, she feels like an outsider looking in on her life.

"Gabrielle," the blonde-haired woman says, "room 444 is open and clean. We can move them into there for now."

"No!" Josie interjects. "Please, not that room! Not that room!"

"Calm down." Gabrielle rubs Josie's back, attempting to calm her.

"It's the numbers ... ," Josie whispers to Gabrielle.

"Okay, okay ... I get it," Gabrielle reassures her. "Brian went to see what other rooms we have. Let's see what he comes up with."

Josie nods, though she remains jittery. Her mind cycles, *What's happened to me? I'm here among people I don't know. I'm all alone except for these strangers! Why am I here?*

"Look, if 444 is open, I'll start moving Sandra into there," Rachel says. "Let's at least get her relocated right now."

"Good idea," Gabrielle says in agreement.

Josie senses they think she's being irrational and she is. She shivers from the cold damp air coming in through the broken window. "May I have a blanket?"

"Oh, of course." Gabrielle takes a blanket off Josie's bed and wraps it around her. "Are you sure you want to wait for another room?"

"Yes, I'm absolutely sure," Josie says, quietly.

Gabrielle then brings Josie into the bathroom. She gathers several towels and starts to clean Josie's wounds. She pulls out a new pack of gauze and throws the other saturated one away. She applies a new pressure bandage over Josie's head wound, wrapping it around Josie's forehead. Her appearance in another setting could confuse her for a soldier injured in battle.

While Gabrielle works, a voice comes into the room via intercom. "Gabrielle, room 425 is open, but it's a private one."

With the words, "private room" and the number "425," Josie's heart surges with gratitude. She wouldn't have to room with Sandra anymore nor would she have to move to the dreaded room numbered 444.

"That's fine. We don't have a choice, and privacy is probably what she needs right now," Gabrielle calls back. "Did anyone notify the ER and the on-call psychiatrist?"

"Yeah, we did," the voice says, then muffles out.

Gabrielle helps Josie into the wheelchair. She quickly gathers the few belongings Josie had stowed in the room. In one efficient trip, she moves Josie to her new patient room down the hall.

Upon arrival, her new room looks similar to the old one—same plain blue gray walls, same sparse fixtures. The dimensions though were smaller and it contained just one bed. She hears a noise outside of her room as Gabrielle is helping her into bed.

Another new voice calls in from outside the door. "Hey, I brought you the suture cart."

"Benjamin, my man, thanks for bringing it up so promptly," Gabrielle calls back to him.

Benjamin peeks in the room. "No problem, Bell. I'll just leave it right outside the door here. Let me know when you're done and I'll come back and get it."

"Sure thing," she says.

After Josie's belongings are put away, she hears more noise outside of her room. There is a clanking din from the clamor of medical instruments, the rummaging sound of metal and glass, and drawers opening and closing.

Gabrielle is at the bedside sink, wringing out a washcloth. "You have some dry blood crusted around your eyes. Let's wash that off before your eyes become stuck together permanently." Gabrielle smiles wide and reassuringly. Josie notes Gabrielle has a gold tooth on the top right, thus adding to her vibrant character. Gabrielle brings the washcloth over to her. "Close your eyes so I can work the blood off of your lids. I promise to be gentle."

Josie closes her eyes per Gabrielle's instruction. She touches Josie's lids gently with the warm wet cloth. As Gabrielle works, Josie hears a set of heavy footsteps coming into her room. They stop at the side of her bed.

"Hello, I take it this is the patient," a male voice says. Josie takes in its familiarity, noting the voice is deep as a radio newscaster's.

"Yes, sir, this is Mrs. Reilly," Gabrielle says. "Josie, this is Dr. Chase."

"Hi," she says, not interested in saying more, she's exhausted.

"He's the ER doctor and he's come to suture your wound," Gabrielle adds.

"Oh, okay, I guess," Josie says, although she'd rather go to sleep.

"And thank you, Dr. Chase, for coming. We do appreciate it." Gabrielle continues to wash the blood off of Josie's closed eyelids.

"It's no problem at all. It's a slow night down in the ER," he says.

The more he speaks, the more Josie is certain she knows this voice. It whispers, plays and repeats in her mind, shifting her emotions from apathy to relief, from sorrow to joy. She hears liquid being poured into a metal bowl.

"You can open your eyes now," Gabrielle says, "I'm all done."

Josie, slow to open her eyes, afraid of what and who she will see. Once open, everything appears hazy. However, as the doctor's face comes into focus, her eyes grow wide. Out of the blue, Josie breaks into a fit of coughing making her throbbing head pain worse.

"Here, have a drink of water." Gabrielle hands her a Styrofoam cup of water.

Josie drinks it up. Her heart is leaping and skipping beats, punctuating the surprise now evident in her eyes. *You know him,* a voice bellows inside of her head. She isn't sure if it's her own voice or another menacing spirit.

You know him, the voice in her head speaks again.

"Oh, my." She's unable to say anything else. It is him, only cleaner cut than the last time she saw him at the store. His hair is combed, yet his sideburns are still present and in her opinion, they remain too long for his face. He is wearing a white physician's lab coat over a dark blue golf shirt.

"Are you all right, Mrs. Reilly?" Dr. Chase asks and smiles. "You are entertaining," he says under his breath.

Josie hears him and grows more puzzled. In the meantime, Gabrielle has left her bedside and is too busy washing her hands to notice. Unable to produce a single word, Josie's inner voice begins to churn through a multitude of questions. *He is here by my bed? How did he get here? Did he follow me? Should I be scared? Why do I feel as though I miss him? Who is he?*

"She's looking a bit pale," he says to Gabrielle who is over by the room's sink. "Have you checked her pressure lately?"

"Not since she fell and it was fine then." Gabrielle shrugs. She dries her hands with a paper towel and approaches the bed. She touches Josie's cheek. "Hmm, she does feel a little cool and clammy to me now."

"Let's lower the head of her bed and check her pressure again," he says, pulling up a chair to the metal stand by the side of the bed.

Gabrielle lowers the head of Josie's bed down to almost flat. She takes the blood pressure cuff and wraps it around Josie's right arm. Josie watches Dr. Chase draw-up the numbing agent into a syringe while Gabrielle pumps the cuff tight around her arm. Releasing the valve slowly, Gabrielle watches the numbers on the pressure dial fall, the squeezing pressure around Josie's arm relents. Gabrielle takes off the cuff.

"Her pressure's okay, a little low, 92 over 70." Gabrielle holds Josie's wrist and takes her pulse. After a few seconds, she adds, "Her pulse is a bit fast but it's regular."

"How fast?" he asks.

"It's about 120."

"Let's keep her reclined for now and recheck her pulse and BP in about fifteen minutes—after she calms down a bit." He begins to examine her gash with an instrument and probes it with his sterile gloved fingers. At the same time, Gabrielle positions a light over Josie and shines it directly on her forehead.

Josie is noticeably silent; preoccupied with her search for why he triggers these emotions in her.

"Mrs. Reilly," he says, "you are allowed to speak. My work doesn't prohibit you from talking."

She grunts out an okay, consumed by the mystery of him.

"I'm going to numb up the gash on your head now, it will sting for a few seconds and then you shouldn't feel a thing."

She winces from the initial piercing of the needle into her forehead. It quickly goes away as the medication sinks in. "Please ... call me ... Josie." Each word comes out like they are the first words she's has ever spoken in the English language. Why can't she pull herself together?

"It appears that ice ball really nailed you," he says, picking up the needle and suture thread.

Josie doesn't reply. Every time he speaks, her memory comes alive, as if paging through segments of audio and video for the piece that matches the familiarity of his voice.

After a minute or two Gabrielle leaves, stating she needs to check on her other patients but will return. When she exits, there is an uncomfortable silence in the room. Josie keeps her eyes closed and tries desperately to think of other things. But as he sews, her mind's engine revs. *Why is he here? What other bizarre coincidences are coming my way? How will I ever show my face again? How will I explain it to other people when they ask me how I got hurt?*

"Hmm," Dr. Chase breaks the silence, pausing his suturing to examine her wound again.

"Maybe you should consult plastics?" she says. *Please do not leave an obvious mark.*

"The wound's jagged but definitely within my sphere of competence. Do you doubt my ability?" he asks.

"Well, a woman's face is all she's got—please don't screw mine up." Her acid tone surprises even her. She has a desire to push him away and pull him in, all at the same time.

"Oh, and by the way, did you fix your cell phone?" he asks.

She chokes on her breath. *He remembers me?* "Yes ... it's all back together. So, you, um ... remember me?" She spits it out in disconnected phrases, ashamed to admit she's the same hysterical woman he met at the store.

"How could I forget? How could anyone? You made quite a scene."

"So ... that was you?" She doesn't know what else to say.

"Yes, I think we covered that," he says.

She tries to sink deeper into the bed, embarrassed. "I checked out not long afterwards."

"I know, I saw you." He looks down at her wound, continuing to sew. The room is dim except for the procedure light focusing on her wound. The only sound is the tug of suture line through the layers of her skin.

"You were watching me?" *Why?*

"You're making me sound like a stalker. I was watching to make sure you were all right. You were distraught. It seemed like the responsible thing for me to do."

"I guess ... but I wasn't all right. After all, I'm here." Josie's face flushes from humiliation. "How come I didn't see you?"

"I don't know. Maybe you didn't want to see me?"

The overwhelming and strange sensation she felt at the market comes over her again. She doesn't know him but there's a sense they've had a common connection in the past. A past so distant to her that she can't determine the time or the place their meeting may have occurred. Out of nowhere, he appears at Wilson's when she's in a personal crisis and now here he is again, in the hospital when she's in another personal crisis. She wants to believe he's an arrogant jerk, to resist him, but he isn't a jerk. There's a closeness and trust compelling her toward him. To her, it is just plain unexplainable and ... weird.

"Do I know you ... from somewhere other than the grocery store?" She avoids direct eye contact with him in order to keep her emotions in check.

"I thought for sure *you* could come up with a better pick-up line." He smirks at her.

"Uh, I'm married, thank you very much," she says, quick to remind him—and herself—of her marital status. "I used to work in the ER here. I thought perhaps we might've worked together."

"Doubt it. I started about a month ago." He resumes suturing her wound.

"Oh."

It is quiet again for a few more seconds. "I just thought ... I might've met you before," she adds.

He abruptly stops and turns away. She decides it is safe to look and see what he is doing. He takes a gauze pad and wrap from the stand. As he turns back, their eyes unintentionally meet—she notices they are an interesting shade of gray, like tarnished silver or pewter. The longer their eyes meet, the more her heart pounds.

Heat from her jittery nerves rises up her neck and turns her face flush again. *What the hell is wrong with me?*

He gives her a brief smile as he finishes bandaging her wound. "You need to get some rest, Josie." He looks at his watch.

"Are you all done?"

"Yep."

"What about my pulse?"

"It's fine now."

"How do you know?"

"Once again, you doubt my skill. Check it yourself. It's 88 beats per minute and regular." He takes off his sterile gloves with a snap and throws them into the trash. He gives her one more glance with a twisted half-smile walks out of her room.

She checks her own pulse. It is 88 and perfect.

CHAPTER 37

Her fingers glide over the bandage covering her wound, careful not to aggravate or press too hard on it. She recalls the chaos of the night before. Gently, she removes the caked and crusted blood from above and below the gauze wrap with a damp wash cloth. She can't shower as the sutures could come apart if they were to get saturated. She washes the rest of her face by dabbing the damp cloth on her skin then takes a long look at herself in the mirror. *This wound is not going to heal anytime soon,* she thinks and wonders what it looks like now under its covering. Yet, despite her curiosity, she leaves the bandage alone, remembering Gabrielle's instructions that she gave her at the end of her night shift. Josie had to keep it on until Gabrielle returned the next night.

After, she dresses in a clean pair of jeans and a fleece pullover. She's certainly not at her best but at least she's presentable in case she runs into Dr. Chase. Their middle-of-the-night encounter was nothing but a strange coincidence. Yet, in an odd way, she would like to see him again. She wonders why she cares and knows that she shouldn't. It is against the rules—relationships with doctor and patient are to be kept strictly professional. And it goes against everything she believes in—her solemn commitment to her marriage and family. Furthermore, there isn't a reason for him to come to the psychiatric unit unless, of course, there was another emergency—like an overdose or a suicide attempt—an unlikely scenario given all the precautions the psychiatric staff took to protect patients from their worst enemies—themselves.

The schedule on her door indicates breakfast starts at eight in the unit cafeteria. Meals, to her dismay, are communal. The morning nurse's words play over in her head. *Mental illness is isolating enough— it's a good opportunity for you to be social in a safe environment.* Even so, Josie arrives at the cafeteria and selects a vacant table. She isn't up to meeting the strangers around her, and it was best to stay away from Sandra given what happened during the night.

She gathers a plateful from the buffet—toast, pancakes, eggs and a blueberry muffin along with a big cup of decaffeinated coffee with cream. She didn't have orders to allow her to have caffeine yet. Her first mission of the day was to get an order from her doctor to allow her to have caffeine and her second mission—obtain off-unit privileges. All this restriction made her feel like a captive and in truth, she was.

Her psychiatrist arrives to the cafeteria just as she tosses her leftovers into the trash. He approaches her with a chart in his hands and a pen over his ear.

"Good morning, Josie, I'm Dr. Shapiro." He holds out his hand to shake hands with her. He is average in height but imposing in an educated way. He is dressed in a crisp pair of khaki pants and a basic blue-striped, buttoned-down dress shirt.

"Good morning," Josie says and shakes his hand—unsure if the morning is truly good or not. *Funny,* she thinks, *he doesn't look I though a psychiatrist would, except maybe for his round-lensed glasses.* A glint of light catches her eye. It reflects off the gold Star of David that rests on the hollow of his neck. *Just my luck, he's Jewish.* Of course, she has nothing against Jews or their faith. She merely realizes it will be tough for him to reconcile her encounters with Saint Therese and the Virgin Mary.

"I'd like for us to get to know each other this morning. There's a room down the hall where we can talk. Follow me," he says.

She nods but she knows some things will be better kept to herself.

They walk down a long corridor, passing patients rooms and the unit's community meeting room. They round a corner and stop at the first door on the left. He unlocks it with a key. They enter a private office and it is just as uninteresting as her patient room. The room contains a couch, a matching recliner and a desk and chair. There are no visible restraints, nothing too intimidating that might scare off an especially paranoid patient. A window faces out the room toward hall, where passersby are able to see in. It is evident that safety on the unit always takes priority over privacy.

"Have a seat," he says.

Josie nods and moves to the couch, assuming that's where he wants her to sit. She notices his gray thinning hair, imagining he has heard many unusual stories over the years. Perhaps she is wrong about him about not believing her. Maybe her story will not be so out of the ordinary.

She sits down. The comfortable cushions exacerbate her fatigue, given her lack of sleep. The doctor walks over to the room's window and pulls down the blinds. She feels better having seclusion, however marginal. He takes a seat in the recliner across from her.

"How was your breakfast?" he asks.

"It was great. I'm stuffed." Josie realizes for the first time in a long time she has eaten a full meal.

"Did you get to meet or talk with any of the other patients?"

"No." She isn't there to make friends. "Well, except for Sandra. She was my roommate until the window in our room broke."

"I'm so sorry that happened to you. It's too bad you started your admission that way. How are you feeling now?" He scans her appearance.

"I'm a bit worn out but that's all." She touches her bandage.

"Your internist will be in to check on you later this morning. I prefer that your primary care doctor handles anything related to your injury."

She nods. "I'm really okay—he doesn't need to come see me." One less doctor in her life is fine with her.

"I think it would be best, just to be safe. You do look tired. Feel free to lie down while we chat. Can I get you a blanket?"

"No, thank you. I prefer to stay sitting." She straightens-up her posture. "Listen, if you don't mind, I'd like to get on with it." Their conversation is notably strained from the few words they exchange. To her, it is a contrived give and take. She must do this in order to go home.

"Then let's get started. I promise to keep this first session brief so you can get some rest."

"First session?" *First? They'll be more?*

"Yes, we'll be meeting every day while you're here."

"Why?" *Every day? How many?*

"Well, to talk of course, about your ... situation." He pushes his glasses up higher on his nose. He takes the pen from behind his ear and opens her chart.

"I guess I understand, sort of ... sorry, I'm not usually this disagreeable."

"I can tell you're exhausted. If it would help, I could leave an order with your nurse allowing you to rest for today instead of attending group. Would you like me to do that?"

"Yes, please ... did you say *group?*" Her question reveals more irritation because every time he speaks, he reveals a distasteful, obligatory activity for her to do.

"Yes, it's expected that you attend at least two group sessions a day, one morning and one afternoon plus one occupational therapy class. It's all part of your treatment." He hands her a piece of muted yellow paper which lists out the schedule of group sessions for the week, the same one that is posted on the door to her patient room.

Good grief. She did not want to attend any sort of session with others.

"I think you'll find a lot of support in group, it's all part of the process."

She cocks her head to the right, knowing this was his way of telling her she didn't have a choice. They look at each other briefly and say nothing. She is weary and beaten down, reluctant with his plan for her "recovery." Her eyes shift away from him, toward the blue carpet below her feet. It is worn as if someone paced a path from the door to the couch and back.

"What are you thinking? Do you have a question?"

"I'm wondering why a lot of people are here. They don't seem to be all that sick, I mean some do, outwardly, but most are actually ... ," she stops to find an appropriate word.

"Normal?" He laughs.

"Yes, I guess so." She's embarrassed by her prejudiced view of the mentally ill. At breakfast, she observed that few patients fit the image of the stereotypical psychiatric patient, or at least the image she formed in her mind. The ward was nothing like what she saw in the movies of the old institutions with their white walls and barred windows filled with patients muttering out loud to no one or catatonically staring out into space. Most here appeared stable and ordinary. It also helped that everyone, including the staff, wore street clothes. The only thing that set the staff apart from the patients was their ID badge and maybe a stethoscope in their pocket or around their neck. And, she was one of them now. It was absurd to pretend she wasn't.

"Of course they are, and my saying so in no way is meant to minimize what they're going through. The problems they face are serious but they're people like you and me." He scratches the top his head to think. "Now, let's see. Tell me what happened and why *you* agreed to be hospitalized?"

She touches her silver cross on her neck and prepares to keep the part about her exorcism to herself. "Isn't it in my chart?"

"Yes it is, but I'd like to hear it from you ... in your words." He holds out his hands as if to say, *come out with it.*

"I did not want to be admitted, if you want to know the truth."

"No one ever does."

She grows more agitated. Why does she need to repeat her story again and again? Doing so isn't going to help her get better any faster. Above all, she wants to go home to her children. "Look, Dr. Shapiro, I don't like talking about it and I'm tired. Can't you just give me some medicine? It'll make my husband happy and then he'll let me come home."

"Are you telling me you're here because of your husband?"

"Well, yes ... and no. I don't want to talk about it."

His brow furrows. He prods again. "I wish it were as simple as giving you a pill and sending you on your way but it's not. Let me rephrase, tell me what you think you're being treating for?"

"I think I'm being treated for depression and anxiety." Although, this information she provides him with gives little insight into her dilemma. The depression and anxiety are already documented in her chart.

"Okay, good," he nods. "That's correct. Is that all?"

Perhaps I should dilute the truth or this guy might never let me go home. "You think I have a psychosis, don't you?" It comes out from her mouth as an accusation.

"Based on what you reported to Susan, you do appear to be having some symptoms that are indicative of a psychosis. It's nothing to be ashamed of. It can happen to anyone, Josie." His voice is deliberate and kind in attempt to smooth things over with her.

"I know it can happen to other people but *it's not* happening to me. I think I can tell the difference between fiction and reality." Her tone takes on an increasing edge of hostility. Uncertain why she is angry with him, she channels it by taking the piece of paper with the group schedule on it and scrunches it into a ball. She throws the crumpled ball of paper into the basket. She realizes he is only here because he is the doctor assigned to her case—he had the unfortunate luck of being on call.

However, Dr. Shapiro isn't the least bit intimidated by her. He ignores her rebellion and proceeds. "Josie, it doesn't matter what we call it. If you don't like the term psychosis, we don't have to call it that, so long as you understand what we need to do here."

"All I know is that I need to shut off the noise and static in my brain. I can't focus any more. I can't remember details. I can't function and it's making it hard for me to take care of my kids." She closes her eyes and rubs her forehead with the tips of her fingers.

"Then there's something we can agree on. I can help you with that."

While she can tell he is trying with her, she isn't ready to give in. "Dr. Shapiro, may I ask *you* something now?"

"Sure, go ahead."

"Do you believe in God?"

"Well, that's a loaded question. Why do you ask?"

"If we can't see God but we believe He exists, then why is it so hard to believe people like me exist with the ability to communicate with the dead?"

"That's quite a leap, Josie, believing in God and believing people can communicate with the dead are separate ideas entirely."

Dr. Shapiro wears the Star of David only to please his wife. Like a radio blast to her right ear, a male voice randomly speaks to her in her head.

She reaches and touches her ear, *Geez ... who was that?*

He's an agnostic. The voice speaks again in her thoughts.

"So, you don't believe in God?" she asks.

"That's not what I said. Communicating with the dead and believing in God are two different things. Why does this matter to you?"

"How can you help me if *you* question the existence of God? You obviously have doubts." Someone is inciting her to provoke him, she doesn't know who or why. Maybe that's why she's becoming angry. Maybe, she thinks, there's some spirit entity here egging her on.

"I didn't say ... what ... how did...?" He stammers, frustrated by her obstinate behavior.

"Actually, I think it's rather odd you're practicing at a Catholic hospital," she says, lifting her brows. In her mind, she screams at the provoker...the one who is putting these thoughts in her head. *No! Don't let them in. Not here. Not now.*

"Look, Josie, what I believe or don't believe isn't relevant to *your* treatment. I assure you that your illness is entirely physiologic and can be treated with tangible scientific methods."

"So, what you're telling me is that tangible therapies, like medication and counseling, will make this all go away?" She gestures with her hands, waving them like a magic wands.

"Yes," he says, firmly.

"And prayer won't?"

"I'm here to treat you with methods that are scientifically proven. However, you're free to pray, to worship or even to speak with the hospital's chaplain. I can have the nurse ask him to come see you."

"That won't be necessary." *I've already talked to one priest and look where it got me.*

"Is there something else you want to talk about?" he asks.

"I guess that's the point, isn't it?" she asks, looking back at him.

"How so, what do you mean?"

"We don't have to agree on the existential. I'm free to choose what's going to work for me."

"Yes, of course. If you feel that prayer will help you in your recovery, then please use it. However, as your doctor I have a responsibility to advise you in the best way I know and that's with medication and counseling. It's that simple." He regains his composure and takes on a steady, professional exterior, outwardly appearing that she hasn't ruffled him in the least.

She closes her eyes again, thinking about this potential unseen entity. *I rid myself of this hatred. In the name of Jesus, I command you to leave.*

Suddenly, all her anger vanishes. She sees that Dr. Shapiro truly wants to help her. He may or may not believe in God and what does it matter? They both agree the noise and distraction in her head needs to stop. It makes no sense for her to be contrary with him. She's is free to believe in God and the power of prayer as much as she wants. He is not obstructing her from her belief system. And although it may be okay to challenge Dr. Shapiro, she isn't about to challenge God. God gave her the gift of modern medicine and she intends to use it.

CHAPTER 38

Until we die, anything and everything can happen.
—Italian Proverb

After her session with Dr. Shapiro, Josie returns to her room, satisfied she got what she wanted ... for the time being. He wrote an order allowing her to drink regular coffee and another allowing her to leave the unit for outdoor walks and exercise, provided she is accompanied by a responsible adult— either hospital staff or an adult family member. It is a minor victory but these bonus privileges make her happy as if she's won a major coup for "Team Josie."

She's sitting on her bed reading *People* magazine when someone knocks at her door.

"Josie?" Nora calls in to her from the doorway.

Josie sits forward and peeks her head around the corner toward the door. "Come on in.'

Nora enters. Her hair is long again and her face pale despite her exposure to Arizona sunshine, a byproduct of her continued faithful use of sunscreen.

"What happened to your head?" Nora asks, embracing her.

"Oh," her hand goes up to the bandage. "I got hit with a hail ball."

"How?" Nora steps back to look at her face.

"It's a long story, I'll tell you some other time. Who has the kids?" she asks.

"Michael is at school and Anna and Jacob are home with Declan."

"That's right. It's Monday isn't it?" Josie kept losing track of the days of the week, life was such a blur. "Declan? Why isn't he at work?"

"He stayed home to assess the damage from the storm last night."

"Damage?" She didn't realize the storm that hit her hospital window also hit her home as well.

"Yeah, you know ... the hail storm, the same one that apparently pegged you in the head."

"What? It was that bad?" She hadn't watched the news or read a paper this morning.

"It was bad." Nora sits down beside her on the bed. "The news said the storm damaged homes and property throughout the entire county. Apparently, there was hail as large as baseballs."

"I know." Josie rubs her head. "How's our house?"

"Declan thinks there's a good chance you guys will need a new roof and new siding."

"A new roof?" Josie dreaded her next conversation with Declan, more than she already did. This would put him in an even fouler mood but it also confirmed something she already knew—he wouldn't be calling her anytime soon.

The two sisters sat for a time, paging through the magazines that Nora brought from home. They discussed their father's declining mental status, how he was unable to carry on conversations anymore that weren't a word salad—a stream of nonsensical and disconnected speech. Sadly, he barely recognized Nora and their brother Tony when they came to visit him. He couldn't talk on the phone with Josie either so her only way to connect with to him was through Nora's reports. Despite their focus on their father, in the back of Josie's mind, she wondered if Nora would believe her tale if she were to tell her everything.

"Hey, before I head out, is there anything special you need me to watch for or do for the kids while you're here?" Nora asks.

"Not really," Josie thinks for a moment. "Actually ... ," then out Josie's mouth came every minute detail of the kids' routine and habits as if she had sprung a release valve. She covered everything from Jacob being fussy if he doesn't get his warm milk first thing in the morning to Anna having a slice of bread and butter at night before bed. She breathed in to catch her breath. "Keep in mind, Michael's a picky eater, so he'll want the same thing all the time but don't get upset, this is normal for him. Just be sure he takes his vitamins. Actually, be sure ..."

"Will you relax? I've got it," Nora says.

"Are you sure? I could write it all down for you? I'll have to borrow a pen from the nurse's station. They won't let me keep pens or pencils in my room."

"Look, we'll figure things out. Just relax, okay?"

Josie nods.

"Why can't you have any pens or pencils?"

"They think I might use it as a weapon."

"A weapon?"

"Yeah ... a weapon ... against myself. You know, like I'd try to hurt myself with it."

"You wouldn't do that, would you?"

"Of course not, but they don't know that and they aren't going to take any chances, too much ... liability."

"Oh?" Nora furrows her brows. "You're kidding me, right?"

"Nope."

"Anyhow, you know I'll take care of them, I always do. I'm sure Declan can fill in the blanks if I get stuck."

"Hard to say if he will," she says, "he's pretty mad at me."

"Perhaps, but he's not mad at the kids. He'll help."

However, Declan didn't know their routine the way Josie did. He went to the office and she had primary responsibility for their children, traditional role divisions but it worked. Nevertheless, Josie was sure that Declan would bolt as soon as he could, probably leave for a business trip now that Nora had him covered. He would rather avoid their problems than face them.

"Is there anything you need me to do for you? Do you need me to bring you anything from home ... clothes, shampoo, a book?"

"No, I'm good. Well, there's one thing."

"What's that?"

"I need you to make a doctor's appointment for Michael."

"How come?"

"I want his peanut allergy rechecked. If they ask when you make the appointment, tell them we're coming in for that.."

"When?"

"The week after next. I'll be home by then and able to go with him."

"I'll see what I can do. Hopefully, they'll have something available."

"The number for his allergist is posted on our refrigerator. Call the number for Dr. Neal."

"Okay, got it."

"Oh, and one more thing. Don't tell Declan."

"Why?" Nora says, befuddled. "Why can't Declan know?"

"Nora, if I tell you, you've got to keep it between you and me."

She drew in a deep breath. "Do I want to know?"

"When they recheck Michael for his peanut allergy, I know his allergy will be gone." Josie pauses and watches Nora's face.

"How is that possible? I thought they told you Michael wouldn't outgrow his allergy. That he had it for life?"

"Yeah, I know but I'll prove them wrong. And I'll prove to you and Declan that I'm not crazy. Michael's tests will be negative."

"How can you be so sure?" Nora's looks at her skeptically.

"Faith."

"I don't know if I can do this for you."

"You're acting like you're my accomplice in a crime. All I'm asking you to do is to make an appointment. It's that simple."

"I'll think about it." Nora presses her lips together.

"Oh, forget it. I'll make the appointment myself."

"No, I'll do it but you're going to get me in trouble with Declan."

"Why would he care if I was taking Michael in for a check-up? For all he knows, I've had the appointment for months. He doesn't do doctor's appointments with the kids."

Nora grumbles. "Fine."

"All I need is this one little favor, okay? Do it for me, your sis." Josie is more than aware that Nora doesn't have to negotiate with her but by pulling the "sis" card she knew Nora would give in.

"All right." Nora sighs.

Ah, success. Josie smiles. If Michael's cured, then no one can doubt her story ... not even Declan.

CHAPTER 39

"Josie, it's time for dinner."

She hears Susan's voice calling to her from the direction of her doorway. At first, Josie's eyes are narrow slits. They take in the light slowly then open wide.

"Hey there," Susan calls again and walks into the room. She stands by Josie's bed. "Did you have a have a good rest? I think you've been asleep since I started my shift at three."

"Wow," she whispers. When she sees her surroundings, her mind hadn't prepared her to wake in a hospital room. Habit had her waking-up in her own bedroom at home. But when she arouses to her new environment, everything is a tangled jungle. Nothing is what her mind has trained her to expect. For the first twenty seconds or so, she is lost.

"You better get to the dining room before they stop serving dinner. I let you sleep as long as I could," Susan says. "I should have warned you about the meds, sometimes they can make people confused when waking up. You were in a pretty deep sleep. And coincidentally, it's time for your second dose." Susan then passes Josie a few pills.

"What are these? Are they different?" Josie examines her pills in the medicine cup.

"They're the same pills you took earlier plus one new one. The first two are for your depression and to quiet the noise in your head. The new blue one is to increase their potency. It will make the first two work faster."

"Do you think they will silence the invisible voices I hear?"

"That's the goal. And once you adjust, they won't make you so groggy after sleep. Your body just needs time to get stabilized."

"Oh." She trusts Susan is right. She swallows the pills with a drink of water.

Susan then walks with her to the unit cafeteria and finds her a seat next to a window overlooking the hospital parking lot. It isn't much of a view but it's the best seat left in the room.

A stout woman wearing a black hairnet and white apron delivers a meal tray to Josie at her table. Tonight's meal is meatloaf and gravy, a bun with butter and fruit cup—the syrupy kind with mushy grapes and maraschino cherries. Josie picks at it and thinks it's too bad they didn't serve alcohol. She craves a glass of wine.

On the upside, she feels that her medications are already working, even if the new one couldn't have taken effect yet. Her thoughts were becoming more focused. She hadn't heard voices since her morning encounter with Dr. Shapiro. *Who knew?* She thinks. *Those tiny pills must crack a punch, hard enough to kick those menaces out of my head.* The "receivers" she once felt on top of her head, waving around like invisible antennae, felt as if they were retracting and shutting down. She wonders if the relief will last because, for once in her life, her mind feels free of its burdens. Ironically though, her body's trapped on the psych ward.

Outside the cafeteria windows, the sun is starting to set. The sky is mostly clear except for a few billowy clouds. She is anxious to get off the unit and obtain some fresh air. She finishes what she intends to eat, drinks her carton of skim milk and gets up from the table to dispose of the tray. She notices several patients leaving the cafeteria for the unit's community living room at the end of the hall. Instead of following them, she sets out to find someone, anyone at all, to take her outside and decides to approach Susan first. She finds her by the nurse's station.

"What's up, Josie? Did you get enough to eat?" Susan's asks.

"Yeah, it was fine. Hey, I know you're pretty busy but is there any chance you can take me for a walk? Or do you know anyone on staff who can?"

"Oh, I'm really sorry because I do think a walk would do you some good. It's just time for six o'clock meds so I can't take you but I'll check around and see if I find another staff member who can take you," she says, apologetically.

Josie understands. If Susan had the time, she would've taken her. She was that kind of nurse—always positive, always thinking of her patients. And Josie isn't sure she would want to go with someone other than Susan. If she waits until Susan could go, it would be dark which would be too much to ask of her. The hospital is in a decent neighborhood but after dark, it could get dicey.

Out of boredom, Josie wanders into the community living room. Several patients are seated on a large sectional couch in front of the over-sized TV screen. Across the room is an exit door. Maybe, she thinks, she could leave on her own? She could take a quick walk where no one will miss her and come right back. With her luck though, she'll set off some alarm by going through it. Then again, she's on the fifth floor. It's doubtful the door leads anywhere but to a fire escape. Probably not a risk she should be taking right now.

She approaches the exit door anyway and notices a small sign, "Smoking Terrace." Technically speaking, St. Catherine's was a non-smoking hospital. Apparently, one exception to this rule was for the mentally ill. She decides to try the door and pushes the lever down. It lets out a loud creak when she opens it.

"Josie, I didn't know you were a smoker," a voice comes from behind her.

She startles and turns around as if caught doing something wrong. It's him standing in front of her—the flawless Dr. Chase with his hideous sideburns, worn jeans and another concert t-shirt. This one was U2. *At least*, she thinks, *he has good taste in bands.*

"No, I'm not a smoker," she says.

"Then where are you going?" he asks.

"Not that's it any of your business but I want to go outside. I need some air."

"Air saturated with nicotine vapor?" he scoffs.

She ignores him and returns to the door to open it further. However, as she opens it the rest of the way, a layer of gray, smoky fog floats toward her face. She coughs.

"Don't say I didn't warn you," he says, with a smart grin.

She shuts the terrace door and gives up. "What are you doing here anyway?" She crosses her arms, frustrated by her ill-conceived attempt for a brief escape and his interruption. "Hey, Bono called, he wants his t-shirt back."

"What's wrong with U2?"

"Nothing. You docs get all the breaks—wear whatever you want to work. Nurses would never get away with that."

"I don't wear t-shirts to work."

"Then, you hang around the psych ward in your free time?"

"I'm here to check on my handiwork. I can't do that when I'm seeing new patients in the ER."

"Oh, you're just one of those thorough docs, huh?"

He shakes his head. "Whatever. Do you mind if I have a look at your wound?"

"Right here, in the middle of the living room?" She didn't know why she was being so rude to him, it seemed to come naturally.

"We can go to your room if you want privacy."

Creepy. "No, you can check it here. Go ahead."

She places her hands on her hips and leans her head forward. He carefully begins to remove the bandage covering her forehead.

"Shouldn't you be wearing gloves?"

He ignores her and continues to peel the bandage off one piece at a time. "Hmm, just as I thought."

"What? What's wrong? Did it get infected? I knew you didn't know what you were doing."

"No, actually ... it's healed."

"Healed? It can't be. You mean—it's healing." *It can't possibly be healed!* It was far too raw and jagged.

"Look for yourself." He points her toward a crooked mirror on the wall.

Josie walks over to the slanted mirror. The suture threads still punctuate the length of the wound—but the wound no longer exists. There's no scar, no blood and no tissue damage. "How can this be? How did you do—"

"Do what?"

"There's no wound!"

"Shhh, keep it down. I still need to take out those sutures for you."

"But there no scar," she snarls, "there's nothing but thread sewn into skin."

"What can I say?" he shrugs. "I'm pretty good at my job."

"No, you're not that good. What's going on?"

"Just come with me," he says and takes her by the hand, not hard but firm and leads her into the hall. His hand is warm and oddly, she wants to let him hold it. However, she pulls it back.

He walks on and she follows. They stop in front the office door where she had her earlier meeting with Dr. Shapiro.

"Let's get out of here," he says.

"What's going on? I don't get it, I had a major injury and now it's gone. I'm not going anywhere with you until you tell me how you did this."

"I don't know how I did it. It's just something I'm able to do."

"Well, I can't just leave. I don't even know your first name." She finds herself wanting to go with him. What was she doing? Who was he? And why does she feel overwhelming joy whenever he is near? She pushes the emotion down, disallowing any chance for it to rise up and express itself outwardly.

"Andrew," he says.

"Andrew?" she says, confused, as she's already forgotten her earlier question.

"Yes, that's my name, Andrew Chase."

"Oh," she says, blankly.

"Let's go where I can explain. Just don't make a scene."

"You're scaring me," she whispers in a firm tone. "Just what is it that you want from me?"

"Look, I'm not going to hurt you. God knows, I would never do that ... and now that I've found you–"

"Found me?" Josie hadn't set eyes on him before this week. *He was looking for me? Why?*

"I won't touch you ... I promise." His eyes are intent on hers.

"I demand you tell me where you're taking me." She knew she shouldn't go anywhere with him only there was no stopping her, it was as if she was under a spell.

"Anywhere you want," and crosses his heart in a promise "except home."

CHAPTER 40

To consider persons and events and situations only in the light of
their effect upon myself is to live on the doorstep of hell.
—Thomas Merton

efore they leave, Andrew removes her sutures at the nurse's station. The staff hovers around them as if enchanted by his presence. They gush over his witty jokes and boyish charm while he plucks each suture out of Josie's forehead. Susan, Josie thinks, would relinquish her firstborn if he asked her as she becomes overly grateful when Andrew offers to accompany Josie on her desired "walk." She even offers to tag along to assist him, as if he needs it.

Josie finds this most interesting. Susan had been so definite about being unable to take her. Stranger yet, besides Susan's behavior, is that no one notices Josie's wound is completely gone nor the fact she hasn't any residual scaring. The staff appears oblivious to Josie while in his presence. She wonders, *What patient with a laceration like mine would heal in a day?* Andrew's persuasive charm, charisma or some other factor is purposefully distracting the others from viewing the inexplicable disappearance of her wound.

When he finishes, they breeze out of the psychiatry ward with nary a word of opposition and an 8 p.m. curfew. He takes Josie through an apparent short-cut, by way of back halls and an exit stairway. They end up in the rear of the main lobby. As she walks through the lobby with him, they see other staff and visitors. She becomes nervous. Nevertheless, he handles every encounter with amazing ease. While he has worked at the hospital for only a month, everyone seems to know this fascinating Dr. Chase and fortunately no one seems to know her.

Once outside, he asks, "Where to?"

"How about Clancy's?"

"A dive bar? Hmm, I don't think alcohol is a sensible choice."

"Ah, yes, you're the wise physician, I had forgotten. I suppose I'm being reckless enough by leaving the hospital with you."

"If you don't behave, I'll be forced to take you back."

"No, I assure you, I'll behave." Her determination to steal away from the hospital for a brief mental break outweighed any need for alcohol.

They proceed down a long sidewalk toward the arboretum near the hospital. The springtime air is crisp and invigorating, far better than the sterile air of the psychiatry unit. The temperature is warm and the sun is half-set. The sidewalk is clear of leftover snow and ice from winter. The leaves are budding on a canopy of maple tree branches along their path. They walk parallel and arms-width from each other, maintaining a safe personal space as they tread over remnants of leaves left from the previous fall.

If anyone sees us, she comforts herself, *they might not think we are together. Yeah right, who am I kidding?* Her thoughts whirl like a dervish. *What am I doing here with him, this other man?* Why does he attract her curiosity? Is it the familiarity of his voice? She feels as though they have a past but she doesn't remember being there. Or, is it the excitement he brings to her otherwise pedestrian existence? Is she desperate for a cheap thrill?

She hopes she isn't this easy—or ungrateful. Her life is blessed. She has everything she ever wanted. So, why is she here? Yet, the more she grapples with her choice, this choice to walk with him, the more anxious she becomes. Adrenaline surges in her body, her conscience screams, *Go back!* It is taking all she has to maintain a calm and steady exterior. Her palms sweat. She wipes them incon-spicuously on her pant legs and then clutches the tissues she stashed in her pockets. If she listens close enough, she can hear her heart pounding over the tranquility of the evening air.

When they reach the far south corner of the hospital grounds at the arboretum's entry, he stops. Behind him is a group of tall birch trees. What remains of the setting sun illuminates through the branches and forms an outline around his body. It casts an incan-descent glow about his face. It becomes hard for her to see his expression because in looking at him, it's as if she were looking into a bright light. It stings her squinting eyes although the sun itself is disappearing beneath the horizon line. His gray eyes become radiant silver and above his head hovers an emblazoned aura of white. Bewildered, she looks away and rubs her eyes. Certain her imagina-tion playing tricks on her, she begins to laugh. *It must be my medica-tion,* she thinks.

"What's so funny?" he asks.

"You standing there," she says, facing him again. Puzzled, she notices his appearance had returned to normal. "Um ... the sun is ... well ... it was giving you a sort of halo."

"And what's so funny about that?" He scrunches his brows, looking cross but humored.

"You with a halo—you hardly seem the holy type."

"And you are?"

"I never said I was but something tells me I'm closer to holiness than you." Inside, she worries. Is her ability to see auras returning? She had hoped the medication would stifle any psychic abilities she had left.

"I guess I'm glad you find me amusing," he says, tips his head to the side and shrugs.

"For now ... let's just say, I find you perplexing."

"Perplexing? I don't think I've had a woman call that me that before. I've been called some interesting things but never perplexing."

She begins to walk again only this time he stays behind by the birches and doesn't follow. "Aren't you coming?" she asks.

He shakes his head and gives her a quirky grin as if engrossed by her presence. *Of all the peculiar things, why he is looking look at me in this way?* Her eyes meet his stare—his body sculpted, almost reverent. He waits for her to say something more, seemingly knowing she needs to make a decision. In an uncomplicated sense, apart from the guilt she feels, she is enjoying a simple walk. And, according to her chart, she's a suicide risk. Thus, she isn't permitted to go anywhere outside the hospital psych ward alone. He is her legitimate excuse, her guide for the time being and for this reason alone, she convinces herself that being with him is justifiable.

"So, you still haven't told me where we're going," he says. He places his hands in his jacket pockets, keeping them to himself as promised.

"For a walk around the block, I thought." She shrugs.

"Do you have anywhere else in mind?"

"Well, you turned me down on Clancy's, so how about Milwaukee?" Her answer is only partly in jest.

"I don't think we should wander off that far. You might get me into trouble."

"I thought you didn't mind getting into trouble."

"This is true." He nods and looks toward the street cars passing by and then back to her. "We could go for a short drive." He jingles his keys in the pocket of his jacket.

She thinks about his offer for a long minute, a drive is tempting. How did she know he wasn't planning to take her somewhere and kill her? For what she knew about him, which was virtually nothing, he could be a pathologic serial killer. And what about the fleeting brilliance about his head and body? Why was it there and where did it go?

"Seriously, trust me," he says, his words flow like satin.

"Trust you? Why should I?" *Here it is again*, she thinks, *could versus should?* She could but should she? And truly, she couldn't escape him, he was too persuasive—his voice, his smile, the way he looked at her. It was a thrill she had long forgotten, times like this no longer existed for her. She was the mother of three. Her husband, the ambitious and restrained lawyer, had discarded such rapture in her presence. The uncertainty and exhilaration Andrew suddenly brings to her life is irresistible. Her thoughts become fragmented and her body weak and conflicted, about to send her hurling to the safety of the hospital's four-walls.

"Have I lied to you before?" he asks.

"I don't think so but then again, we just met. You haven't had a chance to." She surveys the surroundings, noticing there is no one around but them. Anxious, she clings to one thought to keep her grounded—the thought that if she could be anywhere in the world at this minute, she would choose to be with her children. Perhaps he could drive her near home, drop her off somewhere close so that she could walk by or watch them play from afar. But what if Declan sees her? What if her children see her? What will she say? How will she explain? And Declan wouldn't have it—he'd take her right back to the hospital.

"Where's your car?" she asks. Momentarily, she considers taking a razor to his face to shave his unruly sideburns. Fortunately, she didn't have access to razors right now.

"Here."

"This one?" *Smooth.*

They happened to have walked directly to his car. And, while a drive sounded harmless, her mind races. She never took risks, at least none like this. It wasn't in her make-up. She never dreamt of being unfaithful to her husband, physically or emotionally, but somewhere in the course of their marriage, she became a given—a reliable "employee." She entirely forgot what it felt like to have your head get dizzy when you see that one person who makes you feel like the sole object of their desire. She was entering serious emotional violation territory. The thought of Andrew was enough to grant her a scarlet letter.

"Interesting choice of car, not one I would have pictured you in," she says, raising her brows. Given his attire, a worn leather coat and jeans, she was sure he would have driven something less slick to match but he didn't. He drove a conspicuous midnight blue convertible BMW, albeit an older one but impressive just the same.

"It's good for picking up chicks."

Josie coughs out a laugh. "So, you're shallow and a womanizer."

"I'm kidding—it was a gift from my parents when I graduated from med school. I've had it a very long time and you're right. It's downright pretentious for a guy like me to be driving this. I need to trade this in for something more ... practical, something with four-wheel drive, like a Jeep or Explorer."

She nods, knowing it isn't good for her to be so judgmental.

He pops open the passenger door when she suddenly freezes. She can't lift an arm. She can't move her legs. His magnetic presence, coupled by her desire as well as her fears, becomes instantly staggering. She knows once she gets in, she is a traitor even if she doesn't do anything at all. The damage will be done with the simple act of getting in his car. Above all, her feelings for him, be it infatuation, confusion, curiosity, or even compulsion—are regrettable. She will never be his nor would he ever be hers because there are her children. They will always and forever come first in her life, even if her marriage were to come apart.

Andrew perceives her hesitation. "We don't have to go for a ride, Josie. We can keep walking if you want?"

Strange, she thinks, *he's not pushing me to do this.* He is willing to do what she asks—if she only knew what she wanted. He touches her shoulder with his hand. She flinches and lurches away from him.

"I'm sorry, I didn't mean to ..." he stammers and drops his hand to his side.

His hand's brief touch on her shoulder cripples her into further paralysis. "If we keep walking, someone will see me, either someone I used to work with here or someone my husband knows or—"

"Or what?"

She closes her eyes for a brief moment as her mind spins through a flurry of thoughts. If she stands there with him any longer, they may become a spectacle. Other people will see them and she doesn't want to churn the hospital rumor mill or any other rumor mill for that matter. She reaches for the car door and hesitates.

"Lighten up, Josephine. We're going for a ride, that's all."

"This is no simple ride," she says and gets in.

CHAPTER 41

After he starts the car, Andrew reaches for the radio. "What sort of music do you like to listen to?" he asks.

"Oh, I don't know, you pick." She motions for him to make the choice. Music selection is the last thing on her mind.

"But you must have to have a style of music that you like?" he asks again.

She relaxes back in her seat. Her eyes look up as she thinks.

"C'mon, this isn't that difficult. Which is it? Country? Rock? Alternative?"

"Alternative rock and ... grunge," she says almost reluctantly.

"Grunge? I never would have guessed." He pulls an iPod from his glove compartment and plugs it into the car's upgraded music system. "Let me see what *grunge* I've got here." He shuffles through some songs. "Here, I found a mix you'll probably like," and he turns on a song by the Stone Temple Pilots.

They drive for a time listening to the music without conversation, winding down the long and often narrow country roads south of the city. She scans her surroundings, nothing looks familiar. Nevertheless, it doesn't to matter to her. The warmth of good feelings pulsates through her. The music, the cool breeze and the farms they pass along their way—all calm her anxious mind.

She sees why Andrew attracts her and everyone else's attention. It's clearer here than it was back at the hospital. He is the embodiment of what every female finds attractive in men—wit, intellect, effortless looks, topped off by a shadow of the unconventional. In fact, he is much like her Declan, but she could already tell he measured success differently. Andrew was far less concerned with outward appearances and what others thought of him. Declan, on the other hand, was wound tight like a spool of unopened thread. And around Andrew, she didn't have to measure her words before they came out of her mouth.

Despite all of this, a tremendous hole grows inside of her heart. She misses her children and the time in her life with Declan when it was uncomplicated and carefree, before careers and obligations. She thinks about Nora and how she's probably getting her children ready for bed. She misses hugging little Jacob and his tiny hands clutching her neck. She misses Anna's giggles and Michael's butterfly kisses on her cheek. Her heart aches for them. The love and joy her children bring to her life fill her in a way no man ever would and ever can. And yet, she's drawn to Andrew. She knows her decision to be here in this car is about to irrevocably change the course of her life as well as that of those already in it.

"Is everything all right?" he asks.

She wipes new tears from her face. "You tell me. What do you think?" Out of nowhere, she spews anger and disgust. She doesn't know why except for her own horrible guilt. And anger is safe, much safer than attraction and longing.

"What did I do?" Andrew's voice inflects an octave higher as if blindsided by the unmistakable and rapid change in her mood, clearly ignorant to her inner conflict—dedicated mother or betraying wife. He presses down on the accelerator.

She hears the engine kick over. "Are you ever going to tell me how my gash became non-existent?"

The RPMs on the dash module climb higher, the engine grows louder.

"Oh, c'mon, you must be sore?" He drives faster, careening and hugging the curves tight.

"No. Not one bit. It's like it *never* happened. By the way, this isn't the Daytona, slow down!"

He continues to speed and take the curves too fast, skidding occasionally onto the narrow shoulder and back to the pavement. "Well, maybe it didn't," he says, stridently. His expression is flat; his eyes are fixed on the road ahead.

"Please Andrew, stop! Stop all of this!" she screams.

"Me? You want *me* to stop? What about you?" he shouts over the thunderous engine vibration.

The car accelerates further, the wind rages by them and over them. The force makes her hair a tangled mess, not unlike her life. She attempts to pull it back from her eyes, but the car is going so fast, it's impossible to keep it off her face. The seatbelt tightens from the swerving of the car. She lets go of her hair and braces her body, pressing one hand against the dash and the other grips her seat. She's too small to take a major hit from an airbag if they crash. And worse, she remembers the car's age. Perhaps there is no airbag. She's certain ... she's going to die.

"You're the one shrouded in mystery," she shouts. "I'm an open book. I haven't hidden a damn thing from you. But, but you ... *you* know something and I want to know what it is!"

"You want to know? Are you sure?" He takes every bend hard, the car swerves then fish-tails. The tires squeal.

"I need to know what the *hell's* going on before I die in a wreck!"

"You should stop the swearing. It's not becoming of a lady of your stature," he says, sharply.

"Tell me or I'll jump out of this car. My blood will be on *your* hands!"

"Josie, I know who you are." His hands hold the steering wheel so hard that his knuckles are white.

"Good, now that we have that out of the way," Josie says sarcastically.

"No, I know who you are in a way that *you* don't."

"What do you mean?" If looks could kill, her eyes would have burned a hole in the side of his face. Did he really have the answer? Why did the scum of the spirit world drive her mad? Why would her house need an exorcism? Why did she encounter the Virgin Mary in her bedroom? "I demand you tell me everything now!"

The car screeches to a stop on the banks of Lake Winnequah. He stares straight out the windshield at the water. He revs the engine.

"Don't!" she screams.

"What, Josie, don't drive into the lake? Well, if we die, I know where I'm going ... do you?" He looks directly into her eyes and appears to have no compunction about drowning them both.

Her heart beats faster, not knowing if she will live or die.

He shuts off his car. "Calm down ... I'm messing with you. You take *this life* too seriously."

"You're a lunatic. You're the one who belongs in the psych ward, not me!"

"I told you to trust me, I didn't lie. I'd never lie to you. It's the car, I can't help myself." He lets out a laugh as if possessed by the sheer power of his German racecar.

"Take me back," she says, not knowing what to make of his erratic, volatile behavior. "I said, take me back!" *I should've never left the hospital.* "Wait a second, what did you mean by *this life?*"

"Josephine ... you're a saint."

CHAPTER 42

If any one of you is without sin,
let him be the first to throw a stone at her.
—Michael 8:7

"Saint? You are nuts."

"Yes, a saint," he says, flatly.

She narrows her eyes, wary he's taking her for a fool. "And I suppose you're going to tell me that you're an angel."

"You're a saint and you're living a parallel existence." His straight face reveals nothing; he may as well be giving her the weather report. "As for me, angel doesn't exactly capture what I am but it will do for the time being."

"You've definitely lost your mind. What's next, reincarnation?"

He laughs, "In simple terms, we are spiritual beings. We are capable of living in multiple alternate dimensions."

Her eyes open wide giving a window to her thoughts. *What have I done? How will I get back to the hospital?*

"Let me try to explain. Our frame of reference on Earth always includes a finite beginning and end. That's why when people have memories or dreams of their *other* lives they believe them to be *former* lives. It's hard for us to understand because everything in our world is subject to temporal constraints. Try to think of what it would be like to live without the barrier of time? What if a lifetime in another plane equaled a day in the alternate world?"

She looks at him skeptically. Nevertheless, what he's telling her draws her in, this enigmatic tale leaves her struggling against a battle of wills, to believe him or not.

"Reality is far bigger than our immediate experiences. Beyond the here and the now, there are many more dimensions than our own. And yes, some of our parallel lives will share similarities and we may even carry certain talents or traits across dimensions. But each existence takes an alternative path—where things end up differently."

"I'm not following, this is very confusing."

"Did you ever see *It's A Wonderful Life?*"

"Of course. It's one of my favorite movies of all time."

"George Bailey gets to see the alternative of his choice, where he chose not to be born. His brother dies, his wife becomes an old maid—"

"Are you saying we make choices and sometimes, the choice we don't take spins off into its own alternate reality?"

"Correct, and the realities may overlap, like the Venn diagrams we learned about in high school math class."

"Bizarre."

"Yes, I know it is."

"No, you're bizarre. Why should I believe you? Where's your proof?" she says, challenging him.

He shakes his head and appears exasperated as he looks out at the water. The music fills the void. Josie, on the other hand, tries to stay strong, calm and rational as a storm of doubt brews in her head. She reaches over and shuts off the radio. It's a distraction and she needs all her faculties to process his preposterous claims.

"Andrew, let me address your initial outrageous claim ... how can I be a saint?"

"True, I understand, you are hardly perfect."

"And you are? That's not what I meant. What I was trying to say before you so rudely reminded me that I'm imperfect is that I'm alive and yes, I am a sinner. Saints are canonized after they die, correct? So, am I a case of reincarnation?"

"Possibly, but I can't be sure. I am not privy to such information. You see, when we incarnate into a physical body, we are bathed in the River of Forgetfulness. We are given access to only certain memories of our other lives, others remain closed for the mere reason that it may be revealed at some later point, if at all, in the process of what we are here to do."

"Then how do you know I'm a saint?"

"To be more accurate, I know you're a saint and immortal in another dimension—the one people on Earth call Heaven." His eyes move to hers, his face is serious. And yet, he's still not providing her with the clarity she seeks.

"Have you been there?"

"Yes."

"Recently?"

He laughs. "Heaven is not subject to time."

The effort she's expending appears to be in vain, it's not likely she will ever understand his claims. Her mind ponders leaving but where will she go? She hasn't a way back unless she tries thumbing a ride from a stranger, a prospect she's never considered before. Further, the closest well-traveled highway is a long walk away. She wonders if his tale is a lure to get her alone in this relative wilderness. *Go ahead and kill me now, just don't let me suffer.*

"Come on—let's get out of the car. I have something you might want to see." He exits the driver's side and comes around the front of the car to the passenger's side. He places his hand on her door and opens it.

She hesitates before getting out. Her face is stone cold in warning, *Keep your distance.* She steps out of the car.

He moves to the side and grants her physical space. She stays standing next to the car door and faces the water but away from him.

"Look, I know you think you made a mistake coming here with me and ... I'm sorry if I frightened you."

She looks at him, reluctantly, since he sounds sincere for the moment. She breathes deep and sighs. His piercing gaze gives rise to the inner emotional conflict she aptly fought back in the car minutes before given his insane behavior. She thinks about running from him only she knows he will catch her. She was not much of a sprinter and once caught, she'd be incapable of escaping–whether she wanted to or not. *How can he know these things? Does he have any evidence?*

She didn't know what to feel anymore, attracted or repelled, excited or angered? Just one time, she wished she could touch him––touch the supple ridge on his chest where it met the base of his neck and run her fingers through his wild hair. While she could only imagine it, it already felt wicked and real in her soul. *Josie—get a hold of yourself! This isn't healthy, he's nuts!* Her thoughts prod, attempting to reason with her escalating and irrational desires.

Andrew smiles in response to her hesitation. "You're a funny, funny girl."

Indecision is scrawled all over her face. "Why do you say that? You unleashed your wayward charm on me and then placed me in this racecar bound for Armageddon. I'm as funny as you're stable."

"Please forgive me. C'mon—the ride was fun wasn't it?"

"That answer would be no," she glowers. *Is he always such a contradiction?*

"Will you relax? I won't bite, I promise." He holds out his hand for her to walk with him.

She accepts, deciding to trust him for the moment. The alternative means she'll be stuck on the banks of Lake Winnequah without a flashlight, blanket or a cell phone. And, if there's a degree of truth in his claim, it might explain as to how he was able to get her wound to vanish into thin air. Her mother always taught her that saints and angels could heal people. And who's to say he wasn't an angel of some kind? Didn't the Bible talk about how angels come to us in disguise? But were all heavenly beings as erratic as he was?

One thing is certain, I can't tell anyone about this, not even Nora. I need to be discharged before Sunday. Josie desperately wants to spend Easter Sunday with her children. Sharing this story will guarantee she will not be able to leave the hospital anytime soon.

They stroll along the rocky shoreline. She refrains from talking as she tries to digest everything he has told her thus far. The ground, moist and thawing from winter, is soft wherever she steps. Josie notices the temperature is falling, especially with the descending sun. She starts to shiver and rub her arms. Gooseflesh spreads up her arms and neck. He takes off his jacket and places it around her shoulders. She didn't expect to need a coat when they left the hospital. His feels warm from having just been on his body.

Josie continues to grapple. What if all of this was just a way to get her out here to murder her? She has no evidence of his sanity or credibility. How will her husband and children feel if her body is found near a lake far from the hospital? Will they think she was skipping out on them? It feels so deceptive, this isn't like her and she doesn't feel right about it.

She stops, rotates around and begins walking toward to the car. Andrew continues ahead toward the lake. And then she hears them.

Donnnggggg ... .donnnggggg ... donnnggggg ... the bells echo as if some ethereal cathedral is smack dab in the middle of the nearby woods. They reverberate through the surrounding trees and foliage and then drift outward across the lake.

"Andrew, do you hear that?" He is now several feet ahead of her getting closer to the docks. The wind picks up, it whips and swirls. Loose branches and leaves tumble across the rocky shore and spill into the water.

Abruptly, he turns back with decisive steps and returns to where she is standing. The closer he approaches, the greater the luminescence surrounding him becomes. The sky grows darker, the howling wind rocks the boats tethered to docks in the distance. They creak, back and forth, back and forth. He draws her to him and kisses her hard on the lips. She falls into his embrace and then pulls back, "Andrew, no!"

He clutches her arms in his hands. "I hear them, too."

She swallows and closes her eyes, then shakes her head. She knows he'll release her if she tries to break free ... but she doesn't.

"Josie—we're miles from any church." The wind continues to howl and whip.

"Does anyone else hear them? Besides us?"

"No ... just you ... and me."

She feels herself becoming weaker and before he can kiss her again, she steps away from him. She covers her mouth in a stunning testament to his kiss. She takes a tissue from her pocket and begins wiping off the stain of her betrayal.

"That's not going to make it go away," he says.

"Andrew, this can't happen. Not between us, I'm married and I have three beautiful children. I made a commitment. I can't and I won't." She looks out across the restless lake water and sits down on the rocks of the bank and cries.

"If I have to, I will wait for you. I'm not sorry for kissing you. You've always been with me."

"What? You don't know me. How can you say such things?" She wipes her nose and tries to regain a fragment of composure.

"That's where you're wrong, I know you better than anyone ... anywhere. Our spiritual selves have traveled and lived in other worlds together, many, many times and even the one we are living now. The problem is—this is your alternate reality. This is the one where I died."

CHAPTER 43

Eye has not seen ... nor ear heard,
what God has prepared for those who love him.
—1 Corinthians 2:9

"You look very much alive to me. Were you raised from the dead?" she asks, half-jokingly.

"Yes."

"What? What do you mean?" she exclaims in frustration from yet another astonishing claim.

"Death doesn't mean one is secured an immediate passage into eternal peace. Some of us have additional work to do beyond our physical death. I wasn't supposed to die."

"Lots of people die when they aren't supposed to. Are they then raised from the dead as well? I think not!" she mocks.

"All I know is in exchange for the life I have now, I became a living guardian of the light."

"A guardian of light?"

"Yes."

"So, are you claiming to be immortal?"

"No, I'm not physically immortal. Our souls are immortal."

Beyond them, the lake waters continue to be restless but the wind dies down. He sits down on a patch of dry grass and picks up a stick. He uses it to poke the weeds and rocks at his feet. As ludicrous as his statements sound, she can see he clearly means them. But, for the moment, Josie decides not to ask anything further as she's afraid of what his answers will be to her numerous and unending questions.

"I'll be right back." He stands back up and begins to walk to his car. She stays and waits for him, trusting he'll return. The sky is in full darkness with very few stars and while the moon is bright, it illuminates only a short distance in front of her.

She hears his steps in the dark coming toward her where she is sitting on the ground.

"Will you come with me to my boat?" he asks, flipping on a flashlight he is carrying. He hands her a flashlight for her to use.

"You have a boat? Out here?" she asks, looking up at him.

"Yes, why else would have I driven us to this place?"

"How would I know that's what we were doing?"

"I thought you were the psychic?" he jokes.

"Touché," she says.

"I wanted to check to make sure it didn't get damaged in the storm last night. Although, I suppose I won't be able to see much now."

She stands up then brushes the dust and debris off of her pants from sitting on the rocks and dirt. At least now she knew he had a true purpose for bringing her here besides leaving her for dead. They begin walking when she sees it in the moonlight, slightly hidden beyond the natural curve of the shoreline and behind the tall grassy weeds. She shines her flashlight on it. His vessel is neither a small motor boat nor a sleek flashy speedboat. And it isn't what she expects. It is a marvel of water transport. Among all of the boats docked nearby, his has the largest profile. She surmises it's probably larger and more elaborate than most of the boats afloat anywhere else in Minnesota. She just couldn't see those vessels in order to compare.

He takes his flashlight and shines it on the yacht. She notes it has incredible features—an upper deck for the captain, a large lower deck with passenger seating as well as a diving platform. There was an entry door off of the lower deck to what appeared to be the yacht's living quarters. Given her limited maritime experience, she could only imagine what a boat like this was worth.

"I suppose this was another gift from your parents?" she asks with sarcasm. She had never been up and close personal with a yacht before.

"Not quite, I spent many years working for my family's fishing business. My father decided to sell it a couple of years ago. I bought the yacht with a portion of my proceeds from the sale."

"Wow, it must've been some business." Josie couldn't help but be impressed even though she tried not to show it.

"It was initially my great-grandfather's business, my father inherited it. He hoped to leave it to me but he knew what I wanted was to be a doctor."

"Didn't you have a brother or sister who wanted to run it?"

"No, I was adopted. I'm an only child."

"So, you're telling me you're rich and you were raised from the dead. Are you Lazarus?"

"No, of course not." He laughs.

"Aren't saints or angels, or whatever you are, supposed to live in poverty, forgo material comforts and the rest?"

"I'm trying, but I'm human like you. I'm loaded with faults. I've allowed myself a couple of expensive things, my car and my boat. And, I love to fish. One day, I hope to live on this boat year-round, just as soon I get to a warmer climate, but that'll be awhile." Suddenly, he leaps in one swift motion from the dock onto the yacht's platform.

"Where are you planning to move? Didn't you just get here?" she asks.

"Yep, but my stay here is temporary. I'm filling in for a doctor who's on leave with the Doctors for World Relief program. I also plan to work for them just as soon as he returns." He extends his hand to help her come aboard.

"No thanks, I think it would be better if I wait here on the dock."

He appears somewhat disappointed by her choice to stay on the dock but it's safer for her to be away from him. She doesn't want temptation to pull her in any deeper.

"What is Doctors for World Relief?" she asks.

"They're a humanitarian organization. They place doctors in areas where access to medical care is nonexistent, places of desperate poverty." He heads up a few steps to the upper level deck, shining the flashlight along his path. He inspects every corner and crevice of his so-called boat with the limited light.

"It sounds like a big commitment," she says.

"You could say that. And, I have to stay in my assignment for at least a year ... to start."

Josie didn't know whether to feel relieved or sad that he would eventually leave the Twin Cities. Without him around, she wouldn't have to face the temptation of wanting to be with him or the confusion of her conflicted emotions. "Do you know where they'll place you?"

"Not yet, hopefully someplace warm. Maybe somewhere in South America ... they have a lot of options for me there although all of them entail a high level of risk."

"Oh, I see. When will you know?"

"I'm hoping within the next twelve months." He returns to the side of the boat facing her.

"Why then did you come to St. Paul if you're supposed to work for this organization?"

"When I applied for the job with DWR, they told me about the opening in St. Paul. They wanted me to get more experience before they shipped me off to some remote area. See, I've been working in the ER for only a couple of years. DWR needed a doctor to replace a St. Catherine's ER doctor for a limited time who was coming to work for them. It's a long story but let's just say I'll eventually work for DWR—one way or another."

She sighs. "Interesting. You are clearly motivated by risk."

"I guess so." He shrugs.

Still, inside she is burning with questions, starting with, *Are you for real? And what in God's name is a "living guardian of the light?" Adopted and raised from the dead? Who are his parents? They must be extraordinary people to raise such a strange child.* While she wanted to know, part of her didn't want to hear any more of it. She couldn't possibly live up to the expectation of sainthood—in her past, present or alternate reality. She felt incredibly substandard already in this life but she wished she knew more about this "other" life he spoke of.

Once his inspection is complete, he leaps back onto the dock and leads her back to the shoreline. Again, they walk side-by-side, parallel without touching but the emotional tension and physical attraction could be cut with a knife. She can feel it radiating back and forth between their bodies. Before they go too far, she turns around to view his yacht one more time by taking her flashlight and shining it across its surface. It shoots through her heart like an arrow. In large, clear, black script across its bow is the name, her name ... *Josephine.*

CHAPTER 44

They return to St. Catherine's at about 8:15 p.m., sliding in shy of her assigned curfew. Since neither of them knew what to expect, given their marginal tardiness, they use Andrew's electronic doctor's ID badge to enter through the back door of the hospital—the one used for deliveries. He waves the card in front of the infrared eye and in a split second, the door unlocks with the sound of a click.

They slip through the vacant and dim unloading area. It reminds Josie of the inside of a warehouse or a large garage. They pass through another set of doors, leading to a stairway. He grasps her hand and quickens the pace. They ascend several flights until they arrive at the fourth floor emergency exit. She hasn't passed through this portion of the hospital before, it never occurred to her it was there.

He waves his badge once more, opening the exit door. It enters directly into a hallway on the psychiatry unit. She creeps through it first, privately hoping no alarm will go off.

"Aren't you coming?" she asks, turning back she sees him still in the doorway.

"No, it would be better no one sees us together now," he says.

She nods, with an unexpected twinge of regret. She walks on, passing several doors that lead to other patient rooms until arriving at her own. She glances to see if he's waiting in the opening of the emergency exit and he is, she gives him a slight wave. He closes the door. She returns to being alone.

In the distance, she sees Susan down the hall talking with another patient. Josie hurries into her room and sits on her bed, pretending to read a magazine. No sooner she obtains her prop, she hears Susan outside her door.

"Josie?" Susan calls into the room.

"C'mon in," Josie says, feigning interest in her *Better Homes and Gardens* magazine.

"Hey, girl, it's time for your bedtime meds and vital sign check," Susan says.

"Already? Sure." Josie sets down her magazine and raises an arm for Susan to wrap the blood pressure cuff around it.

"Somehow the unit clerk missed you come in." Susan places the stethoscope ear buds in her ears getting ready to take Josie's blood pressure.

"Oh?"

"Dr. Chase was supposed to sign you back in when you returned, but he must've forgotten." After she takes Josie's blood pressure, Susan pops the thermometer into Josie's mouth. While waiting for the thermometer to read her temperature, Josie examines Susan's face. It wasn't so much as suspicion Josie observed in her face but disappointment. Susan wasn't wearing a wedding ring.

The thermometer beeps. "98.4, just fine and dandy." With a "pop" and a "click," Susan drops its disposable cover into the trash.

"I'm sorry, I didn't know he was supposed to sign me back in. Next time I'll–"

"Next time?" Susan says with surprise.

"Um, yes, next time, I'll be sure *whoever* takes me for a walk signs me back in." Josie wasn't competing with her for Andrew. Susan could have him as far as Josie was concerned; it would release her of her feelings for him knowing he loved someone else. But given what happened at the lake, she didn't think he returned Susan's affection.

"Anyhow, here's your medication." She hands Josie a small medicine cup containing her sleeping pill. She takes the tablet from her and swallows it quick, washing it down with a cup of water. "By the way, you received a phone call while you were out."

"Oh, was it my sister? I need to call and say good night to my kids before it gets any later."

"No ... it was your husband."

"He called?" Her mouth falls open. "When was that?"

"It was at least an hour ago, maybe more."

"Did you tell him where I was?" *Okay, don't give it away.*

"I told him one of our doctors took you for a walk since the weather was so nice."

I hope that's all she said. "Did he want me to call him?"

"He didn't say. He wanted me to tell you he's leaving tonight for some out-of-town meetings. He said your sister will be looking after your children."

"He left?" Josie had a feeling this was coming. No doubt he was relieved he didn't have to tell her himself. "I guess I better call home."

"Yeah, it's probably a good idea. Are you upset about your husband's message?"

"Yes and no. I knew he'd leave but I was hoping he would've stayed with our children while I was here." Josie felt like a hypocrite, here she left with Andrew tonight and yet she was upset Declan left home.

"I've seen it before, Josie, he'll come around. It can be hard for a man to accept his wife's mental illness. Even worse, men don't accept their own mental health problems. Have the two of you thought about marital counseling? It might help him to learn to understand your illness. Maybe it will help him to be more suppor-tive of you."

"Declan isn't one for therapy. Oh, sure, he thinks it okay that I do it, because I'm a woman. To him, couple's therapy—in any form—would be an admission of weakness."

"I'm very sorry to hear that," Susan's hand touches Josie's shoulder and gives her a sympathetic squeeze. "Call your children. I'm sure they want to say good night to you. Let me know if you need anything or if you want to talk some more. I'm on until eleven."

"Thank you." She appreciates that Susan knows when enough is said. And somewhat guiltily, Josie envies her. Josie possessed baggage, a life already underway and far too late to turn back. Susan is fresh for the picking—smart, young, pretty and unattached. *Why wouldn't Andrew want her instead? She's available. Grow up, Josie!* She scolds herself. Divided and confused, she wonders if it's Andrew she wants or to be desired by her husband. It had been weeks since Declan and she were intimate. He was always busy with work and when he wasn't working, he was traveling ... for work. Josie was tired from taking care of three small children, most days on her own with not much help from anyone else. Nevertheless, things between them were stable and secure, good in their routine way.

But now, there was uncertainty. It was scary ... and exhilarating. Josie couldn't stop thinking of Andrew, his arms, his hands, his voice and best—and worst—of all, his passionate kiss. The attraction she felt for him during their momentary embrace was dangerous. It would lead to thoughts of other things. Things she knew weren't possible for Andrew and her. She attempted to ground her mind in the present, a married mother of three with responsibilities ... and liabilities.

Josie picks up the phone to call her children. *This will bring me back to reality.* Nora answers. After their initial greetings, Josie asks the dreaded question. "Did Declan leave yet?"

"Yeah ... he did," Nora says.

Josie cringes. Declan left and dumped the responsibility of the kids on her sister.

"He took off just a little while ago."

She grumbles, although she is somewhat thankful not to have to talk to him.

"It pretty much went like this, Jos—he got home from work, went for a run, played ball with the kids, showered, packed and left."

"Did he say anything about why he was leaving?"

"All he said was that he wouldn't be home again until Saturday. He was going to visit two of his client's headquarters, one in Detroit and one in Chicago over the next few days."

Josie's stomach turns. It is bad enough she abandoned her children, but Declan? And she didn't abandon them by choice—he made her. What was so important that he had to leave and strand Nora? Although, deep down, she knows she's the last person who should be pointing fingers. She isn't exactly the pillar of sanctity or maternal responsibility.

Josie hears the kids start to chatter and grab for the phone. "Josie, the kids want to talk to you," Nora says.

"Put them on, I miss them so much." Her heart sinks as if she's miles away. Even though they are in the same city, she can't touch them, hug them or give them a goodnight kiss.

"Hi, Mommy," a little voice says.

"Michael?"

"We miss you, Mommy. Are you coming home soon?" Michael asks, sadly.

"I hope to be home by Saturday."

"That's when Daddy said he'd be back, too," Michael's voice lowers further as if disheartened by the news, neither parent will be home any sooner.

"It's okay to be sad but don't worry, I'll be home in a few days, I promise."

"You promise you'll be home by Saturday?"

"I promise. Aunt Nora will take good care of you and your brother and sister while I'm here, okay?"

"Okay," he mumbles.

"Call me tomorrow when you get home from school. I want to hear all about it. Oh, and make sure Aunt Nora checks the snack for you at school tomorrow morning."

"Okay, she will. Mrs. Thompson is very careful about it, Mom. You don't have to worry."

"I know, but I do anyway." Josie didn't feel right giving other people the responsibility of checking her son's snack. The last thing they needed was another allergic reaction. Josie remembers, two more weeks. *Will his allergies really be gone?* She could only hope ... and pray.

After her conversation with Michael, she chats with Anna and promises her as well that she will be home by the weekend. Then, following their good-byes, Nora returns to the line.

"Is the therapy helping?"

"It seems to be although I haven't had much therapy yet. I think the meds are working."

"Good."

"Nora, thank you. Thanks for being there for me and for my children. I know Declan doesn't show it, but I know he's glad you're there, too."

"I suppose, for the mere reason, it allowed him to make his hasty exit. He got spooked by people wondering where you were and he clearly didn't know what to say. I overheard heard him on the phone. He told a couple of your friends you were in the hospital with a kidney infection."

"A kidney infection? You're kidding me." She couldn't believe it, and then again, she could. Declan was notorious in his ability to spin a good story but usually this applied to his work, not to their marriage.

"No, I'm not. Look, I know he's a good provider and most of the time, he's a good father ... but truth be told, lately he's being selfish."

"Nora, please ..."

"Don't worry, the kids can't hear me. Michael and Anna went to brush their teeth and Jacob, he's with me but he can't understand."

"Well, he might ..."

"I will say this for Declan, he does look good since the last time I saw him. He's trimmed down a bit from all the running. Too bad it hasn't helped his attitude."

"What do you mean?"

"You know—his *all about me* attitude. He changed when he took that job, you know. When you met him, he wasn't like that."

"I know in my heart, he's still a good man."

"Yes but the demands of his career have taken over. Josie, you guys need to think about your priorities. Does he need this job or could you guys make do with less? I think you'll both be happier with less."

She decides not to answer, she can't answer. The words become lodged in her throat, to concede Nora was right would require a level of bravery she didn't have.

"Are you there?" Nora asks.

"Um, yeah." *Change the subject, Josie.* "What about you? Are you okay staying alone with the kids? Do you want me to hire some babysitter help?"

"No, I'm fine and it's better this way. Declan can focus on work and himself, you can focus on your recovery."

Josie's somewhat thrown for a loop. She didn't realize how much Declan irritated her sister but how could she not? His behavior lately was less than optimal and she was finally ticked off enough to tell him.

ABOUT AN HOUR LATER, WITH DETERMINATION AND ANGER ON her side, she dials his cell phone. She figures he will have landed by now—wherever he was going—be it Detroit or Chicago. She let it ring and it clicked immediately over to his voicemail, "Hello, this is Declan Reilly with ..." She waits for the beep.

"Call me." She says no more than that. He should've answered but either he was avoiding her or he wasn't there yet because of a delay. Her money was on avoidance.

At ten minutes to 10 p.m., the phone rings. She hesitates for a long second. *Let it ring three times.* She picks it up on the fourth ring. "Hello," she says.

"Hi," he says and adds nothing further.

"Where are you?" she asks with indignation, as if he had gone rogue on their children.

"I'm at O'Hare, on my way to my hotel."

"Why did you leave? I didn't know you needed to be out of town this week."

"I wasn't planning to. I got called to an urgent meeting."

Josie hears a muffled voice in the background, as if someone is talking to Declan at the same time. "I feel bad that Nora's with the kids alone at the house." She hears the voice again.

"You'll be home soon," he says, distracted.

Then she hears him mumbling. He was half-talking to her and half to another. He is engaged in another conversation on the side.

"I don't know, they haven't told me." Josie listens closer, growing more annoyed by his inattention to their conversation and his attention to the other. "Declan, who are you talking to?"

"Huh? What? I'm talking to you."

"But I heard you laugh, like someone ..." and then she hears the voice again, it's distinct and female.

"Thank you," the unknown female says.

"No problem at all." Here he is, simultaneously polite to this *other* woman and yet bothered by her.

"Declan, who is that?" She had been under the impression he was traveling alone because he almost always traveled alone.

"I was helping my assistant get the luggage off the belt."

"Assistant?" A sick feeling hits her stomach, for her to attain emotional stability hinged on his being there for her when she got home. What if he wasn't?

"Yeah, Sheila. She just joined the firm."

"Is she a new paralegal?"

"No, she's a lawyer. I just hired her on for my division."

"Oh, did anyone else go with you?"

"Nope, just Sheila." His voice is short. "She's handling some of my accounts going forward—she's here for meetings, too."

Josie is silent. He is alone with another woman in another city, far from home and no witnesses. *C'mon Josie, it's professional, above board, right?* She reminds herself there were occasions, although rare, when his partners traveled with him ... but they had always been male.

"Look, I gotta run," he says, evasively.

"Wait ... before you go, I have a quick question."

"What?"

"Declan, I heard you've been telling people I'm sick with a kidney infection."

"Hold on," he says. Then she hears Declan put the phone to the side. "Give me a minute here," he says to his traveling partner. A second later he returns. "Look, I figured you wouldn't want me telling people the *real* reason you were in the hospital. I thought you preferred to keep this whole matter private."

"You mean *you* prefer to keep this whole matter private. There's nothing wrong with mental illness—it's part of life. Let's not perpetuate the stigma."

"Are you're insinuating that I'm perpetuating the stigma?" he scoffs.

"You've already done it. Let's be honest about this; you don't want this to affect your reputation," Josie says, haughtily.

Click.

All she hears is the hollow echo of dead air.

CHAPTER 45

Josie lies in bed, facing her digital clock. Its bright red display shows the time is 7 a.m. The sun is peeking through her window, scattering a few flinty rays onto the linoleum floor. She examines her room and it is evident, she is still in the hospital. She wishes she could've been magically transported home during the night while she slept but no such luck. She could hear the rush of voices and footsteps coming close and then passing by her door. The day shift is starting morning rounds. It is time for her to get up and get this show on the road. She pushes back her sheets and blankets and sits up. Her first full day of therapy is ahead of her. "Terrific," she grumbles. *Not.*

She gets out of bed and places her bare feet on the floor. Her room is cold, her body shivers and she looks for her robe. She finds it in her closet, bundles up and goes into the bathroom. The shower stall is small and the tile worn. She pulls the lever on its faucet, letting the water run until warm before she gets in. While listening to the purr of the shower water, it sparks her memory of a dream, but it could've been a vision. She isn't certain as it occurred as her body was rousing for the day. She recollects spotty and vague parts of it. By and large, it was a fragmented picture: an enormous body of water full of cresting waves, an opaque sky, an untamed shore-line, and primitively crafted boats drifting across the water. She watches from land, wearing leather sandals and an ankle-length brown tunic. In the background, she hears the swish and sway of the waves coming in and going out.

She removes her robe and pajamas, uses the toilet first, then steps into the shower. The warm water trickles over her head and then down over her body. She lathers-up her hair with shampoo when another image flashes in her mind from her dream. This time the image is of Andrew, only he looks different, more savage— much like a sixties hippie at Woodstock. His brown hair is long and wavy, resting in an unruly heap on his upper back. He has a tangled beard, worse than his current under-groomed sideburns.

Thinking of him, even given his organic appearance, made her feel vulnerable and achy. It was not unlike the feeling of falling in love only this time she resists the urge. She can't permit herself to a dizzy free-fall. There's too much at stake, her marriage, her children, her reputation as a good mother and a faithful wife, and most of all, the promise she made to God and her husband in front of 250 people ten years earlier. Yet, she wonders if she'll see Andrew again. She wants to see him, for all the wrong reasons. Although it would be better if she didn't, he knew things, things she needed and wanted to know. If she could somehow get beyond their attraction, perhaps she could focus on learning the bits and pieces of the puzzle that he seemed to have in hand. And then she thinks of Declan.

She finishes her shower and towels off then slips on her robe and slippers. She walks back to the bed, sits down and cries, more out of frustration and confusion than out of sorrow. Her mind can't let go of the last conversation she had with her husband. Why does he harbor such anger for her? What happened to him—and them— along the way? Where did they get lost? Where did she get lost? She felt as though they hardly knew each other anymore. While they lived in the same house and shared the same children, in many ways they had become strangers. She pulls together and wipes her eyes. Today is not the day she will wallow in despair. It takes took too much energy, energy she must conserve and put toward her recovery. It's not that she doesn't care, rather because she cares too much. Today she must put that aside and focus on becoming whole again.

GROUP THERAPY BEGINS AND THE TIME PASSES SLUGGISHLY. SHE keeps her eyes on the clock more than she should and twiddles her wedding ring about her finger. She even provides her therapy mates with a genuine performance, does a lot of "uh huh'ing" and occasionally throws in an idea or two, committing herself to share a few small parts of her incomplete life: her children a blessing, her husband emotionally missing, her mother dead, a father whose mind is failing, a brother she rarely talks to and a sister, the glue who holds the family together.

Josie is far luckier than most who attended group therapy with her and she doesn't want to look like an ungrateful brat for being there. She really didn't belong. Her life was not hard enough to qualify for their ranks. So she kept what she added short, not allowing herself to indulge in self-pity.

Once group therapy was over, she moves on to occupational therapy. It is easier to avoid sharing the details of her life there. Instead, she focuses on painting small ornaments for each of her children while listening to the chatter of the fractured lives around her.

Intermittently, she looks for Andrew in hopes he might show up and save her from her mandatory therapy sessions but he never does. He never said he would but nevertheless, she feels disappointed and somewhat misled. Given all her years of experience with men, she was still reduced to the mentality of a naïve teenage girl—*did he mean what he said?* She had no recollection of him before their encounter at Wilson's. As the day wears on, she becomes convinced she's a fool for believing him. She over-analyzes every word, every action and every one of his advances.

That's it, she decides. Going forward, she will make a concerted effort to think about him in only one context, of what he knows that she doesn't. It is the first mature decision she's made in the last 48 hours. He obviously knows more than she does about what was happening to her and she needs answers. If she sees him again, she'll corner him into to telling her everything. There was one problem, he never did say when or if he'd be back.

DR. SHAPIRO COMES BY LATE IN THE DAY SHORTLY AFTER SHE finishes eating dinner in the unit cafeteria. He had told her Tuesdays were his clinic day and on those days he saw patients in his office from 7 a.m. until 5 p.m. She shouldn't have expected him to arrive to the inpatient psych ward much before six but she did, having forgotten what he told her the day before about Tuesdays. He arrives wearing a white oxford-collared dress shirt, khaki pants and sneakers. His dress and wire-rimmed glasses made him look more like a college professor than a psychiatrist. They return to the room where they met for the first therapy session, with its gray couch and recliner, worn rug, and plastic blinds covering the window that faces the hall outside.

"How did your day go?" Dr. Shapiro asks, pushing his glasses up higher on the bridge of his nose.

"Very well, thank you. It was ... educational." *Interesting choice of words.*

"How so?"

"I learned a lot about myself."

"Such as?"

"I heard some stories that put some things about my life into perspective for me."

"Really?" He appears encouraged but not convinced.

"At group, there were people who shared some awful details about their lives like enduring child abuse. It was heartbreaking."

"Yes, group therapy does help put things in perspective."

Josie notices his forehead creases when he talks. She isn't revealing much beneath the surface and he appears to want more meat to her answers.

"Did you learn anything else? Did you have any realizations about *your* condition?"

She gives a heavy sigh. "I know I've always had it ... to varying degrees at different times in my life."

"Probably so ... but, maybe you were able to keep it in check?"

"Well, yes ... but there's more. Everything got worse when I deliberately engaged my extrasensory abilities." *I might as well tell him, I have to tell someone.* "You see, I've always been hyper-aware. I call it telepathy, intuition and the like, only I've never spent any time exploring it. It happened, haphazardly, when I didn't expect it. It would pop into my head at random times."

He stares back at her when she stops talking and then jots some notes on a chart he holds on his lap. The silence makes her nervous and causes her to spew forth details she hadn't ever shared with anyone. "The minute I paid attention to it, it expanded further to the point where I couldn't process everything coming at me. When I channel—that is, when I try to communicate with those who have died—my mind is open to all kinds of communication and I know now that it can't sort through it all. I became over-whelmed by it."

"What do you mean?"

"The messages come to me all at once, like a tossed salad. And when I try to sort them, I tend to reach for strongest messages and well, it's not reliable."

"Okay?" He raises one brow.

"The messages that are strongest are the ones closest to the Earth. I've become convinced these messages are actually coming from souls who are earthbound. So, like in a salad, the flavors of onion and green pepper take over and you miss the nuances of the subtle spices in the dressing. The lost or earthbound souls are louder because they're closer to us in the here and now, their messages are more intrusive. The quieter souls are like the subtle spices in the dressing, they're harder to reach but they're there if you listen closely."

"Interesting analysis," he says, making a slight thoughtful frown.

"Only here's the catch, the quieter souls can't be heard or felt with the mind. They can only be felt and heard within the heart and, if we're truly aware, with our soul. At the risk of sounding *New Age,*" using finger quotes around her words, "our soul is the focal point. If we use our mind to channel, it's like talking on the phone with the wrong end of the receiver. Hearing with the soul isn't like hearing a voice in your ears or even in your head. It's a sense of knowing."

"Why do you think that is?"

"Channeling with the mind only distracts the receiver from the messenger. It's the easy way out. Unfortunately, the easy way delivers the wrong result, a lot of noise, a confusing blur of messages."

"Hmm, sounds like you've given this a lot of thought."

"I have."

"And it's a convincing argument. I see that you've convinced yourself of this hypothesis."

She doesn't know how to respond. Is he saying to her that she believes her own manufactured delusion? Is he patronizing her?

"Would you like to hear *my* analysis?" he asks.

"I guess so." It's only fair for her to allow him an opportunity to explain his position. She prepares to hear his psychoanalytical reasoning by again, twirling her wedding ring about her finger.

"Josie, based on my medical training and the current research on the subject of psychosis, I believe your symptoms were precipitated by a severe form of generalized anxiety disorder. Your anxiety has been building since your mother died four years ago. Motherhood, in the absence of having your own mother to mentor you, fueled a cascade of emotions, such as insecurity, fear, low self-esteem, grief, and loneliness. Would you agree?"

"Yes, I'd say that's true."

"These emotions were left 'unchecked' for a long period, and as a result, another underlying condition, obsessive compulsive disorder or also known as 'OCD' emerged."

"Okay," she says but isn't sure if she agrees with him.

"OCD was your mind's way of trying to regain control over your emotional state, thus a coping mechanism. It's very reinforcing. OCD tells you if you do this one thing, everything will be all right. Then you do that one thing and things are all right but only temporarily and so you have to do it again, and again, and again."

"But what did I obsess about?"

"You fixated on your intuition and ultimately, your desire to communicate with your dead mother."

"But if I'm obsessive, why didn't my mind pick something more mundane like washing my hands over and over?"

He glances down at her twisting her wedding ring about her finger.

She notices this and sees the raw red mark on her finger beneath her ring.

He smiles.

"Point taken," she says.

"It's not just what you do with your ring, that's just one symptom of a very complex condition. OCD is deeply rooted. It's related to your life experience. You said your mother was superstitious and you were brought up in a strong religious home. Your life experience was influenced by a supernatural belief system and for some reason, your mind, under severe stress, triggered an obsession with it."

His arguments, or more accurately, his convictions did make at least some sense to her. Only she knew he couldn't render a logical explanation for her exorcism and the casting out of lost souls from her home by heavenly beings, unless this was one grand hallucination. Above all, what about her children? This didn't mesh with the fact that her children heard these invisible menacing wanderers as well. But she couldn't tell him that. She just couldn't.

"Now, there's a catch to OCD as there is with your theory. OCD works sometimes. It's employed by the mind to regain control of whatever is going out of control through the use of ritualistic or repetitive behaviors. In your case, OCD wasn't a successful strategy. It's natural for the mind to gravitate toward OCD in overwhelming situations such as in cases of abuse and physical illness. When OCD fails, as in your case, the situation grows worse. The behaviors escalate and can lead to a more severe condition."

"And what's that?"

"Psychosis. Psychosis is a survival mechanism."

"So, I moved straight from being unable to cope to barely being able to survive?" While his analysis sounds rational, his reasoning in her opinion, is far too complicated. In his divergent view, she's lost all contact with reality but in hers she is more than aware of co-existing realities—the physical and non-physical dimensions. However, she did admire his tenacity.

"Josie, did anything traumatic happen to you before your mother died."

"No, nothing that serious comes to mind."

"You're certain."

She rigorously peruses her memory, still not capturing anything distressing.

"Look even farther back, did anything occur in childhood?"

"If you're referring to abuse, I was never abused in any form."

"What about loss? Did you lose anyone significant to you before your mother passed?"

"I lost several aunts, they all died of cancer, and my mom had cancer when I was a little girl but she recovered."

"This is good. This helps me to understand where your focus with death and the afterlife comes in. Usually in cases like yours, there's a history from childhood that provides the original trigger event. Did you ever try to channel your aunts?"

"No, I wasn't all that close with my aunts. I knew they were my mother's sisters and the whole thing was upsetting but I can't say that it caused me a lot of emotional pain or grief. I think I was too young to understand."

"Was there anyone else important to you that died during or around that same period?"

"Andy." His face pops into her head. Of course, how could she have forgotten her beloved friend Andy? During that period, she was incredibly lost. When he died, she couldn't comprehend the "never"—to never see him alive again—because she was so young.

"Who?"

"I had a friend who drowned in the pond near our house."

"How old were you?"

"I was nine and he was eleven."

"Okay, now we're getting somewhere."

She sighs because she knows Dr. Shapiro isn't getting it, nor is she getting him. His explanation of her illness works for him because he can validate it with hardcore scientific research. He is a rationalist and the view that there's more to life than what meets the eye is irrational. Therefore, her skewed thinking is an excuse for living in a fantasy world, a world with an all-knowing, all-powerful supernatural being she calls God. He can't comprehend the interplay between those living in the form of a soul and those living in a physical body. To him, the presentation of her bizarre symptoms (that is, her psychic ability) is a representation of some suppressed memory or denial of some truth that she can't face head-on, a manifestation of her severe anxiety disorder. In one small way, he is correct. She is avoiding something—her fear that her husband no longer loved her, the fact she doubted herself at every juncture and despite all of the people around her, she felt incredibly alone in the world.

AFTER THE HOUR OF A MODEST ATTEMPT AT SELF-REVELATORY therapy with Dr. Shapiro, she hunkers down with a book that she found in the unit library earlier in the day. It's one of those grocery store romance novels, "junk food for the mind" and it's exactly what she needs. She skips the evening movie preferring to escape into the wispy tale of Lady Ciara and Sir Sean in a medieval castle in Ireland. At least there is love somewhere that will last forever, even if it is between the pages of a paperback novel.

She calls home at about 8 p.m. and speaks with her children. They say their good nights and after they hang up, she reads about an hour more. When her eyes become droopy, she shuts off the light above her bed and places her head on her pillow. Sadness fills her heart, teardrops drip from the corner of her eyes and onto the pillow case. It has been a long and lonely day. All she wants is to go home.

CHAPTER 46

I have been all things unholy. If God can work through me,
He can work through anyone.
—St. Francis of Assisi

The naked branches of silver oaks and maples encircle the frozen pond like skeletal creatures hovering over their prey. The pines, heavy with snow and ice, allow a bare hint of sun to enter through a thick cover of clouds. Alone, she skates. She hears his voice call to her, "Skate faster, Josie!"

The cold wind presses against her face. Her sight dims. Soon, all she sees is black. There's the sound of cracking. She drops to her knees and struggles, attempting to use her hands for a guide. She hears screams.

"Hold on!" She crawls in her blindness in search of him. The ice stings her fingertips. "Andy!"

There is no response. She collapses in grief.

A small and gentle hand touches her hair. Her vision clears. A young boy takes shape before her. He sits beside her weary body. His small arms wrap around her like mercy bestowed by an angel. She looks into his gaze and sees her own image reflecting back at her. The child helps her from the ice. His small, frail body transforms. The child, no longer a boy, is taller, older, and becomes the man she calls Andrew. He speaks to her and while she doesn't hear any words, the simple and pure sound of his voice seizes her heart. He holds her in his arms in the light of the coming dawn.

JOSIE SENSES SOMEONE STANDING BY HER BED. SHE RUBS HER eyes and opens them. Her breath cuts short. A silhouette of a figure shadows the wall beside her.

"Andrew?" she whispers.

"Yep," he says. His figure is ghost-like, the quality of an apparition. His eyes in the dark have a glow as if they contain their own light.

"What are you doing here?"

"I'm working so I don't have long. I waited all day to come."

Josie is sluggish and sleepy. She turns to look at the digital clock and then back to him. "It's almost two."

"I know it is."

"Couldn't you have come before … midnight?"

He bends toward her, coming within a few inches of her face. She pulls back and sits upright then switches on the light above her bed.

"Sorry, I didn't mean to startle you." He backs away.

She nods once. While his approach feels natural, she can't allow it.

"I knew you didn't want people to see us together … I figured the cloak of darkness would provide me with adequate camouflage." He raises one brow and smiles in a way that tempts her to surrender.

She shuts her eyes in delirium, resulting from the hormonal rush that develops whenever he is near. How can she be so weak in her commitment and so strong in desire? "Please, go away," she says.

He takes a step back. "Wow, I didn't expect that. I was hoping you'd be happy to see me."

She opens her eyes to look at him. "I am happy to see you," and more than she's willing to admit. "I'm sorry—"

"It's fine." He offers her a half-smile. "When I came in, you looked as though you were having a bad dream."

"I was, sort of." The image from her dream of Andy and Andrew flip back and forth like a playing card in her mind.

"Do you want to talk about it?"

She shakes her head and avoids looking at him directly. Instead, she watches the rise and fall of his chest at the V-neck opening of his faded earth-green scrubs. His black Littman stethoscope is slung around his neck and rests upon his chest. There is something different about him. His appearance is almost angelic, a da Vinci coming to life. It's as if she's seeing his face for the first time.

"I thought about you a lot today." He leans against a chair adjacent to her bed.

"Was it while driving like a maniac in your BMW?" she says, in half-jest.

"I told you, I can't help myself, its powerful engine takes over me."

"You can say that again." Her lips curve up at the corners, revealing the fringe of a smile.

"See, I knew I could make you smile."

She rolls her eyes and gives him a quick once over. His skin is mildly sunned and thinks he probably returned to work on his boat during the daytime. His cheek bones are more defined as are his other features: his jaw, chiseled, his chin, mildly squared. All of a sudden, it hits her. His sideburns are missing.

"Yes?" He points to the spot his sideburns once occupied as if he's reading her mind. While he still has a tuft of hair on each side of his face, it is within the realm of a normal sideburn for a man. Nevertheless, it is far reduced from the obnoxious distraction that previously grew on his face.

"How did you know?" She didn't remember indicating to him that she disliked sideburns.

"I knew, so I shaved them off."

"You did that for me?" *This is not good.*

He steps closer to her bed. His body is near enough to touch, even inadvertently. Gently, he uses his fingers to brush the loose hair away from her eyes. His light touch causes her limbs to tingle. How quickly she disavows her day of earnest and grown-up decision making.

"You're him, aren't you?" While she can't figure out how, she knows he is the Andy of her youth.

"Yes," he nods.

"But how? This makes no sense!" She can't wrap her mind around it but understands it in her soul, in the same way she described earlier to Dr. Shapiro. There was no doubt, Andrew is also Andy. "You ought to be much younger than you appear if you're Andy. Andy died at age eleven. I was nine when he died."

"Remember, what I told you. Andy wasn't reincarnated."

"Oh, yes, of course, you rose from the dead," she says, skeptically.

"Yes. I am both Andreas as well as Andy."

"Andreas? Who?"

"Okay, admittedly it's complicated. My parents adopted me from an Israeli orphanage and changed my name to Andrew when they brought me to the States."

"How the heck did you end up in Israel? Andy died and was buried in Upstate N.Y."

"Yes, I remember each horrific moment of my drowning death."

She is befuddled on a number of levels. "Why would they go all the way to Israel to adopt you?"

"My mother is of Israeli descent, she felt compelled to help her people. One way she knew how was to adopt a child orphaned by the Israeli-Palestinian conflict."

"Oh," she says and pauses to process what he is telling her. "But couldn't you have these memories and not be Andy? Couldn't you be aware psychically of his life without being him?"

"According to the orphanage staff, they told my parents I was amnesic when they found me at the gates of the orphanage. They estimated that I was about the age of ten or eleven. No relative came forward to claim me and they weren't able to locate a birth record. The assumption was that my parents had been killed in the conflict and that my memories were erased because of the physical, and emotional, trauma I endured."

"So, it's a mystery. I understand, but again, rising from the dead?"

"As I grew older, I learned what happened. My body and soul passed intact through a tunnel, basically a portal, and I remember being in the dark briefly. Most of all, I remember what happened before I entered this portal. I spent time in heaven with other children and with ... you."

"Me, I was there? How? I'm alive and have been for thirty-five years."

"Remember, souls do not have boundaries."

"Is this when you learned that I was a saint?"

"No, I only knew you held a special place in the heaven realm. After a time there, I assume it was only days, I awoke in Israel, literally on the pavement and not quite certain how I arrived there. I knew my name was Andy and that was about it. I didn't remember my visit to heaven or my prior life until after—"

She holds up her hand and stops him from speaking. "Why should I believe you?" Could she trust him? Here was "could verses should" once more. Was he just another demon sent here to mess with her mind?

"I'm not asking you to believe me. I'm telling you the truth. Whether you believe me or not, is up to you."

"This is so confusing." Her overwhelming attraction to him couldn't be sufficient criteria for her to believe him. "Then tell me this, are you a saint, too?"

"I'm a living guardian of the light, a mortal being. I am here in this life to be a conduit of healing for those who suffer physical pain and suffering. Healers bring the light of God's power to the afflicted. Like a safe, I carry the light within me and protect it. If I die, the light dies with me. There's only one thing more satisfying to Satan than eliminating God's light carried and protected by living guardians."

"And what is that?" A memory tugs the edges of her mind. *...the Healer's touch. The Healer will be with you....*

"To eliminate the saints. If there aren't any saints, there is no one to carry the prayers to heaven for those who don't know how to pray or who can't pray for themselves. Saints are interpreters on behalf of mortals. Without saints, there would be no interpreters for those who have the most difficulty reaching God."

"If mortals are the ones who need help praying, why do lost souls persist in bothering me?"

"The lost souls haunt you because they are removed from God's light. They need someone to communicate with God on their behalf and save them from their eternal wandering. However, the demonic influences are so powerful in the borderland between heaven and hell that they are overcome by them. Instinctively, these souls gravitate toward you. They can't reach the saints in Heaven. This is in part, their doing and in part, from the dark influences around them. However, these same lost souls are able to reach you in the earthly realm."

"But I'm not a saint in the present?"

"That doesn't matter, you're a saint in heaven and they know it."

"I live in two places, one mortal and one immortal?"

"Yes, but you're only conscious of the life you lead here. However, your immortal self is helping you at this time only you aren't aware of it."

"Is this true for all people?"

"No, every soul is different."

While he continues to explain, her chest grows heavy with each beat of her heart. His presence warms her, disorients her and most of all, it intoxicates her. She refocuses back to her immediate priorities: to find out why now and why here? But before she can ask more questions, he pulls in his arms, holding them close to his body and his hands clench into fists. His knuckles blanch white. Beads of sweat form on his head, he grimaces and pants.

"What's the matter? What's happening to you?" She gets up out of bed, not sure if she should help him or run, when her mind lands on an extraordinary revelation.

"Andrew?" She mouths his name in a silent shock, "You are the apostle, Andrew, and I loved you."

"Yes ... and you ... were Peter's wife." He grunts between words.

Oh, my God! Is this what this is all about? She steps closer to him and carefully looks him over. His eyes are scrunched shut as he moans. "Andrew, I demand you tell me what you know, all of it! What's going on?"

His legs buckle, he falls to the ground, splinting his arms and hands against his chest. He cries out quietly in agony and writhes on the floor.

She doesn't know if she should be sympathetic or angry. How can she believe his absurd stories? His rising from the dead, her being a saint, her being married to Peter in a previous life, all during the time of Jesus Christ? *I was faithful in body, but unfaithful in heart? What does this make me?*

"A human being!" Andrew cries out from a fetal position on the floor, again as if he hearing her thoughts.

"How did you know?"

"Sometimes ... I know," he moans and struggles, "what you're thinking."

"I can't believe it! None of this can be true!"

"Do you ... need me ... to prove it?" He breathes hard and fast, then with great effort, he slowly stands while still clutching his hands and arms to his chest.

"Yes, prove your story, the one which gets more and more absurd with every word you speak! And healing my head wound yesterday doesn't count!" She denies him mercy. Why? She didn't know except that after experiencing so much deceit in her life, especially the deceptions that led her to being hospitalized, she worries he's the Devil's own sent to finish her off.

He groans. "Are ... you ... sure?"

"Yes! Damn it, prove it!"

Blood drips from his hands onto her bed.

In horror, she covers her mouth.

His hands continue to drip ... drip ... drip. He reaches for a towel from the sink by her bed. Again with great effort, wincing, grunting and panting, he opens his arms, palms up toward her. In the center of each palm, bright red blood seeps from a hollow wound.

CHAPTER 47

Her eyes examine his torn flesh. No church bells ring out. No heavenly voices sing. Her room grows dark even though the lights are on. All she feels is grief, a sorrow beyond any sorrow she has known before. She wants to lie down and die.

"It's the stigmata," he says. Blood continues to drip. He wraps the towel around his right hand and then another one around his left.

While her expression reveals a multitude of questions, her gaping mouth will produce no words.

"During the eight nights before Easter, my palms are torn open as if they are pierced by invisible iron nails," he says in an oddly, relaxed way. His pain appears to be relenting.

"But why? Why you?"

"I don't know why this happens to me except that maybe, I'm supposed to feel the same excruciating pain Christ felt when they nailed Him to the cross. Maybe I'm meant to share this with others, I don't know. Fortunately, I feel only the pain Christ felt in his hands. I can't imagine having all the wounds at once. Like the flogging, the crown of thorns or the nails driven into his feet. I know I wouldn't survive."

"Are you still ... in pain?"

"No. When wounds initially form, it's horribly painful but it lasts for only a minute or two ... thank God." His eyes look briefly up at the ceiling and then back to her. He continues to press the towels to his wounds.

"Why do I feel this way?" she whispers. "I feel such intense sadness ... absolute hopelessness."

"For me, I feel the physical pain of the nails in Christ's hands. I imagine you're bearing the suffering of the women at the foot of the cross on Calvary that day."

"I was there?"

"Yes, you were there."

"I've never felt like this. I know I'm emotional but this is beyond anything I've experienced before."

"It's because we're together, that's why I'm here now. I suspected you would feel something unusual, that's why I wanted you to see it happen with your own eyes. I knew telling you about it would not be the same as seeing if for yourself." He looks at his hands bound up in the towel. "Would you like to touch them?"

Her eyes widen. She can swallow the saint thing and perhaps the rising from the dead as they can be explained away by psychotic delusions, but the Stigmata? Here before her is a tangible wound which wasn't there when he first walked into her room.

"Go ahead, don't be afraid. You can put your finger right through the wound to other side."

Slowly, with the fingers of her right hand, she probes the center of each of his palms. Like the wounds on the hands of Jesus, the nails leave a hole. In awe, she watches her right forefinger go right through his palm all the way to the other side. She looks at her fingers, now covered in his blood. She holds them up in front of her face and sees his blood sliding down her fingers and pooling into the creases of her palms. He walks to the sink and puts disposable gloves on over his own bloody hands. Then he takes a clean towel and wets it.

"When will the wounds go away?" she asks.

He takes the wet towel and begins to wash her hands of his blood. "At 2:01 a.m., they stay for eight minutes and then disappear. You'll see."

The clock shows it is 1:59. He pulls off his gloves and places his hands back in a clean towel but opens it so she can see the gaping wounds.

"The wounds form at 1:53 a.m.? Every night ... for eight days and eight minutes?

"Yes, eight."

"Why eight?"

"The number eight is symbolic of beginnings."

"It is?"

"Christ rose on the first day of the week. The first day of the week is Sunday but it's also the eighth day, and the first day of his new life ... of a new order in the world. Eight is also infinite, a continuous and unending loop. Symbolic of the cycle of our existence, a cycle of continuous beginnings…"

"But why 153?"

"One always represents God the Father and three represents the Holy Spirit, in particular, the culmination of God in the Trinity."

"And five?"

"Five represents Christ, the Word made flesh."

Her face twists with a puzzled expression.

"Five signifies the five piercing wounds of Christ's crucifixion. And, there are five foundational books in the New Testament—Matthew, Mark, Luke, John, and the Acts of the Apostles. But for me, most of all, 153 connects me to my first life. It's associated with one of the miracles after the resurrection."

"What miracle is that?"

"In my first life, after Jesus died and returned to us alive, we saw him on the shore and didn't recognize him. We hadn't caught any fish for over a day and were about to give up."

"And?"

"We caught 153 fish."

Wow. It's the same thing Josie experienced before coming into the hospital. The unseen world communicates in a wholly different way, it is subtle and symbolic, revealing and linking itself in pieces to the living. And yet there is an order about it. It seems nothing is coincidence.

"Andrew, when did you first receive the stigmata?"

"When I was twelve."

"Do your parents know that this happens to you?"

"Of course."

"Did they try to help you somehow?"

"Sure, they tried. Soon after it happened the first time, they took me to our priest and then to our bishop. They strongly advised my parents to keep it confidential. We made a pact—they and my parents. They knew it held an enormous supernatural component and to alert the conventional medical world about me was not worth the cost of our privacy and my remaining childhood. Once I became an adult, I decided to keep my condition private as well. I sort of disappeared into the Vatican's woodwork of the unexplainable."

"The Vatican knows about this?" Josie's says.

"They do. I'm guessing there are others. I don't know who they are though. We've not had the benefit of being formally introduced," he says with a laugh. "And, at this point, I'm not looking for a cure. There isn't one. It's far more important that I live my life in the service of God than try to prove to anyone that God exists because of what He does to my hands at the end of every Lenten season. There's no amount of evidence that will convince an already unbelieving world."

"I suppose, but still, it seems to sweep this under the rug is ignoring God. He has to want others to know about you—it will save more souls."

"Josie, I'm a healer. That's my purpose. If others knew, I couldn't fulfill my purpose. I'd be crucified by the world...both literally and figuratively. I'm trusting you will keep my secret but by the look on your face, I wonder. You think I'm a freak, don't you?"

"I don't," she says. "And, I will keep your secret." However, everything lacked a solid explanation. While his wounds were undoubtedly real, was his story? Is it true? He believes it but could she? Is he the Healer Mary told her about? Was he one of the doctors who tended to Michael last week before she arrived at the ER?

They sit back down on the bed together. She scoots over a few inches so their bodies don't touch. It's better if they kept their distance, if only to keep his blood away from her. How will she explain this one to the nurse? She hopes he plans to take the blood stained towels with him. And so she watches carefully and does not take her eyes off of his hands.

AT 2:01, HIS WOUNDS VANISH. THE BLOOD ON HER BED IS gone. The blood on the towels disappears. His hands return to their normal appearance, leaving no evidence behind. *Incredible.* And with the rapid disappearance of his wounds, she immediately feels her sadness depart. She begins to wonder if the suffering of the women at the foot of the cross is the source of her fragile and emotional nature. Has she borne this sorrow her entire life? It seems she must've carried it with her because when Andrew showed her his hands, it felt as if someone took a hot cattle iron and branded it on her soul.

"Josie, it's important you understand this one critical fact of your first life." Andrew's face turns grave and serious.

"What's that?" *There's more?*

"You were ..."

"What Andrew? Tell me!"

"An apostle. When Peter denied Christ, you stayed. You never left Christ's side."

To believe him meant she'd be accepting his truth and that the extraordinary bizarreness of their encounter is real. "How come I know nothing about her?"

"Your life was erased by the scholars and leaders of the time."

"Why?"

"It was unacceptable to place a woman in a position of leadership."

"They ignored Jesus?"

"In a way, yes. Jesus was a radical. He's not the tidy picture we have turned him into, placed on a wall somewhere to be looked at and not lived. Jesus made no distinction between the role of men and the role of women in building his church. This caused tremendous strife among his followers as well as the leaders of the time. And it continues to this day."

"Is there any record of my life at all?"

"The only record that was preserved was the healing of your mother by Jesus and briefly that you were a believing wife who accompanied Peter on his mission to spread the Word of God. Unfortunately, there's no record of your name."

"I know that in Hebrew, 'Josephine' means *the Lord's addition?*"

"You could have had the same name. I can't say for certain, but you were added among the initial twelve."

"Were all the wives of the apostles also apostles themselves?"

"Not all. But you were brave enough to answer Christ's call." He glances over to her clock. "I have to go but I promise I'll come back to tell you more tomorrow."

"Wait. Before you go, tell me how come you know all of this and why don't I?"

"When I received the Stigmata, my memory of my former, as well as my concurrent lives, was restored. My life made sense to me from that point on."

"I hope I don't have to receive the Stigmata to have the memories of my past or other lives restored."

"No, but be assured, your time is coming. You will have your own cross to bear."

CHAPTER 48

During afternoon group therapy, Josie diligently tries to focus on the other patients in group. Therapy is a sharing time and so much of what people share is gut-wrenching and awful, not to mention, completely confidential. It takes great courage for them to confide in each other and she owes her therapy-mates her undivided attention. Nevertheless, Josie's mind is elsewhere, and in her opinion, most selfishly elsewhere.

Her thoughts insist on churning through the sequence of events leading her to meet Andrew and witnessing his crippling manifestation of the stigmata. It's almost impossible for her to think of anything else. Although, she has heard of people receiving the stigmata—a few saints, popes and priests—never in her wildest dreams did she believe she'd see it with her own eyes. Nor did she realize that stigmatics received the piercings in their palms, stab wounds that were visible to anyone willing to look.

In the middle of group, there is a knock at the door of the therapy room. Mark, the therapy coordinator, stops the session and answers it. Josie overhears Mark talking in hushed tones to the person outside. He opens the door wider. Josie sees Susan standing there, her hair is pulled back in a French braid and as usual, Susan looks natural and gorgeous.

She motions for Josie to come to the door. "You have a visitor," she says, "I thought it would be okay to interrupt you for this particular visitor."

"Oh, who is it?" Josie asks. It is late Wednesday afternoon, who would be coming to see her? Her children? Her sister? Or, maybe Andrew? Perhaps Dr. Shapiro as she hasn't seen him yet today.

"It's a surprise." She smiles, "You'll see."

Josie starts to get excited, thinking it must be her children. She can't wait to see them. She originally didn't want her children to see her in the hospital but it doesn't matter to her anymore, she just wants to hug and kiss them.

When they arrive at her room, Susan instructs her to go inside. "I'll wait out here," she says.

Josie nods and assumes Susan is affording her some privacy. She passes through the short hall into her room. Her breath catches. There, on the bedside table, is a vase containing a dozen long-stemmed red roses. Next to them, sitting on her bed, is Declan.

CHAPTER 49

Declan is his dapper self, wearing a charcoal pin-striped suit and designer tie—it's one Josie picked for him on a recent shopping trip.

"What are you doing here?" she asks. "I thought you weren't coming home until Saturday?"

"That's a nice welcome," he says, giving her a charming frown.

Josie shifts her feet and crosses her arms across her chest, taken aback by the sudden change in his demeanor. Is she supposed to be happy to see him? "But what about our last conversation?"

"Well," he says, sighing. "I missed you and I know ... I was wrong."

She turns her back on him, secretly wondering which one of them is the true crazy person. He is the very last person she expected to see. She starts to walk out the door but he steps into her path. She hasn't a choice but to face him.

"Josie, please hear me out," he says, earnestly.

She directs her eyes at the wall beside him and refuses to look at him.

"I know I've been impatient, not to mention a judgmental royal jerk. I'm sorry."

"Is that all?" she asks, waiting for more.

"I love you. I love our family. The rest doesn't matter."

"You do?"

"How could you doubt that?"

He reaches around her waist and pulls her to him. Her bottom lip begins to quiver as she's determined not to cry. Instead, she buries her face in his chest. He holds her close and strokes her long brown hair.

"Josie, there's something else ... another important reason why I'm here."

She steps back from him. *Didn't he mean what he said? Is he going to bring it all down with a shallow request?*

"Something's happened to your father."

"My dad? What's going on?" Her head aches.

"Your father's had a stroke."

"Is he okay?" She cries out. Her hand goes to her temples.

Susan knocks and enters. "Is everything all right?"

"Josie's father had a stroke this morning," Declan says. "He's in critical condition."

"You should've warned me, Mr. Reilly," she says, "your wife's still in a fragile state, I could've helped you deliver this news to her."

"I can handle it," Josie says. "Is he going to be okay?"

"We don't think so, it happened at about ten this morning. Your brother called Nora. Then she called me right after that. Nora's already left for Phoenix. Maureen has the kids at her house."

"Why didn't Nora call to tell me?" *Why would they keep this from me?*

"She didn't want to upset you and we both know ... how you are."

"What ... emotionally weak?" she growls.

"C'mon, Josie, we didn't mean to leave you in the dark. We didn't want you to be alone when you heard the news. I promised her I'd tell you as soon as I got in today. You see, this morning, we thought your father had time. When it first happened, he was still conscious but in the last couple of hours ... he's become unresponsive."

"I have to go see him ... I have to go now!"

"Tony's last message on my cell was that your dad's gone into a coma. They don't expect him to make it." Declan passes her an envelope. "Josie, you're right, you have to go see your dad right away."

She stares at the envelope, knowing what it is but opens it to be sure. Inside she finds a plane ticket.

"I have a bag packed for you and I'll take you to the airport right now. Your plane leaves in an hour and a half." He looks away from her to Susan.

"This is most unusual," Susan says, "Dr. Shapiro needs to okay this. She can't just leave."

"I know," he says, "he left orders with your supervisor."

"He did? Hmm, seems you've covered all the bases, Mr. Reilly," she says, suspiciously. "I guess I'll be gathering Josie's things stored at the nurse's station." Susan turns abruptly and leaves.

"I'm sorry, Jos," Declan's voice softens. He reaches for her hand and she allows him to hold it.

"My dad doesn't deserve this." Josie shakes her head and sits down in the chair next to her bed. She takes back her hand and bows her head, covering her face with her hands.

"What I meant is I'm sorry about us. I've been so blind. I want us to be together ... always. After you see your father, I want you to come home. I'll be there for you like I promised. We'll get you all the help you need."

"Do you mean it?" She uncovers her face and looks up at him. She wonders who this man is in front of her and what did he do with Declan? What spurred his turn-a-round? Further, she didn't know if she was ready to come home.

"Yes, of course I do. While you were here, I had time to think about us. And, after our last conversation, I had a bit of a wake-up call."

"You did?"

"Yes, I had an awful dream last night. I saw what my life would be without you in it."

"A dream? But you don't buy into dreams, I thought."

He nods. "I know but this one was different. It felt real. I didn't like it at all."

"But what about all of this? The treatment, the medications?"

"Dr. Shapiro said you'll do fine with outpatient treatment so long as you come in like you're supposed to and stay on your medications. You'll see him in his office as soon as you get back."

She nods. While her face reveals grief about her father, she's contending with another emotion, regret. First and foremost, she wants to see her father and her children and yet leaving the hospital means not getting any more of her questions answered by Andrew. Leaving means not saying good-bye.

CHAPTER 50

J osie sees her brother Tony waiting for her by the baggage claim. It is a busy night at Sky Harbor Airport with carousels full of luggage and people milling around. She has déjà vu. Here she is again at the moment of a last breath but now the breath belongs to her father. Josie approaches Tony. He looks handsome in a crisp pair of khaki shorts and a faded orange t-shirt. He is clean-shaven and muscular. His sunglasses are pushed up over the top of his head. The phrase "fit as fiddle" comes to her mind. But Tony's eyes are sad. He walks up to Josie. Her arms go limp at her sides.

"Josie," he says, "I'm sorry. Dad's gone."

THEY HOLD A SMALL PRIVATE PRAYER SERVICE FOR HER FATHER on Thursday afternoon in the chapel of his church. Oddly enough, the name of the church is St. Andrew's. According to Catholic tradition, no funerals can be held between the days of Holy Thursday and Easter. Her father's pastor, Father Frank, makes a compromise by holding the prayer service because, in his words, "God wouldn't want them to be sorrowful on Easter." The funeral rite will be performed the following week at the cemetery before his burial and after Josie returns home. She can't stay because she gave her word to her children that she would be home in time to share Easter with them.

The next day Josie decides to visit the grave of her mother and the future burial place of her father's remains. She borrows Nora's car to make the long trek to the cemetery on the far north side of Phoenix. The drive over there gives her much time to think about how she is going to move forward with her life. What is she supposed to do with it now? She must be destined for something, but what? Perhaps it is right in front of her.

In many ways, she wished she could go back in time, to the time before channeling and start over. Her home is with her children and Declan and because of her love for them above all else, she needs to let go of the time she spent with Andrew. While with him, she was free to accept her supernatural experiences, be they real or unreal, and this will have to be enough for her. She could keep looking for proof of her experiences but it will be to no avail. She'll never find it in the outside world.

She arrives at the cemetery and walks among the various markers looking for her mother's gravesite. The land is stark and arid, nothing like the lush green cemeteries of the upper Midwest. Rather, this hallowed ground is pure desert, made of dirt, gravel and the occasional tumbleweed. It doesn't take long before she finds her mother's burial place. She sees a flat metal plate in the ground engraved with her mother's name, *Giovanna La Fortuna, March 2, 1931–May 22, 2002*. Next to her name is an empty space where her father's name and dates of birth and death will be inscribed. Her parents vowed to be to be buried together.

Most of the surrounding graves are decorated with silk flowers and wreaths, but many have faded under the intense desert sun. Josie sets a bouquet of pink silk roses in the holder next to her mother's grave marker so others will know she isn't among the forgotten. She kneels down to say a Hail Mary when she hears the cawing of a desert crow. It sits on a low-hanging branch of an olive tree, several feet beyond her mother's grave. Josie has grown accustomed to eerie noises and isn't about to let the crow intimidate her into leaving. She's seen and been through enough lately that even an agent of the Devil can't scare her anymore.

She finishes with the Sign of the Cross. When standing back up, she notices her mother's grave is draped by shadows. Clouds drifted in out of nowhere and have blocked out the sun. Under the opaque sky, she asks her mother and whoever else might be listening to her laments on the other side, "How are we to know if there is anything to follow this life?" *For all we know, there's nothing at all. Maybe we won't see those we love again?* To believe otherwise may be a product of her overactive imagination, acting to protect her from a harsh truth.

She places her hand over the silver cross hanging at the base of her neck. The words, *The Sign of Jonah*, pass through her mind. She remembers the story from catechism classes when she was a child where the scribes and Pharisees demanded a sign from Jesus to prove to them he was the Messiah, despite the innumerable miracles he already performed. In their confrontation, Jesus warns it is an evil and unfaithful age that asks for a sign. And he conveys a key message—a sign will not be given except for the Sign of Jonah. As Jonah spent three days and three nights in the belly of a whale, so it will able be for the Son of Man in the heart of the earth. Was Josie, like the Pharisees, coming precariously close to demanding such a sign? Was she going against the Word of God?

Loneliness, doubt, and her own insignificance overwhelm her and as usual, she begins to weep. She wipes her eyes with the wad of tissues she brought with her. Unexpectedly, she sees red on her fingers and scattered on the tissues. She examines her palms, the back sides of her hands, her wrists, and between her fingers. There are no cuts, no wounds, no bruises and no pain. Is she so arrogant to think herself worthy to receive the stigmata? No, she thinks not. She wipes her eyes again but with a brand new tissue. There covering the tissue is more red. Wet and bloody.

She starts to tremble and takes a make-up mirror from her purse. In the mirror, she sees the water of her tears mixed with blood streaming down her cheeks. The tiny mirror in her hand cracks in three. She drops it to the ground. The slow, mournful tolling of bells rings out, donnnngggg ... donnnngggg ... donnnngggg ...

The solemn bells are unlike the cathedral bells she heard days earlier. Within seconds, rain douses her hair and clothing. Lightning fractures the sky in jagged waves of horizontal and vertical fire. Thunder rolls over the cemetery as if angry for the plight of the lost. Her cell phone alarm rings and hurls her heart into a galloping panic. *I never set the alarm on my phone.* She doesn't know how. She pulls the phone from her purse and looks at the time. It is three in the afternoon on Good Friday.

Suddenly, she hears a man speaking to her from behind. "Young woman," he says in a slow, comforting voice. "Please don't cry."

She turns around and is instantly without words. The man wears work gloves and a wide brimmed sun-hat. He is the gardener she met at Como Park on the day of Michael's anaphylactic food reaction. The man's mouth curves with a smile and his eyes dazzle blue but are cloaked by the brim of his hat.

How can the same caretaker of the gardens in St. Paul be here in the desert caring for the cemetery grounds? Her trembling hands wipe her eyes, staining them dark red from the salt and blood of her tears.

"Your mother is not here. She does not live among the rock and dust of the earth. She has left to take her place among the angels," the caretaker says.

"Who are you?" she asks. *Is he a hallucination?* He can't be, as he is tangible, made of flesh and bone. Something falls from his hands to the ground. It makes a soft thud as it hits the pebbles and dirt. It is small and gold.

"Remember the day you encountered the Glory of the Snow?" he asks.

"Yes, I do. But ... how can you? Are you an angel?"

He laughs, "I'm a teacher. You, Josie, are like the Glory of the Snow ... curled and small, waiting beneath the dense bitterness of the frost that belongs to this life and this body. One day you too will emerge and behold the divinity living within you and every human being."

"I don't understand."

"Seek God in all you do, not only around you but more importantly, within you." He points to her heart. "You have a gift. It has accompanied you through the ages. You may freely accept it, it is yours alone to decide but in accepting this gift, you must stay alert. If the spirits come, ask if they are of the light. Command those who are not, to leave. Do not be anxious, rest in knowing I am with you."

"But what if I can't do it?"

"Remember, this world and its affairs are not lasting. In the end, you will realize the soul belongs to God and it will return to Him when its work here is done. Commit yourself, each and every day of your life, to offer yourself as a living sacrifice for the attainment of the glory that waits for you with your Father in heaven. *This* is all that matters."

The man's clothes transform into a flowing robe of dazzling white. His hat disappears, his work gloves vanish. He is young, beautiful and perfect. She recognizes Him, but as she does, He disappears. Like a mirage in the desert, He is gone.

In the seconds that follow, a flood of new memories enter her brain. She runs toward her car, faster and faster. It seems she can't run fast enough. The images appear like a reel from a movie, one frame at a time with lightning speed, becoming a colorful blizzard of flashing lights through her mind. One frame is of a woman, who looks like Josie but she wears a dress of a different time and place. Her hair is much longer and her skin is bronzed.

She stands on the shore of a vast body of sparkling clear water. She doesn't remember going there in this life but can't help but feel she's been there many times before. Another frame shows men in the distance fishing on a small boat. Yet another shows a small boy with her who calls her "mother." The boy looks and sounds like her Michael. A man calls to her, she recognizes the voice. It is Andrew's.

She gets in the car, locks the door and sobs alone. Frame by frame, pictures and sounds of memories from another age, come flying in and flying out. In her mind, she sees herself, she isn't wearing shoes and the sand runs soft and warm under her feet. Draped over her body is an ankle-length brown garment. It is wet on the bottom and drags on the ground. She runs up the shoreline, growing breathless and tired. The weight of her body is heavy. Her steps are weary and lumbered, she is pregnant.

Josie holds her head in her hands as more voices call out to her in her mind. This time they shout *"Peter! Andrew!"* A crowd of people run toward the shore. There are men in other boats and they bring them in closer to a boat holding an enormous quantity of fish. The fish are contained within nets—nets on the verge of bursting. The man they call Peter falls to his knees in front of a luminous man standing in his boat. His tunic is lighter than the others around him and the sun shines precisely on him.

Astounded at what her mind is witnessing, a different sadder image emerges, one of a man on a mountaintop dying on a large wooden cross. In the image, she is kneeling in grief at the foot of his cross surrounded by other grieving women who are also dressed in long earthen brown garments. The face of the dying man is clear. It belongs to the gardener.

Her cell phone alarms again. She looks at her watch. It is 3:08 p.m. In an instant, her grief lifts as if the weight of the world is removed from her. It is a relief beyond recognition. For the first time in her life, she is at peace. She gets out of her car and runs back to the grave of her mother. She kneels before her and asks her one more question, "Is this true?"

The sky parts in a resonant *"Yes!"* The rain ceases and the clouds dissolve, bringing a pure blue sky. She no longer feels fragile but strong and realizes she isn't alone. God and his angels will always be at her side.

The object the caretaker dropped catches her eye. It is on the ground, shimmering and reflecting tiny glints of light toward her. She reaches down to pick it up and recognizes the familiar piece of metal. The inside inscription is still intact, "C & G 2-14-50." It is her father's wedding band. She decides not to ask how or why for it is inexplicably here, perhaps left for her as a symbol of God's grace. She outstretches her arms with her face up toward the sun, feeling its warmth wrap around her as she hopes it will do for the rest of her life.

EPILOGUE
Easter

The children wake early, excited to search for their Easter baskets. Josie gets the camera and switches the setting to video. She films Michael locating his first. His basket is hiding under the kitchen sink and behind the dish soap. Declan takes the camera from Josie so she can help Anna find hers next. Hers is in the coat closet on top of the box of hats and mittens. With the camera in hand, Declan helps Jacob. He pretends for the children that he doesn't know where Jacob's basket could be. Jacob declares his discovery with a screech and a clap. "Here!" he says, finding it in almost plain sight, tucked under an end table.

The children proceed to devour several milk chocolates and jelly beans while moving on to the egg hunt with their father. Josie collects the discarded foil wraps from consumed chocolate bunnies scattered on the living room carpet. *So much for a healthy breakfast before Mass*, she thinks.

Once everyone is dressed in their Sunday finest, including Anna in a pair of white gloves and a new bonnet, the family leaves to attend Mass at a new parish. Josie and Declan decide as a couple it is best they not see Father Anthony. Neither is ready to face him. The events are recent and its closeness is too much for Josie's recovering soul and mind to bear. The children don't seem to notice the change in direction on their drive to church. She wonders if they too want to go someplace new and have a fresh start.

She breathes deep and looks out the passenger side window. The warmth of her family surrounds her. Whatever or whoever had disrupted their home has gone but she worries they have left to find other unsuspecting victims. Nevertheless, her life is as it should be. Easter marks a time of renewal, a new beginning. *It is fitting,* she believes. Purged of the voices and haunting, her mental state is free of the horrid grip of spiritual torment. Still, she thinks of Andrew but not as a lover or a friend. Rather, he is the keeper of their shared secret and past. Perhaps they are together in a parallel life, another world, another time as he suggests.

The life that matters though is the one she's aware of, the one she is living here and now. *It is all for the best.* Andrew will make his way with DWR and set off on new adventures. He will likely find a partner and one, unlike Josie, who won't weigh him down. And certainly, closure isn't necessary between them because there's nothing to conclude. It never started. She loves her husband and her family and would not give them up for anyone.

She peeks at the children seated in the row behind them. They are wearing headphones and watching a Disney DVD on the drop-down screen.

Declan takes his right hand off the steering wheel and grasps her hand. "What are you thinking about?" he asks.

"Everything and nothing," she says. "It's been a full few weeks. I'm glad to be home."

"It's good to have you home." He squeezes her hand briefly and then places it back on the wheel. "Um ... there is something I need to talk with you about but there hasn't been a good time for us to talk without the kids around."

"Their headphones are on, this is about as much privacy as we're going to get."

"I suppose." He glances at the children in his rearview mirror. "Well, while you were away in Phoenix, an opportunity came up."

"What kind of opportunity?"

"I was contacted by a firm in Madison, Wisconsin."

"Madison? And?"

"They would like to fly me down next week for an interview."

"An interview? What's the job?"

"I would be the managing partner of their governmental affairs division."

"What firm?"

"Davis, Cline, and Robertson."

"I've never heard of them."

"They're local to Madison but trust me, they are well-known and respected in the industry."

"So, government affairs rather than corporate mergers?"

"Yep, I think a change is in order and at my age, I think it's time to grow my skills in a new field while I still have the chance. Plus, it's an opportunity that will allow me to be around home more."

"That would be nice for a change. How would you be home more though if you're working out of Madison?"

"Obviously, we would need to move."

She gazes out the passenger window, unsure how to respond. "Madison, Wisconsin, huh?" She turns to look at him. His features are handsome, as always, although he has aged over the last few weeks as has she. Stress has had their way with both of them.

"It's not a done deal. I still have to interview."

"What about all of our friends here?"

"We'll stay in touch and Madison isn't that far away. Plus, I think it will do us good as a family, start over in a new city, a new home. You've always wanted us to build our own house. We could do that there. And, if we're going to move, better now before the kids get settled in a school."

She looks back at Michael. "We'll have to find him a new allergist," she says, quietly, not wanting to cause Michael further anxiety about his allergies.

"I think we'll find plenty of reputable allergists working for the University of Wisconsin Clinics."

Josie is very aware of the medical establishment in Madison, especially the UW Children's Hospital. She knows they have an incredible reputation. She reflects, hopefully they will not have to worry about his allergies in the near future anyhow. His appointment is a week away. She wonders if all of this happened to her, and to them, for a reason. Did this experience serve a greater purpose apart from anything having to do with herself or even her encounter with Andrew? Will she ever know?

"Declan," she says, "I think you should go ahead and interview. You're right, a move will do this family good."

He smiles, pats her leg and gives her thigh a squeeze. "This is going to be great, I can feel it."

She's happy because he is and it's good to have her old Declan back. Relaxed, kind, loving. It's as if the man she fell in love with came to life again. She marvels at the change in him and considers his return a blessing. The spirits must've affected him as well, she thinks, although not as directly as they did her. The dark clouds she observed over his mood and behavior in the previous weeks had lifted.

Declan turns the corner and enters the parking lot of St. Theresa's Parish. She smiles and reflects, *No more what ifs, this is where I'm meant to be.* If all she does with her life is aspire to be the very best mother to her children, then this is the greatest vocation of all. One day soon, she will write in her journal about her supernatural experiences with the Virgin and the angels, the Devil and his minions, and leave it for her children to read once they were older and perhaps, after she is gone. *Maybe that's what saints do?* They understand where they belong in life's fabric. They live it, exemplify it and, sometimes, write about it in hopes they will leave the world a better place and at the end of their days, are at peace with their lives. Why? Because they lived their lives from a place of love. Their devotion to God mirrored in their devotion to their family and to others.

At last she hears them, the ringing of church bells. They belong to St. Theresa's Church. Their melodic song is real and everyone can hear them.

ANDREW
2010

A ndrew buys a cup of coffee and a newspaper and sits down. He drinks a large slug, bitter but he likes it that way. Sugar and cream weaken the taste and this cup is for resetting his clock. Jet-lagged from the time difference after flying half-way around the world, he opens the paper and relaxes in an airport chair. All told, his trip back took thirty hours from Thailand to Chicago. He never expected to be sent there; he had planned on South America. Nevertheless, it was interesting to say the least and feels good to be back in the States. There were times when he wasn't too sure he'd return home in one piece, if at all.

His body is in a strange state of shock as he takes in the surrounding conveniences and decadence of American life. Clean bathrooms, cooked food ready at a moment's notice, gourmet coffee, a newspaper from today and not weeks earlier and, best of all, clean drinking water. After four years as a medical relief physician abroad, he only experienced such luxury in dreams.

He opens the *USA Today* and goes right to the section dedicated to news by State, looking for Minnesota. He can't help himself. Not a day passes where hasn't thought of her or that fateful Saturday when they collided at Wilson's Market. Up until then, he didn't understand how one's life can change in an instant. But from that point on, he knew. He remembers when he saw her, distraught and arguing with someone on the other end of her cell phone. Her long brown hair covered her face but as he passed her in the frozen food aisle, he took notice.

Her presence was beyond memorable, it shattered any rational thought he had left. Then he saw her again, moments later by the checkouts. She dropped her phone. The battery popped off and glided across the floor toward him as if some angel above heard his prayer and granted him the chance of his lifetime. When he bent over to pick it up and hand it back to her, Josie's eyes penetrated his being, rendering him mute. Any woman who came before her no longer mattered. Without question, it was her heart he needed to win ... only to find it already belonged to someone else.

Four years later and he still needs to know about her life, what might be going on around her or even with her. "Ahhh," he says, sighing when his eyes spot the Minnesota section. There is never anything written about her, per se, but he always has to read it, just in case. He smirks, once again, nothing, just more news about Minnesota's forestry industry and the controversial fire practices recommended by the State for targeted forestry management.

While he sits and waits for his connection to Newark, he examines the faces around him hoping maybe he'd see hers mingling in with the crowd. Maybe they will cross paths on this day, in this terminal while he reads the paper and drinks his black coffee.

"Geezus," he says to himself, and then apologizes to God. He knows better than to be taking His son's name in vain. He has tried to live a decent life since he left St. Paul. That is, he hadn't attempted to break-up any other marriages besides Josie's.

She made her choice when she left the hospital, he says to himself. *Who was I to break what God had joined together in her present life?* And yet, after what he witnessed in the world at large in his duties as a doctor, he can't help but have his doubts. Why would God bring them together only to tear them apart again?

I'm a grown man, for God's sake! He isn't a romantic and cynicism is by far one of his more attractive traits. Despite his doubts, he knows why God brought them together this time around. It's taken him years though to accept. He came back into her life to heal her son. Their paths were allowed to cross this one time. He takes comfort in knowing they are living an alternative life somewhere, a parallel reality where she is with him. How does he know? He's been there in his dreams. There, they are together. There, he knows she has a healthy son in this present life because of a guardian of light.

Overhead, he hears the page, "United Flight 111 is now boarding for Newark, rows eighteen and higher." He is looking forward to two weeks of R&R at his parents' home on Cape May. And then he'll be off again to yet another assignment, this time, Haiti.

He stands up and gathers his carry-on bag, tosses what is left of his coffee into the trash and leaves the newspaper on the table by his chair. He figures some other person can read it. This is his personal form of recycling.

"United Flight 111 is now boarding all rows." The pager's voice sounds muffled over the loudspeaker. He wonders why airline personnel have to stick their mouth right on the mike. He pulls out his ticket and is about fifth in line when another voice comes in loud and clear. It's from the television. The screen is over his right shoulder when he hears the name, "Declan Reilly."

Declan Reilly? How could he forget that name, it stirred an anger within him that he couldn't explain. Jealousy? Maybe. Worse, he questioned Declan's ability to care for Josie in the manner he believed she deserved. Andrew wanders closer to TV and lets the people behind him go ahead.

"Late last night, Josephine Reilly, the wife of Declan Reilly, Wisconsin Republican and candidate for United States Senate, was hospitalized for undisclosed injuries she suffered during a campaign rally in Madison, Wisconsin. According to nearby witnesses, a group of protestors entered the rally at the Concourse Hotel. He and two of his campaign staffers were seen attempting to calm the protestors. Soon after, his wife was reportedly taken from the rally by ambulance to the University of Wisconsin Hospital. An anonymous source close to the couple states Mrs. Reilly suffered a head injury during the altercation with the protestors.

"A head injury? Wisconsin? U.S. Senate?" Andrews says out loud to no one but himself. Then he sees her face, her picture on the screen but it is more than that, it's her presence. It fills his heart as if not a single day has passed. *She looks the same.* Declan has a firm hold around her waist, smiling and waving. Andrew presumes it must have been taken at another political rally. But the news that follows is more of what he doesn't expect.

"The same source indicates she's been placed on ventilator support. No further information has been provided to the media at this time. We will update you as this story develops."

Before Andrew allows the strangers around him to witness him falling apart, he proceeds to the nearest flight desk. He starts to speak but no utterance comes.

"How may I help you?" the airline attendant asks. The man who muffled his voice into the mike is now speaking succinctly to him.

"Yes sir," Andrew says, clearing his throat, "I'm booked on Flight 111 that's boarding right now to Newark."

"Yes," the man nods, "and?"

"I made a mistake. I need to alter my itinerary. I would like to change my destination."

"Oh," the man says, befuddled. "Um, sir, you do know you will have to buy an entirely new ticket and it's too late for us to remove your bag from this flight."

"I know. I'm sorry about this, but it's a family emergency." *Well, close enough.* "I'm willing to pay the price, whatever the inconvenience may be."

"To where should I book your next flight?"

"To Madison, please ... Madison, Wisconsin."

ACKNOWLEDGMENTS

Thank you to Victoria Grundle, my editor, and to all the authors who helped me to locate the resources and most of all, the confidence to keep going.

A special thank you to my publisher, Kira Henschel and Henschel-Haus Publishing, for believing in me and my work. Thank you for helping me to realize a life-long dream.

Thank you to all of my friends and family who read and commented on my book (either whole or in part) over the years during its writing and provided me with invaluable feedback. I am forever in your debt.

Author photo by Jody Dingle Photography

ABOUT THE AUTHOR

Margaret Goss is a writer, hockey mom and regis-tered nurse. She has a B.S. in Nursing from Arizona State University and an M.A. in Public Policy and Administration from the University of Wisconsin-Madison. Though Margaret has spent many years on and off working as a nurse, her true calling has always been writing. Her parents, first-generation Italian-Americans, inspired Margaret's early appreciation for the arts. Her father, an English and Journalism teacher, as well as a musician, and her mother, an art teacher and painter, passed on a creative gene that their post-depression era pragmatism could not stifle. She currently resides in Madison, Wisconsin with her husband, three children and their border collie-terrier.

To learn more about Margaret, you can visit her website at
www.margaretmgoss.com or

on Facebook at
www.facebook.com/margaretmgoss.author.

CPSIA information can be obtained at www.ICGtesting.com
Printed in the USA
LVOW11s0954071015

457140LV00003B/4/P

9 781595 984289